Praise for Debbie Macomber's
Bestselling Novels from Ballantine Books

Any Dream Will Do

"Emotional, romantic and inspirational, the latest novel from romance maven Macomber is a must read! . . . Shay's journey is one of courage, and there's something in her story for every reader." —*RT Book Reviews*

"*Any Dream Will Do* is . . . so realistic, it's hard to believe it's fiction through the end. Even then, it's hard to say goodbye to these characters. This standalone novel will make you hope it becomes a Hallmark movie, or gets a sequel. It's an inspiring, hard-to-put-down tale. . . . You need to read it." —*The Free Lance–Star*

"*Any Dream Will Do* by Debbie Macomber is a study in human tolerance and friendship. Macomber masterfully shows how all people have value." —*Fresh Fiction*

If Not for You

"[An] uplifting and deliciously romantic tale with vibrant characters and a wide range of emotions."
—*RT Book Reviews*

"A heartwarming story of forgiveness and unexpected love." —*Harlequin Junkie*

"A fun, sweet read." —*Publishers Weekly*

A Girl's Guide to Moving On

"Debbie Macomber's finest novel. Betrayal and sorrow can happen in any stage of life, and, in this wonderful story, her very nimble hands weave a spectacular kaleidoscope of courage, struggles, and finally joyous redemption and reinvention. Macomber totally understands the human heart. I absolutely loved it!"
—DOROTHEA BENTON FRANK, *New York Times* bestselling author of *All the Single Ladies*

"Whispers a message of love, hope, and, yes, reinvention to every woman who has ever wondered 'Is that all there is?' I predict every diehard Macomber fan—as well as legions of readers new to the Macomber magic—will be cheering for Leanne and Nichole, and clamoring for more, more, more."
—MARY KAY ANDREWS, *New York Times* bestselling author of *Beach Town, Ladies' Night,* and *Summer Rental*

"Macomber is a master at pulling heartstrings, and readers will delight in this heartwarming story of friendship, love, and second chances. Leanne, Nichole, Rocco, and Nikolai will renew your faith in love and hope. The perfect read curled up in front of the fire or on a beach, it's as satisfying as a slice of freshly baked bread—wholesome, pleasantly filling, and delicious."
—KAREN WHITE, *New York Times* bestselling author of *Flight Patterns*

"Beloved author Debbie Macomber reaches new heights in this wise and beautiful novel. It's the kind of reading experience that comes along only rarely, bearing the hallmarks of a classic. The timeless wisdom in these pages will stay with you long after the book is closed."
—SUSAN WIGGS, #1 *New York Times* bestselling author of *Starlight on Willow Lake*

Rose Harbor

Sweet Tomorrows

"Macomber fans will leave the Rose Harbor Inn with warm memories of healing, hope, and enduring love."
—*Kirkus Reviews*

"Overflowing with the poignancy, sweetness, conflicts and romance for which Debbie Macomber is famous, *Sweet Tomorrows* captivates from beginning to end."
—*Book Reporter*

"Macomber manages to infuse her trademark humor in a more somber story that focuses on love, loss and faith. . . . This one will appeal to those looking for more mature heroines and a good, clean romance."
—*RT Book Reviews*

"There's a reason why Debbie Macomber is a #1 *New York Times* bestselling author and with *Sweet Tomorrows,* we get another dose of women's fiction perfection. . . . In the nooks and crannies of small-town life, we'll find significance, beauty, and love."
—*Heroes and Heartbreakers*

"Fans will enjoy this final installment of the Rose Harbor series as they see Jo Marie's story finally come to an end." —*Library Journal*

Silver Linings

"A heartwarming, feel-good story from beginning to end . . . No one writes stories of love and forgiveness like Macomber." —*RT Book Reviews*

"Macomber's homespun storytelling style makes reading an easy venture. . . . She also tosses in some hidden twists and turns that will delight her many longtime fans." —*Bookreporter*

"Reading Macomber's novels is like being with good friends, talking and sharing joys and sorrows."
—*New York Journal of Books*

Love Letters

"[Debbie] Macomber's mastery of women's fiction is evident in her latest. . . . [She] breathes life into each plotline, carefully intertwining her characters' stories to ensure that none of them overshadow the others. Yet it is her ability to capture different facets of emotion which will entrance fans and newcomers alike."
—*Publishers Weekly*

"Romance and a little mystery abound in this third installment of Macomber's series set at Cedar Cove's Rose Harbor Inn. . . . Readers of Robyn Carr and Sherryl Woods will enjoy Macomber's latest, which will have them flipping pages until the end and eagerly anticipating the next installment."
—*Library Journal* (starred review)

"Uplifting . . . a cliffhanger ending for Jo Marie begs for a swift resolution in the next book." —*Kirkus Reviews*

"Mending a broken heart is not always easy to do, but Macomber succeeds at this beautifully in *Love Letters*. . . . Quite simply, this is a refreshing take on most love stories—there are twists and turns in the plot that keep readers on their toes—and the author shares up slices of realism, allowing her audience to feel right at home as they follow a cast of familiar characters living in the small coastal town of Cedar Cove, where life is interesting, to say the least." —*Bookreporter*

"*Love Letters* is another wonderful story in the Rose Harbor series. Genuine life struggles with heartwarming endings for the three couples in this book make it special. Readers won't be able to get enough of Macomber's gentle storytelling. Fans already know what a charming place Rose Harbor is and new readers will love discovering it as well."
—*RT Book Reviews* (4½ stars)

Rose Harbor in Bloom

"[Debbie] Macomber uses warmth, humor and superb storytelling skills to deliver a tale that charms and entertains." —*BookPage*

"A wonderful reading experience . . . as [the characters'] stories unfold, you almost feel they have become friends." —Wichita Falls *Times Record News*

"[Debbie Macomber] draws in threads of her earlier book in this series, *The Inn at Rose Harbor,* in what is likely to be just as comfortable a place for Macomber fans as for Jo Marie's guests at the inn."
—*The Seattle Times*

"Macomber's legions of fans will embrace this cozy, heartwarming read." —*Booklist*

"Readers will find the emotionally impactful storylines and sweet, redemptive character arcs for which the author is famous. Classic Macomber, which will please fans and keep them coming back for more."
—*Kirkus Reviews*

"Macomber is an institution in women's fiction. Her principal talent lies in creating characters with a humble, familiar charm. They possess complex personalities, but it is their kinder qualities that are emphasized in the warm world of her novels—a world much like Rose Harbor Inn, in which one wants to curl up and stay." —*Shelf Awareness*

"The storybook scenery of lighthouses, cozy bed and breakfast inns dotting the coastline, and seagulls flying above takes readers on personal journeys of first love, lost love and recaptured love [presenting] love in its purest and most personal forms." —*Bookreporter*

"Just the right blend of emotional turmoil and satisfying resolutions . . . For a feel-good indulgence, this book delivers." —*RT Book Reviews* (4 stars)

The Inn at Rose Harbor

"Debbie Macomber's Cedar Cove romance novels have a warm, comfy feel to them. Perhaps that's why they've sold millions." —*USA Today*

"No one tugs at readers' heartstrings quite as effectively as Macomber." —*Chicago Tribune*

"The characters and their various entanglements are sure to resonate with Macomber fans. . . . The book sets up an appealing milieu of townspeople and visitors that sets the stage for what will doubtless be many further adventures at the Inn at Rose Harbor."
—*The Seattle Times*

"Debbie Macomber is the reigning queen of women's fiction." —*The Sacramento Bee*

Blossom Street

Blossom Street Brides

"[An] enjoyable read that pulls you right in from page one." —*Fresh Fiction*

"A master at writing stories that embrace both romance and friendship, [Debbie] Macomber can always be counted on for an enjoyable page-turner, and this Blossom Street installment is no exception."
—*RT Book Reviews*

"A wonderful, love-affirming novel . . . an engaging, emotionally fulfilling story that clearly shows why [Macomber] is a peerless storyteller." —*Examiner.com*

"Rewarding . . . Macomber amply delivers her signature engrossing relationship tales, wrapping her readers in warmth as fuzzy and soft as a hand-knitted creation from everyone's favorite yarn shop." —*Bookreporter*

"Fans will happily return to the warm, welcoming sanctuary of Macomber's Blossom Street, catching up with old friends from past Blossom Street books and meeting new ones being welcomed into the fold."
—*Kirkus Reviews*

"Macomber's nondenominational-inspirational women's novel, with its large cast of characters, will resonate with fans of the popular series." —*Booklist*

"*Blossom Street Brides* gives Macomber fans sympathetic characters who strive to make the right choices as they cope with issues that face many of today's women. Readers will thoroughly enjoy spending time on Blossom Street once again and watching as Lydia, Bethanne and Lauren struggle to solve their problems, deal with family crises, fall in love and reach their own happy endings." —*BookPage*

Starting Now

"Macomber has a masterful gift of creating tales that are both mesmerizing and inspiring, and her talent is at its peak with *Starting Now*. Her Blossom Street characters seem as warm and caring as beloved friends, and the new characters ease into the series smoothly. The storyline moves along at a lovely pace, and it is a joy to sit down and savor the world of Blossom Street once again." —Wichita Falls *Times Record News*

"Macomber understands the often complex nature of a woman's friendships, as well as the emotional language women use with their friends." —*NY Journal of Books*

"There is a reason that legions of Macomber fans ask for more Blossom Street books. They fully engage her readers as her characters discover happiness, purpose, and meaning in life. . . . Macomber's feel-good novel, emphasizing interpersonal relationships and putting people above status and objects, is truly satisfying."
—*Booklist* (starred review)

"Macomber's writing and storytelling deliver what she's famous for—a smooth, satisfying tale with characters her fans will cheer for and an arc that is cozy, heartwarming and ends with the expected happily-ever-after."
—*Kirkus Reviews*

"Macomber's many fans are going to be over the moon with her latest Blossom Street novel. *Starting Now* combines Macomber's winning elements of romance and friendship, along with a search for one woman's life's meaning—all cozily bundled into a warmly satisfying story that is the very definition of 'comfort reading.'" —*Bookreporter*

"Macomber's latest Blossom Street novel is a sweet story that tugs on the heartstrings and hits on the joy of family, friends and knitting, as readers have come to expect." —*RT Book Reviews* (4½ stars)

"The return to Blossom Street is an engaging visit for longtime readers as old friends play secondary roles while newcomers take the lead. . . . Fans will enjoy the mixing of friends and knitting with many kinds of loving relationships." —*Genre Go Round Reviews*

Christmas Novels

Twelve Days of Christmas

"Another heartwarming seasonal [Debbie] Macomber tale, which fans will find as bright and cozy as a blazing fire on Christmas Eve." —*Kirkus Reviews*

"*Twelve Days of Christmas* is a delightful, charming read for anyone looking for an enjoyable Christmas novel. . . . Settle in with a warm blanket and a cup of hot chocolate, and curl up for some Christmas fun with Debbie Macomber's latest festive read." —*Bookreporter*

"If you're looking for a quick but meaningful holiday romance that will be sure to spark a need inside you to show others kindness, look no further than *Twelve Days of Christmas*." —*Harlequin Junkie*

"*Twelve Days of Christmas* is a charming, heartwarming holiday tale. With poignant characters and an enchanting plot, Macomber again burrows into the fragility of human emotions to arrive at a delightful conclusion."
—*New York Journal of Books*

Dashing Through the Snow

"Wonderful and heartwarming . . . full of fun, laughter, and love." —*Romance Reviews Today*

"This Christmas romance from [Debbie] Macomber is both sweet and sincere." —*Library Journal*

"There's just the right amount of holiday cheer. . . . This road-trip romance is full of high jinks and the kooky characters Macomber does so well."
—*RT Book Reviews*

Mr. Miracle

"Macomber's Christmas novels are always something to cherish. *Mr. Miracle* is a sweet and innocent story that will lift your spirits during the holidays and throughout the year. Celebrating the comforts of home, family traditions, forgiveness and love, this is the perfect, quick Christmas read." —*RT Book Reviews*

"[Macomber] writes about romance, family and friendship with a gentle, humorous touch."
—*Tampa Bay Times*

"Macomber spins another sweet, warmhearted holiday tale that will be as comforting to her fans as hot chocolate on Christmas morning." —*Kirkus Reviews*

"This gentle, inspiring romance will be a sought-after read." —*Library Journal*

"Macomber cheerfully presents a holiday story that combines the winsomeness of a visiting angel (similar to Clarence from *It's a Wonderful Life*) with the more poignant soulfulness of *A Christmas Carol* to bring to life a memorable reading experience." —*Bookreporter*

"Macomber's name is almost as closely linked to Christmas reading as that of Charles Dickens. . . . [*Mr. Miracle*] has enough sweetness, charm, and seasonal sentiment to make Macomber fans happy."
—*The Romance Dish*

Starry Night

"Contemporary romance queen Macomber (*Rose Harbor in Bloom*) hits the sweet spot with this tender tale of impractical love. . . . A delicious Christmas miracle well worth waiting for."
—*Publishers Weekly* (starred review)

"[A] holiday confection . . . as much a part of the season for some readers as cookies and candy canes."
—*Kirkus Reviews*

"A sweet contemporary Christmas romance . . . [that] the best-selling author's many fans will enjoy."
—*Library Journal*

"Macomber can be depended on for an excellent story. . . . Readers will remain firmly planted in the beginnings of a beautiful love story between two of the most unlikely characters."
—*RT Book Reviews* (Top Pick, 4½ stars)

"Macomber, the prolific and beloved author of countless bestsellers, has penned a romantic story that will pull at your heartstrings with its holiday theme and emphasis on love and finding that special someone."
—*Bookreporter*

"Magical . . . Macomber has given us another delightful romantic story to cherish. This one will touch your heart just as much as her other Christmas stories. Don't miss it!" —*Fresh Fiction*

Angels at the Table

"This delightful mix of romance, humor, hope and happenstance is the perfect recipe for holiday cheer." —*Examiner.com*

"Rings in Christmas in tried-and-true Macomber style, with romance and a touch of heavenly magic." —*Kirkus Reviews*

"The angels' antics are a hugely hilarious and entertaining bonus to a warm love story." —*Bookreporter*

"[A] sweetly charming holiday romance." —*Library Journal*

Summer 2017

Dear Friends,

We all need second chances. Sometimes third and fourth chances. When I think of all the diets I've tried over the years, I can easily lose count of the times I've had to start over.

It was thinking about second chances that made me realize I'd like to write a story along those lines. Readers often ask what inspired a book. I got the idea for *Any Dream Will Do* while in prison. It's not what you're thinking! I spoke at the Washington Corrections Center for Women (WCCW) a few months back. What I realized afterward was that these women were not all that different from you or me. They'd all made mistakes and they were paying the price.

About the same time as I visited the corrections center, our family became involved with Seattle's Union Gospel Mission and Hope Place. My daughter Adele, who is my CEO, has gone out on several Search & Rescue missions serving the needs of the homeless. Several of my staff have since joined her on these nighttime sojourns, ministering to people living on the streets.

And so *Any Dream Will Do* was born. This is a story of redemption, of second chances, of learning from our mistakes, and of moving forward. I hope you fall in love with Shay and Drew the way I did.

This book is dedicated to our wonderful son-in-law Greg Banks. Over a year ago Greg was in a car accident, and the surgery that followed left him paralyzed on one half of his body. This has been a huge life adjustment for

Greg and our daughter Jody. Their faith, love, and support of each other amaze me every single day.

Hearing from my readers is one of my greatest joys as an author. As I like to say, I'm downright friendly, so please don't hesitate to contact me! You can do it a number of ways. The best place to leave me a note is on my website at debbiemacomber.com or on Facebook or Twitter. Or you can write me at P.O. Box 1458, Port Orchard, WA 98366.

Warmest regards,

Debbie Macomber

Any Dream Will Do

DEBBIE MACOMBER

Any Dream Will Do

A Novel

BALLANTINE BOOKS · NEW YORK

2017 Ballantine Books Mass Market Edition

Copyright © 2017 by Debbie Macomber
Excerpt from *A Girl's Guide to Moving On* by Debbie Macomber copyright © 2016 by Debbie Macomber

Published in the United States by Ballantine Books, an imprint of Random House, a division of Random House LLC, a Penguin Random House Company, New York.

BALLANTINE BOOKS and the HOUSE colophon are registered trademarks of Random House LLC.

Originally published in hardcover in the United States by Ballantine Books, an imprint of Random House, a division of Random House LLC, in 2016.

ISBN 978-0-399-18121-4
Ebook ISBN 978-0-399-18120-7

Cover design: Belina Huey
Cover photograph: Judie Long/Getty Images and Miles Studio/Stocksy United

Printed in the United States of America

randomhousebooks.com

9 8 7 6 5 4 3 2 1

Ballantine Books mass market edition: January 2018

To our son-in-law Greg Banks
For his inner strength, integrity, and honor
You bless our family

Any Dream Will Do

PROLOGUE

"I need the money."

My brother's eyes showed a desperation I had never seen in him before.

"Shay," he pleaded, "you don't understand. If I don't have it by tomorrow night they will kill me."

"They?" I repeated. "Who are *they*?" But I knew.

Caden had been waiting for me outside my tiny apartment that I shared with three roommates, pacing in front of my door when I got off work at the bank. I hadn't seen him in weeks, which was never a good sign. In some ways, I was grateful he'd stayed out of my life. This was my chance, the first real one I'd had, and my brother was trouble. "Tell me what happened," I said as I unlocked my apartment. He followed me inside and rammed his fingers through his hair with enough strength to uproot several strands.

"It's complicated . . ."

It always was with Caden. I'd been looking out for him nearly his entire life, but for once I had to think about myself. My gut was churning as I set the teakettle on the stove, afraid of what he was going to tell me.

Caden had met a lot of his bad connections through me and one boyfriend in particular. I'd fallen in deeper with Shooter than I'd ever intended, but through a community program I'd managed to break away from that lifestyle. With the help of one of the counselors I'd landed a job, a good one at a bank. For the first time in my life I had a chance at making something of myself. I had a shot at getting away from the gangs and the drugs and the lifestyle that would eventually lead to either prison or death. I had a small taste of what the future could be if I stayed away from people determined to hold me down. I'd made mistakes. Big ones, but I was working hard to put that behind me.

I should have known it wouldn't work. Not for someone like me. Caden was here to remind me I'd been living a pipe dream.

"Who's threatening to kill you?" I asked again, already anticipating the answer. It was Shooter or one of his gang members.

My brother closed his eyes and gripped hold of my forearm hard enough to cause a bruise. "You know."

"You're hanging with the Angels again?" I'd repeatedly warned Caden to stay away from the gang, which was anything but angelic.

He didn't respond, which was answer enough.

My hands trembled as I brought down two mugs and reached for the tea bags. My back was to Caden. "How much do you need?" I asked as I gritted my teeth. I'd managed to save a few hundred dollars. All I could do was hope that would be enough.

He hesitated before blurting out, "Five thousand."

"Dollars?" I gasped. The figure stunned me to the

point my knees felt weak, as if they were no longer capable of holding me upright. Caden had to know that amount was impossible for me. No way could I come up with that much. "I don't have that kind of money."

"Can you borrow it?" he pleaded. His dark brown eyes, so like my own, were wild, his voice frantic. "I'm not joking, Shay. If I don't hand over the money by tomorrow I'm a dead man."

Doing my best to remain calm, I looped a long strand of my auburn hair around my ear, racking my brain. No one was going to loan me that kind of cash. Working as a bank teller, I barely made enough to get by myself. Between rent and my accounting classes, I was already stretched financially. The few dollars I'd managed to save came from doing without lunch and eating ramen noodles for dinner.

Before I could explain that the possibility of a loan was hopeless, Caden tried again. "What about the bank?" he suggested, his gaze holding mine.

A tingling feeling started at the base of my neck and worked its way down my spine. Even before I answered, I knew what Caden was thinking.

My brother lowered his voice as if he expected someone was listening in through the thin apartment walls. "Can you get the money from the bank?" he asked.

"You mean a loan? No, they aren't going to loan me that kind of cash on what I make. I don't have anything for collateral." While I had a driver's license, I used public transportation. No way could I afford a car. Not even a scooter. Caden knew that.

"Not a loan, sis. The bank isn't going to miss it . . . at least not for a couple days. You take the money, and before anyone notices I'll have it for you to replace, no one will even know."

The knot in my stomach tightened to the point of pain. Surely Caden knew what he was asking me. I had hope for the first time since our mother died and now he was asking me to give it all up for him. The bank would miss that money and it wouldn't take them five minutes to figure out I was the one who took it.

Stiffening my spine, I decided then and there I wasn't going to throw away my future because my idiot brother had gotten himself into this kind of trouble.

"I can't. The bank doesn't work like that. The missing money will be discovered the same day."

"Shay, please. You know I wouldn't ask this of you if I wasn't desperate."

"I'm sorry . . ."

Caden slammed his fist against the tabletop. "Do you want me dead?" he shouted.

I flinched and shrunk back, half expecting him to hit me. It was what our father would have done. "I . . ."

"If you don't help me, you're signing my death warrant."

The kettle whistled as the water started to boil. I removed it from the burner and noticed how badly my hands were trembling. Caden was my brother, my only living relative. I'd looked after him when our mother died and later after our father passed, although his death had been a blessing, as far as I was concerned. Despite everything I had sacrificed for Caden, I tried my best to help him. But it seemed he was determined to continue to make poor choices. I wanted to rant at him for being weak, but then I had been weak, too. I felt responsible for introducing him to the Angels.

"Where will you get the money to repay me?" I asked.

Caden paced the tiny kitchen and ignored the mug I offered him.

"People owe me."

"Five thousand dollars?" I asked, unable to hide my doubt.

"I swear on our mother's life. I'll have the money by the end of the week."

Our mother had been everything to us. Everything. Caden had never sworn on her life before. I wanted to believe him but remained uncertain. He'd let me down countless times and I wasn't sure I should trust him. Not that it would matter. Even if I did replace the money, I'd lose my job.

Burying my face in my hands, I sank into the chair and closed my eyes. "Let me think."

"While you're thinking, the minutes are ticking away." He sounded more angry than worried now, furious with me for not immediately agreeing to his plan. "I can't believe you. I'm your brother. You could save my life and *you need to think about it*?"

I exhaled a staggered breath. "You're the one who got into this mess, not me."

Caden's face fell as if I'd wounded him. He fell to his knees and pressed his forehead against my legs as he'd done as a child after our mother died. "I don't know what else to do," he cried. "They're going to kill me, Shay, and when they do, it won't be quick and easy. They'll want to make an example of me. They'll start by breaking all my bones, and then . . ." He started to cry, his shoulders shaking with fear.

I placed a comforting hand on his back. "Can't the Angels wait a couple days until you have the money?" I whispered, hoping the gang would be reasonable if they knew it was coming. I wove my fingers into his hair the way Mom would have done. "Don't you have some collateral to offer?"

Caden exhaled slowly. "I owe more people than the Angels . . . these people aren't willing to listen to any more excuses. The collateral they'd want is either one of my arms or a leg."

I gasped, wanting to weep that my baby brother had gotten involved with loan sharks. Men who were thugs and criminals. All Caden and I had in this world was each other. If I was desperate, the one person I could reach out to for help would be my brother.

"You said you can replace the money within a couple days?"

He raised his head from my knee, his gaze wide and hopeful. "I swear," he said, gripping hold of my hand and pressing his lips to it.

"I hope you realize what will happen to me if I do this." He had to understand the consequences for me. Best-case scenario, I'd get fired from a job I considered my only shot at a real future. Worst case, I'd be incarcerated, even if I did return the money. No way would that amount of missing cash go unnoticed.

"I promise you, Shay, you won't go to prison," he said. "No way would I let my sister end up behind bars."

—

Two months later, I accepted the guilty plea for embezzling as recommended by my court-appointed attorney. From the Seattle cell, I was placed on a transport bus from King County jail and driven across the Tacoma Narrows bridge to the Washington Corrections Center for Women in Purdy, Washington.

When the prison door locked behind me, the sound reverberated in my head like a thunderbolt, shaking the entire room. I was locked away from any hope for a decent future. Any hope of making something out of my crummy life.

From any hope whatsoever.

My sentence was three years. I'd risked everything for my brother. I had no one to blame but myself. After giving the money to Caden, I hadn't heard from or seen him since. His promise was empty. I'd known it at the time and had still given in. Deep down I accepted that my brother couldn't be trusted. He'd never intended to fulfill his promise, and now I was paying the price.

Helping Caden had stolen my future and sentenced me to a life I had worked so hard to escape.

All was lost.

Any chance for a decent future.

All hope.

I don't know what made me believe there would ever be anything else but struggles and pain for me. Even when I tried to do the right thing, I got kicked in the head.

CHAPTER 1

Shay

Three years later

I was released from the Washington Corrections Center for Women in Purdy at midnight the first week of December. Apparently the state of Washington wasn't interested in paying for my upkeep one minute longer than necessary. No one stood outside the prison gates to greet me. Any friends I'd made while working at Pacific Bank had been quick to disassociate themselves from me, not that I blamed them. My only living family was my brother, and he was the reason I'd gone to prison in the first place.

In all three years of my incarceration, I hadn't received a single letter from Caden. The first letter I'd mailed him had been returned with a notice that he'd moved with no forwarding address. I shouldn't have been surprised. For all I knew he'd taken that five thousand dollars and escaped to Mexico. One thing I could count on was the fact that he didn't have a shred of guilt for what he'd done to me.

Bitterness ate at me, consumed me. I should have ulcers for all the nights I'd lain awake and replayed that final scene with Caden. What an idiot I'd been to let him talk me into stealing money for him. To save his life. Yeah, right. Caden had missed his calling. He should be on the stage. His acting ability was worthy of a Tony.

As much as possible I stayed to myself while in prison. I took accounting classes, although it was probably a waste of time with my record. I sincerely doubted any company would take a chance on hiring me. As for the dream of one day getting my CPA license, that ship had sailed. The best I could hope for now was working as a hotel maid or in a restaurant washing dishes. Whatever it was, I was going to need housing and a job, and I was going to need them immediately.

Right. Like that was going to happen.

I had information on the closest bus stop, walked there in the cold and dark, and waited until daylight. I sat, chilled to the bone, with the wind buffeting against me until I got on the first available bus that would take me to downtown Seattle, over fifty miles away. Everything I owned in the world was in one small suitcase. All I had on me was a few hundred dollars in cash. I was afraid to spend it on anything other than bare necessities, not knowing how long I was going to need it to last.

The one constant for nearly the entire length of my sentence had been letters from an elderly woman named Elizabeth. She was a retired teacher who volunteered for Prison Fellowship, the Christian organization started by Chuck Colson, another felon. In her letters, Elizabeth talked a lot about God and her own life.

I wasn't particularly interested in either, but it was mail. I was desperate for any link with the outside world. While I was grateful, this old lady had no idea of what my life was like. She lived in a lily-white world that was the opposite of my own. I read her letters but basically ignored what she had to say. She seemed to consider it her duty to be hopeful for me, to encourage and inspire me. When I did write her back I pretended to believe her, but I knew better. It was far too late for me. I had no future. The poor woman was delusional. She didn't have a clue. Not a single clue of what my life was like.

In my last letter, I explained that when I was released I would have no place to live, no job, no family to help me. I laughed when I read her reply. She wrote that I should trust God and that she'd be praying for me. Yeah, right, like it had worked so well in the past.

I quickly wrote her back with a page full of questions. Doubts poured out of me until the letter was an entire page, written on both sides. I vented about the injustices that had happened in my life, the unfairness, my anger and fears. My hand could barely move fast enough to keep up with my thoughts. The lead in the pencil broke several times as I pressed it hard against the paper and I blasted at her for being naïve.

This woman was a joke.

In the end, I didn't mail the letter. Why waste a stamp? Elizabeth had this mountain of faith, and my own resembled a pothole in the road. She'd been kind and it felt wrong to lash out at her for not understanding my situation.

I stayed on the bus for three hours until it hit Fourth Avenue in the heart of downtown Seattle. It took that long for the warmth to seep into my bones after my long wait in the December cold.

My first day of freedom and I had nowhere to go. I had

nowhere to sleep that night and no one to ask for help. I stepped out onto the sidewalk and drew in a deep breath. A homeless person was asleep on the sidewalk, tucked up against the bus shelter. That could well be me in a matter of hours.

Breathing in the taste of freedom, I had to admit it frightened me more than anything ever had, including my father's fist. To my surprise, when I looked up I realized the bus had let me off in front of a church.

It was almost comical. A church. Really?

Not having anyplace else to go, I decided to step inside and hope it was warm and that no one would kick me out. I had a list of shelters in Seattle, but spending the night in one was my last resort. From what I'd been told, shelters didn't take people in until nightfall, which was hours away. A church would be a relatively safe place to hang around until I could find someplace else.

I walked up the steps to the church, and thankfully the door opened. I'd half suspected that it would be locked up tight. I wasn't there to pray. All I wanted was to stay out of the cold.

Once inside, I went from the lobby into the interior, which was dark and empty. As I stood in the back and looked toward the altar, the sanctuary felt cavernous. I was sure if I were to call out, my voice would echo back at me. Row upon row of wooden pews lined each side of the center aisle.

I had been inside a church only a few times in my life. Once with my mother, who took my brother and me on Christmas Eve; I must have been four or five at the time. Dad got mad when he found out about it, shouting at Mom. I remembered his anger more than anything that happened while we were at church. They gave me a little Bible, but Dad took it away. I'd wanted to keep it and cried because I'd never had a book before. Mom said I could get another someday, but I never did.

I stood in the middle of the church aisle. It didn't look anything like the church of my childhood memory. The church of my youth had been a small neighborhood one. This was a large city church. Stained-glass windows allowed meager light to flicker against the floors. Unsure what to do next, I slipped into the back pew and sat down. A nativity scene was set up close to the altar and I focused on the figure of the baby. I felt as helpless as a newborn, alone and desperate.

Tears pricked at my eyes, but I refused to let them fall. I was tough by this time; emotion was a weakness I didn't dare display while behind bars. I'd seen what happened to the women who lowered their guard and showed signs of vulnerability. I was determined it would never be me. Consequently, I'd shut down emotionally as much as possible, remaining stoic and indifferent to all but a precious few.

After thirty minutes of sitting and staring into space, I was tempted to get up and leave. I didn't know what I was thinking to come into a church. This was a useless waste of time, but for whatever reason I remained seated.

While it was true I had nowhere else to go, I should be looking for a job or doing something. Anything. Sitting in church wasn't going to solve my problems.

"You got anything for me?" I challenged. I wasn't sure who I was talking to, not that it mattered. It was a ridiculous question.

This was bad. I hadn't been free for twenty-four hours and already I was losing it.

Sagging forward, I leaned my head against the back of the wooden pew while resisting the urge to give in to self-pity. I was disgusted with myself when tears filled my eyes. I was stronger than this. I released a slow, shuddering breath, my chest tight with anxiety and fear.

In that moment something changed. Something in me. I experienced a sense of peace. Or something like it. I hadn't felt peaceful in so long that I couldn't be sure what it was. Of course, it could have been my imagination, but some of the tenseness left my shoulder blades and I felt my body relax.

Shrugging it off but willing to test this strange feeling, I tried speaking again but then realized I had nothing to say.

I needed help. A little guidance would be appreciated. It wasn't like I was looking for God or anyone else to part the Red Sea or to give a blind man sight. All I cared about was where my next meal was coming from and where I would find a bed that night. The thought of sleeping on the street terrified me. A job would be helpful, too.

The more I dwelled on my immediate future, the more tense I grew. Whatever peace I'd experienced earlier was fleeting at best. I closed my eyes and exhaled, searching to find it within myself.

None came. No surprise there. The only person I'd ever been able to depend on was myself. If ever there was a time I needed to pull myself up by my bootstraps, it was now.

Coming into this church had been a mistake. I should

have known better. Churches like this weren't meant for people like me.

I started to get up, feeling a little like Indiana Jones in the movie when he had to step off a ledge in faith and hope that a bridge would appear out of nowhere. As I stood, my purse dropped to the floor, making a loud noise that seemed to reverberate through the church like an echo against a canyon wall. For just an instant I stood frozen.

It was then that I noticed I wasn't alone. Someone else was in the church, kneeling in the front. At the sound of my purse dropping, the man turned and looked over his shoulder.

Then he stood and I froze in shock as he started walking toward me. Without a doubt I knew that whoever this man was, he was going to ask me to leave. I stiffened, determined to meet him head-on. If he was going to toss me onto the street I would be sure to tell him I'd been kicked out of better places than this.

CHAPTER 2

Drew

I knelt in front of the church, broken and lost.

Empty.

My wife was dead, my children were hurting, and my congregation was drifting away. Fewer and fewer numbers showed up each week. In essence, my faith was shot.

On my knees, I poured out my heart in prayer, seeking guidance and help. I'd started out in ministry with enthusiasm and high expectations. My goal was to make a difference in people's lives, to write books based on Scripture that would reach others in their faith journey.

The problem, as best as I could describe it, was this: I couldn't give away what I didn't have to give. I felt bereft, hurting and uncertain. Katie's death had taken a toll on me and the children—that was understood. My congregation had been patient with me. More than patient, but it was three years now and it was no better.

The intense grief had passed, but I realized things were different. Something had changed.

I wasn't the same man any longer.

I didn't have what it took to stand in front of the church each week and speak to the needs of the people. I

couldn't help anyone when I seemed incapable of helping myself. I'd stumbled in my own walk, lacking faith,
lacking trust.

Simply lacking.

Some might suggest I'd burned out, but the fact was
that I hadn't been able to start a fire. There'd been nothing to put out, especially in the last three years. I hung
my head, disappointed in myself, pleading with God to
guide me, show me what He would have me do.

I was half inclined to submit my resignation to the elders. That was an option, of course, but the ramifications to myself and the children would be substantial.
Mark and Sarah had been through enough, dealing with
the death of their mother. The last thing they needed at
this point was to be uprooted from the only home they'd
ever known. Plus, in my current state of mind, I couldn't
be assured another church would be willing to accept me
as their pastor or that I should even continue in ministry.
Maybe it would be best all around if I sought out another career entirely.

I'd talked with Linda Kincaid, one of the women in
the congregation, who worked as a tireless volunteer. She
had retired from teaching and played a major role in the
life of the church. She'd become my right hand, along
with my assistant, Mary Lou. Between the two of them,
they'd kept me afloat this long.

Linda was a trusted friend and a good sounding board.
I don't know what I would have done without her. It was
her hard work that kept the volunteer programs running
smoothly. As I prayed, I thanked God for her and her
willingness to step in and help. She'd suggested I stick it

out, give myself time. She'd once told me that if I felt God was far away, then I was the one who'd moved.

Talk about hitting the nail on the head. What I needed now was to find a way back.

As I continued to pray I heard a noise in the back of the church. I wasn't aware anyone else was in the sanctuary. When I got up from my knees I saw a woman standing at a back pew. Even from this distance I noticed she had the look of a deer caught in the headlights. Her wide-eyed expression made me think she was up to no good.

I started toward her with the elders' warnings ringing in my ears, reminding me of the risk I took leaving the church unlocked during the day. They felt it was an open invitation to vagrants and vandals. I'd won the argument, but now I wondered if I'd made the right decision.

As I drew close I saw it was a young woman. Her gaze skirted mine, which made me suspicious.

"Can I help you?" I asked. "I'm Drew Douglas, the pastor here."

"Pastor?" she repeated as if the word felt awkward on her tongue.

"What can I do for you?" I asked, doing my best to disguise my reservations. The small suitcase by her side was curious. She didn't look like a tourist, and the church, while one of the older ones in town, wasn't exactly a Seattle attraction.

The woman swallowed hard and offered me the weakest of smiles. "I was just leaving. Don't worry, I'll get out of your hair."

She seemed to muster up her courage, and her eyes snapped defiantly.

"I'm not here to ask you to leave."

Her steady look challenged me. She seemed to be saying she didn't believe I'd welcome her in the church.

"Do you need help?"

She blinked hard, as though surprised by the question. "No . . . I don't need anything."

Again, she spoke with a razor-sharp edge, her voice cutting, her shoulders stiff. She might claim otherwise, but I knew she was lying. She struggled to look indifferent, but I read the desperation in her eyes. This woman needed help, but pride prevented her from asking for it.

"Can you tell me why you're here?"

"Ah . . . no, well, yes." She fumbled with her words and didn't seem to know where to start. "The bus let me off in front of the church."

"The bus," I repeated, unable to follow her line of thought.

She lifted her head and looked me square in the eyes. "I was released from prison this morning." As if anticipating me tossing her out, she reached for her suitcase and started for the door.

Years ago I'd been involved in prison ministry, but my work had always been with men.

"Please don't go," I said and gestured toward the pew. "You clearly came into the church for a reason. Let's talk."

She hesitated, as if that was the last thing she expected me to say. "This going to take long?" she asked, with the same brash, uncertain edge.

"Not long at all."

She shrugged as if she was doing me a favor, sitting down in the pew next to me. Unsure where to start, I waited for her to speak. I was patient, knowing if I waited long enough she'd explain her circumstances.

"You should know I'm a convicted felon."

I shrugged. "Don't suppose they tossed you in the clink for jaywalking," I said, dismissing her words. In an effort to encourage her, I smiled. "Do you have somewhere to live?"

She stiffened and shook her head. "Not yet."

"How about a job?"

It took her longer to answer this time. "No." Her shoulders slumped forward before she quickly straightened again.

It would be easy enough to wish her the best and let her go. She wasn't expecting any help and appeared to resent answering my questions. Another lost soul who drifted through the church doors. I couldn't do much for her; we didn't run a shelter and my resources were limited. It would be best to offer to pray with her and let her go. I opened my mouth to do exactly that and found I couldn't. Even knowing the elders were likely to disapprove, I didn't feel I could ignore her need. "Come with me."

Her head snapped up as if she suspected I had some nefarious intention. "Where are you taking me?"

"I have a few contacts who might be able to help you."

She stood, blinked a couple times, and then quickly sat back down. Placing her hand over her heart, she exhaled and went pale.

"Miss?"

"Sorry, I had a dizzy spell. I'm fine."

Dizzy spell? "When was the last time you ate?"

"Yesterday."

"They didn't feed you in prison?" Silly question, because I knew they did.

"I wasn't hungry."

A more honest answer would have been that she was too anxious about being released to eat.

"No wonder you're light-headed." We had a small kitchen in the church office, but we didn't keep much in the way of food there, other than a few snack items. "There are sandwiches in the office kitchen." I didn't mention that she'd be eating my lunch.

"I don't need anything."

This woman was too proud for her own good.

"Please, I hate to hurt Mary Lou's feelings." When she gave me a confused look, I clarified. "She's the one who brings in the sandwiches. She makes my lunch and then adds extra."

"She your wife or something?"

"No, my assistant. My wife died a few years back. Making my lunch is Mary Lou's way of being sure I pause long enough to eat. You'd be doing us both a favor."

"Yeah, right."

She thought about my offer cautiously. I doubted anyone was going to pull anything over on her.

I started up the aisle, expecting her to follow, taking her through the side door that led to my office.

Mary Lou looked up from the computer screen and her eyes automatically went to the young woman who accompanied me.

"Mary Lou, I'd like you to meet . . ." I hesitated when I realized I hadn't asked for the woman's name.

"Shay," she supplied. "Shay Benson."

"Hello, Shay," Mary Lou said, without missing a beat.

"I met up with Shay in the church. Would you show her into the kitchen while I make a few phone calls?" I asked.

"Of course."

Mary Lou stood from behind her desk and led the way down the narrow hallway while I headed into my office.

"Oh, and Mary Lou," I called out, "would you bring out the sandwiches? Shay will be joining me for lunch."

Without a pause, Mary Lou agreed. She looked at Shay. "If you'll come this way."

The woman was a rare jewel. Her easy acceptance of me giving up my lunch made me appreciate her all the more.

Stepping into my office, I closed the door, sat down at my desk, and reached for my phone. The one place I felt would help Shay most was Hope Center, which was run by one of the gospel mission agencies in town. They had high standards, which meant Shay would need to pass a rigorous examination and drug testing.

The ladies' group at the church provided dinner for the residents once a month, and I'd known Kevin Forester, the director, for several years. We hadn't talked in longer than I could remember. It was time to correct that. Like so much else in my life, I'd let friendships slide since I'd lost Katie.

Within a matter of minutes I connected with Kevin. "Kevin," I greeted, "Drew Douglas here."

"Drew." Kevin sounded genuinely happy to hear from me. "How are you, man?"

"Better," I said, exaggerating the truth. "I need a favor."

"Sure. What's up?"

"I found a lost soul in my church this morning." I went on to explain what I'd learned from Shay.

Kevin listened intently and then asked, "Do you know if she has a history of drug use?"

I hadn't done street ministry in years but was fairly sure I'd recognize the signs. "Looking at her, I'd say no, but I can't be sure."

"Alcohol?"

"She actually looks pretty good. Again, it's difficult to tell, but like I said, she looks clean."

He hesitated. "She mentioned a felony charge?"

"Yes. I didn't ask her what it was about and she didn't offer."

"I can find out easily enough. It's all a matter of public record."

I was curious myself but would wait for her to volunteer the information.

"Did you tell her it's a yearlong program?" Kevin asked me, breaking into my thoughts.

"No. I didn't want to get her hopes up until I learned if you had a free bed."

Kevin exhaled. "If you'd called thirty minutes ago, I would have had to turn you away. We have a no-tolerance drug policy here and we found meth in one of the residents' rooms."

The timing impressed me. An opening right when one was needed. "Can I bring her by for an interview?"

"No guarantees."

That went without saying.

"Got you. I don't have any skin in this." It was important that Kevin understand I wouldn't take a refusal personally. Shay's acceptance was up to her and her willingness to work 24/7 in a life-skills program. "If she's approved, great. If not, then I did what I could."

"Right," Kevin said. "Bring her by this afternoon and I'll have my staff do an evaluation. It'll be a few days before we'll be ready to accept her, if we do."

I wasn't sure Shay had anyplace to sleep and said as much. I hated the thought of her spending the night on the street.

"I'll get her into one of the shelters until we get the test results back," Kevin said.

"I'd appreciate whatever you can do."

Kevin hesitated. "It's been awhile."

"It has," I agreed.

"How are you, man?"

"Good."

"Drew," he said, unwilling to let it drop. "How. Are. You?"

I hesitated. There'd been a time when Kevin and I were close. We'd attended seminary together, played basketball, and were ushers in each other's weddings. I'd lost track of the last time we'd talked.

"Empty," I admitted, feeling like a failure. "I feel empty."

"You personally bringing this woman by this afternoon?"

"Yeah."

"Block out the rest of your day."

"Can't," I argued. "I've got meetings set up. There's an electrician coming by to . . ."

"Cancel it. No excuses."

"Kevin . . ."

"Cancel those appointments."

Groaning, I wanted to argue with him. I'd waited a week for this electrician and didn't know how long it would take for him to manage to return. Furthermore, this other meeting was important. It was with Alex Turnbull, one of the elders, who wanted to rehash the budget numbers. With attendance down, giving had dropped substantially. Adjustments had to be made.

It wasn't like I was looking forward to cutting programs. We'd already done away with the monthly newsletter we mailed out. A good portion of the congregation was older and not many were computer savvy, so when the newsletter was delivered via email it had created a problem. We'd cut back on the janitorial services and lowered the heat in the church. My mind raced with the difficult decisions facing me.

Truthfully, I'd like nothing more than to avoid seeing Alex and dealing with the church's finances. The thing was, I had responsibilities, ones that weighed heavily on my shoulders.

"What do you have in mind?" I asked before I stated my argument.

"Basketball," Kevin said.

The word hung in the air between us. He must be joking. It was a good thing Kevin couldn't see me roll my eyes. "I can't cancel these appointments so we can run around a basketball court."

"Yes, you can. There's a thing called self-maintenance. Whether you're willing to admit it or not, you need this. I'm not going to listen to excuses. Either you show or I'm going to come collect you myself."

"It's been years since I played basketball." Before Katie's cancer. Before that even. Years. I was rusty and out of shape. Kevin was sure to run circles around me. My entire life revolved around the church and my family. What Kevin called self-maintenance hadn't been on my to-do list for longer than I could remember.

"You hear me?" Kevin demanded. "I said I'm not listening to any arguments."

I sighed, accepting defeat. I recognized that tone of voice and wouldn't put it past him to come to the office and collect me like an errant teen.

My call had been on behalf of Shay, hoping Kevin would be able to help her. I hadn't expected more than a quick phone conversation. Now this.

For all I knew, Kevin was the answer to Shay's prayers. And to mine as well.

CHAPTER 3

Shay

I wasn't sure what to think when Pastor Douglas told me about Hope Center. Seeing how limited my options were, I agreed to go with him, but my expectations weren't high. Why should they be?

When we arrived I thought the building was a hotel. I assumed the center would look more like one of the run-down shelters. One with cots shored up against the walls and people lined up early to be sure they were there in time for a hot meal and a bed. Not this modern high-rise building.

"Pastor . . ." I stood outside, unsure this was the right place. "This is it? Hope Center?" I called him pastor but I thought of him as Drew. That was the way he'd introduced himself to me and it was the name that stuck in my head.

"Is there a problem?"

I shook my head, biting back my surprise. We'd both been quiet on the drive over and I wondered if he regretted his willingness to help me. I kept quiet for fear my acid tongue would ruin this chance.

We found parking along the side of the building and

then walked toward the entrance. I took in everything I could as we headed in that direction. I saw a line of pre-school children walking with three adults. The children cheerfully bounced along, holding hands. Their smiling faces startled me. It had been a long time since I'd heard children laugh. Drew had mentioned earlier that Hope Center took in mothers with children and I wondered if these little ones were some of those. It didn't seem likely, seeing how happy they looked.

Joyful.

I hadn't known joy, true joy, in such a long time that witnessing it, seeing it in others, struck me like a slap in the face. Not in a hurtful way but more like an awakening. From the moment I'd lost my mother, all sense of comfort and love had been ripped away.

Once inside the building we were greeted by a receptionist, just as if we were registering for a hotel room. Only we weren't given room keys. Instead, we signed in and were handed badges that identified us as visitors. I kept looking around suspiciously, not knowing what to expect. A decorated Christmas tree sat in the corner of the foyer with wrapped packages stacked below it.

My heart pounded like I'd been running uphill, and I knew the reason. I'd alluded to the fact that I'd made mistakes in the past, but I hadn't mentioned what they were. Drew wasn't my confessor and no way was I willing to spill my guts to him—or anyone else, for that matter.

I wasn't proud of the relationships I'd had, especially as a teenager. Part of the reason I'd stolen the money to help Caden had been out of guilt. It was because of me that my brother had fallen into drugs.

I was the one who'd introduced him to Shooter.

At one time Shooter had been my boyfriend. An older bad boy who'd taken a liking to me. I'd never had anyone tell me I was pretty before or think I was anything special. Shooter did, or said so. It wasn't until later that I learned how he got his name. It didn't take long for me to discover he was a younger version of my dad, only instead of alcohol, he was into meth and crack cocaine. When he used, he got violent. It was only after he was arrested that I was able to break free of him. That was the chance I needed and I'd grabbed hold of it with both hands and escaped.

Shooter didn't like me going to school, so I'd dropped out my senior year to be with him. First thing I did when he was sent to prison was get my GED. With the help of a counselor and my diploma in hand, I searched for a job that would support me enough to get away from the life I desperately wanted to escape. The job as a bank teller had been the opportunity I'd only dreamed about, and I'd blown it.

Big-time.

No one was going to be willing to give me another chance and I couldn't blame them. But that was water under the bridge. I couldn't think like that. Elizabeth, my prison pen pal, had once assured me that there would be more chances for me. I didn't believe her. Yet here I was, on the threshold of an unexpected break. Seeing that my history left a lot to be desired, I was afraid, scared out of my wits that I had blown this chance, too.

Drew and I were told to take a seat and I did, sitting on the edge of the cushion, my heart beating so loud and hard I was afraid he would hear it and comment.

He glanced over at me and offered a reassuring smile. "You okay?"

"Of course," I snapped, as if I resented the question. Lies came easily to me, always had. Wasn't sure I could break the habit. Wasn't sure it was possible.

Within a few minutes we were approached by two people. A man and a woman.

Drew stood as they came closer. The man grinned at Drew and the two pumped fists like they were brothers.

"Shay," Drew said, addressing me. "This is Kevin Forester; he's the director of Hope Center."

I met his look and bobbed my head in recognition.

"And this is Lilly Palmer. She's going to handle your evaluation," Kevin said, speaking to me.

Lilly stared at me as if sizing me up and finding me lacking.

Her eyes cut straight through me. So it was going to be like that. Fine, I could take whatever she had to dish out. What little hope I'd held quickly faded. As nuts as it sounded, I wanted to take hold of Drew's hand. The thought stunned me. I wasn't a pansy. I could take care of myself. I had been doing it from the time I was barely a teenager. I didn't need him or anyone else.

Besides, I barely knew the man. I was nothing to him. I was nothing to anyone.

As if he'd read my thoughts, Drew offered me a gentle smile and patted my shoulder. "You're going to do great."

"If you'll come with me," Lilly said, no warmth in her. This woman was cold.

Stiffening my shoulders and my resolve, I followed. A dozen steps and I looked back to see Drew and Kevin deep in conversation. This wasn't like me. I didn't need him. To my embarrassment, Drew must have felt my eyes on him, because he looked up and nodded as if to say that I had nothing to worry about.

Yeah, right.

Lilly led me into a cubicle and gestured for me to take a seat. She sat down on the other side of the desk and set her hands on top, looking me over.

"As you know, my name is Lilly," she said. "I need to ask you a few questions."

"Go ahead." I stiffened but played nice.

"I expect honesty, Shay. If I find out you're lying you will automatically be excluded from the program."

"I'm not a liar," I returned defensively, which on its own was a lie.

Lilly snickered as if she had prior knowledge of every lie I'd ever said. Relaxing against the back of her chair, she looked me straight in the eye. "I think you should know, I sat in that chair myself at one time, full of bravado and attitude. My life was a mess. I was into drugs, alcohol, and bad men. I was going a hundred miles an hour on the road to self-destruction. I've been clean and sober for five years. If you'd told me that was even possible six years ago, I would have laughed in your face."

Of everything I'd expected Lilly to say, it wasn't that.

"This is your chance to make a change, Shay. Your *one* chance. We're here to help make that a reality, but what happens next is on you. *It's all on you.* If you want this, you have to be the one to make it happen. You think you're smart enough to fool me, then think again. You think you're smart, well, I'm smarter. You aren't going to fool me, so don't even bother trying.

"Whatever got you here, you're at the center now and you have a choice to make. Choose carefully. You can change the course of self-destruction or you can continue on the same path. Now, what's it going to be?"

Her words were hard, and her look cut into me as effectively as a knife with a serrated edge. She waited and I gulped. It was as if she had read my mind. It was difficult for me to admit that I needed this program, wanted this program. I'd failed at nearly everything I'd ever wanted in my life. Failed miserably. There was nothing to say this would be any different.

Even getting the words out of my mouth seemed unmanageable. "I want this."

"That's good to hear, a good start. Every woman who steps through that door wants a better life. I'm here to tell you that this isn't going to be easy. You're going to want to quit a hundred times, but if you do you'll go right back to where you started.

"You can succeed, Shay, but you've got to be the one to make that happen. Not a single woman here can do it for you. It's going to mean tearing down that wall, trusting others, opening your life and living in the truth, and that, my friend, leaves you naked and exposed."

She waited, as if expecting me to tell her how grateful I was. Instead, I said the first thing that came to mind. "I am not your friend."

Lilly grinned. "You might not realize it yet, but I'm the best friend you'll ever have. Now, you ready to answer these questions?"

Although I didn't dare say it aloud, I was determined that Lilly would never be my friend. I hadn't known her more than a few minutes and already I didn't like her.

She was abrupt and callous, reminding me of a few prison guards I'd known. Righteous bitches.

Turning toward the computer screen, she set her fingers on the keyboard and threw questions at me, typing in my answers. She wanted honesty and she got it. I didn't hold anything back. Before we were finished she knew more about my family background than anyone else in the world besides my brother.

I told her about Shooter, too, and the fact that he was sentenced to life. For that I was especially thankful, although I didn't mention that.

After I finished the evaluation, I was given urine and blood tests. "You do know I was released from prison this morning, right?" It wasn't like I'd had the chance to buy anything illegal.

Lilly laughed. "You want drugs and alcohol, you'll find them inside and outside of prison walls. I don't care if you stepped off the bus on your way out the door and walked straight into this building—you'd still be tested."

"Okay." What she said was true enough. Drugs were as accessible in prison as they were on the streets.

Once I'd finished with the urine test, Lilly said, "Do you have any questions for me?"

"How long does this program take?"

She shook her head. "You haven't been accepted and you're already wondering how soon you can leave. Not a good sign, sister."

At some point I'd swapped from being a friend to becoming a sister. Wasn't sure if I should read anything into that.

"Twelve months," Lilly told me before I could comment.

"And afterward? What happens to me after I graduate?" I wasn't sure "graduate" was the right word, but it seemed to fit best. A year was a long time, not that I had any other plans.

From everything I'd learned to this point, I was free to leave at any time. The program was structured with a variety of classes, counseling sessions, and work assignments. Everyone did their part to keep the center running smoothly.

"By the time you leave, if all goes well, you'll have a job and housing arrangements."

I felt the faint stirring of hope take root and sprout. I quickly squelched it down. Hope was dangerous for someone like me. It led to pain and disappointment. "I'll be able to support myself?"

"Up to you, my friend."

So I was no longer her sister. Demoted already.

Lilly led me to another part of the building and knocked before entering a second cubicle. A woman I would guess to be in her early fifties glanced up from her desk when we entered. "Brenda, meet Shay Benson. Shay, this is Brenda Jordan."

"Hello, Shay." Unlike Lilly, Brenda's smile was warm and welcoming.

I nodded toward her, keeping my lips pressed together, unwilling to say anything more, seeing that I'd already spilled my guts once.

"Should you be accepted, Brenda will be your case manager," Lilly explained. "She'll be the one who will work with you as you progress in the program. If you're able to follow through, remain in the truth, and be willing to do what's necessary, then Brenda will be the one to help you with life outside these doors. You got a problem, you look to Brenda. You need to talk, and you will, then you come to me. Got it?"

"Got it," I returned without emotion, although I wasn't entirely sure I did. Lilly smiled and nodded.

It was the first time I'd seen the counselor crack a smile. "That's a good start," she said approvingly.

Lilly left me with Brenda. Sitting down with the case manager, I answered a few questions, some of which had already been asked by Lilly. About thirty minutes into our session, her phone rang. Brenda reached for it and after the initial greeting her eyes switched to me.

"Give us five" was all she said.

Sure enough, about five minutes later she stood and directed me to follow her. On the way I happened to get a look at the wall clock and was surprised to realize it was already late in the afternoon. The time had zipped by.

Brenda led me to the front reception area and I returned my visitor's badge. When I turned around I saw Kevin Forester and Drew had joined us. Both were dressed in shorts and had towels looped around their necks. They looked like they'd just finished running a marathon.

Drew leaned forward and braced his hands on his knees as he sucked in oxygen. "You're killing me, man."

Kevin slapped him across the back. "I'll see you next week."

"Come on, Kev, I've got—"

"I'll see you next week," the other man said, cutting him off.

As if he didn't have the wherewithal to argue, Drew reluctantly nodded. "Next week."

"Same time as today."

"Gotcha."

"You don't show, then I'm coming for you."

"I said 'gotcha.'"

Another slap on the back and Kevin said, "Good." He looked to me then. "I've made arrangements at one of the women's shelters for the next two nights," he said.

I blinked, unsure if that meant I hadn't been accepted or what. Then I remembered that either Drew or Lilly had told me that it would take a couple days to have the committee review my evaluation and get the urine and blood tests back.

"Okay."

"I can drop you off at the shelter on my way back to the church," Drew offered.

Nodding, I accepted the ride. I wanted to thank him, but the words got stuck in my throat.

The sense of hope was back again. Unwilling to trust it, I shoved it out of my mind. When I'd first arrived at Hope Center, I hadn't known what to think, especially after meeting Lilly. Now, with everything within me I wanted this chance. I was smart enough to recognize I couldn't do this on my own. I needed help.

I followed Drew back to where he'd parked the car. Like a gentleman, he opened the passenger door for me. It wasn't until he was in the driver's seat that he spoke. "So, do you think Hope Center is going to work for you?"

The center had been adequately named, although I wasn't about to tell him that. I shrugged. "I'm willing to give it a shot."

"Good." He leaned slightly forward, inserted the key, and started the car's engine.

We rode in silence on the way to the shelter. "Will you be the one to tell me if I'm accepted into the program?" I asked.

"No, you'll either hear from Kevin or from Lilly."

"Okay." So this was it. I probably would never see him again, which was fine.

We rode in silence for a few minutes more. Stopping at a red light, Drew kept his focus straight ahead. "It looks like I'll be at the center once a week for the foreseeable future."

"Oh." I wasn't sure what that meant. Perhaps this was his way of telling me he'd be around and he'd have a chance to keep tabs on me. I wasn't sure how I felt about that.

"You going to check on me?" I asked, somewhat defiantly, like that was the last thing I wanted or needed from him.

"No. I probably won't see you again."

"Sure. No reason you should."

He glanced my way again. "I will if you like." The offer seemed genuine.

I shrugged as if it wasn't a big deal. The thing was, I sort of would like it if he did. Knowing he would be around and keeping up on my progress was incentive to do well.

"The church comes in to serve dinner here once a month," he mentioned at the next red light.

"You do that?"

"Not me personally. A group of women from the church see to it. Introduce yourself."

"Oh." As if any of those church ladies would want to meet me.

"Linda Kincaid is the one who manages the program. You won't have any trouble identifying her. She's nearly six feet tall and has a thick head of salt-and-pepper hair."

"Sure thing." I did my best to hide my sarcasm. No way was I seeking out this other woman.

"You need anything, you let her know and she'll tell me."

Not happening.

Drew pulled up in front of the shelter. "Once inside the shelter, give the director your name. There's a bed for you there for the next couple nights."

I looked over and nodded a couple times. "Thank you," I whispered, somehow getting out the words.

"I'm glad I could help," he said.

And then to my complete surprise, Drew turned his head away from me as if he didn't want me to read his expression. "You might think I was the one who helped you, but, Shay, you'll be surprised to know *you were the answer to my prayer.*"

Me? An answer to a prayer? Too stunned to react, I climbed out of the car wondering what he could possibly mean. I wasn't given the chance to ask as he drove away, leaving me standing with my small suitcase on the side of the street.

CHAPTER 4

Drew

Four months later

Kevin insisted I join the basketball team. As much as I wanted to make excuses to avoid it, my friend was bound and determined that I be there. So every Wednesday afternoon, rain or shine, I raced around the court with a bunch of other men, all serving in ministry in one capacity or another. To my surprise, I actually came to enjoy the workout. I found the physical exertion helped sweat away the worst of my frustration and depression.

As difficult as it was to admit, that's what I'd been suffering from—a deep, dark depression. At the time I hadn't realized it, which is probably fairly common. While in seminary, I'd sat through plenty of psychology classes. One would think I'd be able to recognize the symptoms. Unfortunately, I'd been walking around in a thick fog of loss and grief and hadn't been able to recognize what was happening to me.

Once I faced a few home truths about myself, I made an appointment with a physician as well as started weekly counseling for me and my kids. We'd been through hell, and it was time we stopped pretending all was fine when it wasn't. The antidepressants and counseling had done wonders for my mental health. Time with friends and physical exercise had been added bonuses.

As the weeks progressed, Kevin and I started taking time to cool off together after basketball with a cold soda. In retrospect, I was convinced he planned these sessions. We talked about Katie's sickness and ultimate death and about the effect her passing had on the children. Kevin had been the one to recommend the counselor, who happened to be a friend of his.

As a result, both Mark and Sarah seemed to be adjusting and accepting life without their mother a little better. Sarah had been only five when Katie was first diagnosed with stage-four ovarian cancer. The doctors gave her just a few months. She lasted six. In some ways I wish she'd died sooner. That sounds callous, and I suffered a tremendous amount of guilt for thinking that, but those last weeks when she'd lingered were the hardest of my life. It became intolerable to watch her suffer. It killed me in ways I was only now beginning to recognize.

After about a month of the soda breaks, a couple of the other guys joined in. I looked forward to that time as much as I did to playing basketball. As an added advantage, I was in the best shape I'd been in since college.

About a week or so before Easter, when I was arriving at the center for my weekly basketball game, I caught sight of a woman who looked vaguely familiar as I went to collect Sarah from the child-care center. My daughter had accompanied me, since it was spring break. It didn't take me long to recognize the woman helping in the center as the one I'd found in church all those months ago.

She was walking with another Hope Center resident. The two of them were laughing. I smiled and decided to ask Kevin about her.

After the game, as we gathered in the staff kitchen with our drinks, I looked to Kevin. "You remember that woman I brought by a few months back?"

"Shay," he supplied.

"Yeah, Shay. How's she doing?"

"There are confidentiality matters, but seeing that you're the one who brought her here, I can let you know that Shay is toeing the line. Still got attitude, but that's par for the course."

I grinned, remembering how her eyes had flashed with defiance when I first met her. Finding her in the church that day wasn't coincidence, I knew that now. If not for stumbling upon Shay, I don't know what would have happened with me personally. Contacting Kevin had been a turning point in my recovery from the loss of my wife.

Kevin studied me. "How about we talk to Lilly? She's Shay's counselor."

"Sure." I was eager to hear about Shay's progress, and Kevin seemed to sense that.

Kevin disappeared for a few minutes and returned with the woman I'd met the afternoon I'd brought Shay to the center for an evaluation.

"You remember Pastor Douglas, don't you?" Kevin asked.

Lilly raised her chin in greeting. "I do."

"He was asking about Shay. Can you give us an update?"

"Sure." Lilly crossed her arms. "She came with a chip

on her shoulder, which is fairly common. I had to call her on the carpet a couple times, but she does what's required of her. The attitude is more out of fear, I think."

"Fear?" I asked.

"Yeah, Shay's afraid of what will happen to her if she fails. It could mean life on the street, so she's doing what's necessary to stay in the program."

In other words, and I was reading between the lines, Shay was doing just enough to remain in the program. All I could do was hope that the life lessons taught at the center would take hold.

"Is she attending church with the other women?" I asked. I knew church attendance was completely voluntary. It said a lot if she had made that step of faith.

Lilly shook her head. "Not yet, but hopefully she will in time."

"The counseling sessions are going well?" I asked, knowing how much counseling had helped me and my children.

Lilly hesitated before she answered. "They're going okay. She's pretty tightly wound just yet. Given time, I believe she'll let me peek behind those walls." She paused and then looked to me. "You're that pastor she met when she was released from prison, right?"

I nodded.

"She's mentioned you a couple times. I asked if I could pass along any information about her, should you ask, and she was fine with that."

"You say she mentioned me? In what way?"

"Said you helped her. She didn't come out and say it, but I knew that it meant something. With women like Shay, their relationships with men have usually been anything but positive. You may be the first man to actually show any genuine concern for her."

I swallowed back my surprise. I had done so little. I felt a bit ashamed that I hadn't followed up sooner. "All I did was call Kevin. If she's grateful to anyone, it should be to you and Kevin."

Lilly shook her head. "She said you gave her hope." She paused before adding, "It would do Shay a world of good if you gave her a word of encouragement."

"Now?" I was all sweaty and probably smelled bad.

"No time like the present," Lilly insisted. "I'll call her down to my office and give you two a few minutes. That sound good to you?"

Shrugging, I said, "Sure."

Kevin slapped my back on my way out the door, and I followed Lilly to her office. She had me sit in her chair while I waited for Shay after Lilly had called her to her office. I heard Shay before I saw her. Lilly stood outside her office, waiting for her.

"What did I do?" Shay asked with a tone of defiance, challenging Lilly.

"You have a visitor."

"A visitor? Me?" She sounded shocked. "Who is it?"

"Check it out." Lilly opened the office door and I stood as Shay stepped inside.

"Hello, Shay," I said.

Her eyes rounded and she looked dumbstruck. "Drew . . . I mean Pastor Douglas."

"You can call me Drew." I gestured toward the chair for her to take a seat. "I thought I'd check to see how it's going," I said, although I had a good idea from what Lilly had already mentioned.

She shrugged. "I'm okay."

She studied me as if she needed to remember exactly who I was, which seemed odd, given that she'd called me by name.

"You've changed," she said, and then snapped her mouth closed as if she regretted the words as soon as she said them.

It surprised me that she'd noticed. "How so?" I asked, curious as to what differences she saw.

"When we met you looked . . . I don't know, burdened, I guess. It's better now?"

"Much," I said. I hadn't come to talk about myself, though, so I leaned back in the chair and focused my attention on Shay. "So tell me, are the classes here helping you?"

"Yeah, I guess." She sat up a bit straighter. "I've graduated into Phase Two."

"What did you learn in Phase One?" I asked. It'd been years since Kevin had mentioned the details of the program, and I was interested in hearing what Shay had to tell me.

"Right from the start there have been plenty of sessions with Lilly. They want me to talk about my life and all that sh—" She paused. "All that childhood crap. Stuff," she quickly amended. "Especially Lilly," she said and snickered.

"You don't like Lilly?"

"She's all right. Lilly's tough. Like me, she's been around the block more times than the postman. She doesn't take any bull, if you know what I mean."

Grinning, I nodded. "I do."

"There are fitness and nutrition classes, and that's been the best part for me. I think when it comes time to look for a job I'd like to find something in that field."

"Good." I hoped that encouraged her.

She smiled and looked down at her hands, as if she didn't want me to know that anything I said pleased her.

"What's been the hardest part for you?" I asked.

Shay glanced up, met my gaze, and then immediately broke eye contact. "Boundaries, for sure. I don't know why, but somehow it got programmed in my head that if someone needed me, then it was my duty to do whatever it was, no matter what the cost was to me personally. Crazy, isn't it?"

She impressed me. "You're not the only one dealing with those issues."

That small smile came and disappeared just as quickly again.

"Tell me about Phase Two."

"Well, I'll continue to spend a lot of time with Lilly, but I don't mind that as much as I did in the beginning. I'm still not sure I like her, but I trust her. She isn't going to take any guff. I guess it boils down to the fact that I don't always like hearing what she has to say."

I knew the feeling well. I'd come away from my own counseling sessions with the same thought.

"A few times I've been so mad that it takes me a day or two to get over the anger and come to grips with what she's saying. If I disagree, I've learned it's generally because it was something I didn't want to hear."

"I get that."

"I've come to realize I have a lot of anger in me. For instance, the only thing that gave me any hope behind bars was my weekly correspondence from Elizabeth, an older woman who volunteered with Prison Fellowship. Her last letter before I was released really frustrated and angered me, because she had so much hope for my future, and I had none. I never wrote her back, and I've regretted it every day since. This week, I finally sat down and let her know where I am, that her prayers were working, and how much progress I've made. And then, there's my brother."

"Your brother?"

She lowered her gaze. "I embezzled money for him. He was in a bad spot and was desperate for the money. He convinced me he would be able to return it, which was pure fiction. He had no way of getting the money back to me and he knew it. He let me take the rap. I was angry with him. The bitterness ate me alive while I served my sentence."

That was understandable. I was pleased Shay trusted me enough to share what had led to her time behind bars.

"What I didn't realize until I moved into the center is that I have a lot of repressed feelings toward my dad that have come out in self-destructive ways. That's what Lilly tells me. She seems to think that if someone physically hurts me, then I convince myself that I must deserve it." She hesitated and picked at her fingernails before she continued. "I'm not sure I'm ready to buy into all this, but I'm willing to listen and chew on it."

I smiled, encouraging her to continue.

"Lilly claims anger and grief go together. Not sure I buy that, either, but I remember I was angry with my mother for leaving, like she had a choice," Shay added. "Mom died, so it wasn't like she packed her bags and ran off."

My children had felt that same sense of abandonment, and it had come out in negative ways. Hearing that Shay had experienced the same thing after the loss of her own mother helped me realize what Mark and Sarah had been feeling since we buried Katie.

"Of all the classes you've attended, which is your favorite?" I asked.

Shay seemed to mull over my question for a few awkward moments, as if searching for an answer. I feared she would say whatever she felt I would want to hear. "Actually, I've gained the most out of the class dealing with emotional freedom," she mentioned.

Once she got started telling me about the class, Shay had a lot to say. She seemed sincere, and the more she spoke, the more genuine she sounded.

"I don't need to be carrying around the weight of the world. I realize if I have any chance of living a decent life, of making the right choices, then I need to let go of these resentments before I can move on. I've started with my father but have yet to deal with what my brother did to me."

As if reading my mind, Shay added, "I haven't heard from my brother, Caden, in over three years, so I have no idea if he's alive or dead." She paused and glanced down at her hands. "Odd part is, with Caden, I've come to accept that I need to forgive myself, too. I was the one who got him involved with Shooter."

"Shooter?"

"My ex-boyfriend. He's in prison. Doubt he'll come out anytime soon, which is a good thing."

I could see that despite her attitude, Shay had come a long way in the short amount of time that she'd been at the center. "Lilly tells me you're doing well and I wanted you to know how proud I am of you."

Shay's head shot up and her eyes widened with shock. "You are?"

"I had a good feeling that this was the right place for you. I'm glad it's working out. Do you have any family who will visit you over Easter?" I asked.

Shaking her head, she looked down at her hands in her lap once again. "No . . . I don't have any family, well, other than my brother, but like I said, I haven't seen him in over three years."

"You're making friends, though?"

She nodded. "Yeah, I suppose."

"If you like, I'll check on you again in a few months."

"If you want," she said, shrugging as if it wasn't a big deal.

Standing up from the chair, I thought it was time I give Lilly back her small office.

Shay stood when I did. "Before you go, I wanted to mention that I saw the woman you mentioned."

My mind went blank. "I mentioned someone?"

"Yes, the day you dropped me off at the women's shelter. You said the church supplied one dinner a month and that Linda Kincaid was the one heading up the volunteers for the dinner."

"Oh, right." I remembered that now.

"You said I wouldn't have a problem identifying her,

and you were right. As soon as I saw her, I knew she was the one you'd told me about."

"Did you say anything to her?" I asked. I realized I'd never told Linda about meeting Shay, although Mary Lou, my assistant, might have said something.

"No . . . I wasn't sure I should."

"You should," I encouraged. "Linda's big heart matches her height."

"If I see her again I might say something," she offered noncommittally.

"I hope you do," I encouraged. I'd be sure to give Linda a heads-up about Shay so she wouldn't be taken by surprise.

By the time I left the center it looked like it might rain. Sarah was sure to love that. We'd put Easter decorations out earlier in the week, but I hadn't had time to dye eggs with the kids. Tonight would be perfect for that, following choir practice. I did what I could to make their lives as normal as possible without their mother, not that it was easy.

This would be the third Easter without Katie. The first two had been dreadful. The three of us had done our best to put on a happy face and pretend all was well. Sarah was the one who broke down first, crying, saying she wanted her mother and that I didn't do anything right. I comforted my daughter as best as I could. The problem was I needed comforting myself.

For the first time since we buried Katie, I had the feeling we were going to make it just fine. I wasn't sure I could attribute this sense of well-being to my time spent with Shay, but I decided I would.

I vividly remembered the day we'd met and how I'd

felt after dropping her off at the shelter. I'd mentioned how meeting her had helped me. Everything had changed for me and my children after that day.

I collected Sarah and together we left Hope Center. I felt good after talking to Shay. Good for us both.

CHAPTER 5

Shay

One year after being released from prison

Sunday morning, I snuck into the back of Drew's church just as the organ music started to play. The same Nativity scene was in place beside the altar. This was the first time since that day over a year ago that I'd returned to the church. Every time I spoke to Drew, which had been only three times in the last twelve months, he'd invited me to visit his church. To this point I'd never taken him up on his invitation.

Until now.

Having completed all four phases of the program with Hope Center, I was transitioning into the real world, and I admit I was terrified of the future. I'd finished all the program requirements, and applied for and found a job working as a server in The Corner Café. Following graduation, I'd be moving into a tiny house provided by Hope Center. And when I say tiny, I mean *tiny*. It was minuscule. Just enough room for a bed, a sink, a stove, and a bathroom. The idea was that, within a year of graduation, I'd be able to live without any additional assistance from Hope Center. That remained to be seen. A lot was left to the unknown, which made me uncomfortable.

While wanting to believe I was ready to start my new life over without the weight of past mistakes, I remained skeptical. With doubts running through my mind night and day, I wasn't sleeping well. Every time I closed my eyes I was bombarded by worries. All the what-ifs seemed to buzz around inside my head like pesky flies and there wasn't a flyswatter in sight.

Lilly, my counselor, had been supportive, but I'd already failed miserably once, and there was nothing to say I'd be a success this time.

As I slipped into a pew as close to the back of the church as I could get, I recalled my initial meeting with Lilly. I'd scoffed about the possibility of the other woman becoming a friend. Like most everything else, I gradually learned Lilly had been right. Lilly Palmer had become a good friend. It didn't happen overnight, but as we worked together I'd begun to trust her with my secrets and let go of the resentments that I carried around like an extra set of luggage. I'd never had anyone like her in my life. Over the last year, Lilly had become a sounding board and an encourager. Best of all, I was beginning to dream again.

The music ebbed to a close and Linda Kincaid stepped up to the lectern. I recognized her from the Bring-a-Meal program Drew's church participated in. I'd never had the nerve to tell her I'd met Drew. If Drew had mentioned me, then Linda hadn't reached out to me, either. The woman intimidated me. Perhaps it was her height, or knowing Linda was close to Drew and that he depended on her. I wasn't sure what it was.

Although it might sound ridiculous, I felt close to

Drew, too, although those feelings were completely one-sided. After all, I'd talked to the man a total of only four times. But each one of those meetings had played back in my mind a thousand times.

One day I hoped to marry a man like him. Not a pastor but a decent man who wasn't into drugs or cheating or hitting women. Sounds simple, right? Well, from my experience those men were few and far between, and if I did happen upon one, I wasn't entirely sure I'd recognize him.

After everything I'd been through in my life, building a relationship with a man was going to be tough. An even bigger challenge would be exploring a relationship with a Being greater than myself. Yet here I was, ready to do both for the first time as the new Shay.

I focused my attention to the front of the church. Linda Kincaid read the Scripture verse for that morning from Psalm 56 and then quietly took her seat. Caught up in my thoughts, I'd heard only part of the reading.

After Linda left the lectern, Drew approached. He wore a suit and tie, and for a moment I was mesmerized. Every other time I'd ever seen him, he'd been dressed casually. The last three times we'd met at Hope Center had followed basketball and he was in workout gear. I barely recognized him and knew that every unmarried woman in the entire church must have a huge crush on him.

"The topic of this morning's sermon is worry."

Hold up.

Wait a minute.

My mind started to swirl. How was this possible? How did Drew know my head was completely messed up with worries and concerns about my future? I wanted to hit the side of my head to be certain I'd heard him correctly.

"When we worry," Drew continued, "we take reality and move it into the realm of fiction. What is real is transferred into the land of monsters and dragons, which seem far bigger and more frightening than they really are."

I sat up straighter and scooted so close to the edge of the pew that I was in danger of slipping off entirely. I'd been doing exactly what Drew was saying. Because I was moving out of Hope Center, I lived in fear of the future. My head had been filled with scenarios of everything I could do to mess up my life yet again.

I'd been discounting all the tools the center had given me to make a success of my future. I had a job and a place to live and good friends who were willing to guide me along the way.

Yet here I was stewing, stirring up doubts and fears, not trusting myself. With all the stinking thinking that had been going on inside my head, it was like I was about to move into Jurassic Park just before the dinosaurs broke loose.

The rest of Drew's sermon seemed as if it'd been written just for me. I felt dumbstruck. Just before he finished, it looked like his gaze zoomed to the back of the church and landed squarely on me. I could have been off base, but it seemed that his smile was meant solely for me.

At the end of the service there was more music. Drew left the front of the church and walked down the center aisle, and then stood at the door to shake hands with the congregation as they exited the building.

Because I'd come for a specific purpose, I waited until there were only a few stragglers before I approached him. I watched as he interacted with each person, greeting them by name, shaking their hands, and asking pertinent questions.

He really was good at his job, making everyone feel welcome. I wanted him to know that I appreciated everything that he'd done for me. I doubted I'd be able to tell him that. Because of him I'd been given another chance.

All too soon it was my turn. As I approached, Drew recognized me and his face lit up with a warm smile.

"Shay," he said, taking my hand in both of his. "I see you finally accepted my invitation."

"Yes." Color invaded my cheeks. I could feel the heat coming up from my neck.

"It's good to see you."

"You, too." My hand felt warm in his. He held my gaze for an extra-long moment and his smile seemed to cut into me, breaking through my hesitation.

"From what I understand, you're about to graduate," he said.

I nodded. "Actually, that's the reason I'm here."

"How do you mean?"

He released my hand as if he'd forgotten he was still holding it. I immediately felt the loss of his touch.

All at once I was unsure this was the right thing to do. He was a busy man. A single father, and I was about to ask him . . .

"Shay," he said, calling attention away from my thoughts. "What's going on in that head of yours? From the way you're frowning I'd guess it's nothing good. Are you having troubles at the center?"

"No, no, nothing like that. I came to invite you to my graduation. It's no big deal if you can't come. I just thought, you know, that because you . . . well, you know." I exhaled, convinced I'd made a mess of this invite.

His smile was immediate. "I'd be honored to attend."

"You would?" As soon as the words escaped my mouth I wanted to pull them back. I'd worked hard on being confident, and the question made me sound weak and vulnerable.

"When is it?"

I was about to tell him when a little girl in pigtails came racing up to him.

"Can we go home now?" she asked, looking up at Drew.

I knew Sarah from the times she'd been at the center. During the summer months Drew's daughter had accompanied him on Wednesdays when he played basketball with Kevin and the others. Sarah went to the children's center, where I pitched in when needed. I wondered if she'd remember me. She looked adorable in her Sunday best, with her pretty dress and Mary Jane shoes.

Drew reached down and placed an arm around her shoulder. "Sarah, I want you to meet a friend of mine. Her name is Shay."

The little girl beamed me an awkward smile. Her front teeth were coming in and she was apparently self-conscious about the big gap in the front of her mouth.

"I know Miss Shay," Sarah said, smiling up at me.

"You do?"

"From the center. She worked with the kids and she was lots of fun."

It pleased me that she remembered. "Hello again, Sarah."

"Hi. The first time we met you told me how much you liked my name, remember?"

"Of course. It's a pretty name."

"It's from the Bible."

"Is it?" I'd suspected it was from somewhere in the Bible. I wasn't completely sure where, though. The child probably knew better than I did.

"Her name used to be Sari."

That was something else I didn't know.

"That happens," Sarah explained. "God changes the names of people sometimes."

"Why?" I asked, genuinely curious.

"I don't know," she said and looked to her father. "Daddy, why did God change Sarah's name?"

Drew smiled down at his daughter. "It usually happened when God was about to do something big in their lives. With Sarah it was because she was about to have a baby."

"Oh." His daughter readily accepted his explanation.

Drew looked to me. "Shay has invited us to attend her graduation."

Sarah's eyes widened. "That sounds important. Do you need a new name?"

The question took me by surprise. "I might," I said, smiling back at her.

The youngster's eyes widened with excitement. "Can I help you choose?"

I noticed Drew's grin. "Sure," I said.

"Daddy, can we invite Shay to have dinner with us? Please?" she pleaded and grabbed hold of my hand. "That way I can help her choose her new name."

Automatically I shook my head. "No, no, I can't."

Sarah was looking up at her father, her eyes wide and pleading. "If you're going to choose another name, then this is serious business," Drew said, directing the comment to me. "It would mean a lot to Sarah if you'd agree to join us."

Still, I hesitated. "You're sure?" He didn't really know me, and it was a leap of faith for him to invite me to meet his family.

"Very sure," he said.

"Say you will," Sarah pleaded, tugging my hand as if needing to garner my attention. "Dad puts it in the Crock-Pot," she explained, and then lowered her voice. "He isn't a good cook, but he tries."

"In other words," Drew joked, "we're never quite sure what we're getting, although the Crock-Pot seems to work best for me."

"You'll come, won't you?" Sarah asked, wrapping her arm around mine and tilting her head back to look up at me.

"Okay," I said. I probably shouldn't have agreed, but I hated to disappoint Sarah.

The little girl tightened her hand around mine and pulled me along, apparently eager to be on our way. "We live next to the church in the parsonage."

"Where's your brother?" Drew asked his daughter.

"He went to the house. I told him it was his turn to set the table."

Drew shared a look with me. "She's a little bossy at times," he said under his breath.

"Am not," Sarah argued.

Drew ignored her rebuke. "Why don't you wait here a few minutes and we can all walk over to the house together. I have a couple things to finish up." Looking my way again, his gaze connected with mine.

"All right." I remained overwhelmed first by the invitation, and also by Sarah's easy acceptance of me.

The little girl led me to the door leading out of the church, chattering the entire time. "Did you know my mother died?" she asked.

"I did and I'm sorry."

"I hardly remember her anymore," she said sadly. "But she's looking down from heaven and watching over me. Daddy told me that I can still talk to her if I want but that she won't be able to answer. Sometimes I go to sleep telling her about school. She always wanted to know that stuff. I wonder if she's made friends with the angels."

"I'm sure she has," I said, hoping to sound reassuring to the child. She was small and didn't look to be more than six or seven, although I knew she was nine from the times she'd been at the center.

Drew returned and walked with us outside. Just as she'd said, the parsonage was next to the church, tucked in the back of the property. I'd noticed it before but didn't realize it was a residence. It was built of brick, the same as the church, which must have been constructed before earthquake building codes were passed. We were at the front door when someone back at the church called for Drew.

He turned and answered. "Go on in. This will only take a moment."

Sarah opened the front door and ushered me into the house, which was surprisingly neat.

As soon as we crossed the threshold, she called out to her brother, "Mark, we have company."

A boy appeared who didn't look to be anywhere close to thirteen. He looked too small for thirteen, and had a smattering of freckles across his nose. He looked at me and blinked.

"That's Mark," Sarah said. "He's a brat."

"Am not," Mark growled.

"I'm Shay," I said and held out my hand. Mark took it and gave me one hard shake before releasing me.

"Did you set the table?" Sarah demanded with hands braced against her hips.

It didn't take me long to figure out who the dominant sibling was. Sarah ruled this roost.

"We have our big meal Sunday after church," Sarah explained, leading the way into the kitchen. "Today it's pot roast. Dad wakes up early on Sundays and gets everything cooking before he leaves for the church, otherwise it would be hours and hours before we could eat."

"Good idea." Looking around the kitchen, I could see that Drew had taken care of almost everything well in advance. Serving dishes lined the countertop along with the necessary serving spoons.

Mark got another place setting out of the silverware drawer and added it to the table while Sarah opened a second drawer and removed a pen and pad.

"What's that for?" he asked his sister.

Sarah looked over at me and offered me a toothless smile. "We're choosing a new name for Shay because . . ." She hesitated and looked to me. "Did you tell me why you wanted a new name?"

"Because I'm graduating and starting a new life."

"What do you want your name to be?" she asked,

scooting out the chair and setting the pen and tablet on the table.

"I'm not quite sure yet," I admitted.

"Do you like the name Dory?" she asked. "She's one of my favorite characters."

"She doesn't want to be named after an animated fish," Mark tossed out, sounding disgusted with his sister.

"It would be hard to change my name completely," I explained, "because it's my legal name and everything is listed under Shay Benson. I was thinking." I paused and pressed one finger against my bottom lip. "Maybe we could add something to the name I already have."

"Good idea," Sarah said approvingly.

"Give me an example," Mark said as he set an extra plate on the table.

This wasn't as easy as it sounded. "Well . . . because I'm starting over I'm looking to make wise decisions. I want to be confident, too." Both children studied me as I mulled over other names. "Your father's sermon this morning had to do with trust and I want to include that."

"I have an idea," Sarah said, tapping the end of the pencil against the pad as if to keep up with her thoughts. "You could add those words to the end of your name."

I didn't get it. "How do you mean?"

"Keep your real name, like you said, but add to it. Shay the graduate."

"That's stupid," Mark grumbled. ··

"No, it isn't," his sister insisted.

"You might be onto something, Sarah. How about Shay, a wise, trusting, and confident woman?" I asked.

That wasn't me, but it was the woman I hoped to be one day.

"Yes," Sarah said excitedly. "That sounds perfect."

I heard the front door open and I looked up as Drew entered the house.

"Daddy, Daddy, we have a new name for Shay only it's still Shay because she said she had to keep that for some reason. We decided to add the new names to her already name." When she finished speaking she was breathless.

Drew placed his arm around his daughter's shoulders. He looked to me. "So what's your extended name?"

I hesitated and so Sarah filled in for me. "Shay, a wise, confident, trusting woman. Isn't that good!" the youngster said, looking well pleased with herself.

"It's very good," Drew said, holding my gaze. "I couldn't have chosen better myself."

"When are we going to eat?" Mark asked, sounding bored. "I'm hungry."

"I am, too," Drew said and headed for the Crock-Pot. He glanced over his shoulder. "It's nothing special, so don't get your hopes up," he warned me.

The truth was, just spending time with Drew and his children was special enough. He could have been serving sawdust for all I cared.

CHAPTER 6

Drew

Mondays were technically my day off. *Off* being figurative. While I wasn't involved in church business, unless there was an emergency, I often used my free day to catch up with housework as much as possible.

This Monday, like most Mondays, I was knee-deep in laundry. I had three separate loads piled on the floor in front of the washer and dryer. As soon as I finished those I would need to run two extra loads for the bedsheets. I couldn't put off getting groceries another day, either. The cupboards were shockingly bare. I'd need to find time to squeeze that in between a dentist appointment for Mark at eleven-thirty and when I needed to be at the elementary school. I'd volunteered with Sarah's class to help with an art project.

I'd volunteered. What *was* I thinking?

Being forced into the roles of both mother and father physically and emotionally drained me. Some days, when the frustration felt overwhelming, I had to remind myself Katie hadn't opted to die. She didn't want to leave our children. Or me. Doing so broke her heart.

It had nearly broken me, too. It'd taken all this time to

come out of the blue funk I'd sunk into. These days, I was able to deal with the needs of the children that would normally fall into Katie's hands without the anger. It was the unreasonable irritation with Katie that had once clung to me like an insidious spiderweb I couldn't seem to free myself from. It was much better now. I'd learned to adjust, hold on to the good times, and remember how deeply she'd loved me and the children.

She was gone and I was left to face life without her, taking on all the responsibilities she'd carried in our family, and feeling grossly inadequate to do them half as well as she had.

It'd been four years now and I would never stop missing Katie. She'd been the perfect pastor's wife: devoted, loving, kind, godly. I felt like a part of me was missing every single day. The grief wasn't suffocating the way it had been that first year. I still missed her terribly, but I'd forged a path through that overwhelming loss, and as with most pain, I'd found rewards as well. A deeper understanding of myself, of all that I had for which to be grateful, the good years Katie and I had shared, the love we'd found, our children. These were small jewels I'd picked up along the way toward healing. I could remember her now and not feel the anchors weighing me down. I could even laugh and joke again.

And one day, God willing, I would even love again.

By the time I'd finished folding and putting away the laundry, buying groceries, and taking Mark to the dentist—he was going to need braces—it seemed I was rushing from one point to another. Before I headed to Sarah's school, I popped dinner in the Crock-Pot and made a mental list of everything else I needed to accomplish that day. My head was spinning out of control. Back at the house, I stripped the beds and put the sheets into the washing machine. I'd need to make the beds later. Mark promised to get the sheets into the dryer while I dropped Sarah off for her violin lesson.

After dinner, while the kids did their homework, I put the freshly dried sheets on the beds and loaded the washer with our towels for the last load of the day. It would help, I realized, if I was able to spread out these chores over the rest of the week, but that never seemed to work well for me.

I was more than ready to sit down and relax when Sarah asked me to read her a story before she went to bed. It'd been a long time since I'd read my daughter to sleep, seeing that she was reading at a fourth-grade level herself all on her own.

As I was sitting on the edge of her bed, she surprised me by crawling onto my lap and laying her head against my shoulder. This, too, was out of the norm and left me wondering if she was coming down with something. I never felt more inadequate than when one of the kids was sick.

"You not feeling well?" I asked. This clinging little girl wasn't like my take-charge nine-year-old daughter.

"No," she answered, her voice so low I had to strain to hear her. "I'm sad."

I kissed the top of her head. "What are you sad about?" I asked, thinking something must have happened at school.

She turned and buried her face in my chest.

"What is it, pumpkin?" I asked, using the pet name I had for her.

Sarah released a wobbly breath as if struggling to hold

back tears. "I heard Mrs. Gallon tell another teacher that I was a motherless child."

I stiffened. "Mrs. Gallon is wrong."

Sarah cocked her head so she could look at me, her eyes wide and questioning. "My mommy died, though."

"Yes, she did, but you have a mother, Sarah, one who loved you very much. She just isn't here any longer." My words hung in the air between us as my daughter absorbed them.

"I'm not motherless?"

"No, you most certainly are not."

The tightness around her eyes relaxed. "I remember her," Sarah whispered.

Katie's photograph sat on Sarah's dresser. The picture was taken shortly after Sarah's birth. Katie held our infant daughter and smiled into the camera. I'd always loved that photo of my wife, and looking at it now, I felt more than a pang of loneliness.

"She used to read me stories and sing to me."

My arms tightened briefly as I remembered Katie singing in the shower and as she moved about the house. It seemed she was filled with song. "Your mother had a beautiful voice."

"Was she in the choir?"

"Oh yes." To my mind, the choir had never sounded the same without Katie.

"I don't remember what her voice sounded like," Sarah whispered, and again it seemed as if she was close to tears.

I kissed the top of Sarah's head and sighed. I hadn't thought to record Katie's voice before she died. The cancer had claimed her far too quickly, even though she'd battled valiantly. When she'd been told she had only a few months to live I'd been in shock and denial, refusing to believe she would die. Talk about someone burying his head in the sand! I didn't want to believe, let alone accept, that I was about to lose my soulmate.

"All you need to remember," I advised my daughter, "is how much your mother loved you."

"And I'm not a motherless child," Sarah stated emphatically.

"Right," I assured her.

Sarah covered her mouth as she yawned.

"Do you still want me to read you a good-night story?"

She nodded. "Please."

Forty minutes later I crept out of Sarah's bedroom and decided to check on Mark. My son was a quiet boy and hadn't been as open in dealing with his feelings when it came to the loss of his mother.

Mark sat at the kitchen table, an algebra book open in front of him. Both Mark and Sarah were intelligent children. I never had to worry about their grades. "How's it going, buddy?" I asked, coming to stand behind him. I rested my hand on his shoulder.

"Okay."

He almost always answered questions with one word. I'd learned the key to communicating with him was to ask questions that required thought on his part.

Pulling out the chair, I sat down next to him and looked over the problems. Mathematics had never been my strong suit. Mark was already working equations that were above my skill level. I didn't volunteer to help should he need it, which, thankfully, he didn't.

"So what do you think about getting braces?" I asked.

He shrugged. "It's all right, I guess."

It would mean a lot of dentist appointments, not to mention the expense. That reminded me I needed to check our dental coverage to see how much of the cost would be covered by the plan . . . if the plan even included braces.

"How about a bowl of ice cream?"

Mark glanced up and paused as if he needed to clear his head before he considered the offer. "We have ice cream?"

"I got groceries today." Scooting back the chair, I headed over to the refrigerator and opened the freezer. "You want some?" I asked, pulling out the container.

"What flavor?"

"Vanilla."

"No thanks." Mark slouched his shoulders forward as he bent over his math homework.

Really, what kid refused ice cream? "You don't like vanilla?"

"It's okay. I'm not in the mood."

"How about a banana?" Fruit never lasted long at our house.

"No thanks."

I'd noticed he hadn't had much of an appetite lately, and that didn't seem right. If this continued, I'd make a doctor appointment.

"Mark," I argued. "You're a growing boy. You need to eat more."

My son slapped his pencil down on the table with such force that it shocked me.

"That's the problem, Dad, I'm not growing. I'm the shortest boy in my class and I hate it."

So that was it. Well, this was an area I knew well. "Hey,

kiddo, I was short at your age, too, and look at me now."
I was proud of every inch of my six feet. Setting the ice
cream back in the freezer, I joined Mark at the table. "I
didn't like being short when I was your age, either."

Mark held on to the pencil with both hands with such
force that I was convinced it was about to snap in two.

"When did you start to grow?"

My son wouldn't want to hear this, so I fudged a bit.
"High school."

This was a white lie, although there is no such thing. A
lie is a lie. I didn't get my height until the summer after
I'd graduated. The growth streak hit just before I left for
college.

"High school." Mark groaned and, bending forward,
pressed his forehead against the tabletop. "I have to wait
that long?"

Offering sympathy, I patted his back. "I'm sorry, son,
but most likely you will."

It went without saying this wasn't what he wanted to
hear. Like Mark, I'd been as skinny as a beanpole, too.
Short, skinny, and something of a nerd. Unlike Mark,
my grades weren't anything to write home about. Thankfully, in that area our son took after Katie, who had always earned top grades. In fact, we'd met in college when
I'd needed a math tutor.

"Isn't there anything I can do to grow quicker?" Mark
pleaded. "Aren't there growing pills I can take?"

"Not that I know of." There probably were, but I wasn't
about to mention that to my son.

Mark closed his eyes, shook his head, and then slammed
his textbook closed. "I'm going to bed."

Hesitating, I wasn't sure if I should follow and try to

encourage him or not. Until now I hadn't had much success in offering him reassurances. He didn't want reality and I didn't blame him.

At his age I'd been impatient, too. I was a senior in high school before I'd asked a girl out on a date, and the main reason was because nearly every girl in my class was taller than I was.

The house was quiet when I sat down in front of the television with a bowl of ice cream. I liked to watch the late news for the weather report so I'd know how best to help the kids dress in the morning. Mark didn't need help as much as Sarah. If it was up to her, Sarah would wear a summer dress every day. She was a girly girl who liked dresses and her hair done up fancy.

Thinking about her hair made me want to cringe. My daughter wanted to keep her hair long, which was nothing but a hassle for me. I knew this desire was partly because of the picture Sarah had of her mother. Before all the cancer treatments Katie'd had long, thick, dark hair. This was Sarah's way of being like her mother. Unfortunately, my daughter's hair tangled easily and she hated having me brush it out. For all the crying and whimpering she did while I fussed with her hair, I was surprised I hadn't been turned in to Child Protective Services for child abuse.

The weatherman stood in front of a map of western Washington and the entire half of the state showed cloud cover. Rain was forecasted for the remainder of the week, typical of winter in this part of the state. Naturally, my children wanted it to snow, but snowfall was rare in Seattle.

Even before the news finished airing, I felt myself

drifting off. My day had been full, and it would be morning before I knew it.

Checking to make sure all the doors were locked and secure, I turned out the lights and headed to my bedroom. A half-hour later I crawled into bed and nestled against the pillow. Closing my eyes, I murmured my prayers. As always, Mark and Sarah were the first ones that came to mind. I asked for wisdom as their father, how best to guide and shape their young lives. I worried about fulfilling their needs, being a good father, and feared I overcompensated because they had lost their mother.

The church family was next. My concerns there were multiple. Our numbers were growing, not by leaps and bounds by any means, but there was a slow increase and that was encouraging. We'd gone back to mailing out the monthly newsletter. Funny how a little thing like that could make a difference.

Linda had headed up the Christmas program and the choir was practicing for the Christmas Eve service. I hoped to get the tree up and decorated following church Sunday afternoon.

As I was rounding out my prayers, Shay Benson popped into my mind. My thoughts came to an abrupt halt and my eyes opened. Seeing her in church on Sunday morning had boosted my spirits. Although I'd spoken to her only a few times over the last year, I'd kept tabs on her through Kevin.

Shay had fulfilled every requirement. According to Kevin, she'd made significant progress in the last few months. She had found employment at The Corner Café, which was situated about six blocks away from the church. With help from Hope Center, she would move into one of the tiny houses supplied to graduating residents in the transition phase. He'd told me she'd be allowed to live there for a year with minimal rent until she could afford a place on her own.

Kevin had warned me not to get my hopes up when it came to Shay. The real test would come once she left the center and mingled with the real world. He was optimistic, but he'd seen too many promising women return to their former lifestyles.

Kevin never lost heart, though. I wasn't sure how he did it. His faith was strong; I wished I could be more like him, resilient and unwavering in his efforts, refusing to let the weight of discouragement keep him down.

I wanted to believe the life lessons Shay had learned at Hope Center had taken root. Kevin had assured me she would face more than one trial in her efforts to build a new life. The good news was that as long as she maintained a good support system, attended group meetings, and stayed out of trouble, she would do well. For her sake I prayed she would.

Graduation was the following weekend. I was pleased Shay had come to personally invite me. Remembering how quickly Sarah had taken to her brought a smile to my face. Having her join us for a meal had been a big move on my part. It was the first time since we'd lost Katie that I'd invited a single woman to our home. Not until after she left did I realize what I'd done, but I had no regrets.

We'd all enjoyed her company.

Even Mark.

I noticed my normally somber son had actually smiled a couple times as Shay and Sarah told me about choosing a new name for Shay.

Bunching up my pillow, I smiled into the darkness. I'd had a full day. It seemed I'd been on the run from the minute the alarm sounded until I placed my head back on the pillow. I should be exhausted.

I was exhausted.

At the same time, I was smiling, thinking about Shay.

And feeling pleased that I'd be seeing her again soon.

CHAPTER 7

Shay

The Thursday before graduation was the Bring-a-Meal
night. As soon as I stepped into the cafeteria I realized
the volunteer group serving was from Seattle Calvary,
Drew's church. The woman he'd mentioned several times,
Linda Kincaid, was busy supervising a group of servers.

After I'd eaten I built up my confidence enough to seek
her out. Cleanup was going on around me when I approached her. "You're Linda Kincaid, aren't you?" I said.

She turned and looked for the source of the voice until
her gaze caught mine.

"Yes." While her words were clipped, her eyes were
friendly. "Have we met?"

"No . . . not formally. Drew . . . Pastor Douglas suggested I introduce myself." I needed to remember not to
use his given name, although that was the way I thought
of him.

"You attend Seattle Calvary?"

"No . . . well, I did last Sunday, but that was the first
time."

We were interrupted when one of the volunteers asked
Linda a question. "Put it in the van," she instructed. She

reached inside her pocket and handed the other woman a set of keys before returning her attention to me.

"I'm sorry, what were you saying again?"

"Nothing, really. I wanted to meet you. Drew . . . sorry, Pastor Douglas, has mentioned your name several times. He told me how much he relies on you."

"He's a good man and I'm happy to help him," Linda said. "He's carrying a heavy load."

"He is," I agreed. "Does he ever come to one of the BAM nights?" He hadn't in the year that I'd been at Hope Center.

A touch of sadness flitted in and out of Linda's eyes. "He routinely did, but that was before his wife got so sick. Now he feels it's more important to have dinner with his children. Why do you ask?"

I looked down at my feet, wondering how much I should say, if anything. "He's a good cook." I quickly amended that. "Perhaps I should say his Crock-Pot skills are finely tuned."

Her mouth opened and closed as though she wasn't sure what to say. "He's cooked for you?"

It was then that I realized I'd said too much. I hadn't meant to imply anything, but it was clear from her shock that she'd read more into my words.

"It wasn't like a date or anything," I hurried to explain. "Pastor Douglas invited me to the house . . . he called it a parsonage, after church last Sunday." I hesitated before adding that I'd invited Drew to attend my graduation from Hope Center.

"That was kind of him," Linda said.

Uneasy now, I studied the other woman. "I hope I didn't speak out of turn."

"You didn't," Linda assured me. "I'm pleased to meet you, Shay."

"I'm sorry now that I didn't introduce myself sooner." I'd been intimidated . . . no, that was too strong a word. Hesitant maybe, daunted. Perhaps it was because she was the epitome of a good Christian woman who gave unselfishly to others. And maybe, again, it was because she towered over me. But then I suspected I wasn't the first person taken aback by her dominating presence.

We chatted a few minutes longer, the conversation friendly and light. She learned that I would be graduating that Saturday.

"I'm working as a server at The Corner Café," I told her.

"Lloyd and I stop by there for lunch every now and again. We'll come by one day next week."

"That would be great." I couldn't keep the smile off my face, pleased with how well our conversation had gone.

All told, we didn't spend more than ten minutes chatting. When she left, I felt like I'd made a friend. Those were few and far between. Yes, I'd bonded with several of the women at Hope Center and those ties were strong. Linda, however, was a friend in the real world and I had shockingly few of those.

Saturday morning, a volunteer hairdresser arrived to help each of us get ready for the graduation ceremony. My hair had grown in the last year and I was more than ready for a trim. It reached just past my shoulders. I got

French braids on both sides, and then pulled them up and attached them at the crown of my head.

While in prison I'd gotten out of the habit of wearing makeup, which I couldn't afford, but for graduation I used a bit of eyeshadow and lip gloss. When I'd finished I put on the pretty dress I'd found at Goodwill. Staring at my reflection in the mirror, I thought about the Taylor Swift song with the lyrics that mentioned standing in a pretty dress and looking into the sunset. While the melody ran through my head, my thoughts drifted to Drew. I wondered what he would think when he saw me. I immediately put the thought out of my head. I wouldn't let myself hope that he'd show. I'd been disappointed before and didn't want to set myself up for another letdown. It would mean the world to me if he came, but I wasn't counting on it. As I looked into the mirror I realized I wanted to look pretty for Drew . . .

Stop. My musings screeched to a halt.

Not happening.

I put an immediate end to those thoughts. No way was Pastor Douglas romantically interested in me. The sooner I accepted that he was off-limits, the better for my mental health. Letting myself even consider romance as a possibility between us was setting myself up for a painful shot of reality. My goal was to be a wise woman, and letting myself fall for Drew would be foolishness in the extreme.

Still, as I walked into the room where the graduation was being held, I couldn't help searching the audience. When I saw him with Sarah and Mark at his side, I couldn't swallow back a smile. It was big enough to make my face hurt. My heart swelled with joy, an emotion I hadn't experienced in such a long time that I was barely able to identify it.

He'd come. I should have known he would, and, even better, he'd brought his children.

As soon as Sarah saw me, she clapped and clapped until her father leaned down and whispered in her ear. Only then did she stop.

Mark looked bored. He wore a suit and tie like his father and shuffled his feet as if he would rather be any-place in the world than here. Can't say I blamed him. Later I'd let him know how much I appreciated that he'd come to witness my big day.

Dr. Kevin Forester, the director for Hope Center, started the ceremony with opening comments. Then two of the counselors spoke. My name was mentioned twice as someone who had worked hard to make the most of this opportunity. I couldn't have been more proud. Because I'd given up the chance to graduate with my high school class, this ceremony was as close as it would get for me. I savored every minute.

When it came time to receive my certificate, Dr. Forester called out my name, "Shay Benson, a wise, confident, and trusting woman."

My gaze shot to Drew and the children and I watched as Sarah slid off the folding chair and applauded as hard and loud as her tiny hands would allow. Drew did nothing to contain her enthusiasm. Even Mark smiled and straightened in his chair to get a better look at me as I stepped forward to accept my certificate.

As I returned to my seat, I looked into the audience. My eyes locked on Drew and he smiled and nodded, letting me know he was proud of me. There it was again, that feeling of joy, real joy. It had become an elixir, an emotional high and strongly addictive.

Following the graduation ceremony, the center had a small reception for the graduates and their guests. Drew and his children were the only ones I'd invited. Actually, they were the only ones I knew to invite. No way would I ask anyone from my past life to come.

As soon as we were free, Sarah raced to my side. "Shay, Shay, you look so pretty," she cried, as if she couldn't get the words out fast enough.

"Thank you." I was surprised Drew wasn't with her. "Where're your dad and brother?"

"They went to the car," Sarah explained as she hugged my middle.

I placed my arms around her and hugged her back. "Would you like some juice and a cookie?" I asked.

"Not yet," Sarah said, grabbing hold of my hand. "You need to stay here until Dad and Mark get back, okay?"

"Okay," I said, wondering what this was about.

Within a couple minutes both Drew and his son returned. Mark carried a large bouquet of flowers in his hand. He approached me with them. "These are for you," he said, thrusting it toward me.

For one wild minute I was afraid I was going to tear up. I rarely cry. I'd learned it was a sign of weakness, and when my father beat me, any show of pain fed into his abuse. Blinking, I held back the wetness that gathered in my eyes and stared at the flowers in his hand.

Mark kept holding the flowers with sprigs of holly tucked into the foliage and looked to his father as if he wasn't sure what to do next.

"Take them," Sarah whispered. "We got them for you."

I managed to croak out my appreciation and took the bundle from Mark, laying them across my arms like a beauty queen. "No one has ever given me flowers before," I told the thirteen-year-old.

"Dad bought them," Mark explained, his face reddening with embarrassment.

"They're from all of us," Drew explained.

"Dad went to Costco because they have the biggest bouquets there for the same money as the grocery-store flowers. They're especially big because of Christmas."

"I'm nothing if not practical," Drew whispered.

We shared a smile and then I noticed Mark glancing longingly toward the table where the cookies and juice were being served. "Would you care for some refreshments?" I asked.

Mark nodded eagerly, so I escorted the children to the table. They each took a small plate and we all sat down together.

Once we were seated at one of the tables, Sarah looked at her father. "Daddy, see Shay's braids? That's the way I want you to do my hair."

"Pumpkin," Drew muttered and motioned helplessly with his hands. "That's a bit fancy for me. I'll try if you want me to, but I don't know that I can do yours nearly as pretty as Shay's."

Sarah's head fell.

"I could fix your hair for you," I offered, eager to do something to show my appreciation for Drew's support. I laid the floral bouquet on my lap and couldn't help glancing down at it. The flowers meant more than he would ever know.

The nine-year-old beamed me a big, toothless smile. "You could? When?" she asked eagerly. "I want to have it done like that for school. Could you come to the house Monday before I leave for class?"

I shook my head. "I can't, sorry. I work on Monday morning at the café."

Disappointed, her sweet, young face fell.

"But I could come on Sunday and do it for you and if you're careful, it would still look pretty on Monday."

Sarah turned to look at her father. "Can she come, Daddy? After church like last week. Can Shay eat with us again?"

Drew hesitated and frowned.

Rather than put him on the spot, I quickly intervened. "It would probably work best if I did your hair later in the day, Sarah. That way the braids will stay nice and tight until morning. Does that work?"

Again she looked to her father.

"That would be great. This is kind of you, Shay," he said.

I wished there was some way of letting him know that I was the one who should be grateful.

"Can I have another cookie?" Mark asked.

Drew nodded and his son returned to the refreshment table.

"Kevin tells me you're taking an accounting class," Drew commented after he sipped his coffee.

"Yes." I was surprised he knew about that. Lilly had encouraged me to use my evenings to broaden my education at the community college. My job went from five-thirty in the morning until two in the afternoon. I had reservations about taking classes, but I'd always been good with numbers, which was why I'd applied for a job with the bank.

"I'm happy to hear you're looking to the future, Shay."

"It's probably an exercise in futility," I admitted, "but Lilly says that I can't let my past define me."

"Lilly is right," Drew said.

"Brenda Jordan, my case manager, has contacts, and she says she would highly recommend me for a position once I've completed the course."

Drew nodded. "You're going to do great, Shay."

His confidence in me was reassuring.

After about thirty minutes, Drew and the kids announced that it was time they left. I didn't want them to go, which was selfish of me. Drew led a busy life and I had no reason to detain them. I walked them to the reception area. "Thank you again for coming."

"You'll braid my hair tomorrow, right?" Sarah asked, wanting to make sure I'd keep my promise.

"I wouldn't miss it. And I'll sleep in mine so you can see what it looks like on the second day."

The youngster nodded eagerly.

I stood by the window and watched them walk away in the drizzling rain. It wasn't even four yet and it was already dark.

"He your dream man?" Sydney, another one of the residents, asked.

I shook my head. "I wish," I whispered.

"He brought you the flowers?"

I glanced down at the bouquet in my arms. "Yes."

"I think you should keep wishing then, girlfriend. A guy who brings you flowers is more than a friend."

It was a nice thought, but I knew a romantic relationship between Drew and me wasn't likely. Then I remembered that he knew about me taking the accounting class. I doubted that Dr. Forester would have volunteered the information. It could only mean that Drew had asked.

CHAPTER 8

Drew

Sunday morning Linda Kincaid waited for me following the eleven o'clock worship service. Over the last few years, I'd come to rely on her more and more. In addition to being a tireless volunteer, Linda had become a sounding board and a wonderful help to me as a single father. Since Katie's death, Linda had stepped in and bought Christmas gifts for the children, a task I found heart-wrenching.

Not that I avoided shopping. I actually enjoyed it. Well, for the most part. Shopping without Katie was what I found especially hard. Buying Christmas gifts was something the two of us had always done together. We'd looked forward to it.

Without Katie, Christmas and all the other important holidays had become just another slap in the face that reminded me I was alone. For the past three Christmases, I'd barely held it together. If not for Linda and a few others in my church family, I don't know what I would have done.

This year felt different, and in a good way.

"I met your friend," Linda said.

"Which friend would that be?" I asked as I finished checking over the deposit slip for that week's contributions. Lloyd, Linda's husband, was the one who counted out the money each week.

"That woman," Linda continued, "the one at Hope Center."

Just thinking about Shay brought a smile. "I hoped she'd introduce herself. The children and I attended her graduation."

Surprise flickered in Linda's eyes. "Really? That was kind of you."

"She's come a long way. I'm proud of the positive changes Shay has made in her life." I was tempted to explain that finding Shay that morning in the church all those months ago had been a turning point for me, too. That meeting had reconnected me to Kevin, which led to gym time with the guys, which had resulted in a small group gathering with fellow pastors where we encouraged and supported one another. It'd been like watching a series of dominoes falling. One event led to the other.

"I understand you brought her to the house," Linda said, and her eyes bored into mine as if waiting to hear if that could possibly be true.

"I did," I admitted, surprised by the censure I heard in her voice.

"Is that wise, Drew?" she asked.

"How do you mean?"

"Is this really someone you want to expose your children to?"

Linda looked mildly uncomfortable. Knowing her as well as I did, I realized this wasn't a casual question but one she'd been mulling over for several days.

Immediately my hackles went up with the need to defend my decision. "Shay has been nothing but wonderful
with my children. I'm surprised at you, Linda. I would
hope you wouldn't prejudge someone by their past."

She took my criticism with a gentle nod. "I'm prone
to err on the side of caution. It surprises me that you
haven't, is all."

"In this case, I don't feel it's necessary."

"Perhaps," she agreed with some reluctance and followed me out of the church.

As far as I was concerned it was a closed subject. I was
eager to get to the parsonage, where Mark and Sarah
were waiting. We had plans to decorate the tree this afternoon. Later, Shay was due to arrive to fix Sarah's hair
with those fancy French braids my daughter had admired. In fact, Sarah had talked of little else all morning.
In light of Linda's feelings, I didn't mention Shay's visit.

"Actually, I stopped to ask what you had in mind for
the children this Christmas. I'd like to do the shopping a
bit earlier this year instead of waiting until the last minute."

This was in reference to the previous year, when I'd left
everything until three days before Christmas. Thankfully, Linda had stepped in anyway. While I was grateful
for the help, Linda was more the age of my parents and
really didn't have a clue when it came to appropriate gifts
for their age group. The children were thankful for the
gifts under the tree, and they didn't complain, but I knew
they would have appreciated videogames and electronics
more than stuffed animals and board games geared to a
younger age group.

"You know, Linda, I think I'm up to doing my own

shopping this year. I'm thankful for the offer. Your willingness to help has made a big difference in the last several years."

In a gesture of friendship, she patted my back. "If you need me to do anything, don't be afraid to ask."

"I could never thank you enough for all you've done for me and my family." I would reach out if needed, but I felt good—better than I had since I'd lost Katie. I trusted Linda and relied on her, probably more than I should. When it came to Shay, however, she was off-limits. I'd seen the changes in her from when we'd first met, the personal growth. I believed in her.

Mark and Sarah were impatiently waiting for me when I finally made it back to the house. Early that morning, I'd pulled out the tree decorations and, unable to wait, the two had already started placing the ornaments on the tree.

For practical purposes, I'd purchased an artificial tree and hoped Katie would forgive me for not getting a fresh one. I'd set it up in the corner of the living room after the kids had gone to bed the night before.

"Did we do good, Daddy?" Sarah asked, proud of their efforts.

"You did great." I would need to add the ornaments that were higher on the tree and out of their reach. The tree already had the lights attached, so it was easier to decorate. I'd add a couple of those sparkly garlands and that should do. It was almost hassle-free.

An hour after I arrived home, we sat down to a late lunch and I was more than ready to put my feet up and relax in front of a Seahawks football game. They were playing a prime-time game on the East Coast and kickoff would start at about five-thirty.

"When will Shay get here?" Sarah asked anxiously.

I checked my watch. "Any time now."

That was all the encouragement Sarah needed. "I'll get my hair stuff ready," she called as she raced toward her bedroom.

Glancing at Mark, I saw him roll his eyes at his sister. "You going to watch football with me, buddy?" I asked. We never missed a game.

My son had grown quiet and distant the last few months after school had started. I'd tried talking to him about it, but he'd remained tight-lipped. I knew his lack of height troubled him. I hoped in time that he'd open up. Because I was concerned, I'd stopped off at the junior high and asked the school counselor to keep an eye on him. To this date, I'd heard nothing back. I had to assume it was the transition Mark was making from boyhood to being a teenager. It didn't help that he had been especially close to Katie.

The doorbell chimed, and even before I could get out of my recliner, Sarah raced toward the front door so fast she became a blur as she sped past Mark and me. Seeing her enthusiasm, I grinned.

Just as I suspected, it was Shay. Sarah grabbed her hand and nearly yanked her over the threshold and into the house. "I didn't think you'd ever get here," my daughter said, bubbling over with enthusiasm. "I've got everything ready in my room for you to do my hair."

"Hello to you, too," Shay said, laughing.

Sarah stopped mid-step as if she'd missed something. "You still want to fix my hair, don't you?"

"Of course. I brought some hair clips along."

"You did?" For a moment I thought Sarah was going to keel over with joy. "I haven't had hair clips in forever."

"I appreciate this, Shay," I said as she walked in front of me. "Sarah's been counting the hours until you got here."

The two disappeared into the other room and the football game started. The Patriots and Seahawks were evenly matched. Mark and I were quickly involved in cheering for the Hawks. Not until halftime did I realize I hadn't heard a peep out of Sarah or Shay.

"Daddy, Daddy." Sarah raced out into the living room. "Look," she cried and thrust out her hands for me to see. "Shay and I had a spa afternoon. She brought nail polish and she painted my nails and my toes, too."

"You look beautiful," I said, smiling at my daughter, who was bubbling over with excitement. She stood with her weight balanced on her heels to keep the nail polish on her toes off the carpet. "Shay did my hair, too." She whirled around like a ballerina, her long braid twirling with her.

"Move," Mark shouted. "You're blocking the television."

"It's halftime," I reminded my son.

"Can Shay and I pop popcorn?" Sarah asked.

"Of course. Great idea." I wasn't sure I had any of the microwave stuff, but I was fairly confident I had kernels.

Looking nervous, Shay came into the living room. She rubbed her hands together as she spoke. "I hope you don't mind my painting Sarah's nails. She was excited and said you wouldn't mind."

"It's fine," I assured her, more interested now that the third quarter of the game was about to start.

"I would have asked, but it looked like you were wrapped up in the game."

"Not a problem." Glancing over my shoulder, I made my way into the kitchen to show Shay where to find what she and Sarah would need for the popcorn.

Before long the entire house was filled with the scent of popping corn, and my mouth started to water.

Sarah brought me a large bowl and another for her brother before she and Shay joined us in the living room. Shay sat on the sofa between the two kids. Sarah leaned her head against her and Mark looked completely at ease, munching away on the popcorn.

"What's the score?" Shay asked, glancing toward the television.

"The Seahawks are tied with the Patriots," Mark supplied before I could.

"Can you stay a little while longer?" Sarah asked.

Shay looked to me as though seeking my approval. "Stay," I said. Shay had managed to keep my daughter occupied for a good part of the afternoon. That had freed me up to enjoy the game and spend time with Mark. Normally Sarah would be constantly interrupting us. This was the most peaceful Seahawks game I'd enjoyed all season.

"We win this game and we're assured of getting into the play-offs," I explained, leaning forward.

"Did you notice my hair, Daddy?"

"It looks wonderful, pumpkin."

—

Halfway through the third quarter, Sarah grew bored with football. "Will you play a game with me, Shay?" she asked. "It's one my mom and I used to play."

Sarah's request caught my attention. Sarah had played Candyland with Katie and hadn't touched the board game since Katie's death. I waited to see if that was the one she'd bring out from her bedroom, and, sure enough, it was.

For just a moment my chest tightened. Part of me was happy that Sarah had connected with Shay enough to play her favorite game. Another part of me heard Linda's words of caution ringing in the back of my head. Perhaps it wasn't such a good idea to allow Shay to get too close to my children.

By her own admission, Shay had made several mistakes in her life. She'd turned that around, which was wonderful, and I was pleased for her. But the test would come in the weeks that followed Shay's graduation as she lived in the real world outside the protected one at the center.

"Touchdown!" Mark threw his arms into the air and leaped to his feet.

I'd been so caught up in my thoughts about Shay and Sarah that I hadn't paid attention to what was happening on the television screen. I laughed while Mark did a happy dance around the coffee table.

Looking up from the board game that Sarah had on the kitchen table, she rolled her eyes and said to Shay, "Men!"

I had to laugh. It was a stirring moment. This was rare. I was smiling and happy. When I'd buried my wife I assumed this sense of contentment would be forever lost. And yet my children were content, my life was back on an even keel, and the church was prospering. It felt good. Really good.

Shay stayed until after the football game. At the last minute the Seahawks were able to pull out a victory, which made Mark and me happy. When I saw that she had reached for her coat, I walked Shay to the front door with Sarah at my side.

"Thank you, Shay," my daughter whispered. She raised her hand to her head. "I never had my hair look so pretty. Can we do another spa day someday soon?"

"Of course." Shay smiled down at my daughter.

Sarah compulsively threw her arms around Shay's middle and hugged her.

Night had settled in and the darkness struck me. I knew Shay was without wheels. "How are you getting back?" I asked.

"Same way I got here, by bus."

I didn't like the idea of her riding the bus alone at night. "I'll drive you."

"Drew, it's fine, really. I take the bus all the time. It's safe; I'm fully capable of taking care of myself."

Ignoring her, I turned to my children. "Grab your coats, we're taking Shay home."

"Do I have to go?" Mark cried, disgruntled to be torn away from his videogame.

"Sarah, you want to come with me?" I asked.

"My show is on, Daddy."

"Drew, please," Shay protested, "I'll be fine."

"Not happening. It's the least I can do after everything you've done for Sarah. No arguing."

She hesitated and then reluctantly nodded. "Okay, if that's what you want."

"It is." I'd left the kids by themselves before, so this wasn't anything new. If necessary, they knew how to reach me. I got my coat and car keys and called to the kids as I headed out the door. "Be good. I'll be back in twenty minutes."

The night was colder than I expected and a chill raced up my arms. I was glad I hadn't given in and left Shay to wait at the bus stop in this weather, which looked threatening.

She continued to protest, but I wasn't listening. I led the way to where I parked my car, unlocked it, and held open the passenger door for her. She went silent once she was inside the vehicle.

I got in the driver's side and started the engine. It took a few minutes for the heater to kick in, so I asked for her address and entered it into my GPS while we waited for the engine to warm up. Neither of us had much to say, I noticed.

In the close confines of the car it seemed intimate with just the two of us. I glanced over at Shay and noticed she had focused her eyes on her hands, which were folded in her lap. Her head was bent forward and I saw that she was nibbling on her bottom lip. Seeing that stirred awake memories of my first dates with Katie and how it had been with us. We were both awkward with each other in the beginning.

I forced myself to look away. Shay was nothing like Katie and I appreciated that she'd given up a large part of her Sunday to entertain Sarah. I found that I liked Shay, and not just because Sarah was fond of her. I liked her for myself and that surprised me.

I hadn't touched another woman since the moment I'd

met Katie. She'd been my soulmate, the love of my life. Finding myself attracted to another woman shook me. It took me by surprise.

I felt the sudden need to break the silence.

"I'm grateful for everything you did for Sarah today."

"She's a wonderful little girl."

"A bit precocious at times." I found it was necessary to keep the conversation going, needing to keep my mind away from these alien feelings. "Did she happen to say anything about what she wanted for Christmas?"

"Christmas was all she talked about," she told me.

It was apparent my daughter was a subject we were both comfortable enough to discuss. "Did she mention anything in particular?" I asked.

"She did. She claims she's getting too big for dolls but there's this one Barbie doll that caught her eye."

I knew next to nothing about the doll market.

Shopping for Mark was much easier for me. My son enjoyed videogames and I'd recently taught him to play chess. Mark was easy to shop for, but when it came to Sarah I was at a loss.

Stopping at a red light, I glanced over at Shay. "Would you mind . . . seeing how well you know Sarah . . . but only if it's convenient, if you have time . . . I could really use some help with my Christmas shopping, especially when it comes to Sarah."

Shay's gaze flew to mine. "Sure. I guess. I mean, if you'd like."

"Great." I wasn't asking her out on a date. She was doing me a favor. That was all this was.

After dropping her off at the tiny house where she lived among a row of other tiny houses, I headed back to the parsonage, grinning the entire way. As I returned to the house, whistling, both children glanced up at me with a look of surprise.

"What?" I asked.

"You're smiling, Dad," Mark commented.

"Is that so unusual?"

Both children continued to stare at me as if the answer was a given. I'd told Shay I'd pick her up after her shift at the diner the following afternoon and we'd head over to the mall. As I made sandwiches for dinner, I wasn't able to keep the smile off my face.

CHAPTER 9

Shay

Monday morning I arrived at the café and noticed what looked to be someone wrapped up in a blanket, a figure of a man huddled up against the cold, sitting along the side of the building. He had a thin blanket around his shoulders and had his legs tucked up under his chin, with his head resting on his bent knees. This wasn't the first time I'd seen this homeless man at the café. I knew he slept there because of the warm air coming up from a nearby grate.

Sadie, another one of the servers, had shooed him away Friday last week, claiming the homeless discourage customers. I knew she had the welfare of the café in mind, but I couldn't help remembering my own predicament when I'd been released from prison. Just over a year ago, that could have been me doing my best to sleep on the street because I had nowhere else to go.

While Sadie was busy in the kitchen, I kept thinking about the man on the street. I didn't want to get involved. He needed to be gone. Half angry with myself, I poured a cup of coffee, paid for it myself, and took it out to him.

"Here," I said gruffly, shoving the cup of coffee at him.

He looked up and tossed aside the blanket, probably thinking I was giving him the coffee as incentive to leave.

"I'm moving," he muttered, not making eye contact.

"Don't leave on my account. The coffee is to help you keep warm." I squatted down so I could see his face. His eyes had bags under them, as if he hadn't had a decent night's sleep in a good long while. His face was dirty and he needed a shave. "I added sugar and a little cream. Hope you like it that way."

He eyed me skeptically. "You put anything else in there?"

He was afraid I was trying to drug him or something. "No. Just sugar and cream. My name is Shay. I work here at the café."

"I'm Richard." He took the foam cup from me, tasted it, and regarded me suspiciously. "Why you doing this?"

I shrugged and figured he deserved the truth. "Not so long ago I was about to be homeless. I'm not and I'm grateful."

He nodded, holding on to the cup with both hands. "Coffee tastes good. Thank you."

"You eaten lately?" I asked.

"I'm okay. I'll head to Sally's for breakfast."

"Sally's?" I didn't know of any restaurant in the area by that name.

"The Salvation Army. We call it Sally's around here."

That explained it. "You take care."

He nodded and saluted me with the cup. "Thank you."

"You're welcome."

I headed back into The Corner Café and found Sadie waiting for me, hands braced against her hips. I respected

Sadie; she called it like she saw it and didn't take any guff from the customers or the staff. We worked well together.

"You're encouraging that old man to hang around here," she said, cutting me with a look.

"Just bought him a cup of coffee. In case you didn't notice, it's cold out there."

"I noticed." Glancing over her shoulder, she looked into the kitchen. "Don't you let Frankie know what you're doing. He doesn't take kindly to the homeless hanging around here."

"Gotcha," I whispered back.

Sadie started filling the napkin dispensers at the counter. "That soft heart of yours is going to be a problem. You can't save the world, Shay."

"True," I agreed, "but I can give one old man a cup of coffee."

Sadie threw back her head and let out a roar of a laugh. The door opened and we had our first customer of the morning. We did a bustling business between six and nine, both of us running our feet off.

I didn't have time to think of anything else other than getting those breakfast platters out while the food was hot. At ten-thirty, business had slowed down to a trickle. It was the break Sadie and I needed before getting hit with the lunch crowd.

Frankie, the owner, had a reputation for serving comfort food and for giving customers their money's worth. One of his breakfasts would feed me for three meals. My one meal a day came from the café and I made sure it lasted. I was saving my money for business classes. Tips were decent, and collecting a paycheck helped me meet expenses.

"What are you doing for Christmas?" Sadie asked, while resting her feet and sipping a cup of coffee. Because she was older and had seniority, she got the first coffee break.

"I'll be with friends." Lilly Palmer had invited me to join her family. I'd hardly known what to say when she'd asked me to come to her house. The invitation had been unexpected. It showed her belief in me that she was willing to open her home and introduce me to her family. Her trust was a gift, same as it had been with Drew and his children. It made me more determined than ever not to disappoint her.

After my own break, which was shorter than I would have liked, the lunch crowd started to arrive. Frankie baked his own bread, and his sandwiches were some of the most popular items on the menu. I was sure the special, his meatloaf sandwich, would sell out before noon.

I served the counter while Sadie and Alice managed the floor. As soon as one seat emptied, someone else took the spot. After removing the dirty dishes and wiping the area clean, I looked up to greet my new customer.

Drew.

I nearly dropped the water glass, and right away my heart started this crazy staccato beat that echoed in my ears.

"Hi," I said, trying desperately to hide my nervousness.

"Hi." He reached behind the sugar canister for the plastic-coated menu.

"What can I get you to drink?" I asked.

"Coffee."

"You need cream?"

"No, thanks."

I poured him a cup and returned the glass pot to the heater. The ding behind me told me an order was up and I quickly turned, hoping it was one of mine. I needed an excuse to move away and calm my pounding heart. Unfortunately, it was Alice's order.

"What's the soup today?" Drew asked.

"Cream of broccoli."

He scrunched up his nose. "How's the chili?"

"I haven't had any complaints." I hadn't sampled it myself, but it appeared to be a popular menu item.

"Anything you'd care to recommend?"

"Sandwiches are popular," I told him. "Frankie bakes the bread himself. Today's special is a meatloaf sandwich."

Drew nodded and I reached for my ordering pad and the pencil tucked behind my ear. "I'll give the chili a try."

"How about some cornbread with that?" I asked. Sadie had been after me to upsell as much as possible.

"Is it homemade?" he asked.

I nodded. "Frankie does all the baking here."

"Then the cornbread it is."

"Great," I said. I tore the order off the pad, placed it on the circular device, and whirled it to be sure Frankie and Jim, his assistant, had it in plain view.

While I waited for Drew's chili and cornbread to come up, I gave the man two stools down from Drew his check and collected the dirty dishes from the customer at the far end of the counter. The whole time I worked, my hands trembled as if this was my first day.

The kitchen had Drew's order up in minutes. I knew it wouldn't take long. I delivered it with the plate of cornbread and brought him the dish with foil-wrapped pats of butter.

Noticing that his coffee cup was half empty, I reached for the coffeepot and automatically filled it.

"Are you still willing to go shopping with me later this afternoon?" he asked.

I nodded. "Sure."

"What time do you get off?"

"I can be ready to leave here by two-fifteen."

"Okay, I'll stop by and get you then."

I hesitated. I'd rather not leave from the café, especially wearing my uniform. "Would it be all right if I went home and changed clothes first?"

He nodded. "Sure. You want me to pick you up there?"

"Please. Make it at three. You remember where my place is?"

Reaching for his spoon, he grinned and nodded.

"See you then."

After that I got busy, and other than leaving Drew the check, I didn't get a chance to talk to him again.

As Sadie, Alice, and I finished cleaning up just before closing, Sadie sidled up to me. "You want to tell me about that good-looking guy who had you all flustered?"

I wanted to pretend I didn't know who she was talking about but I knew it would be a waste of breath. Little slipped by Sadie. She'd been waiting tables for nearly twenty-five years and had been the one to train me. I was still new enough for her to keep tabs on me and my interactions with customers. She'd been quick to tell me what I was doing wrong, and equally quick to compliment me when I did well.

"That's Pastor Douglas from Seattle Calvary."

Sadie's eyebrows shot up to her hairline. "You got the hots for a man of God?"

"I . . . he's a friend." I could feel the heat invading my cheeks.

"He's eye candy."

"Sadie!" I cried.

"He married?" Alice asked, joining us.

"Widowed. He asked me to go Christmas shopping with him for his children."

Sadie and Alice exchanged knowing looks.

"Don't make anything more of this than it is," I warned my friends. "Drew isn't interested in me romantically."

"Drew, is it?" Alice asked.

Right away I realized the mistake I'd made by calling him by his first name. I wanted to groan. While I wanted to believe that Drew might be interested in me that way, I was realistic enough to know it was unlikely. Again I warned myself that letting my thoughts wander in that direction would be ill-advised.

Thankfully Sadie and Alice didn't bombard me with any more questions. As soon as my shift was over, I hopped the bus and hurried home. I showered quickly and changed into jeans and a sweater. By the time Drew arrived I was dressed and ready.

He parked outside my house, and not waiting for him to get out of the car, I stepped outside and walked over to where he'd parked. To my amazement, he climbed out and came around to open my door.

Dumbfounded, I stared at him. No man had ever done that for me before. It was such a simple gesture, kind and thoughtful. I was tempted to say something and found I couldn't get the words out. I couldn't imagine Shooter or any other man I'd been with doing anything like that.

Once inside the car, we seemed to struggle with a topic of conversation. I was afraid he might have regretted asking me to shop with him. Wanting to ease the tension, I asked him about his lunch.

"The chili was great."

"I'm glad. I'd feel bad if I steered you wrong."

The exchange was followed by a tense silence, as if we were both uncomfortable. "I checked online for the doll Sarah mentioned."

"You have a computer now?" he asked.

"No. I got a smartphone. It was a gift from Sadie when she upgraded."

Drew glanced over at me. "That's great."

"Yeah. It's a good thing."

"I thought I'd buy one for Mark this year," Drew said. "From what I understand, all the kids at school have them now. He's never mentioned wanting one, but I figure it's time."

"That's a good idea." Actually, I was surprised Mark didn't already have a phone.

"His own phone and a couple videogames for his Xbox and that's all he needs. Sarah's the one who has me worried."

"I think she'd enjoy getting her ears pierced," I suggested.

"Sarah? She's only nine."

He sounded shocked at my suggestion. "It's just a thought." But it was one thing I knew she'd like.

"Did she mention it?"

I nodded. "In passing. Just that a friend of hers had

Dory earrings. You could buy her the earrings with the promise of getting her ears pierced after Christmas."

"I suppose that will work," he said, as though still mulling over the suggestion.

Drew drove to the mall at Northgate, and once we found a parking spot we were on a mission. Within two hours we had purchased everything he'd mentioned and a few items more.

My one purchase was a pair of gloves for Richard, the homeless man I'd met that morning. I'd noticed how chapped his hands were when he held the coffee.

As we headed back to the parking lot, Drew hesitated as we walked through the cosmetics section of Macy's. Frowning, he stopped and studied a display of perfumes.

The sales clerk appeared as if by magic. "Can I help you?" she asked.

Feeling a bit awkward, I stood back and waited.

"I need a bottle of . . . I think it's called *Beautiful*," he said, as he continued to study the display case.

The clerk brought out several sizes and mentioned if he purchased the eight-ounce bottle he would receive a free gift. The price was over a hundred dollars, but Drew didn't hesitate.

"This is for someone special," he said, and handed over his credit card.

If I ever needed the reminder that I was out of Drew's league, this was it. Whoever was getting the expensive bottle of perfume was someone he'd known a long while and whose taste he was familiar with.

No, this perfume was for someone special in his life.

And it definitely wasn't me.

CHAPTER 10

Drew

The Christmas Eve service went off without a hitch. With Linda Kincaid heading up the program, the evening was in good hands. I knew she'd enjoy the perfume, and while it was above what I would normally spend on a gift, she deserved it for everything she did for me.

In the program, Mark played the role of one of the Three Kings and Sarah had a speaking part as one of the angels who'd come to announce the baby's birth to the shepherds.

It was moments like this when I felt Katie's presence more than I did her absence. I felt certain she was there with me, beaming with pride at our children. I missed her dreadfully, but I was learning to live without her.

Christmas morning Sarah was awake before six. "Daddy, Daddy, get up so we can open our gifts."

I rubbed the sleep from my face and did my best to hold her off. "Give me five minutes, okay?" It was the line she gave me when I had to wake her to get ready for school.

"Daddy, it's Christmas."

"I need coffee," I grumbled. It'd been nearly midnight

before I got all the gifts wrapped and under the tree, and I would gladly have slept another couple hours.

"Mark's making you coffee, so get up. Get up."

Muttering, I tossed aside the covers and climbed out of bed. Sure enough, when I wandered aimlessly toward the kitchen my son stood in front of the coffeemaker, waiting while it brewed me a single cup.

"I'll sort through the gifts," Sarah said, eager to get to the presents.

"Give me a chance to wake up," I complained, doing my best to hide a smile at my daughter's enthusiasm.

"Hurry, Daddy," she cried impatiently. Taking me by the hand, she led me into the living room and patted at the recliner, indicating that I needed to sit there. No sooner had I sat down than Mark delivered my coffee. I took a tentative sip, not wanting to burn my lips.

"Can we get started *now*?" Sarah implored, holding the largest gift under the tree in both hands.

"Okay, sure," I said. While I wouldn't let the kids know it, I was just as eager as they were to have them open their gifts. Shopping with Shay had been an eye-opener. Her insights into my children's needs and wants had made the expedition fun. I don't think I'd laughed that much in months. I'd enjoyed spending time with her.

Later I thought to buy her a gift to thank her. Something small. Nothing personal. I mulled it over for a couple days, wondering if it would be the right thing to do. My gut said I should, but I wasn't sure it would be appropriate—me buying Shay a gift. It could easily be misconstrued.

I knew what Linda would say if I mentioned it to her,

and I trusted her judgment. In the end I decided against it. I hoped I wouldn't regret it later.

"Open this one first," Sarah said, racing to my side. There'd been a Santa Workshop at the school for students to purchase gifts for their parents. I knew Sarah had been saving her allowance to buy me something special and was eager for me to unwrap it. My little girl had spent copious amounts of time wrapping and taping my gift with great care. She was obviously proud of what she'd chosen for me.

"You want me to open my gift first?" I asked as she handed me the present. She'd wrapped it with enough paper to circle the living room twice over. I tore it away with both hands. "I can't imagine what you'd get me," I said eagerly. Sarah stood so close to my side, she was nearly sitting on the arm of my recliner.

"You're going to like it, Daddy."

When I was finally able to tear away the excessive paper, I found a flashlight. We'd had a power outage a few months back and I hadn't been able to locate a flashlight. I actually needed one.

"Sarah, thank you. This is perfect."

She tossed her arms around my neck and squeezed me with all her might.

Mark had me open his gift next. He got me a Seahawks coffee mug and a Seahawks key chain. I smiled and thanked him. Mark wasn't nearly as exuberant as Sarah, but I knew he was proud of the gifts he'd gotten me and I wanted him to know I appreciated them.

I watched anxiously as the children opened their gifts. Sarah gasped when she saw the earrings along with the promise she could have her ears pierced.

"Daddy, oh Daddy, I've been wanting my ears pierced forever and ever. It's on my wish list." Once again she threw her arms around me and squeezed until I found it hard to breathe. She was equally thrilled with the Barbie Shay had mentioned.

When Mark opened his phone, he stared at it a long time. I knew he was pleased.

"It's ready to go. I've got important numbers already programmed into it for you," I explained.

"Thanks, Dad."

"You're welcome, son."

It was Sarah's turn to go next and I didn't recognize the wrapping. "Who's that from?" I asked.

"Shay," she said, ripping aside the paper.

I frowned. "When did you see Shay?" I asked.

"Yesterday while you were at the church. She stopped by and asked me to put these under the tree and I did."

"You didn't tell me she was here."

"I forgot. When you got back it was time to get ready for the program. Shay said she knew you were busy and didn't want to bother you."

I wished I'd known about her visit; I would have liked to talk to her.

Sarah continued unwrapping her gift and beamed a huge smile. "She got me fingernail polish and some hair clips," she said, holding everything up, proudly displaying her gifts. "This way we can do another spa day, just us girls." She looked pointedly at her brother.

Ignoring his sister, Mark opened his gift from Shay next. It appeared to be a thick magazine of some sort. "It's a book of mathematical puzzles," he explained, "and a set of pencils. Cool."

Cool? Further proof that Shay knew what my children would want better than I did. Mark excelled at math, but it never dawned on me that he would enjoy the challenge of mathematical puzzles.

"What did we get Shay?" Sarah asked, looking intently at me.

This was a bit embarrassing. Now I wished I'd given in to the impulse and gotten her something. Thinking quickly, I said, "I thought we'd take her to dinner one night, just the three of us."

Sarah cocked her head to one side. "But taking her to dinner isn't something she can open. Did anyone get Shay presents?"

"I don't know."

Sarah sat back on her haunches. "That makes me sad. Where is she going for Christmas dinner?"

I didn't know that, either. "She didn't tell me."

"What if she's all alone, Dad?" Mark asked me.

"I'm sure she has friends, Mark," I said, hoping I sounded more confident than I felt. I should have considered that myself. Should have realized she was probably spending the day alone.

"Could we invite her to come to dinner with us to Mrs. Kincaid's house?" Mark asked.

I shook my head. I wished I'd thought of Shay sooner. "I'm afraid not, son. Seeing that the Kincaids are hosting dinner, they would need to be the ones to invite Shay."

Both of the children looked disappointed.

"Tell you what," I said, "first thing tomorrow we'll have breakfast at The Corner Café where Shay works and we'll invite her to dinner. How does that sound?"

"It's not Christmas Day, though."

"No, it's not," I agreed.

"Can we go to her house and thank her for our gifts when we leave for the Kincaids?" Sarah asked.

I needed to think about it. If Shay was home and alone, the children wouldn't want to leave her. As much as I wanted to, I couldn't invite her to join us at the Kincaid house. It wasn't my place.

"We'll stop off to see Shay on our way home," I decided.

The children looked disappointed but agreed.

"Daddy, please. Shay is our friend and we didn't even buy her a Christmas gift."

It surprised me how guilty I felt. "We'll do better next Christmas," I promised.

Dinner with the Kincaids was great, as always. In addition to being my right hand when it came to matters at the church, Linda was an excellent cook. She had gifts for me and the children, but I knew the doll she bought Sarah was one geared toward someone much younger than my daughter. And the camera she wrapped up for Mark was unnecessary, since he now had his own phone. Still, she was thoughtful, and I made sure they showed their appreciation. She bought me a book I'd been wanting to read, although I didn't know when I'd find the time.

The traditional prime rib dinner was excellent, but as soon as we were finished I could see that the kids were antsy and ready to leave. If we left too early, Linda would wonder, so I delayed our departure as best I could without disappointing my children.

As soon as we were in the car, Sarah leaned into the front seat.

"Seatbelt on," I reminded her.

"I know, Daddy, I know. I wanted to ask if we can still stop by and see Shay. Please."

I hesitated and then nodded. "Okay. But you have to remember her place is small and there won't be room inside for all of us."

"That's okay," Mark said. "I just want to thank her."

"Me, too," Sarah chimed in, "and tell her I'm sorry I didn't buy her a gift and that I will next year."

"I'm sure Shay didn't expect us to buy her gifts, Sarah," I said, hoping to ease her guilt. If anyone should feel bad, it should be me. "Besides, we're going to take her to dinner, remember?"

"But that's only because we didn't think of doing anything sooner," Mark said.

Mark caught on quickly. He surprised me.

"I'm going to write her a story. One just for her," Sarah announced.

"That's a wonderful idea." I headed in the direction where Shay lived. It wasn't in the greatest neighborhood, but I knew it was the best option for her. She was proud that she was able to pay rent and live on her own. That had been important to her.

When I parked outside of Shay's little house, I had the kids wait in the car while I went to the front door. It didn't look like there were any lights on inside. After knocking and waiting a couple minutes I could only surmise that she wasn't home. I assumed the children would have been happy to know she wasn't home alone for Christmas.

I was wrong.

"Where would she go?" Sarah cried. "She should be with us."

"Like I said earlier, I'm sure Shay is with friends."

"You don't know that for sure," Mark commented.

"No," I was forced to admit.

The rest of the ride home was spent in silence. While eager to get back to the house, both children went to bed early. I set the alarm determined to get up in time for breakfast at The Corner Café and to see Shay.

I expected complaints when I woke up the children the following morning. Mark grumbled until I reminded him we had a breakfast date. That was all it took to get him out of bed and dressed.

"Can I order waffles?" Sarah asked as we climbed into the car.

"If that's what you want." Although the café was a short six blocks away, the weather was too cold to walk.

"What are you going to order, buddy?" I asked Mark. Eating out was a rare treat for the children and me.

"Blueberry pancakes," he said, "with a side of bacon."

"You two are going to bankrupt me," I teased.

"What are you going to have, Daddy?" Sarah wanted to know.

"Probably hash and eggs." That was a favorite of mine, but I couldn't be certain it was on the menu.

As soon as we arrived, Sarah hurried into the café and looked around until she spotted Shay, who stood at the counter, taking an order. I had to grab hold of my daughter's shoulders to keep her from racing over to Shay's side.

"She's busy with customers now," I whispered as I led the children to an open booth. Actually, we were fortunate to find one available. The little café did a good business. It had been packed when I'd stopped by the other day for lunch.

After speaking to another one of the servers, Shay made her way to our booth. By this time we'd already read through the menu. Both Sarah and Mark had changed their minds a dozen times. As soon as Mark and Sarah saw Shay, they thanked her again and again for their gifts. Sarah stood up on the booth and hugged her and Mark politely shook her hand.

"Good morning, Shay," I said, smiling at her when the children had finished their greeting.

She returned the smile with a shy one of her own.

"We came to your house," Sarah told her, "but you weren't home and we wanted to thank you for our presents."

"I'm happy you liked them."

"I've already solved three pages of puzzles," Mark told her.

"You've got a great brain," she said, smiling at my son. "Now, what can I get you for breakfast?"

"Daddy," Sarah said pointedly. "Aren't you going to ask Sarah to dinner?"

"Ah, yes." I cleared my throat. "The children and I wanted to take you out to dinner," I said, feeling more than a little foolish.

"You can choose any place you want," Sarah added, "but Mark and I like Chinese."

"Sarah!"

"Mexican is okay, too."

Shay grinned. "You don't need to take me out."

"We want to," Mark said. "To thank you for our gifts. They were awesome."

Shay looked to me for confirmation. "Would you consider having dinner with us?" I asked.

She nodded, took our order, and then left the table.

Another one of the servers approached us, an older woman who wore a name tag that said SADIE. She glared at me with what I would call an evil eye, as if looking straight through me.

"That girl is a gem. Don't you be leading her on, you hear?"

"No way," I promised, amused by the older woman's censure.

"Good," she said, and nodded before she left the table.

"What did she mean, Daddy?" Sarah asked, cuddling close to my side.

"Nothing, pumpkin. She's just a friend of Shay's, too."

The thing was, I'd done a lot of thinking about Shay since our little shopping expedition. I'd enjoyed being with her and been impressed by her thoughtfulness, buying gloves for her homeless friend.

I wasn't sure I was ready for a relationship, but I liked Shay and was comfortable with her. Perhaps it was time to consider dating.

CHAPTER 11

Shay

This dinner with Drew and the children wasn't a date.

I was forced to remind myself of that a dozen times as I dressed for this evening six days after Drew had shown up at the café with the children. I'd hesitated before buying the children Christmas gifts, afraid Drew would feel bad because he hadn't gotten me anything. My gut had been right. The only reason he'd asked me to dinner was out of a misconstrued obligation to reciprocate. Even knowing that, I'd eagerly accepted.

I'm sure if I'd have mentioned my feelings about this dinner to Lilly she would have been all over me. This was that little girl inside me who sought love and acceptance, popping her head out and seeking attention. I'd done my fair share of beating her down in the last year, but every now and again she'd escape me and I'd give in to her whims.

Tonight was one of those times. Here I was doubting myself. Doubting Drew's intentions. Struggling with my insecurities.

Drew let me know he'd be by to pick me up at about six. I was ready an hour before that, fussing with my hair and makeup and then berating myself for worrying about how I looked. Repeatedly I had to remind myself, *This is not a date.*

Watching out the window, I saw him pull up to the house and automatically reached for my coat and purse. I had the door locked before he reached the porch.

"You didn't need to come out. I would have come to the door," he said.

"That's all right. I was ready and waiting."

The gentleman that he was, he opened the passenger door for me and I slid into the front seat.

"You smell good," Sarah said, leaning over from the back, where she sat with Mark.

"Thank you," I returned. "It's a new perfume."

"Was it a gift from a boyfriend?" Sarah asked.

"No, but a friend gave it to me. It's from Lilly Palmer. She was my counselor at Hope Center. I was with her family for Christmas."

"You weren't alone," Sarah said with a relieved sigh. "I was afraid you were. I wanted to invite you to come with us to the Kincaids', but Daddy said you couldn't because it wasn't our place. I wish we had, though. It would have been a whole lot more fun if you'd been there."

"Thank you, Sarah. That's a sweet thing to say."

"It's true," Mark added.

Looking over my shoulder, I smiled at both children.

"Do you have a boyfriend?" Sarah asked.

I mulled over my answer, thinking about Richard, who had become a real friend. "Sort of."

"What's his name?"

"Richard."

The ever curious Sarah continued with her questions. "Do you go out on dates?"

"Sarah," Drew grumbled, "it isn't polite to ask personal questions."

"I don't mind," I assured him. "Richard and I have coffee every morning, but that isn't really a date."

"Oh." Sarah's voice dropped as if she was disappointed.

"I haven't had much time to date between work and my classes. That's why your dad had to wait almost a week for us to have our dinner."

Drew pulled into the restaurant parking lot. I'd chosen Chinese on Sarah's recommendation. As it happened, I was fond of Chinese food myself. I couldn't remember the last time I'd tasted almond chicken.

Drew came around and helped me out of the car. The kids joined us and Sarah slipped her hand in mine as we entered the restaurant.

"Doesn't Shay smell good?" she asked her father.

Drew grinned at me. "She does."

I think I must have blushed, and as a distraction I asked, "Who knows how to eat with chopsticks?"

"I do," Drew said. "What about you?"

"I try each time but it's been awhile."

Once we were seated inside and had placed our order, we all tried practicing using chopsticks. Drew did amazingly well. Mark was pretty good, too, but Sarah and I were hopeless. By the time the food arrived, we'd all dissolved into giggles.

"I'll starve if you make me eat with these," the little girl protested.

Leaning close, I whispered in her ear, "I bet they have forks, too."

"Good."

The meal was a lot of fun and we ate until it felt as if our stomachs would burst wide open. Both Sarah and Mark leaned back in their chairs and planted their hands over their middles. I was stuffed and Drew declared that he was as well. He had the server package up the leftovers.

As we headed toward the parking lot, Sarah looked up at me and claimed, "This was the most fun ever."

"I think so, too," I told her. In truth, I couldn't remember the last time I'd had an experience like this. I'm sure we'd gone out to eat as a family before my mother died, but if we had I didn't remember it. What I recalled was the yelling and the fighting and then later the hitting and the verbal abuse heaped on me by my father.

My thoughts automatically turned to my brother and all I'd done to protect him over the years. It made me sad to think about him. I had no idea where Caden was now or even if he was alive. My fear was he was in prison, dead, or an addict living on the street the way Richard did. I'd mentioned Caden to Richard and Richard told me he'd ask around. I said that wasn't necessary, but Richard insisted that he might be able to help him. This was his way of thanking me for the coffee I brought him, I suspected.

To this point, Richard had nothing to report. I didn't like to think about Caden because any thoughts of him invariably weighed down my heart with feelings of anger and resentment, although I'd been working on letting go of those emotions.

Drew drove me back to my house. When he turned off the engine, I placed my hand on his forearm. "You don't need to get out."

"Sorry, manners say that I do. I wouldn't want to disappoint my mother by not escorting you to the door," he teased.

I knew it was important for Drew to demonstrate to his son how to properly treat a lady, so I quietly sat until he came around to my side of the car and opened the passenger door.

Drew walked me to my front door.

"I had a great time," I told him, and it was true. "Thank you."

Drew looked down at his feet and then glanced up. "Maybe we could do this again sometime?"

"Sure," I said. "I'd enjoy that. The kids would, too." If we used chopsticks often enough, perhaps Sarah and I would eventually get the hang of it.

I assumed Drew would hurry back to the car and was surprised when he lingered. "Without the kids."

"I'm sorry?" I didn't understand what he meant.

"I mean the two of us having dinner or lunch or whatever and not bringing along Mark and Sarah."

To say I was stunned would be an understatement. I opened my mouth and closed it when no words came out. I'm rarely at a loss for words, but Drew had me tongue-tied. The oddest sensation came over me, and emotion whirled around me until my throat thickened. I'd never dated as a teenager. I'd hung out with guys, but they didn't take me to dinner or pay my way into a movie. We did drugs or smoked pot and did other things that I was ashamed of now.

"Unless, I mean, you mentioned this guy you're see-ing," Drew said, rushing the words together as if he was as nervous as I was. "The one you have coffee with in the mornings. I wouldn't want to intrude on that relation-ship."

That made me smile and the tension eased from be-tween my shoulder blades. "Richard is a homeless man, old enough to be my father. He sleeps outside The Cor-ner Café. I bring him coffee and we talk."

"Is he the one you bought the gloves for?"

"Yes."

Drew smiled then and his gaze held mine. "How about Friday night?" he asked, sounding more confident now.

My heart fell. "I can't. I've signed up to go to a Search & Rescue event with the Seattle Gospel Mission. We hand out food to the homeless. Have you ever gone?"

"No, but I've wanted to. Kevin has invited me several times."

"Then join us," I said, having a hard time disguising my enthusiasm. "I've gone before."

"I'd like that," Drew surprised me by saying. "Kevin claims it's an eye-opening experience."

"It is." I'd been with the group twice now and always came away feeling blessed by the gratitude and humility of those we helped.

"What time should I pick you up?" he asked.

My heart was doing jumping jacks, and I was happier than I could remember being in a long time. "The van leaves at seven-thirty, so seven should work."

"Dad." Mark rolled down the car window and shouted at his father. "What's taking so long?"

Drew looked toward the car. "I'll be right there."

"Are you going to kiss Shay?" Sarah shouted from the other side. "You should."

"I better go," Drew said. "I'll be by to pick you up at seven on Friday."

I nodded, excited to the point I wanted to do a happy dance on my top porch step. Drew started toward the car when I stopped him. "Be prepared, Drew. We often don't get back until after midnight."

"Good to know."

He left then. I stood in the doorway and watched him pull out. He glanced my way and smiled. I grinned and waved.

I couldn't argue with myself. I had a date. A real date. The first one in my entire life.

The next morning I met Richard, bringing him his morning cup of coffee.

He took it from me and held it with both hands. I noticed he had only one glove. "Did you lose a glove?" I asked.

He avoided eye contact and shrugged.

"Richard," I said, squatting down so he couldn't help but meet my gaze. "Did someone take that glove from you?" I knew theft could be a real problem among the homeless.

"No one took it," he assured me, but he kept his focus on the coffee cup and not me.

"Then what happened to it?"

"You gonna be mad if I tell you?"

I came up with the one scenario that would upset me. "Did you sell it?"

"No." He seemed offended by the question.

"Then tell me."

"Got a friend. Chuck. A veteran like me. I gave him one glove so he could keep his hand warm. One is better than nothing, right?"

"Oh Richard. How could I possibly be angry about that?"

"Didn't want to upset you." He sipped his coffee. "I was afraid if you got mad you wouldn't bring me coffee. I've kind of gotten used to this. I told Chuck what you do and he said he might come by some morning. Don't worry, I'll share the coffee with him. Wouldn't want you to have to buy two cups."

"I'm not going to withhold your coffee," I said, hiding a smile. "And if Chuck joins you I'll get another cup. Frankie hasn't been charging me anyway."

Richard's eyes brightened. "I'll tell Chuck, then."

"Okay."

Richard sighed. "Wanted you to know I've been asking around about your brother but I haven't heard anything yet. Don't you worry, if he's around, I'll find him and let you know how he's doing."

"That isn't necessary."

"I know."

Caden was bad news and I couldn't allow myself to get caught up in his troubles again.

Richard grinned, something he didn't do often, and I could see he was missing several teeth. Then, because I was excited, I mentioned my date. "I'm bringing a friend along with me Friday."

"You handing out sandwiches again?"

"Yup."

"Hate to tell you this, Shay, but that's not much of a date. What's a matter with this guy, can't he afford to take you to dinner? A fine girl like you deserves a man who will treat you right."

"He's one of my best friends."

"You like him?"

"I do." More than I probably should, but I didn't say that.

"You gonna be at the regular stops?" Richard asked.

"Think so."

Richard nodded. "I'll come by and check him out for you if you'd like."

"Sure," I said. I didn't tell Richard, but I had the feeling Drew wanted to check him out, too.

"If he's sober, I'll bring Chuck with me."

"That would be great. I'll see what I can do to get him a pair of his own gloves."

Richard gave me another spotted-tooth grin.

"Hope this date of yours knows you're a good person."

I had to wonder that myself. "I believe he does."

"If he doesn't, you be sure to let me know."

"I'll do that," I promised, smiling at the thought of Pastor Drew Douglas being checked out by my homeless friend.

CHAPTER 12

Drew

I got the call on Wednesday from Joan Sullivan, the wife of an old friend. Joe was dying. It looked like he had only a few weeks left to live.

"Come now," Joan urged. "He wants to see you."

Glancing down at the weekly calendar Mary Lou put together for me, the only day I could manage would be Friday.

My heart sank.

I had hoped to go out with Shay in a Search & Rescue van that night. No way could I drive to Spokane and be back in time to be with her. Not if I planned to make the five-hour trip in a single day, and really that was what I would need to do. Ten hours on the road and I couldn't guarantee I'd be back before seven to pick her up.

"I'll come Friday," I assured Joan.

We chatted a few minutes longer before ending the call. I hadn't seen Joe in eighteen months or longer. At seventy, he'd been a good friend to my father and a mentor of sorts to me. Joe had been a constant encourager in the bleak days when Katie had been so desperately ill. I knew he had cancer and we'd kept in touch via email.

Not wanting to burden him, I let him assume all was well in the darkest days following her death. Thankfully, I'd been in a much better frame of mind lately.

I had Shay to thank for that, too. I had a lot to thank her for.

Sitting back in my chair, I exhaled, saddened to hear this news about my friend and mentor. I'd hoped he would rebound, but clearly that wasn't to be the case. Thinking it would be best to break the news to Shay personally rather than over the phone, I decided to stop by The Corner Café for lunch.

"I'm taking a lunch break," I told Mary Lou as I headed out of the office.

"The Brownes are coming in at one for marriage counseling," my assistant reminded me.

"I'll be back in plenty of time," I promised, and glanced at my watch to make sure that was true. Timing should work out fine. I decided to walk the six blocks, feeling the exercise would do me good. The thought of losing Joe filled me with sadness, and at the same time I dealt with the disappointment of needing to break my date with Shay.

It might be for the best, though. It'd been years since I'd last dated and I felt rusty. Even now I wasn't sure it was a good idea for me to get involved with Shay. My fears were wrapped up in what others would say or think about her. Certainly, she wasn't like any woman my church family would expect me to date. Still, this was my life and I should be comfortable dating anyone I wanted.

The thing was, I liked Shay and the way I felt when I was around her. She was good for Mark and Sarah, too. Sarah, especially. With Mark it was harder to tell. He kept his feelings bottled up most of the time, which was another concern. I could laugh with Shay and I was comfortable around her.

I knew people would talk. There would be questions about how appropriate she was for me and my children. Worries bounced around inside my head like a ping-pong ball gone wild. Yet, I couldn't stop thinking about her. Given the chance, I would like to know her better.

The long drive to and from Spokane would give me the time I needed to mull over these doubts about what I was doing. My life and ministry had become complicated in ways I hadn't anticipated since I'd lost Katie. How I wished I could talk to her about our children and how to be the best parent possible. A good majority of the time I felt inadequate, lost as to what was best for them.

When I arrived, The Corner Café was busy, and once again the only option available to me was a stool at the counter. Thankfully, Shay was stationed there and bustled about taking care of her customers with an ease and friendliness that drew me in immediately.

When she noticed me, she paused and a big smile came over her as if she'd been waiting all day for me to arrive. I told myself that her smile was for every customer and not just me. I wasn't successful because I wanted to believe that I was the one she'd been looking for. Me.

Right away Shay reached for a coffee mug and brought it over along with a fresh pot of the brew.

"Special today is shepherd's pie," she said.

"Sounds good," I said, not bothering to look at the menu. Bottom line, I wasn't all that hungry or interested in lunch. The reason I was there was to talk to Shay.

She put in my order and it was up within a few minutes. When she set it before me, I asked, "Do you have five minutes to chat?"

Shay glanced at the counter with every stool filled and reluctantly shook her head. I read the regret in her eyes.

"Sorry, not really."

I should have known better than to come at the busiest time of the day. I'd hoped she could take her break so I could explain in more than a few words.

"If you like, I could stop by your office after work."

I mentally reviewed my afternoon schedule and realized I had meetings the rest of the day. "That won't work, either. It's about Friday . . ."

We were interrupted when another server told Shay she had an order up. She reluctantly left me to deliver the plate to the guy at the other end of the counter. Needing an excuse to return, she came back and refreshed my coffee. "What about Friday?" she asked.

"I'm afraid I won't be able to make it."

Her eyes immediately flew up to meet mine. She seemed to forget what she was doing and overfilled my coffee mug, spilling the dark liquid all across the counter. Right away she set the coffeepot aside and reached for a rag to clean up the mess.

"I'm sorry, Shay." She had no idea how sorry.

She shrugged as if it was nothing. "No, it's fine. Not a problem. Really."

"I have a sick friend." That sounded incredibly lame and I immediately regretted explaining it that way. It sounded as if I'd told the teacher the dog ate my homework. Rushing to explain, I said, "Joe lives in Spokane and I need to make a one-day trip out of it and—"

Shay set her hand on my forearm. "It's fine, Drew. It's not a big deal; we'll make it another time."

The shepherd's pie might have been an award-winning recipe, but it tasted like burned rubber to me. Although Shay made a gallant effort to hide it, I could see she was disappointed. Her reaction gave me pause. My fear was that she'd put more stock into my asking her out than warranted. I felt like rubbing my hand down my face. I didn't know what I was doing. I liked Shay and being with her made me feel lighthearted and happy.

Lighthearted. That made me sound old. It was a word Joe would have used.

Joe. My heart sank at the thought of letting him go.

While Joe had asked to see me, I was the one who was grateful for the opportunity to talk to my friend. I needed his advice and welcomed the chance to bare my soul.

Shay remained busy, working the counter. Once I was served, she set the tab by my plate and basically ignored me the rest of the meal. I wasn't given a chance to talk to her again. With time running short, I was forced to leave soon afterward. Because I'd waited longer than I should have, I speed-walked back to the office and arrived a scant five minutes before the Brownes.

Friday morning, I got the children off to school, checked in with Mary Lou, and then headed out to drive to Spokane. Linda Kincaid had offered to pick up Mark and Sarah after school, feed them dinner, and then take them back to the house and wait for my return.

Frankly, I don't know what I would have done without her. When Sarah learned I wouldn't be home on Friday, she asked if Shay could be her babysitter. Right away Mark complained that he didn't need a babysitter.

Thinking about the children, I gassed up my car and headed out. Traffic was reasonable once I got out of the Seattle morning rush, and the lengthy drive was pleasant. The biggest concern was making it over Snoqualmie Pass. Winter months could be tricky. Thankfully, the weather forecast was good and the roads were clear and dry.

I arrived just after one and Joan thoughtfully had a tuna sandwich waiting for me. Knowing me, she was well aware I wouldn't stop along the way to eat, and she was right.

Joe was in his recliner in the living room, and I was stunned at the first look at him. He was terribly thin, his face gaunt. When I first arrived he was asleep, something he did more and more, Joan told me. He didn't stir when Joan brought me into the room. She lovingly placed her hand on his shoulder, kissed his cheek, and whispered, "Drew is here."

Joe's eyes fluttered open, and when he saw me he attempted a weak smile. "Drew," he said, his voice feeble and thin. "Thank you for coming."

"It's good to see you, Joe." I scooted the ottoman closer to his recliner, which Joe righted. I didn't ask him how he was doing or how he felt. It was clear he was deathly sick, and as Joan had explained it was only a matter of weeks now. Hospice had been notified.

We talked for several minutes about the church and how matters were progressing. As always, he listened, asked pertinent questions, and had the ability to read between the lines. I was happy to tell him Sunday-morning attendance was up and that financially we were meeting our budget. That was a great relief to me. Finances were a constant worry.

"Enough about Seattle Calvary," Joe said. "I want to know about you. How are you doing?"

"Much better," I answered without explaining.

He studied me for an uncomfortable moment, letting me know I shouldn't have hesitated to come to see him. Neither one of us said it, but we both knew why I hadn't. All this was communicated without either of us uttering a single word.

After a few moments, Joe asked, "It's been how long now since you lost Katie?"

"Four years." The longest, most miserable years of my life, but that was understood as well.

A couple times Joe closed his eyes while talking and I was afraid I was tiring him out. He rebounded quickly, though, and maintained his caring and loving attitude.

"Almost five years since she was diagnosed," he repeated after one of his short eye-resting breaks. "Have you met anyone?"

I don't know what it was about Joe. He had the uncanny knack of sensing the very subject most heavy on my mind. Over the years, he'd done it again and again. It felt, at times, as if he had the ability to read my mind.

"Funny you should ask."

He responded with the faint semblance of a smile. "So there is."

For the next thirty minutes I told him about Shay, starting with how we met in the church that morning last December, over a year ago. I explained that in helping her get into Hope Center, I'd rebounded from the spiritual slump I'd suffered. The feelings of worthlessness, of loss and anger.

Joe arched his brows, nodded a few times, and then asked, "What about Shay appeals to you?"

"Sarah—"

Holding up his hand, he stopped me. "I didn't ask about Sarah, I asked about what attracts *you* to this woman."

His question gave me pause and I realized I felt guilty about my feelings for Shay. My thoughts had wandered down paths that were different from the way I thought about other women. Several of the ladies in the church had tried to arrange blind dates for me with their daughters or nieces or the daughters of friends. Not once had I been tempted. Everything felt fresh and new with Shay.

"I can see you're having a hard time answering my question."

"No," I disagreed, "not difficult. I realized something just now." I leaned forward and braced my elbows on my knees. "She's different from any other woman I've ever known. There's an edge to her that comes from a troubled past. She wasn't raised in the church, she came to faith on her own, down a path that would have broken a woman with less grit. She's had to fight her way to where she is now and she still has a long way to go. I admire her."

"Has she met the children?"

I nodded. "They love her, especially Sarah. Mark doesn't say much, but from the things he's mentioned, I know he likes her, too. I love the way she interacts with my children, the way she smiles when she's happy." Her smiles were rare. I was mesmerized every time I saw one and thought she was beautiful. "It's as if she brings light into the dark corners of my life," I added, deep in thought. "At the same time, I seem to want to justify the way I'm attracted to her and worry what my congregation will think if I start to date her."

Joe paused and closed his eyes again.

I waited several minutes. "And guilty," he added, insinuating that I might feel bad because of how deeply I loved Katie.

"Yes, I suppose there's that, too. I loved my wife." I could never deny or discount the intensity and depth of my love for Katie. Every minute with her was one I'd treasured. Had I known before we married that she would die young, I wouldn't have changed a single thing. I would have prized every day with her even more.

"Katie loved you and she wouldn't want you to live the rest of your life alone."

Before her death, Katie and I had talked about this very subject. At the time, I couldn't imagine ever loving another woman with the depth and passion with which I loved her. The subject was uncomfortable and I cut short our conversation, finding it depressing. In retrospect, I wished I'd looked beyond the pain of the inevitability of her leaving us and been willing to discuss the future the way she'd wanted.

"Did you know Joan is my second wife?" Joe asked.

Surprised, I shook my head. "No." Glancing into the other room, I looked at Joan, who was busy baking cookies for me to take back to the children.

"I married young. Too young," Joe told me. "The marriage was a mistake and my wife left me for another man within the first year. The divorce devastated me. Cut me to the core. I was convinced I would be of no use to God in ministry if anyone knew I had a failed marriage under my belt. I did everything within my power to save that marriage, Drew. Everything. In the end it did no good.

"Three years later I met Joan. We dated for two years until she finally wanted to know if I was serious. She loved me, but she wasn't going to wait for me to propose if that wasn't my intention."

Apparently, Joan was listening in on our conversation because she brought in a plate of cookies still warm from the oven. She set it down on the table next to me and said, "I ended up proposing to him."

"I'm no fool," Joe said and reached for his wife's fingers. "I said yes and there hasn't been a day that I've regretted having Joan as my wife."

Grinning, Joan balanced her hand on her hip and cocked her head to one side.

Joe shook his head. "Not a day, Joan. Yes, I've been upset with you and we've certainly had our share of challenges over the years. But not a minute has passed that I've thought I wanted anyone but you."

Leaning down, Joan kissed her husband's forehead, and when she straightened I saw tears glistening in her eyes as she headed back to the kitchen.

"You moved into a second relationship slowly, then."

"It's what I advise you to do with Shay. Give yourself time," Joe advised.

That was exactly what I needed to hear.

"My father gave me good advice following my divorce. He told me to find a woman who loved me and loved God, and that's exactly what I did. You do the same, Drew. I know God has someone special in mind for you. It could well be Shay, but it could be someone else, too. Don't be too quick to assume she's the one."

The one? I hadn't thought of Shay as anything yet. We hadn't so much as held hands. That didn't mean I hadn't thought about kissing her. My thoughts drifted in that direction far more than I cared to admit.

From certain things she'd told me, I knew she was experienced when it came to men and relationships. She once mentioned that she'd gotten involved with a gang member who was currently imprisoned. Their relationship certainly hadn't been platonic.

"She's unlike any woman I've ever known," I admitted.

"Not a bad thing, you know," Joe told me.

I avoided eye contact. "She's been around, if you know what I mean."

Joe locked eyes with me and burst into laughter to the point that Joan came into the room and helped ease him forward, allowing him to catch his breath.

"Sorry, sorry," Joe muttered when he was able to speak again. "My dear boy, God can use us all, no matter what is in our past. He's already used Shay to touch your heart and that of your children. He doesn't ask for any of us to be perfect."

"I know . . . These feelings are unfamiliar, Joe. I'm not sure I have the right to feel the way I do. She's beautiful and smart and she could date anyone."

"Is she dating anyone else?"

This was the question I'd asked myself several times since Christmas. When Sarah had asked about Richard I'd been all ears, interested in what she had to say. When she mentioned his name, my heart had sunk until I learned that Richard was a homeless man old enough to be her father.

The rest of the afternoon passed quickly. We prayed together and I left shortly after four. By the time I arrived back in Seattle I was mentally and physically drained. Thankfully, both kids were involved in a movie. I thanked Linda for stepping in for me and gave the children the cookies Joan had sent home with me.

Sarah crawled into my lap and laid her head upon my shoulder. "Next time we need a babysitter . . ."

"I don't need a sitter," Mark insisted.

"Next time you leave us," Sarah started again, "can we have Shay instead of Mrs. Kincaid?"

I kissed her forehead. "I'll see what I can do."

Laying my head on top of my daughter's, I thought about Shay. She hadn't been far from my thoughts the entire drive home, and I wished, with an almost hungry need, to spend time with her as soon as it could be arranged.

CHAPTER 13

Shay

"You have a visitor," Sadie said, coming back into the kitchen to get me. We were ready to close for the day and I'd already checked out.

"A customer?" I asked and wanted to groan. We were minutes away from locking the doors.

"By the looks of him, I doubt it."

Him? I hoped it wasn't Richard. Frankie wouldn't take kindly to Richard coming inside the café. I wiped my hands on my apron and headed out front. It didn't take me long to see Drew's son, who sat in a booth with his back to me. Mark's head was bowed and he didn't look at me when I approached.

"Mark? Shouldn't you be in school?"

He looked up and I gasped. His left eye was nearly swollen shut and was turning black and blue. "Mark, oh my goodness, what happened? Wait, let me get some ice. It will help take the swelling down." Rushing behind the counter, I grabbed a plastic bag and filled it with ice.

The young teen groaned slightly when I set the make-shift compress against his face.

"It will feel better in a few minutes," I assured him as

I checked him for any other injuries. It looked like his lip was cut, too, as there was evidence of blood.

"School's out," he said, answering my question.

"I take it you got into a fight?" I continued to hold the ice against his face and gently pushed back the hair from his forehead. "Do I want to see the other guy?"

The question brought a hint of amusement, but then he grimaced, as if smiling caused him pain.

"I don't want to go home," he murmured, not making eye contact. "Dad's going to be mad."

"You sure about that?"

Mark nodded. "He doesn't believe in fighting."

"He's right, you know. If there's another way out of a confrontation, then you need to take it."

"That sounds good in theory," he muttered.

From what I knew of Mark, I strongly suspected he wasn't a fighter. I'd wager that whatever happened hadn't been instigated by him. "But it isn't always possible to avoid a fight."

"You're telling me!"

I laughed, and after a few minutes I removed the ice to see if the swelling had gone down. It had, but only slightly. "You're going to have a doozie of a black eye."

His shoulders sagged, as if this was the last thing he wanted to hear. "I was afraid of that."

As much as I longed to hug and comfort him, I didn't think Mark would appreciate it. "You want to tell me what happened?"

"Not really."

I was tempted to reach for my phone and text Drew. Because both our schedules were busy, mine with work and night classes, we'd taken to communicating by texting several times a day.

"Would you come home with me and talk to my dad?" Mark asked, keeping his head down, but he raised his eyes up to meet mine as if he wasn't certain what I'd say.

I had night classes that evening, ones I couldn't miss. "I'll go to the church office with you so *you* can talk to your dad, if that's what you want." I wanted to give Drew a heads-up that we were on the way, but I knew he was busy that afternoon.

Mark's shoulders fell when he realized he was going to have to be the one to explain the fight to his father. Slowly he nodded. "Okay, but you'll still come with me?"

"If that's what you want."

"I do. Dad won't yell as hard if he sees you."

That was nice to hear, although I doubted it was true. "Give me a few minutes and I'll walk to the church with you." I'd be able to catch a bus to the community college from Fourth Street easily enough.

I returned to the kitchen, finished up what I needed to do, and bid Sadie, Alice, and Frankie goodbye before collecting my purse and coat.

"The kid okay?" Frankie asked before I joined Mark. Apparently, he'd caught sight of Mark's shiner.

"I think so. He wants me to go with him while he talks to his dad."

"His dad that preacher guy? The one who comes in, orders the special? The one you can't keep your eyes off of?"

My gaze shot to Sadie. It seemed she'd mentioned my fascination with Drew to Frankie. My friend didn't even pretend to look guilty. I was sorry I'd said anything to

Sadie. I couldn't be upset with either of them, though. Frankie refused to let me pay for the coffee I brought to Richard. He didn't get upset when Chuck started showing up every so often, either. He was gruff about it, not wanting my appreciation or Richard's.

"Yes, Mark's dad is the pastor of Seattle Calvary."

Frankie grumbled something under his breath. "Well, then, don't keep the boy waiting."

Grinning, I scooted out of the kitchen. When he saw me, Mark slid out of the booth and headed for the front door. I noticed a couple boys his age hanging around across the street. Both were much bigger than Mark, who was small for his age. I wondered if those were the boys he'd tangled with earlier. I was about to ask but decided against it. As soon as they saw me, the two other boys took off in the opposite direction. That got me to wondering if Mark had come into the café in order to avoid another confrontation. Maybe having me walk with him the rest of the way home was a safety measure.

When we arrived at the church office, Mary Lou looked up from her computer and gasped. "My heavens, Mark, what happened?"

He shrugged, avoiding answering her. "Is my dad here?"

"He's in a meeting." She glanced down at the corner of her computer screen. "He'll be out shortly; do you want to wait?"

"Okay."

He took a seat in a small waiting area and I sat in the chair next to him. He looked small and his shoulders were slumped forward again, as if he dreaded confronting his father. The wait probably wasn't helping any.

"Have you finished any more pages in the math puzzle book?" I asked, making conversation, hoping to take his mind off talking to his dad.

Mark nodded. "All of it."

"The entire book? Already?"

He chanced a look in my direction and grinned. "They were easy."

"Were not," I argued. Before I'd purchased the book, I'd flipped through the pages and read a few of the word problems and felt they might be too complex for Mark. Heaven knew they were well above my own capabilities.

Mark was about to say something more when the door to Drew's office opened. A man and woman stepped out. Drew followed, caught sight of his son, and did a double take. Right away his gaze shot to me. It seemed, and I could be wrong, but when he looked at me, his eyes softened.

Without a pause, Drew turned his attention to his assistant. "Mary Lou, make an appointment with Mr. and Mrs. Wilkens for next week at the same time."

"Will do."

Not speaking, he gestured to his son to come into his office.

Mark looked to me and I stood with him.

Drew noticed and raised questioning eyes to me. "Mark asked me to accompany him."

As soon as we were in the room, Drew closed the door. Mark stood in front of his father's desk and straightened his shoulders. He looked like a young soldier ready to face a firing squad.

"You hurt?" Drew asked his son.

Mark shrugged. "I'm okay. My eye hurts, but the ice Shay put on my face helped."

"I have aspirin in my purse, but I didn't want to give it to him until I'd talked to you," I interjected.

"You need aspirin for the pain?" Mark asked his son.

Mark shook his head.

Standing behind Mark, I placed my hands on his shoulders while Drew leaned back in his chair and waited, finally expelling his breath. "You want to tell me what happened?"

Mark was quiet. "Not really."

"Could you have avoided the fight?"

Mark answered with a shake of his head. "I tried, but as you can see, that didn't work out so well. Are you mad?"

Drew locked eyes with me. "No. But I'm disappointed you let this get physical."

Mark tensed and I suspected he'd clamped down hard on his jaw as if biting back an explanation. "In that case, I'd rather you got mad and shouted."

Time was fast approaching when I'd need to leave. I hated to go and glanced at my wrist, silently praying that I'd be able to catch a bus quickly.

"Head on home, Mark. We'll talk about this more later."

Mark stood steadfast. "I'd like to get this over with now, Dad. I don't want to sit at home, wondering what you're going to do. It's all right if you want to yell, but I'd like it if you did it all at once. Okay?"

"I'm so sorry," I whispered to them both. "I need to leave or I'll be late for my class."

Drew's focus was on his son. He nodded, letting me

know it was fine for me to go. Giving Mark's shoulders a gentle squeeze, I turned and left the office. As I waited for the bus, I had a sneaking suspicion that there was more to the story of Mark's black eye than he was letting on. I remembered the two bigger boys who were waiting on the other side of the street when we'd left the café. If he'd gone up against those boys, he wouldn't have stood a chance. My thoughts remained troubled and I felt the need to tell Drew what I'd seen and share my suspicions.

Once on the bus, I took my seat and reached for my phone, texting Drew.

Can I give you a call tonight after class?

I hadn't heard back by the time I reached the school and was distracted for the entire class. As soon as class was over, I grabbed my phone and saw that Drew had responded.

Sure.

Not wanting to have the conversation while on the bus, I waited until I was home before I called.

Drew answered on the second ring. "Hey," he greeted.

"Hey," I returned. "Everything okay with Mark?"

"Yeah, I think so, but he wouldn't give me any details of what happened. It isn't like my son to get into a fight. And he didn't have a good reason for not taking the school bus home."

"Drew, the reason I called is because I'm not sure Mark was in a fight."

Drew paused as if he needed to take in my words. "What do you mean?"

It was then that I mentioned the boys I'd seen, who appeared to be waiting for Mark.

"You think those boys might have beat him up?"

"I don't know, but that's my guess. Did he say anything about them?"

"Not a word. In fact, he's remained stubbornly silent about the entire incident. I don't want to pressure him to tell me what happened."

I could understand that. Mark's pride was badly hurt, and talking about the incident would humiliate him all the more. Still, two against one was bad enough, and two much larger boys against a smaller one was grossly unfair.

Drew was silent again. "I appreciate the call."

"Sure, anytime." I was ready to hang up when Drew spoke.

"Do you have plans for Saturday? You aren't working, are you?"

My heart rate quickly accelerated. "No, it's my free Saturday." I worked every other Saturday and Sunday. I'd planned to stay home and study, but if Drew asked me out I'd find another time to hit the books. He'd broken our last almost-date and he hadn't asked me out since.

"I was wondering if you'd mind staying with the kids for a couple hours?"

He wanted me to babysit? Well, that was definitely a letdown. "Sure, I'd be happy to."

"Sarah wants you to do that thing you do with her hair again, if you would?"

"Of course." To the best of my ability, I hid my disappointment.

"Great. Does eleven-thirty work for you?"

"Sure."

"Great, I'll see you then."

Drew sounded chipper and pleased with himself.

My heart sank with disappointment.

So much for him asking me out on a real date. I'd apparently been relegated to the friendly babysitter.

CHAPTER 14

Drew

Marion Rowden was eighty-five years old, a widow, and one of the most faithful members of the church. She'd been attending as long as I'd served as pastor and likely thirty years before that.

Years ago, when I'd first started in ministry, Joe had mentioned that he'd been inspired and encouraged in his role as pastor to spend time with the older members of the congregation. He claimed he'd learned a lot from their own walks of faith. Joe's advice had sounded solid at the time. It wasn't until my recent visit with my friend and mentor that I remembered what he'd said. For the life of me I don't know why I had never followed it.

Marion lived in an assisted-living complex. I arrived shortly before noon and I went up to her room to collect her. I knocked on her door and waited for her to answer. She didn't move as quickly as she once had, but I was patient.

She came to the door dressed to the nines, complete with a hat and white gloves. "I see you're on time."

"Always," I assured her. "I wouldn't want to keep my date waiting."

Her smile was warm enough to melt the Arctic ice cap. I extended my elbow, and she tucked her hand there as I escorted her to the elevator.

"Where are you taking me?"

"Best restaurant in town," I assured her. I wouldn't dream of anything less. Well, what was in my budget, at any rate.

"Mickey D's," Marion teased.

I laughed. "Actually I was thinking of Denny's. A bit more upscale than McDonald's but within my price range."

"I was hoping you'd say Denny's," Marion told me. "My husband and I used to dine there every Saturday night. God rest his soul. Miss him, I do, every single day. Nothing feels the same without him."

Marion chatted as I drove to the closest Denny's, and I listened as she told me about the love of her life, a man whom I'd never met. From what I remembered, Anton had died in his mid-fifties, and she still grieved for him. I could identify.

Once inside, we were escorted to a table. I pulled out Marion's chair and took my own seat. I studied the menu and was surprised to see Marion didn't.

As if reading my mind, she said, "I always order the same thing. You take your time. I'm in no rush."

When the server stepped to our table, I waited for Marion to speak first.

"I'll have the bourbon bacon burger." She grinned sheepishly and looked to me. "That's about as close to drinking hard liquor as I'll get. Anton would have loved that. Unfortunately, it wasn't a menu item when he was alive."

Although I'd had something else in mind to order, I asked for the same thing.

My time with Marion was a delight. We had an entertaining two-hour lunch. She did most of the talking, and I listened. She told me about a negative experience she'd had with a judgmental church when she was a young teen. I marveled that she hadn't allowed it to taint her attitude toward church and other Christians and told her so.

"My dear Drew," she said, looking me square in the eyes. "I never confused God with the church. We're all human. We all make mistakes. The key is not allowing anyone to stand in the way of how we view our Lord."

"How wise you are," I whispered, determined to thank Joe for this suggestion once I returned home.

Following our lengthy lunch, I drove my date back to the assisted-living complex and walked her to her room. "I had a delightful time, Marion."

"I did, too," she assured me. "Next time we should invite Nancy to join us. She's one of my best friends."

"I'll do that," I promised, determined to continue dating Marion and the other widows. I was far more familiar with the older men in the congregation. This was my effort to correct that oversight.

Eager now to return home, I drove back to the parsonage. I'd barely said hello to Shay before I had to leave to collect Marion. I appreciated her willingness to stay with Mark and Sarah. My daughter had been giddy with delight when she learned Shay was coming. Mark didn't show any emotion one way or the other, but I could tell he was pleased.

Shay insisted it wasn't necessary that I pick her up; she

was accustomed to getting around town on the bus and was coming from breakfast with Lilly, the woman who had served as her counselor. Apparently, the two remained in close contact. My hope was that she wouldn't need to leave right away, as I was looking forward to spending time with her. My schedule and hers had made it hard to find time to see her. I'd stopped by The Corner Café a couple times, and that served only to frustrate both of us as she was busy and too distracted to carry on any kind of conversation.

The minute I walked in the front door, Sarah came running toward me, her face bright and full of excitement. "Daddy, Daddy, look at my hair." She whirled around for me to see the French braid. "Shay did it."

"Who else would have done it?" Mark asked sarcastically. "The Tooth Fairy?"

"Very funny," Sarah shot back.

"You look lovely," I told Sarah, "and your hair does, too. Where's Shay?"

"I'm here," she said, her voice flat and emotionless. She had her coat on and her purse strap was wrapped around her shoulder as she headed for the front door with determination.

"You're leaving?"

"Yes." The words were barely out of her mouth when she started to leave.

"I was hoping you'd be able to stay a few minutes longer." Disappointment bled into my voice and I didn't bother to hide it as I followed her outside, hoping to convince her to change her mind.

"I need to get home" was all she said.

Before I could say anything more, Shay was gone.

Stunned, I looked between my two children and wondered if something had happened. Whatever it was had upset Shay to the point that she could barely stand to be in the same room with me.

"Mark. Sarah. Can you tell me why Shay is upset?"

Sarah shook her head. "She was fine until you got home, Daddy."

There had to be more to this than they were telling me. "Mark, do you have any idea?"

He scrunched up his face as if deep in thought. "We were eating lunch and talking and after that Shay got real quiet and sad."

"Sad?" I repeated. "Did she get a phone call?"

Sarah shook her head. "She put her phone on silent."

The only thing I could deduce was something one of the children had said. "What were you talking about when Shay got quiet?" I asked.

"Your date," Sarah told me.

"My date?"

"Yes, I told Shay you were on a date."

Groaning inwardly, I looked to Mark. "Watch your sister, I'll be right back."

Not caring that I'd removed my coat, I grabbed the front door and raced into the cold, running toward the bus stop, silently praying that Shay hadn't already caught the bus.

I was relieved to see her standing, waiting. Slowing my steps, I approached her. "Shay, I believe there's been a misunderstanding."

A bus approached and she looked eager to board it.

"Please give me a chance to explain," I pleaded. "Don't get on that bus. We need to talk."

Hands tucked in her pockets, she ignored me and stepped forward, as if the bus couldn't open its doors fast enough to suit her.

"Please," I tried again, a desperate feeling attacking the pit of my stomach. The thought of hurting her was unbearable.

To my surprise, she whirled around and confronted me. "I don't believe there's anything to say. You did nothing wrong, Drew. Sorry, I mean Pastor Douglas. If there's anyone at fault here it's me. I was the one who let reality get away from me. Really, why would I dare to think that someone like you would possibly be interested in me? How presumptuous of me. How ridiculous."

"Shay, that's not true." My mouth felt dry and I realized how badly she was hurt. "I took Marion—"

"It doesn't matter," she said cutting me off.

"It does to me. You matter to me." There, I'd said it, and I meant it even more than I realized.

"Sure, I matter. I make a damn good babysitter." She looked up at the sky as if seeking something. "Honestly, I don't know what I was thinking."

"What? I don't understand."

"I don't belong here."

"What are you saying? Belong where?" I was confused, not understanding anything of what she said. She wasn't making sense.

"Forget it. It's nothing . . . I feel like an idiot. I don't ever seem to learn."

"I'd like to explain," I said, afraid anything I said now was too late and wouldn't help. She was hurt and angry and I didn't know how to make it better. One thing was clear: Shay was in no mood to listen.

"Like I said, it isn't necessary. Don't worry, I get it. I'm an ex-con, a felon. It's a wonder you even allow me around your children."

As she spoke, several at the bus stop turned to stare at her. My instinct was to pull her into my arms and hold her, to protect her from prying eyes. I reached for her arm, which she jerked away. Her message was clear: She wanted nothing to do with me, and she certainly didn't welcome my touch.

"I learned at Hope Center to stand up for myself," she said tightly. "I am unwilling to give others the opportunity to use me. You used me, Pastor. I am nothing more to you than a convenient babysitter. I think the world of Mark and Sarah, but I am not going to give you the chance to hurt me. Not happening."

"You couldn't be more wrong. Shay, please, if you'd just listen."

"No. There's nothing you have to say that I want to hear."

Another bus pulled up just then and Shay was the first one to board. I watched as she marched to the back and took a seat, staring straight ahead.

Defeat and frustration washed over me. There'd been only a few times in my life when I'd felt this uneasiness in my spirit, knowing I'd hurt another person. Everything she said was off-base. So wrong, and I didn't know how to convince her otherwise.

I don't know how long I stood in the cold. It was only when someone approaching the bus stop bumped into me that I realized I'd remained frozen in place. It felt like my entire body had iced over.

When I returned to the house, both Mark and Sarah were waiting for me.

"Did you talk to her, Daddy?" Sarah asked, wide-eyed.

"I tried." I sank onto the sofa and plowed my fingers through my hair, not knowing how to fix this.

Sensing my distress, Mark sat down next to me and patted my knee. "Girls are hard to talk to. I know."

Grinning, I nodded. "You're wise for your age."

"What did you do when you had trouble talking to Mom?" he asked. "That might help."

The fact that I was getting advice about girls from a thirteen-year-old spoke volumes. Certainly, Katie and I had had our share of differences through the years. One trick that seemed to work when she was hurt or upset was to kiss her. I strongly suspected that wouldn't work with Shay. She was liable to punch me if I tried.

Sleep didn't come easily that night. I didn't expect to see Shay at church the next morning, and I was right.

Knowing I was heavyhearted, Sarah stood at my side following the service after the church had emptied. As was her habit, Linda Kincaid was one of the last to leave. She approached me with a concerned look.

"You weren't yourself this morning, Drew. Something troubling you?"

Before I could answer, Sarah popped up. "He had a fight with Shay."

Linda's eye shot to mine. "I don't think I realized the two of you were involved."

"It wasn't a fight so much as a misunderstanding." I'd unintentionally hurt Shay and it bothered me to the point that even my congregation noticed something was wrong.

Linda patted my shoulder sympathetically. "It's probably for the best."

Her comment stunned me. "Why is that?" I asked, ready to defend Shay and needing to bite my tongue to keep from doing so. Linda had no idea how far Shay had come, the inner strength the woman had shown in the last year. She wasn't the same woman I'd met all those months ago, seeking warmth in the back of the church, defiant and ready to lash out at the world for the unfairness of life. She was stronger now, finding her way, and I admired her more than any woman I had met since Katie. Knowing I'd foolishly lost her because of a simple misunderstanding, a lack of communication on my part, didn't sit right with me. I felt off-kilter and lost as to how to make this right.

"Why?" Linda repeated. "Drew, really, I know you like Shay. I do, too, but you can't deny her past."

"I like Shay," Sarah piped up. "She did my hair."

Right away I could tell that Linda disapproved of Shay having anything to do with the children. She didn't need to say it. I saw it in her eyes.

"That's not how I look at people, Linda," I said, doing my best to keep the emotion out of my voice. "Shay has come a long way, and as Christians we should be the first to encourage and support her."

As I knew she would, Linda took a moment to consider my words. "You're right, Drew. I apologize."

Sarah tugged at my sleeve. "Daddy, that's what you need to do with Shay. You need to apologize. Tell her you're sorry and that you'll never date Mrs. Rowden again."

I wrapped my hand around my daughter's shoulder and wished with everything in me that Shay would listen to my apology.

Linda left and I closed the church. As we walked to the house, Sarah had another idea.

"Can we take Shay for Chinese food? She likes almond chicken, but let her use a fork and don't mention chopsticks."

"Maybe that will work."

As we approached the house, Sarah looked up at me, frowning. "If Shay is mad at you, does that mean she's mad at me, too?"

"No, pumpkin."

"Will she braid my hair again?"

"I don't know." It wasn't in my heart to tell my daughter it was doubtful.

Sadness settled over me and I didn't know if I was willing to accept that Shay was out of our lives. The problem was, I didn't know how to make things right with her.

CHAPTER 15

Shay

I attended worship service with Lilly Palmer on Sunday morning at her church. If she suspected anything was different with me, she didn't ask and I didn't volunteer. If she was waiting for me to spill my heart, then she had a long wait. From the time I could remember, men had used and abused me. I'd come too far for this. No way in hell was I going to let it continue. If I talked to anyone about what had happened between Drew and me it would be Lilly, but I wasn't ready to tell anyone.

What had I been thinking? No way was someone like Drew ever going to be interested in someone like me. It was time I put on my big-girl panties and accepted that I'd been living in a fantasy world. I'd been entertaining visions of sugarplums and romance because his little girl liked the way I braided her hair.

What shocked me was that I'd believed I'd come so far only to realize how little progress I'd made. Well, no more. I'd wised up. Never again was I going to allow a man to mistreat me. I'd walked down that path for a good part of my life and it was over. I was wiser now. Stronger. The key was to remember the lessons I'd learned at the Hope Center and use them.

What surprised me was how quickly I'd reverted to my old ways when I'd assumed a man was interested in me. Despite all the texts, secret smiles, and gentle looks, Drew would never be romantically interested in me. I got it, I really did. But I should have gotten it a whole lot sooner.

When Sarah mentioned that her father had taken another woman on a date for lunch, I nearly blew a gasket. If I needed any evidence that I had grown emotionally in the last year, it was that I'd managed to keep my cool until Drew arrived home.

He'd been gone nearly three hours. He and his date must have enjoyed quite a lunch. Well, good for him. From what I understood, he'd been a widower for four years. It was time he got back in the game and started dating again. I wished him well.

Friday night was another Search & Rescue event with Seattle Gospel Mission. Lilly asked me to accompany her and I agreed, even though I had to be up by four-thirty to get to the café in time for the morning shift.

I left the café, ready to head home and prepare for a cold night on the street, seeking out the homeless to deliver food and hot drinks. I noticed Richard hanging outside the restaurant.

He wouldn't be there if something wasn't right. "Problem?" I asked, thinking Chuck might need help. His friend couldn't stay away from the bottle.

His eyes grew sad. "Not good news, I'm afraid. I think I might have heard something about your brother."

My heart slammed hard against my rib cage. "I don't want to hear it," I said, and then I couldn't help myself, I had to know. "Is he alive?"

"What I heard is he's doing hardcore drugs, selling and using."

This was exactly what I'd expected. Best I keep him out of my life entirely before he dragged me down to his level. I'd learned my lesson with my brother and I didn't need that kind of trouble in my life.

Before I could say anything more, Richard continued. "Person I spoke to said it'd been three months since he was last seen. Dwayne thinks your brother might have drifted south to California. Warmer there in the wintertime."

Probably for the best. "Thanks for letting me know, Richard. It's better for the both of us that we don't have any contact with each other." Rather than dwell on what was happening to Caden, I abruptly changed the subject. "Will I see you tonight?"

"Yup. Both Chuck and I will be out."

"I'll look for you."

Richard glanced down at the sidewalk. "You'd already guessed your brother was using, though, didn't you?"

I nodded. "He was using before I went to prison. It's better for me that I keep him out of my life. He messed me up once and I won't let him use me again."

"You're a smart girl. You want me to let you know if I hear anything more?"

"I don't know . . . probably not."

"Your choice," Richard said, and then his eyes filled

with concern. "You ain't been yourself all week. Something up I don't know about?" he asked. "Seems like the light's gone out of your eyes and there's a hurt radiating off you like you got blisters on your heels."

Sadie had been saying basically the same thing. It seemed I wasn't nearly as clever at hiding my feelings as I thought. "I'm fine, Richard, just had a bit of a disappointment is all; nothing important. I'll be over it soon enough."

"Over it?" Richard asked. "Or over him?"

I decided to leave the question unanswered. "I'll see you later tonight," I said as I started toward the bus stop.

The Seattle Gospel Mission's Search & Rescue nights were done with vans that traveled to areas where the homeless congregated. As soon as the easily recognizable van rolled into an area, people appeared. The winter night was bitter cold and I'd wrapped up as warmly as I could. We'd stopped at a freeway underpass, and I'd given my scarf to one woman who had to have been close to my age.

All too soon another woman appeared, and I offered her hot cocoa and a wrapped sandwich.

"Do you need anything else?" I asked after she drank the hot drink and took the sandwich.

"You have any candy?"

I knew candy was a popular item because the sugar rush helped when coming down off a high.

"Sorry, we ran out of sweets earlier." I noticed her hands were badly chapped from the cold. I had lotion and wipes with me and offered her one, which she took and used to clean her hands.

"Thanks," she said, using a fresh wipe over her face. "This winter has been hard on my hands and face."

I reached for her hand, spread some lotion on the top, and rubbed it into the red, cracked skin.

"Should have a place of my own soon," she said as I continued to massage her hands. "Never thought I'd be on the streets this long. Gonna find a place soon, though."

"Good. You need socks?" I asked her.

"Not me, but Laurie could use a pair," she said and glanced over her shoulder. "The only shoes she's got are too big and her feet get cold, especially on nights like this."

"No doubt. Wait here and I'll get you those socks."

I found the kindness factor among those who lived on the streets humbling. For the most part the homeless never took what they didn't need. Often, if they knew of someone else who was doing without, then they would accept it to hand off to another.

"I'm Shay," I told my newfound friend.

"Irene," she answered.

I removed my gloves and gave them to her. "These will help keep your hands warm," I said, pressing them into her palms.

Irene looked up. "But they're your gloves."

"I have another pair. Take them, please."

"Thanks." Her voice was warm with gratitude.

"I'll look for you again," I said, and then remembered what she'd said. "That is, if you haven't found an apartment."

"Right," she said, grinning now. She accepted the wrapped sandwich and the socks for her friend and continued back to where her tent was tucked under the freeway overpass.

I found it curious that those who lived on the street rarely thought of themselves as homeless, and Irene was a good example. They considered it a temporary situation, a transitional period when they did the best they could with what they had. Most everyone I spoke to mentioned that it would only be a matter of time before they had a permanent address.

If I hadn't met Drew that day, I easily might have ended up in one of these camps myself. If for nothing else, I would always be grateful to him for the guidance he'd given me. Because I'd found my way into Hope Center I'd never had to live on the street, but if I had, my attitude would have been the same. I would have considered it a temporary situation just until I was on my feet financially.

At eleven, we were scheduled to meet up with another van at a recently established tent city. I knew this was the area where Richard and Chuck were most often found.

Sure enough, the two men were waiting for me when the van arrived. The second van hadn't made an appearance yet but would be by shortly.

"We spread the word you were coming," Richard said, greeting me as I climbed out of the vehicle.

I could see that was the case by the number of people who had already lined up for food, water, and clothing. Bottled water was the most requested item, as there was no running water in the tent cities.

"If you want, we can escort you into the camp," Chuck

offered. Volunteers were never to enter a homeless camp alone. We always went with a partner. Over time I'd learned that our work was about building relationships. We were welcomed and it had nothing to do with what we brought.

"Sure, that would be great," I told Richard's friend. The other man shuffled along with Richard. I'd learned that Chuck was a man of few words.

Lilly Palmer ventured into the campsite with me while Richard and Chuck accompanied us as if they were our bodyguards. We stopped along the way to chat with a few others. Richard called out to people, introducing us.

As we started back to the street, I saw that the second van had arrived but didn't have time to greet the other volunteers. Both Lilly and I were busy passing out sandwiches and hot chocolate. When we finished, I gave out the wipes and rubbed lotion into the winter-chapped hands of those who needed it.

When I felt someone behind me, I looked over my shoulder and saw that it was Drew. Seeing him was completely unexpected, and I nearly dropped the container of lotion. He set his hands on my shoulders, leaned forward, and whispered in my ear.

"We are going to talk, so don't even try to put me off again."

I stiffened and tried to jerk his hands free of my shoulders.

"Just so you know," he continued, "my hot date last Saturday was with an eighty-five-year-old woman."

My mouth dropped so fast and hard it was a wonder I didn't dislocate my jaw. Tingling started in my feet that had nothing to do with the cold. I felt light-headed, as if my blood pressure had suddenly dropped significantly. I realized it was relief I was feeling. I'd convinced myself any explanation he offered wouldn't make a difference. I hated the sense of hope that instantly filled me and how susceptible I was to Drew.

"I told Lilly Palmer I'd drive you home, so wait for me."

"That won't be necessary," I insisted, needing to be strong. I was finished allowing men to dictate how I lived my life.

A hurt look instantly bled into his eyes. "Please."

I wavered, uncertain. I'd been strong all week—strong and miserable. From the pleading look he gave me, I knew he'd been just as depressed.

"Okay," I agreed, unsure if I was doing the right thing.

His relief was immediate. "Thank you."

We didn't get a chance to talk until after the vans returned to the Gospel Mission complex. By then it was after midnight and I had to be at the café early that morning. I'd be lucky to get in four hours' sleep, if that. No matter. I needed to see Drew, to talk to him, to straighten out this misunderstanding.

I found him waiting for me in the parking lot. We were the only two volunteers who hadn't left.

He stood beside his vehicle, waiting for me to join him.

When I was at his car, all we seemed able to do was stare at each other. This week had felt like the longest of my life. Longer even than my first seven days in prison. I'd been strong, but my heart hurt with the knowledge I would never be part of his life. I hadn't realized how much Drew had come to mean to me.

After a few minutes, his cold hands cupped my face

and I realized that, like me, he'd probably given his gloves away. Before I could form a clear thought, he lowered his mouth to mine as if he couldn't wait a second longer.

I'd fantasized what it would be like to have Drew kiss me, how I would feel if it were ever to happen. Nothing could have prepared me for the strength, the intensity, the beauty of his kiss. His lips were as cold as his hands, but the minute they touched mine, I felt a warmth spread through me like water soaking into a sponge. His touch. His kiss. Everything about him was beautiful.

I parted my lips to him and he groaned softly, deepening the kiss. Wanting to be closer, needing my arms around him, I circled his waist. This felt so good, wrapped in a cocoon of gentle sensation.

When he broke off the kiss, he held me, my head tucked beneath his chin. "We probably should have talked first," he whispered, "but if I had to wait a second longer to kiss you I think I would have gone crazy."

I found it impossible to speak. I was surprised at how much I longed for his kiss and how much it meant to me.

He rubbed his chin over the top of my head. I'd given away my hat along with my gloves before half the night was over. It appeared Drew had, too.

"You're dating an older woman?" I asked.

I felt Drew's smile against my hair. "I am, but that doesn't mean I wouldn't do just about anything to spend an evening with you."

Smiling, I hugged him closer. "I thought you only wanted me as a babysitter, that you were using me." *Like every other man in my life,* I wanted to tell him but didn't.

"I should have explained what I was doing earlier. I don't know what I was thinking."

"I'm not—"

He stopped me by kissing me again, leaving me breathless. When he broke it off, he said, "I don't know what it was you were going to say, but the way you looked up at me gave me a clue. Don't discount yourself, Shay. If you're about to tell me that you're not like other women, then good. I don't want other women. I want you. You're the one who fills my head, who makes me feel alive. You're the one who makes me smile and laugh when I didn't know if that was ever going to be possible again."

Closing my eyes, I savored his words, holding them tightly against my heart.

"I don't know what I'm doing," Drew admitted. "I've only loved one woman. Katie and I . . . she was my only serious relationship. The thing is, Shay, I am sort of lost here."

"If that's the case, we're in deep trouble."

"I was afraid of that."

"My only relationship worthy of a mention," I explained, "was with a man who is currently serving a life sentence for murder, so my own experience is limited in the extreme."

Drew kissed the top of my head. "The one thing I can say is that I couldn't leave matters as they were."

The crazy part was that there were often several days when we didn't have a chance to see each other. Our only communications were random texts or phone calls. I'd missed those and knew he had, too.

"I've felt miserable myself."

"I tried to explain," he reminded me.

"I know, but I was in no mood to listen."

"The kids missed you, too. Both Mark and Sarah offered up ideas on how best to win you back."

I couldn't hold back a smile. Separating myself from the children had been the worst part of this breakup.

"Sarah believed all it would take was an order of almond chicken."

A giggle escaped me. "What about Mark?"

"First off, my son told me he found it hard to talk to girls, too, and that the other sex is difficult to understand. He felt I needed to be patient, and then just the other day he thought I should do something romantic to win you back."

"Something romantic?"

I could hear the amusement in his voice. "I asked for a few suggestions and he thought a Starbucks gift card might do the trick, or leaving you notes at the café so you'd find them when you came in to work."

"Not a bad idea."

"I considered it," he admitted, "until Sarah insisted it would be easier just to order Chinese."

"And to think all it took was a kiss," I told him, grinning like a silly fool.

Drew lifted his head and I raised my eyes to his. "Maybe it should take two or three or even more."

With that, he kissed me again and it was even better than before.

CHAPTER 16

Drew

Saturday morning I felt like a new man. After settling matters with Shay, I swear I could have leaped over tall buildings in a single bound. I couldn't remember any kisses that affected me as strongly as those I'd shared with Shay in the middle of an abandoned parking lot practically in the middle of the night.

When I finally woke and wandered out of the bedroom it was already after nine o'clock. Both kids were up. Sarah had plopped herself in front of the television and was watching cartoons, nestling a bowl of cold cereal in her lap. She still had on her pajamas. Mark was dressed and sat at the kitchen table, reading from his iPad.

Coffee was first on my mind and I headed for the kitchen. "Morning," I said as I passed my son, ruffling the top of Mark's head.

He immediately jerked, which was his way of letting me know he wasn't a kid and didn't want me doing that any longer. I hated to tell him this, but he would always be a kid to me. I could see myself doing the same thing when Mark was thirty, whether he liked it or not. The thought made me smile.

"Hey, pumpkin, what are you watching?" I asked as the coffee slowly dripped into my cup.

"*Minions.*"

"Can I talk to you kids for a minute?" I asked, after my first reviving sip of coffee. I cradled the mug with both hands as I leaned against the kitchen counter.

Something in my voice must have alerted them that whatever I had to say was serious. And it was.

"Are we in trouble?" Mark asked, looking up from his iPad.

"Whatever it is, Mark did it, not me," Sarah piped up.

"Did not," Mark cried, glaring at his sister.

"No one is in trouble," I said, holding up my hand. I wasn't awake enough to deal with their squabbles.

Sarah glared at her brother. "Mark made a face at me."

"Would you two kindly be quiet for two minutes?" Taking another sip of coffee, I realized I probably should have waited for this discussion, but I was anxious to talk to my children. They knew I liked Shay and was upset that I'd hurt her. I hadn't been able to hide my feelings. What they weren't aware of was the way she'd become important to me over the last several weeks since my visit with Joe. Before I moved to the next step, I needed to discuss the matter with my children.

"What's up, Dad?" Mark asked.

Sitting on the sofa, I gathered the two of them around me. "As you know, I went out last night."

"With Kevin in the van," Sarah added.

Before I left I'd talked to the children about where I

was going and what I'd be doing. Both thought handing out food and clothes to the homeless was a cool idea. What I hadn't told them was the real reason I'd agreed to accompany my friend.

"Did you meet a lot of people and give them stuff?"

"I did, but I wanted to volunteer for another reason. Shay was going to be there, too, and I wanted a chance to talk to her."

Sarah's eyes widened. "You saw Shay?"

"I did, and we talked."

"Is she still mad at us?" Mark asked.

"No." It did my heart good to be able to reassure them.

Sarah tossed her hands in the air. "Oh good. Can she come over today?"

Mark grinned and nodded approvingly. "Good going, Dad."

"Thanks."

"Can I call her?" Sarah asked.

"Perhaps later, pumpkin, but first I need to talk to you kids about something else. Something important."

"Okay." Sarah climbed back onto the sofa.

I placed an arm around each of my children. "It's been four years since your mom died. I know how much you loved her and you know how much I loved her. I miss her every single day."

"Me, too," my son whispered.

"I sometimes forget what she sounded like," Sarah said, her own voice small and sad.

"She's been gone a long time and I'm lonely. I would like to start dating again."

Both of the children went still and quiet.

"You mean dating other than the widows from church?"

I grinned and explained. "Yes, women my own age this time, or close to my age."

"You mean you want to fall in love with someone else?" Mark asked.

That wasn't the way I would have put it, but basically, yes. "I suppose so. No one will ever be able to replace your mother, but it would be nice to have a woman around here again, don't you think?"

"Someone who can do a French braid," Sarah inserted, "and a mom who knows how to bake cookies."

"You like Shay," Mark commented. "Do you think she'd want to date you?"

"I hope she does, but if I date her that doesn't mean I'm going to marry her. I will probably date a few other women, too."

"I vote for Shay," Sarah insisted.

"Yes, I like her a lot, too, but it's still early. The reason I mentioned it is because I wanted to be sure the two of you were okay with me meeting other women and dating again."

Mark's face folded into a frown.

"You have a problem with that, Mark?" I asked.

He took his time answering. "Will Sarah and I have a say in who's going to be our new mom?"

"Of course."

"Not Mrs. Kowalski's niece, okay?"

Evelyn Kowalski had practically tackled me one Sunday following church to introduce me to her niece. In my entire life I had never met anyone with a more dour look. "No problem," I assured my son.

Heaven knew I was attracted to Shay, but there were

several mitigating factors when it came to a relationship with her. She had shown me I was ready to look for a wife, and that excited me. What I'd said to the children about being lonely was true. I hadn't realized how alone I'd felt until I'd met Shay. The way the children had taken to her was another factor, a sign that they were ready, too. That said, Shay was the only woman I was interested in dating at the moment. But I needed to be cautious and, as Joe suggested, go slow.

"Okay, we're in agreement," I said, kissing them each on top of their heads. "Time to get going on our day. Who wants to go grocery shopping with me?"

Sarah raised her hand. Mark didn't.

"Okay, Mark, you get to vacuum. Sarah, once you get dressed, take the dishes out of the dishwasher. I'll get the laundry going."

"If we get a new mom, will she be doing the housework?"

"Probably not all of it, but some for sure," I said. "I'm not going to choose a wife on how well she keeps the house clean or cooks." The role of a pastor's wife was complex and was far more involved than keeping up the home and raising children. My wife would need to be a partner to me in my work, welcoming and gracious and, most important, living a life of faith. Katie had done it all beautifully. I didn't know if I could possibly be that fortunate twice.

The morning passed with chores. When Sarah and I returned from buying groceries, it was time for lunch. While I put together sandwiches and folded clean clothes, my mind was reviewing my sermon for Sunday. I was about to start a new series based on the gospel of Matthew. I'd written the first two weeks' messages but felt they lacked something. I hoped to read over my notes again before Sunday morning and prayed for inspiration. My goal was to make my sermons relevant and provocative. I wanted to give my congregation something that would grab their interest and enthusiasm but I wasn't convinced this new series did all that.

As soon as the lunch dishes were done, Sarah asked, "Can we please call Shay now?"

"Sure." I had to admit Shay had been on my mind all morning. I was eager to see her again, probably more than I should be at this stage. I couldn't stop thinking about the kisses we'd shared and immediately felt the desire to kiss her again. These feelings were foreign and yet ever so welcome. I couldn't stop smiling. Couldn't stop thinking about Shay.

I reached for my phone and realized she was still at work, dealing with the busy lunch crowd. Knowing she wouldn't be able to answer, I sent her a text instead.

Any chance you could stop by the house after your shift? Mark and Sarah would like some time with you. I would, too.

I didn't expect to get a response anytime soon and I was right. An hour passed before I heard from her. I kept my phone out on the kitchen counter, listening with half an ear.

Sure. Be there ASAP.

Just a few words, and after reading them one would think I held a winning lottery ticket.

"Shay's coming by," I announced to the children. Sarah let out a whoop of delight and Mark, being Mark, smiled and stuck up his thumb in the universal sign of "good job." That was about as excited as my boy got these days, but it was enough for me to know he was pleased.

When Shay arrived, Sarah immediately hugged her waist with both arms as if she hadn't seen her in weeks instead of only a few days. "I'm so glad you're our friend again."

"I'll always be your friend," Shay assured her, hugging her back. "I bet you want me to fix your hair."

"Will you?"

"Of course."

I stood back, hands tucked in my pockets, resisting the urge to hug Shay myself.

"Hey, Mark," she said, looking toward my son. "I brought something for you. It's my favorite movie and I thought we'd all watch it together."

"What movie?" Mark asked.

My son had never taken a lot of interest in movies.

"The Incredible Hulk."

Mark shrugged as if it wasn't a big deal, and to him it probably wasn't.

"I'll pop the popcorn," I volunteered.

"Shay has to braid my hair first," Sarah insisted.

"I can do it while we watch the movie," she told my daughter.

While Sarah gathered her comb and other hair products, Mark lobbed pillows onto the living room carpet and got the DVD player ready for the rented movie. In a money-saving effort, I had the least expensive cable program and we didn't have Netflix.

Shay pulled out the bowls while I started the popcorn. It was tempting to steal a kiss from her while the kids were preoccupied, but I resisted. Not that it was easy. I wanted to kiss her again to test if it would be as good as it had been the first time. That didn't seem likely, though. I was only half listening to the conversation between Shay and Mark.

The Incredible Hulk? Had I heard her correctly?

"Is *The Incredible Hulk* really one of your favorite movies?" I asked.

"Sort of," she admitted, helping me dish up the popcorn. "I thought Mark would enjoy it because of the message."

Message? That was an interesting thought. "And what exactly would that be?"

"The Hulk has an issue with anger," she explained, keeping her voice low. "I don't know what happened with Mark the day he got his black eye. If he was in a fight or if those boys I saw were looking to cause trouble, he never told me. Did he tell you?"

"Not really." I'd quizzed him, but Mark had remained stubbornly quiet. "I have the feeling he lost his cool and paid the price," I said, keeping my voice low, not wanting Mark to hear me. Mark was like that. He held his anger inside until it exploded.

"Anger was certainly an issue with the Hulk, and look what it did to him," Shay pointed out. "There's a spiritual reference in the movie, too."

"Oh?" That was a stimulating thought. Hollywood movies didn't strike me as being anything even close to spiritual.

"Think about it, Drew. It's not easy to let go of our anger. Without all those sessions with Lilly I probably would still be stewing over all the wrongs done to me.

Lilly reminded me that self-control is one of the fruits of the Spirit. It takes time and patience not to give in to our anger. The thing is, if we choose to remain calm then eventually we're able to walk away from fighting."

Shay impressed me with her insights into the movie and into my son. "Do you do this often?" I asked. "Do you see deeper meanings in popular movies?"

"All the time. It's a sort of game I play with myself. I love movies, especially the classics. Modern ones, too, of course."

The popcorn started to pop and I removed it from the stove and set it into a large bowl before adding the salt. Shay had the smaller bowls ready.

"Give me another example," I said.

Over the course of the afternoon, Shay and I discussed several other movies and the spiritual lessons she'd found in each one. I was fascinated by her ability to draw parallels between story and spiritual truth. We discussed *Jurassic Park*, *The Princess Bride*, the entire *Rocky* series, and my personal favorite, *Casablanca*. Her insights sent me reeling.

Shay stayed for dinner. We ordered pizza, which was a treat for the kids.

Because she had to work the following morning, I drove her home, my mind whirling with ideas. I would have kissed her, but Sarah had insisted on coming along with us. I walked Shay to the front door, all the while aware of Sarah watching our every move.

Holding Shay's hand, I gave it a squeeze. "Will I see you soon?" I asked.

"I'm off on Wednesday."

I didn't need to look at my appointment calendar to

know I had meetings and appointments set up for most of the day. "What about lunch?" I asked. I'd do whatever was necessary to spend time with her.

"Sure."

Unable to resist, I hugged her. "Thank you for today, for the attention and love you give my children, and especially for giving me a great idea."

She laughed softly. "And what would that be?"

Pressing my forehead against hers, I said, "I'll tell you later. Thanks to you, I'm likely to be up most of the night rewriting my sermon."

By the time I made it to bed it was almost two in the morning. Even then I couldn't sleep for the excitement I felt. I had Shay to thank for the inspiration.

Sunday morning, I stood at the pulpit and looked out over those gathered to worship. "I'm starting a new series of messages this week," I announced. "We're going to be discussing movies most of us have seen and loved through the years. Movies that you will easily recognize.

"A friend and I had an enlightening conversation yesterday afternoon. Some of you may know her. Shay Benson. She's opened my eyes to look at movies from a spiritual standpoint, and that's what we are going to be discussing. This morning I'd like to start with *The Incredible Hulk*."

CHAPTER 17

Shay

I reached for the coffeepot and refilled Devon's cup. Devon, one of our regulars, worked as a truck driver for a company that made a small part for the 737 Boeing airplane. He generally stopped in two or three times a week for breakfast.

"When are you going to let me take you to dinner?" he asked, not for the first time.

Ever since I'd served him, Devon had let me know he wanted to date me. I had never accepted because I didn't feel I was ready to have a man in my life. Drew, on the other hand, had felt safe, and we were more like friends than in a relationship. Until recently, that is. Suddenly matters between Drew and me had become more promising. I wasn't taking anything for granted, though. Not a single thing. We'd kissed but that was it. Oh, and we sent innocent text messages back and forth a few times a day.

When it came to choosing men to invite into my life, my record wasn't exactly stellar. I was leaving my options open and I knew Drew was, too. We weren't serious. We liked each other and were comfortable together, but that was it. I didn't feel I knew enough about Devon to take him seriously. A lot of the guys joked around about wanting to date me. That kind of teasing was common at the café, especially with the morning regulars.

"You should go," Sadie said as she scooted behind me to collect an order that was up from the kitchen.

"Yeah, what's stopping you?" Frankie called out from the kitchen as he set one of my orders out.

I groaned and glanced over my shoulder, hoping Devon wasn't paying attention.

"Sadie. Frankie. Please," I muttered.

Devon must have heard their comments because he quickly said, "They're right, you know. I'm an upstanding guy. A lot of women would give their eye teeth for the opportunity to have dinner with me."

I laughed and put the ticket for his meal on the counter. "I'll think about it."

"Don't think too hard. I'm a hot commodity. A prize," he said as he scooted off the stool and paid, leaving me a generous tip. He waggled his eyebrows at me before he left.

Once the breakfast crowd had started to thin out, Sadie approached me. "Devon's been coming in for breakfast at the café for years. He's a good guy. Never heard him ask any of the other servers out before now. Seems like you've caught his eye."

"I . . . I don't know."

"You've dated that pastor guy a few times, haven't you?" Sadie knew how I felt about Drew, especially after that one week when I'd been depressed because I thought he was dating someone else and using me as his babysitter.

While Sadie was right—I had seen a lot of Drew—they weren't dates. "I wouldn't call it dating as such." It was hard to explain. "We've had dinner, but that was with his children, and a few other things, but that's it. He did ask me to have lunch with him this Wednesday, just the two of us."

Sadie frowned. "Not a good idea to put all your eggs in one basket, girl. Devon has his eye on you. The least you can do is give him a chance."

"I'll think about it," I told her, and I would. Still, I wasn't inclined to toss my ring into the game with a guy I didn't know all that well. It was definitely something to think about, though. My one drawback was the attraction I felt for Drew. Since we'd cleared the air, my feelings for him had grown stronger. When it came to him, more and more I found my thoughts drifting down avenues that were emotionally hazardous. My one comfort was knowing he had genuine feelings for me.

Wednesday, right at noon, I met Drew at a downtown restaurant. It made sense for us to meet there rather than have him pick me up at the house. He could afford only an hour away from the church office and it would be a waste of precious minutes if he spent half that time battling the Seattle traffic, taking me to and from.

Lilly Palmer helped me choose what to wear. I wore a floor-length navy-blue-and-green plaid skirt, black boots, and a black sweater. Lilly looked me over and gave me her seal of approval.

"You look mah-va-lous, darling," she droned, giving a

passable impression of Billy Crystal. "Now go knock Drew's socks off."

Expelling a pent-up breath, I reached for my coat and purse and headed out the door. My morning had been spent at the center. First with Kevin, and then later with Lilly. I was eager to see Drew and share my news.

When I arrived at the restaurant, Drew already had a table. Ever the gentleman, he stood as I approached and held out my chair for me. "Wow, you look great."

I blushed at his compliment, pleased and unable to keep from smiling. "Thanks."

"Missed you."

"Me, too," I admitted.

"I talked to Kevin this morning," I said, unable to hold it in a second longer.

"Kevin—you mean Kevin Forester at Hope Center?"

"Yes." I'd assumed Drew would automatically know who I meant. "He told me the bookkeeper for the center is retiring in a few months and wondered if I'd be interested in applying for the job." This was everything I had hoped for, everything I wanted.

When I'd been arrested for stealing the cash from the bank it was more than the loss of my freedom that had been taken away from me. No one was going to hire me for a position of trust after they learned of my record.

Although I continued with the accounting classes, I suspected they were a waste of time. Nevertheless, it was what I'd been drawn to. With encouragement from Lilly, who clearly knew about the bookkeeper's retirement plans, I'd signed up for the course and had done exceedingly well.

Drew did his best to disguise a grin without much success.

Everything fell into place then. "You already knew."

He arched his brows as if this were a game.

"Drew Douglas, not only did you already know, you're the one who suggested my name, aren't you?"

Leaning back and crossing his arms, he broke into a full-sized grin. "Not me, Shay. It was Lilly. I'll confess that she talked to me and Kevin before she made the recommendation and we both thought it was a wonderful idea."

I put my hand to my mouth and blinked back tears, hardly knowing what to say.

"Are you upset?" he asked, frowning slightly as though worried.

"No, I'm just so grateful." That the three of them would agree and be willing to recommend me meant the world. Lilly was a good friend, the best, and her faith in me meant the world. We still met nearly every week and spoke frequently on the phone. I'd come to know her family and was grateful for her friendship.

The server came to take our order and we both asked for the seafood salad.

Once the server left the table, I continued with our conversation. "When I first came to Hope Center, Lilly asked me what my dreams were. At the time I was in a dark place and unable to see my way out of this black hole. Any dream I'd ever hoped to have had been destroyed. There was no going back." I paused when I saw a sad look leak into Drew's eyes. "That was how I felt at the time. Do you know what Lilly said to me?"

"Tell me," he urged.

"She said any dream would do. And so I gave her a list of what seemed like impossible dreams that I once had before my life went to hell in a handbasket. And a funny thing started to happen. The longer we talked, the more I felt hope creeping into my heart. It astonished me to learn that all it took was a few discussions with Lilly. My hopes for the future, things I had once set in my mind, dreams that had seemed forever lost, all at once they felt real. Achievable."

"What are your dreams, Shay?"

I felt a little silly talking to Drew about them. "Mainly I want to build a life and a future with a man who will love and cherish me. I want a home, a family. When I was in school, I enjoyed anything having to do with math. Many of my friends hated math, but I loved working with numbers. They made sense to me; I've always wanted a job where I could work with numbers, which made book-keeping the perfect choice."

My dreams were simple. What I longed for most were the same things others did, well, maybe not the numbers part, but that sense of belonging, of becoming part of a family unit. I yearned to contribute to life, to making a positive difference in the world.

"What about you?" I asked.

Drew brightened and started to talk about his own dreams for the future when we were interrupted by the server who delivered our food. He paused and waited a moment before picking up the conversation again. "Actually, this is probably as good a time as any to mention this."

That was a curious opening. "Mention what?"

"Saturday, before you arrived, I had a talk with Mark and Sarah about me dating again."

I was afraid the bite of my salad was going to get stuck halfway down my throat. "Oh?"

"After we'd kissed, I realized I was ready. I hadn't had any desire to get involved in a relationship, and then there was you and our kiss and all at once I was interested. More than interested.

"I loved my wife and until now the thought of dating, of seeking another life partner, held no appeal. Zilch." He hesitated, as if he'd said too much. "Shay, I need to tell you, those kisses." Again he paused as if he didn't know what more to say. "Wow. They blew me away."

I looked down but couldn't hide the happiness that seemed to make my heart swell to twice its normal size. "I felt the same way."

"I like you, Shay. I mean, I really like you."

"The feeling is mutual. You have to know that."

"I'm glad because what I say next might upset you, and that's the last thing I want."

This didn't sound good. Setting aside my fork, I clasped my hands in my lap, waiting.

"My feelings for you are a bit overwhelming and I need to test them."

"Test them?" I repeated, hardly knowing what to think. "How?" I had a bad feeling about this.

"Until I met you, until we kissed, I had no idea how lonely I've been. Spending time with you has been an eye-opener, but I need to know: Is it you? Is it me? Is it us? I need the answer to these questions before I can move forward."

As far as I could tell, he was talking in circles. "What are you saying, Drew?"

He reached across the table and I gave him my hand. "I'm going to ask a couple other women out. I need to do this for my own peace of mind. That said, I want you to know it's you I'm attracted to, you who is foremost on my mind. I don't mean to hurt you. That would devastate me." His eyes pleaded with me. "Please tell me you understand."

Surprisingly, I did. Without giving my response too much thought, I said, "I appreciate that you're being up front about this, Drew. Honesty works best with me."

"You aren't upset?"

"No. You're basically the only man I've ever dated." Shooter was the exact opposite of everything I wanted in a man. "I believe it's a good idea for us both to see other people, to test this attraction we share. One of the regulars at the café has been asking me out for some time and I keep putting him off."

"It doesn't surprise me," Drew admitted, frowning slightly. "Are you going to accept?"

I nodded. "Given this conversation, yes. It will be good for us both."

Drew reached for his fork and then set it back down on the table. "Shay, I have to admit the thought of you dating another man isn't sitting right with me." His shoulders sagged. "I feel like a hypocrite telling you that. It isn't that I expect you to sit at home and wait while I date other women. That would be grossly unfair."

"Yes, it would."

He pressed his palm against his chest. "My heart is pounding so fast right now."

"Mine is, too. It's a good thing, Drew. We're both new to this dating thing. Every relationship I've been involved in to this point has been a disaster from start to finish. You're the first decent man I've ever known. Is it you? Is it me? Is it us?" I parroted his words back at him, knowing he would understand.

"When's your first date with this other guy?" he asked, the lines around his mouth tightening.

"I don't know. Probably this week sometime." I wasn't prepared to tell Drew when I went out with Devon, nor was I eager to hear the details of his dates played back for me.

The salad was a masterpiece of taste and freshness. The seafood was artfully arranged atop the lettuce and I wasn't about to let it go to waste. I started eating and noticed it took Drew a couple minutes to follow my lead. While Drew might have assumed I'd be upset, I wasn't. In fact, I felt good about our conversation.

He took a bite and then looked up. "Did I mention how beautiful you look this afternoon?"

"Yes, you did." He couldn't seem to take his eyes off me, especially now.

Wanting to change the subject, I asked him about matters involving the church.

"We're having trouble making budget," Drew admitted. "It's always tough after Christmas, but it's getting better. We need to find a way to make up the shortfall without asking the congregation for more. One of my least favorite tasks as pastor is to preach on giving."

"Seems to me that's God's problem, not yours," I told him.

Drew gave me the oddest look and then burst out laughing. "You're right, so right. I've been stewing about this for weeks. One of the elders suggested we rent out the apartment that's in the church basement, but it hasn't been used in years and is full of storage. I vetoed that idea." He sighed and looked up heavenward. "All right, God, I'm giving this back to You. This is Your church, not mine, and therefore the budget shortfall is Your problem."

I'd always admired the free-flowing conversational style of prayer Drew had with God.

"Thank you, Shay. I feel better already."

"You're welcome. Now enjoy your salad." I was certainly enjoying mine.

As we continued talking, the subject turned to Mark and Sarah. Drew had no trouble discussing his children. I learned that he'd signed Mark up for karate classes but his son hadn't taken well to the sport. "Mark told me Monday afternoon that he doesn't want to go any longer."

"Are you going to let him quit?" I asked, unsure how I would handle the situation. I didn't see Mark as a quitter and for him to want out of the class told me he was utterly miserable.

Drew shrugged as if he wasn't entirely sure what to do, either. "I don't want to force Mark to attend. He clearly isn't enjoying himself. I'd hoped he'd take to it, but I should have realized he's an indoor kid. He never has been physically active. I don't want him to feel like I'm disappointed in him because he'd rather be a member of the chess club than play basketball."

"He's really smart, Drew." I was probably telling him

what he already knew about his own son. "Did you know he's completed that mathematical puzzle book I got him at Christmas? He told me they were all easy, but those story problems were anything but. They challenged me."

"He used his allowance to buy more," Drew told me, grinning proudly. "Sarah is just the opposite. She does fine in the grades department, but she loves being outside. She does have an interest in learning how to bake cookies, though. Do you think you could manage to spend time with her on your next day off?"

"I'll see what I can arrange," I told him. When it came to Drew's children, I loved them already.

All too soon our hour was up. Drew reached for my hand as we left the restaurant. Warmth crept up my arm at his touch. I walked with him part of the way.

"I don't want to leave you," he said, voicing my own thoughts.

"I know." I was feeling much the same.

"Any chance we could meet up later in the week?" he asked.

Seeing that I was determined to accept Devon's dinner invite, I wasn't sure what to tell him. "I'll let you know. Sound good?"

"No." He raised our clasped hands to his lips and kissed the back of my hand. His eyes bored into mine. "I hope you know that I'd give just about anything to be able to kiss you right now."

I knew the feeling because I felt the same powerful urge.

"I'll call you," he whispered. "And I'll make it soon."

"Okay."

He released my hand, and while still facing me, retreated two steps. "I'll be in touch."

Rather than respond verbally, I nodded.

My mind was working at the speed of light as I headed back to my small house to get ready for my classes. I'd finished my homework long before to distract myself from thoughts of Drew and him seeing other women and me accepting a date from Devon. Caught up in my thoughts, it took a moment to realize the buzzing sound coming from my pocket was my phone. A glance at caller ID told me it was Lilly.

"Hey," I said, happy to hear from her. "I had lunch with Drew earlier and he mentioned that you—"

"Shay."

Just the way she said my name, cutting me off, told me something was wrong.

"Have you had the news on?"

"Ah . . . no. What's the problem?" My thoughts immediately went to my brother. He'd been found dead or arrested for a heinous crime. Caden was on a path I was determined to avoid, but I still cared what might have happened to him.

"There's been a computer glitch in the prison system," Lilly said, her voice tight with concern. "Over a hundred felons have mistakenly been set free."

My entire body froze and I was barely able to get out the words. "Is . . . is there a list of names?"

"Yes."

I held my breath, waiting for her to continue.

"The name you mentioned, the one you called Shooter."

"Was someone with that name released?"

"Yes."

My eyes slammed shut. No, this couldn't be happening.

"I thought you should know right away and take precautions."

Letting go of a long, slow breath, I forced the tension from my shoulders. "I'll be fine," I said with a false sense of bravado. "Shooter will have more on his mind than finding me. We haven't been in contact for years. There's no reason for me to think he'll come looking for me."

"You need to be careful, though."

"Of course."

"I mean it, Shay."

"I know." Again, I did my best to sound confident, convincing Lilly that I had nothing to fear from Shooter.

I only hoped I was right.

CHAPTER 18

Drew

Brittany Beckman sat next to me at the symphony. This was my second date with her and she was nice enough, I suppose. According to Mary Lou, my assistant, Brittany and I would be perfect together.

I squelched a yawn. It wasn't that I didn't appreciate classical music. I did. My problem was that I preferred being more familiar with the composer. I'd studied the program before the start and didn't recognize the title of a single piece. Britt, as she preferred to be called, had gotten the tickets as a gift and had invited me to join her.

The violins played and my eyes started to drift shut. Jerking myself awake, I did my best to sit up straighter and pay attention. From all outward appearances, Britt was completely enraptured by the music. I should have been, or at least tried to make more of an effort to enjoy this opportunity. Instead, my head was whirling with all the things I should be doing.

Sarah needed help with her spelling homework and I wasn't sure Jada, the babysitter, had the patience to drill her with her work. And then there was the sermon for Sunday that I had yet to complete.

The series I'd started on the spiritual lessons found in popular movies was a hit with the congregation. I'd gotten a lot of positive feedback. Word had gotten around and I'd heard from a couple pastor friends, who asked how I'd come up with the idea. Of course there were a few naysayers. No subject matter was going to please everyone.

Thinking about the sermon reminded me of Shay, not that she was ever far from my thoughts. Although she hadn't talked about it, I suspected she'd already gone out with that guy she'd met at the café. When she'd first mentioned him, I'd downplayed my reaction. Having her date other men didn't sit right with me, which was completely unreasonable, seeing that I was currently with Britt at the symphony. As much as I wanted to ask Shay to date only me, that would be utterly unfair.

At the end of the exhausting evening, I returned to the house, paid Jada, and slumped onto the sofa, my nerves shot. Britt was a nice woman, but there was no spark between us. Zero chemistry.

Getting up, I turned off the living room lights, when my son wandered out of his bedroom.

"Did I wake you?" I asked Mark. He was a light sleeper and I often saw evidence that he'd been up in the middle of the night. When I asked him about it, he generally brushed it off, irritated by my questions.

He rubbed his eyes and blinked at me. "I heard you and Jada talking."

"I didn't mean to wake you." He had school in the morning and as a growing boy, he needed his rest. "Can I have a glass of milk?" he asked. "It helps me get back to sleep."

"Sure." Tired as I was, I could use a glass myself. "Mind if I join you?"

"Okay."

Mark climbed onto a stool at the kitchen counter while I brought down two glasses and poured each about half full.

"How'd your date go?" he asked when I handed him the milk.

I shrugged. "Fine, I guess."

"You like her?"

I wasn't sure how to answer that. "She's a nice woman."

"Is that your answer?" Mark asked before he sipped his milk.

"Not really." While I did my best to figure out how to explain my feelings, Mark asked another question.

"You like Shay better?"

Why I should feel guilty admitting that was beyond me. "I do."

My son grinned as if he knew something I didn't. "I thought so."

Seeing that Mark had never met Britt, I was curious how he'd determined my feelings. "And you know this how?" I asked.

"Dad, seriously?" He shook his head from side to side as though I had no clue about human nature. "When you got ready tonight, it looked like you were going to attend a funeral."

That wasn't as far-fetched as it sounded. Not that I was willing to admit it. "Did not."

"Did too."

Chuckling softly, I had to agree my son had read me like a text message. I hadn't been interested in seeing Britt again. She was the one who'd contacted me about the symphony tickets. Caught off guard, I couldn't think of a way to refuse and not offend her. That wasn't a mistake I planned to repeat. After our first date, I'd known the two of us didn't click.

"You talk to Shay recently?" Mark asked.

"We text."

"You tell her it isn't working with Britt?"

"No." I wouldn't, especially since she hadn't mentioned anything about her dates with Devon.

"Why not? You two need to talk."

"She's dating another guy, and every time I text about us getting together, she's busy." I hadn't mentioned this to Mark and Sarah.

Mark's eyes widened with surprise. "Are you kidding me? This is a joke, right? What happened?"

"Ah . . ."

Holding up his hand, Mark stopped me from explaining. He looked at me with what can only be described as impatience that bordered on disgust. "Listen, Dad, you like Shay. Sarah and I like Shay. If you let some other guy step in and steal her, then you deserve to lose her."

It was again a sad commentary when I was listening to advice on romance from my son, who was barely in his teens. "When did you get so smart about women and relationships?" I asked him.

Mark shrugged. "That's just common sense."

"We decided not to date exclusively, to explore other relationships." I regretted mentioning anything about this to my son. It wasn't only Britt I had to contend with. Word had leaked out that I was starting to date. Single women and their advocates were all over me. Not a day had passed without a friend or church member wanting to make an introduction. At this rate, I could go out with a different woman every night for the next two weeks.

"Shay suggested this?"

"We both thought it was a good idea." It seemed less of one with each passing day.

Mark muttered under his breath, "I'm surprised at you, Dad."

"I . . ." I didn't know what to say.

Mark shook his head as if becoming aware his father was a total loser. "Whatever."

His support for Shay took me by surprise. As far as I could tell, he hadn't shown strong feelings toward her one way or the other. Sarah, on the other hand, had taken to her like a hummingbird to sugar water. "You like Shay that much?"

"Yeah," he said and shrugged. "She's okay. I like her better than anyone else I've met from church."

"Such a recommendation," I returned, grinning.

"I'm a kid and I don't know that much about women, but Shay is nice and she thinks about other people."

"Yes, she does." I'd watched her interact with others, including Richard, and was taken with her empathy. She was strong—stronger than she realized. When Kevin talked to me about the possibility of hiring Shay, he'd mentioned how she'd become a leader with the women in her class. It was clear that Sadie, Frankie, and the others at The Corner Café had become her advocates as well. She didn't judge people and was generous to a fault.

—

As the week went on, all the phone calls with offers to set me up with single women of family and friends only became worse. There was a constant barrage of suggestions and offers of introductions. On Wednesday evening, minutes before I left for the church to talk with the choir director before practice, the doorbell rang.

For one hopeful moment I thought it might be Shay.

It wasn't.

Instead, a woman dressed in jeans and a plaid jacket and wearing a hard hat stood in front of me, holding a casserole dish with two pot holders. She smiled brightly. I swear I'd never seen her before in my life. She looked like she might work on the Seattle wharf.

"May I help you?" I asked.

"I brought you my special chicken-and-rice dish." She edged past me and made her way into the kitchen. After she set it down on the counter, she looked around the kitchen and shook her head disapprovingly.

"And you are?" I asked, following close behind her.

"Dee Miller. I believe my aunt Sally mentioned me."

For the life of me I couldn't remember anyone named Sally. "I don't think so."

She walked over to the stove and peered at the outlet and made a comment that my kitchen was below code, whatever that meant. "Sure you have to remember," she argued. "Aunt Sally told you what a great cook I am. She told me about your conversation and so I thought I'd bring you dinner so you could judge my skills for yourself."

"I appreciate—"

She cut me off. "I don't mean to be blunt or come on

too strong here, but the fact is I'm thirty-five, as healthy as an ox, and I'm ready."

"Ready for what?"

"For marriage," she answered, as if it should be obvious. "Aunt Sally explained the competition is going to be steep, and I thought I'd take the initiative and introduce myself before another woman snatches you up."

I opened and closed my mouth, too stunned to find words. By now both Mark and Sarah had come to stand at my side. They seemed as shell-shocked as I was.

Dee glanced down and smiled at them. "I've never been married. I'm educated, have all my own teeth, and work as a construction electrician. I have no objection to kids."

Sarah scooted closer to me.

"Thanks for the casserole, but . . ."

"It's my specialty."

As best I could, I eased her out of the kitchen and toward the front door. "I was just about to head over to the church."

"I'll go with you."

Mark looked at me and rolled his eyes as if to say I was getting exactly what I deserved.

"Dee, listen, I'd rather you didn't follow me to church. I can't remember ever talking to anyone named Sally, and while I appreciate the thought, I'm not comfortable feeding my children dinner made by someone I don't know."

She stiffened and frowned at me. "Are you saying you're not interested?"

"To be blunt, yes." Normally I'd be a bit more polite, but I could tell this woman would need to hear it straight with no chance for miscommunication.

She accepted my rejection with little more than a shrug. "You can't blame a girl for trying."

"No, you can't. I appreciate the thought, but I think it would be best if you took your chicken and rice home to share with your aunt Sally." *Whoever she might be,* I added silently.

Dee collected her dish and was gone. Closing the door behind her, I sighed with relief.

Sarah raced to my side and hugged my waist. "Daddy, please call Shay."

She didn't need to ask me twice. I was finished with this little experiment.

As soon as the kids were down for the night and I was fairly certain Shay was home from her classes, I called.

"Drew?" she answered almost right away.

"Hey," I said, sighing with relief just hearing her voice. It was as if I'd been trapped in a cave with no communication from the outside world when she answered her phone.

"You okay?"

"No, actually, I'm not." I had yet to figure out what I'd been thinking to suggest this crazy idea.

"What's wrong?"

"Everything," I said, but didn't elaborate. "How'd your dinner date go with that other guy?"

She hesitated. "It went fine."

"I need more than that. Have pity and indulge me."

I wasn't certain, but I thought I might have heard her chuckle. "Devon was the perfect gentleman and I had a delightful evening."

That, most definitely, wasn't what I wanted to hear. "You did?" My spirits sagged.

"How about you? How's it going with you?" she asked.

"Fine." Pride demanded that I downplay what a miserable failure my dating experiences had been.

"From the sound of it, you're not having much luck?"

"You could say that." Seeing that I probably sounded pitiful anyway, I decided I might as well own up to the truth. "If you must know, I met a construction electrician who literally burst into the house with a casserole dish. She outlined her qualifications and informed me I needed another outlet in my kitchen to meet code."

As I expected she would, Shay laughed.

"She offered to check the rest of the house, but I declined." Feeling it was important, I added, "I made her take the casserole with her, too." I'd noticed she'd used a ceramic dish, which would entail me returning it. As far as I could see, no good would come from accepting the meal. She might have expected to join us for dinner, but that was speculation on my part.

"I'm sorry you're having troubles."

"No you're not," I challenged.

"Okay, the truth, you're right. I'm secretly trying not to laugh."

"The least you could do is tell me you've missed me."

"I do miss you," she offered, her voice low and soft. "When you asked me to the movie I was depressed that I couldn't go."

"Thank you for that." Her words were like salve over a sunburn.

"You're welcome."

I exhaled, not sure where to go from here, especially

since Shay had had a much more positive dating experience.

"So," I said, dragging out the word, "are you going to be seeing this guy again?"

"He asked and we had a great time."

"Oh." It felt like I'd been kicked in the stomach.

"I didn't say I accepted."

"You're toying with me, Shay, and that isn't kind. Be straight with me because I'm miserable here and regret ever suggesting we do this. I'm more than ready to throw in the towel, surrender, and move forward with you."

She sighed and went silent. "Are you serious, Drew?"

"Never more so. Even Mark is annoyed with me. He said if I lost you then I didn't deserve you in the first place."

"Mark said that?"

"Scout's honor."

The line went silent again before she spoke. "I'm pretty miserable myself, thinking about you with other women. Especially when I come with a whole lot of baggage."

"Thank God. I don't want to date anyone but you."

"Are you sure?"

"After the last week I've never been more confident of anything." I hesitated and then felt I had to ask: "What about you?"

"I feel the same."

The relief was overwhelming. I couldn't have been happier. For the first time in a week, I slept like a baby and woke feeling refreshed and rejuvenated. I didn't know where a relationship with Shay would take me, but I was more than ready to find out.

CHAPTER 19

Shay

I was feeling pretty good about life, especially the way things were developing with Drew. We'd both learned a valuable lesson in the last couple weeks. Like Sadie had mentioned, Devon was a good guy. I enjoyed his company, and under other circumstances I wouldn't have minded getting to know him better. My feelings were wrapped up in a certain pastor, though, and it would be wrong to lead Devon on. He took the news with a shrug of his shoulders and wished me well.

"You let this guy you're seeing know he's one lucky fellow," Devon told me when I spoke to him.

I'd never thought of myself as a catch, certainly not with my personal history. His words helped to remind me that I'd come a long way from the girl who hung out with gang members and flirted with drugs. Prison changed me and Hope Center showed me the way to a better life. The center was well named. I'd left hopeful that the positive changes I'd made would stick.

Just before Valentine's Day, I got off the bus and headed toward the café. It was still dark this early in the morning and I kept a cautious eye out walking to the café, aware of my surroundings. It'd been two weeks since I'd heard about the computer glitch that had released felons into the general public. The news had been full of details. Several had been apprehended, but an equal number were still on the loose. The identities of those who remained at large were published in the paper, and that was where I saw Shooter's name.

Perhaps I was foolish not to worry about his release, but I no longer lived in the same neighborhood or associated with the people I once had. It'd been nearly five years since I'd last seen him. My prayer was that he'd forgotten about me. While I wanted to believe I was safe, I wasn't completely convinced Shooter wouldn't come looking for me.

I looked both ways when I stepped off the bus. If Shooter found me, this is when I would be most vulnerable. The street was quiet and silent as I started toward The Corner Café. As I approached, I saw Richard and Chuck against the side of the building, still asleep.

I could see inside the café that Sadie and Frankie were busy getting everything in order before opening.

"Coffee's ready," Sadie told me as I came in from the cold. She knew I'd be taking coffee to Richard and Chuck.

I poured them each a cup and added sugar and cream. Both Navy veterans liked their coffee sweet, so I added extra sugar.

When I returned with the two cups, both men were awake and waiting for me.

"How'd you sleep?" I asked. I didn't know how it was

that they managed to get any rest, leaning against the side of the building. They claimed it was as good as any bed, but I suspected they were exaggerating, not wanting me to make a fuss. I'd grown close to these two, especially Richard. More than once I'd suggested they go to a shelter, but neither seemed interested. I never understood that and didn't ask.

"You're an angel," Richard said, gratefully accepting the coffee.

A shadowy figure stepped out from the dark. "You got that all wrong, old man."

A chill went up my spine. I'd recognize Shooter's voice anywhere. He stepped purposefully toward me, his look menacing. He was thinner than I remembered and had a large snake tattoo that wrapped around his neck.

I froze and swallowed hard.

"Cat got your tongue, Shay?" he growled. His eyes were dark and cold. The man was soulless.

"You leave her be," Richard insisted.

"Shut up, old man, before I take out whatever teeth you've got left."

Not willing to risk physical harm, Chuck scrambled out of sight. Richard, however, stood his ground, refusing to leave me.

"It's all right, Richard. Go," I urged. The last thing I wanted was for Shooter to hurt my friend.

"You heard her. Get lost," Shooter said and shoved the older man aside. "I need to talk to my woman."

"It's been five years, Shooter. I'm not your woman any longer."

He slapped me hard across the face and I tasted blood. "You're my woman until I say you're not."

Holding my hand against my cheek, I asked, "How'd you find me?" Why knowing that was important, I couldn't guess.

"You think you can hide from me?"

"I tried," I whispered, spitting a mouthful of blood onto the sidewalk. Richard sent me a sympathetic look, but no way could he help me.

Shooter got in Richard's face and screamed as he shoved him aside, "Leave."

"No."

"Richard, please."

Shooter slapped me again and I stumbled backward, seeing stars.

"I'll keep hitting her until you disappear."

"I'm not leaving her," Richard insisted, running into Shooter and hitting him with his shoulder.

The impact didn't budge Shooter.

"I don't care what you do to me, Shooter, just leave him alone."

"You care about this old man?" he asked me, grabbing hold of Richard by the scruff of his coat, lifting him off his feet to the point where he was choking. Hot coffee sloshed out of his to-go cup onto the sidewalk. Richard struggled to break free, but it did no good. He was too old and feeble to put up much resistance.

"Okay, okay," I cried. "What do you want from me?"

"Where's Caden?" Shooter demanded.

"I don't know," I said, growing frantic. "I swear."

"Don't feed me a crock of sh—"

"I don't know," I shouted again, enunciating each word. "I haven't seen my brother in years."

"I don't believe you. That sniveling piece of crap clung to you like you were his mommy. You know where he is, so tell me, otherwise . . ." He left the threat hanging there.

"I swear, I don't know."

Shooter released a short, sick laugh. "You always did have a soft spot for your baby brother. You think I don't know that you're protecting him?"

"I'm not, I swear it."

As best I could, I edged away from Shooter, taking tiny steps in retreat. I prayed that Sadie and Frankie would wonder what was taking me so long and come to investigate. This side of the café was dark and without windows. My chances of escaping were nil. Leaving Richard wasn't an option.

Shooter released Richard, who staggered and fell against the side of the building. With his arm free, Shooter's fist shot out and hit the side of my face with a punch that sent me flying backward. "This is the only thing you're good for. Weak. Spineless. White trash."

I went down like a brick, seeing stars. As soon as I hit the sidewalk, Shooter kicked me in the ribs. Turning away, I tried to get up on my knees, but his fists kept me down. Grabbing me by the hair, he slammed my forehead against the sidewalk.

Richard screamed. Maybe it was me.

Shooter was going to kill me. Having already received a life sentence, he had nothing to lose.

"Give him up, woman." The side of my head crashed against the concrete.

"Step away from her *now* or you'll regret it."

I heard someone speak, but the voice seemed to come from a long distance away. I was having trouble staying conscious. It sounded like Frankie, but it couldn't have been him. He was inside the café in the kitchen, preparing for the breakfast crowd.

A siren sounded in the distance. I blinked and saw that Frankie held a baseball bat in his hand. Chuck stood next to him with what looked like a mop. I wanted to laugh that he thought he could defend me against Shooter with that. I loved him for trying, though.

I started to sit up when Shooter swore and kicked me in my ribs again with his heavy boot. Pain blasted through my side. I gasped and my knees shot up and I cradled my stomach to protect myself. It was then that I felt the darkness chasing after me. I fought it, but it was no use.

I don't know how long I was out. Probably only a minute or two. When I regained consciousness, Richard was kneeling on the sidewalk next to me with tears in his eyes.

Sadie was on the other side of me, holding my hand.

"Hold on, Shay," she whispered. "An aid car is on the way."

I blinked up at my friends, wondering at the worry I saw in their eyes. "I'm . . ." I tried to tell everyone that I was okay and found that I couldn't.

"Sorry, Shay . . . so sorry," Frankie said. "I didn't know. I would have come sooner . . ."

I offered him a weak smile, letting him know I understood.

Everything hurt. My head throbbed like someone had slammed a hammer into my skull. Blood flowed from my head wound into my eyes. I read the fear and concern on their faces and knew I was in much worse shape than I realized. Breathing was difficult and everything blurred as I struggled to remain conscious.

Somewhere in the back of my mind I figured I must have a concussion. Shooter had hit my head hard. Kicked me, too.

Years ago I'd heard it was important to remain conscious after a head injury. Who'd told me that? A teacher? No. Had I signed up for a first-aid class? When was that? Couldn't remember. Couldn't keep my eyes open, either, despite every attempt. They closed and I couldn't make them move.

Voices drifted my way.

Different voices. Not Sadie or Frankie. Unfamiliar voices. One voice sounded like it was from a policeman. I could tell from the questions he asked. Cops always did ask a lot of questions.

Then I was being lifted off the sidewalk. A floating sensation came over me. I didn't remember that I could fly. Who knew? Maybe I was one of the characters in the book *Peter Pan*. What was that girl's name? Couldn't remember that, either. I should read more. Wendy, that was it. Wendy. Nice name.

More voices, strange ones. Their words were slurred and grew loud and then soft. Had they been drinking on the job? Someone needed to report them. I tried to lift my hand, but it wouldn't move. Straining, I tried again, but to no avail.

"Shay, we're taking you to the hospital now," the man with the slurred voice told me.

If I couldn't move my hand, I should be able to open my eyes. Hospitals were expensive and I really couldn't afford this.

Shooter should pay. That was it. I'd make him pay.

No. I never, ever wanted to see him again. Him or Caden. My brother. If Shooter found my brother, he'd be killed for sure. I didn't want Caden dead.

Fear and adrenaline shot through me as I remembered the way Shooter had looked at me. He'd wanted Caden.

All at once Shooter was there again. Evil radiated from him.

I tried to scream but nothing came out. He looked straight through me and reached out and grabbed hold of my throat with both hands, strangling me.

Panic attacked every nerve as I struggled to escape. I couldn't breathe. Couldn't move, and no one was helping me. Why weren't the men who were drinking trying to stop Shooter before he killed me?

"She's convulsing."

Someone, not Shooter, was talking.

I wasn't convulsing. I was doing everything within my power to escape Shooter. They should get him off me. Couldn't they see what he was doing?

Why had they let him near me again? Couldn't they see the damage he'd already done to me?

A piercing sound hurt my ears. A fire siren? I welcomed it because it sent Shooter away and I could relax. Relief washed over me.

My head hurt like no pain I'd ever experienced before. The pain so intense it blinded me.

I tried to open my eyes. I really tried, and couldn't.

It was impossible to stay awake any longer, and while I wanted to do what I'd learned in first aid, I couldn't. Although I fought it, I surrendered to the darkness.

CHAPTER 20

Drew

My sermon notes were coming along nicely when someone knocked on my office door.

"Yes."

Generally, if someone came into the office, Mary Lou
would let me know via the intercom.

My assistant opened the door and let herself in, closing it behind her. Something was definitely up.

Before I could ask, she spoke. "Two men are in the
lobby demanding to talk to you. They claim they know
you."

"Is there a problem?"

Mary Lou looked uncomfortable. "They look like
homeless people."

That she would hesitate surprised me. "I'm sure it's
fine. Let them in."

Still, she paused, as if questioning my judgment. "You
sure? I can ask them to leave. They look agitated and
upset. When they arrived I considered calling the police.
I still can if . . . you think it would be best?"

Mary Lou tended to be a lion at the gate, as far as I
was concerned. When I could I'd explain that the night

I'd gone out on the Search & Rescue, I'd met any number of the homeless. I'd told them who I was and where they could find me if the need arose. Perhaps I should have mentioned this to my assistant, who continued to look uncomfortable and unsure.

"I'll take care of it," I said, getting up from my desk.

Once I entered the foyer, I saw my visitors were Richard and Chuck, Shay's two friends. I was about to welcome them when they jumped to their feet and rushed toward me, both speaking at once until I stopped them.

I held up my hand, silencing them. "One at a time."

"We did what we could, but she's hurt," Richard blurted out. The side of his face was swollen and had started to turn black and blue.

"She's hurt bad, Pastor. Real bad," Chuck added.

"Shay's hurt?" They could only mean her.

Richard nodded and his eyes clouded with tears. "I tried to stop him, but he was a big guy and he threw me down like I weighed nothing."

"I ran and got help," Chuck inserted. "Richard wouldn't leave her. No siree, not Richard. He stood up to that brute. He was a hero, a real hero." The other man looked at his friend with pride shining in his eyes.

"What's happened to Shay?" I demanded. They could tell me about their own efforts later. What I needed was to find out about Shay.

"The aid car came and took her to the hospital."

"Which one?"

The two old coots shrugged. They didn't have a clue.

"Who hurt her?" I demanded.

"Don't know his name," Chuck said.

"She called him Shooter," Richard supplied. "He knew

her from a long time ago . . . he wanted her to tell him where to find Caden, her brother. She tried to tell him she didn't know, but he didn't believe her and then he kept hitting her. Nothing I did would stop him."

My stomach pitched like I was on a sailboat in the middle of an Atlantic storm. Quickly returning to my office, I reached for my coat and told Mary Lou I'd give her a call as soon as I had information. I knew she must have overheard our conversation.

"I may need you to cancel my afternoon appointment schedule."

"But—"

I didn't stick around to listen. Richard and Chuck got in the car with me, both talking at the same time, adding more details. Chuck had come after Shooter with a mop, but Frankie had a bat, I learned.

Getting to Shay was what was most important, and making sure she was going to be all right. The best place to get further information was The Corner Café. If Sadie and Frankie had been at the scene they would be able to tell me which hospital Shay had been taken to by the aid car. Thankfully, it was the lull between breakfast and lunch at the café.

As soon as I walked into the café, Sadie looked up as if she'd been expecting me. Although the incident had happened hours earlier, the server remained pale and drawn. As soon as she saw me, she covered her mouth as if she was about to break into tears.

"Which hospital?" I asked without preamble two feet inside the door. I didn't have time for small talk. Sadie could tell me the role she'd played and what she knew later. Right now, I felt a burning need to get to Shay.

"Swedish," Sadie called out.

"Thanks." With a quick reversal I started back out of the restaurant, nearly running directly into Richard and Chuck.

The two men looked stunned, as if they weren't sure what to do next.

"You coming?" I called over my shoulder.

"Yes," Richard agreed automatically.

"You think it'll be okay?" Chuck showed hesitation.

"Your decision." I wasn't inclined to talk him into accompanying me if that wasn't what he wanted.

Both Richard and Chuck followed behind me, scrambling to keep up as I rushed back to where I'd parked the car. I noticed how uneasy Chuck was in the car, shifting his weight every few seconds.

Luckily, I knew a good spot to park at Swedish and pulled right in. Before I lost Katie I'd volunteered as a chaplain and was familiar with the area and the staff.

Richard and Chuck trotted along behind me as I headed toward the ER entrance, knowing that was where the paramedics would likely have delivered her. The two men remained in the waiting room while I walked past the receptionist. No one questioned my being there, as I was known and respected.

It didn't take long for me to find Shay in one of the cubicles. Seeing how badly beaten she was, I instantly felt light-headed and dizzy. I thrust out my arm to grab hold of the wall in order to steady myself.

"Drew?"

Looking up, I saw Dr. John Carson.

"Someone you know?" he asked, looking toward Shay.

I nodded. "Yes. She's a friend. A good friend." If I ever

doubted my feelings for Shay, seeing her battered face and the blood matted in her hair was all the answer I needed. For a moment I thought I would be sick.

That someone would beat her, would dare to hurt her, filled me with a rage so strong it demanded every iota of resolve I possessed not to slam my fist through the wall. I wanted to hunt down this animal and give him as good a beating as he gave Shay, if not worse. By nature, I'm not a violent man, but in this instant I could easily have lost it.

"Drew? You okay?"

Inhaling a stabilizing, even breath through my lungs, I forced myself to remain calm and levelheaded.

"How badly hurt is she?" I asked Dr. Carson.

"I'm waiting for the test results now."

"She's unconscious?" Shay hadn't stirred since I entered the room. True, I hadn't talked to her directly yet. But if she was awake, she would have heard my voice and recognized that I was with her.

"Your friend is in a coma, Pastor. Although I'm waiting for the test results, I'm fairly certain she's suffered a fractured skull."

A fractured skull was serious business. I swallowed against the shock and the fear. "Surgery?"

"Don't know yet, but it's possible."

The physician patted me on the shoulder. Carson was a good doctor and a good man. He knew about my wife, and while he specialized in emergency medicine, he'd sat with me toward the end with Katie.

"We can't let you stay back here," he told me gently.

"I know." I'd half expected to be kicked out before now. "Can I talk to her for just a moment?"

He hesitated. "Not more than a minute."

Stepping toward the gurney, I lifted Shay's limp hand and raised it to my lips, kissing the inside of her palm. "I'm right here, sweetheart. You're going to be okay, you hear?" Overwhelmed with emotion, my voice cracked. I hated leaving her, but there was no other option.

Dr. Carson led me out of the room. "I'll let you know what I can as soon as the test results are in."

"Thanks." I backed out of the room, every step filled with reluctance.

Once I returned to the waiting area, I found Richard and Chuck. Richard sat by himself in a corner off to the side. Chuck hung out by the door like he wanted to be sure he could leave quickly. As I approached, they looked up, their eyes full of questions and concern.

"How's our girl?" Richard asked, walking toward me. Chuck joined him but kept his eyes trained on the sliding glass door.

"Not so good." Slumping down in the chair, I hung my head. Part of me wanted to chastise them for not preparing me better. In my confusion, I'd thought Shay might need a few stitches and gotten a bruise here and there. This was far worse.

Reaching for my cell, I called the office. Mary Lou answered right away.

"Cancel my appointments for the rest of the afternoon," I told her. For that matter, I'd need to take it one day at a time for the rest of the week. It all depended on what future treatment Shay would need.

Another hour passed, though I swore it felt like five or six hours. I paced up and down the hallway, impatient, afraid, praying and pleading with God to let her be okay.

Finding the coffee machine, I bought myself a cup and then one for Richard and Chuck. They tried to tell me what had happened, but I couldn't listen, couldn't bear to hear the details. The evidence of the violence against Shay was savagely written across her face.

When Dr. Carson appeared I rushed toward him and nearly toppled over an elderly man in a walker. After I apologized profusely, I found my way to the physician.

Recognizing his look as serious and troubled, I feared the worst.

"As I suspected, Shay has a fractured skull. The pressure is building in her brain. After consulting with another physician, it's been decided she's going to require surgery."

My throat immediately swelled shut and I couldn't speak. I feared if I tried to talk my voice would come out as a squeak, so I remained silent.

Dr. Carson continued. "Your friend is being prepped for surgery now."

Richard and Chuck came to stand on either side of me, looking to me to explain the details. "She's going into surgery," I said, as soon as the fear loosened my throat enough for me to be coherent.

The surgery unit was up several floors. Knowing there was nothing more they could do but wait, Richard and Chuck decided to leave the hospital. Being here clearly made them uncomfortable, Chuck especially. I promised to let them know how everything came out.

"Shay's strong," Richard assured me. "She stood up to that bully. I . . . I wish I could have done more." I knew Richard had done everything within his power to protect her. I told him so and the old man's eyes flooded with tears.

"If I had a daughter, I'd want her to be like Shay," he whispered, rubbing at his eyes and sniffling. He ran his coat sleeve beneath his runny nose.

The surgical waiting area was large and a hospital volunteer manned the desk, ready to answer questions and check with staff if necessary. The room was full when I first arrived.

After a couple hours, I stepped into the hall and reached for my phone. When I'd served as the chaplain, cellphones hadn't been allowed. The restriction had apparently been lifted. I'd seen others using their cells and no one had questioned it.

Linda Kincaid answered after the second ring. I trusted her and knew the children would be well cared for while I was away for the evening.

After a quick exchange of greetings, I asked her, "Would you mind watching Mark and Sarah after school?"

"Of course. When should I expect you?"

That was hard to answer. "I can't be sure. I'm waiting for a friend to get out of surgery."

Her sympathy was immediate. "I'm sorry. Anyone I know?"

"It's Shay. She was attacked this morning."

"Shay?" she gasped. "Why would anyone attack her?"

Rather than go into a lengthy explanation, I avoided the subject altogether. "It's serious. As much as possible I want to be here for her."

"Of course. I'll do whatever you need from me."

"Thank you," I whispered, grateful beyond words. "As soon as I have information, I'll let you know."

Another ninety minutes lapsed before I got the news that Shay was out of surgery. By then Lilly Palmer had joined me. We both silently sat together. Soon we were the only two people left in the room.

"I told her to be careful," Lilly whispered. "I was afraid something like this would happen. She's come so far . . ." The rest of what she intended to say faded. Lilly was tough emotionally, but I could see how upset she was. When she first joined me, her eyes were bright, as if holding back tears. I knew the two of them were close and was grateful Shay had such a good friend.

The surgeon entered the room and both Lilly and I stood, anxious for a report on Shay's condition.

"Are you family?" the physician asked.

"She has none that I'm aware of; I'm her pastor," I said. I was more, but I didn't mention it.

"I'm her friend," Lilly volunteered.

The surgeon explained the details of the surgery at length and what had been necessary to relieve the pressure on Shay's brain. The bottom line was that Shay's prognosis was good, but it would be several hours, if not days, before she awoke.

Once she was out of recovery and in a room, we would be able to see her.

With family obligations, Lilly had to leave, but I promised to give her an update as soon as there was anything to report.

I walked Lilly to the elevator and once I returned, I found that Shay was out of recovery and in her room. Pulling a chair next to her bed, I held her hand and prayed as fervently as I had been doing ever since I'd received word she'd been hurt.

Sometime during the second day, Kevin came and we prayed together. Lilly Palmer stopped by every day and Richard did, too, but not Chuck. Thankfully Linda kept watch over the children.

For Mark and Sarah's sake, I went home at night and answered their questions. Sarah prayed for Shay and I suspected Mark did, too, but not kneeling at his bedside the way my daughter did.

Shay didn't come out of the coma for four days, and in that time I'd come to realize I'd fallen in love with her. Frankly, I don't know how long it would have taken me to accept the truth if not for the time at her bedside. As I sat with her, I became more and more aware of how important she had become to me and to my children.

Now I just needed to find a way to let her know.

CHAPTER 21

Shay

When I woke all I could see was glaring light. I opened my eyes and quickly closed them again.

"Shay? Are you awake?"

That was Drew's voice. He was here with me? But where was I? My mind was muddled and I couldn't figure out what had happened, and for the love of heaven why were there all these bright lights focused on me?

Someone reached for my hand and was kissing my fingers. I had to assume it was Drew, but I wasn't opening my eyes with those lights blinding me.

"If you can hear me, squeeze my fingers."

I squeezed Drew's hand.

"Thank you, God. Thank you," he whispered with such heartfelt emotion that I had to wonder what had happened.

My throat felt parched. He seemed to read my thoughts because I felt a straw at my lips and I sucked greedily. "Where . . ." I wasn't able to finish the question, but apparently Drew knew what I was asking because he answered.

"You're in the hospital. You've had surgery to relieve

the pressure on your brain after you were attacked. You had a skull fracture."

I'd been attacked? I had no memory of that. Who would want to hurt me this badly?

"I need to let the nurse know you're conscious." He released my hand and I heard the door open and close as Drew left the room.

Once more I tried opening my eyes, but I couldn't against the intense brightness of the light. I felt like I was staring into the sun.

It didn't seem that Drew was gone more than a few seconds when he returned with a nurse who immediately started taking my vital signs and talking to me. It didn't take long for me to feel the urge to sleep, though. Voices surrounded me and whoever was speaking sounded reassured and pleased.

I attempted a smile. Pressing questions were asked of me that demanded answers I didn't seem to have. I could feel the darkness inviting me back into the comfort of sleep again. Ah well, I was in no hurry and figured Drew would be able to explain it all to me later.

The next time I awoke, I again heard voices. One belonged to Lilly Palmer and the other was someone I didn't recognize. I enjoyed listening in on their conversation. Lilly was telling the second person how we'd met over a year ago at Hope Center. She talked about how I'd arrived with attitude and how that had gradually changed. There was pride in her voice that made me realize how far I'd come, and at the same time, how far I had yet to go.

I wanted to explain that I'd had plenty of help along the way and much of that assistance had come from

Lilly. The woman should have been a drill sergeant for the Marines. She'd pushed and prodded me until I'd wanted to scream, run, and hide. It wasn't calisthenics she drilled into me, though. Lilly forced me to face the emotional garbage I'd been dragging around with me for years. Resentments, anger, fears—nothing was ignored or pushed aside. There'd been plenty of pain and tears but in the end it had been worth it. At one point in our counseling session I remember getting angry enough to stand up and scream at Lilly. She'd pushed me too far and I wasn't going to take it any longer. What shocked me was the big smile that had come over her face. That moment had been the turning point for me.

"I hate that this has happened to her," Lilly said.

Yes, interesting. I'd like to know what had happened to me, too.

Lilly continued, "From what I understand, the guy hasn't been caught."

"Do the police know who's responsible for hurting her?"

"It's a man from Shay's past. He goes by the street name Shooter."

Shooter. Shooter? My mind exploded and I must have cried out, because Lilly grabbed hold of my forearm. "Shay? Are you all right? Do you need me to get someone?"

I managed to shake my head. Shooter was the one who'd hurt me? How was that possible when he was supposed to be in prison? And why couldn't I remember what had happened? None of this made sense.

After a few minutes I must have fallen asleep again.

When I next woke, the lights weren't as bright or debilitating, and I was able to open my eyes for more than a few seconds. Right away I saw Drew sitting at my bedside. He had his Bible in his lap and appeared to be reading.

"Hi," I whispered.

He looked up and a big smile came over him. Setting down the Bible he stood and looked down on me. "You're awake."

I attempted a smile.

"Would you like more water?"

"Please." As he had before, he positioned the straw at my lips, and I took a long sip.

When he set the container aside, I raised my hand to my head and felt the bandages. As soon as I did, a bit of my memory returned. I remembered that Richard and Chuck had been with me and was immediately concerned they might be hurt.

"Richard?"

"He's worried sick about you. He's been at the hospital every day. He stands in the doorway and won't come into the room. Haven't quite figured that out yet. It's very kind of him, though. He looks at you from the hallway, sniffles, and walks away, and then comes back, looks some more, sniffles, and leaves."

"Richard tried to save me. Is Chuck okay?"

"Both are fine. I heard what Richard did. The man has a lot of courage." Drew looked at me and a slow grin came over him. "I've been waiting a long time for you to wake up and talk. Now that you have, I don't think you've ever looked more beautiful."

I couldn't help it, I snickered. "Yeah, I'll bet. How long have I been out of it?"

"Awhile. Four days. Three of the longest days of my life."

He touched my cheek with a look of such tenderness that I bit down on my lip, afraid I was going to start crying. Everything that had happened threatened to overwhelm me.

"The police haven't found Shooter?"

Drew shook his head and his face darkened. "Not yet. It's only a matter of time until he's caught."

I swallowed hard. "He's looking for my brother." Seeing that I'd managed to survive this attack didn't mean Shooter wouldn't try again. He knew where I worked and it was highly probable that he had my home address. Fear immediately gripped hold of me in a vise so strong and tight that I found it difficult to breathe.

"How do you think he found you?" Drew asked.

That was the same question that had played in the back of my mind ever since I learned Shooter was responsible for my injuries. "Richard. He's kept his eye out for Caden. I don't want anything to do with my brother, but I wanted to know if he was in the area. Richard had asked around about him. I think he hoped to find him, help him if he could without involving me. I tried to warn him. As much as I love my brother, he's on a path I can't follow. I thought I was helping him before, but I was the one who ended up paying the price."

Drew's frown thickened.

"Shooter believes he can get to Caden through me and he won't stop until he gets what he wants." I knew Shooter and he wouldn't take no for an answer. He refused to believe me before, which was why he'd attacked me. There was nothing to keep him from trying again, and when I

lidn't give him the information he needed, I'd pay the
price. Shooter would think nothing of killing me. He
had nothing to lose.

"I'm not going to let that happen," Drew insisted.

With everything in me, I wanted to believe I was safe,
but experience told me otherwise. "He probably knows
where I live."

"Not anymore."

His answer hung in the air. I blinked, uncertain at the
implication. "What do you mean?"

"You're not living in the tiny house any longer."

"What?"

Drew's shoulders relaxed as he reached for my hand
and held it in both of his. "I don't know if you remember
this or not. Awhile ago I mentioned that there was a
small apartment in the basement of the church. At one
time the youth pastor lived there. It's a tiny space, but it
has all the essentials."

"I don't remember anything about any apartment."
Well, maybe vaguely I recalled Drew mentioning something about it, but that had been weeks ago.

"It's been used for storage for the most part. The elders thought it would be a good idea to rent it out. The
extra income would help the church meet its budget. In
the beginning I was against it because it would require a
lot of work to ready for a tenant. I've since changed my
mind."

"You want me to move to that apartment?"

"Yes. Actually, I made that decision for you as soon as
I heard what had happened and that Shooter hadn't been
apprehended."

"You did?"

He gripped hold of my hand, squeezing my fingers. " refuse for you to be in danger. Linda Kincaid and Lilly Palmer and a couple other volunteers have been working tirelessly to get the apartment ready for you to move in If Lilly has anything to say about it, you'll be completely moved by the time you're released. You won't even go back to your old place."

"My job . . ."

"Will be waiting for you when you're ready to go back only I'll be driving you there in the mornings and picking you up when you're finished with your shift."

"Drew—"

"If you plan on arguing with me, then save your breath," he said, cutting me off. "It's all been decided Not one of us is willing to give Shooter another chance to get close to you. The church basement is secure, with an alarm system. I had new lighting installed as well. Plus I'm practically living next door."

The idea of being close to Drew and the children appealed to me on a number of different levels. "Thank you," I whispered, overwhelmed by the love and care shown to me by my friends.

"You're welcome," Drew said. "Oh, and before I forget, Sarah drew you a picture." He turned away and reached for it.

I laughed out loud when I saw it. The nine-year-old had drawn me as a stick figure, lying in a bed with my head twice the size of my body. She had an IV pole next to the bed with a nightstand with a Bible on it. Then in large letters below the drawing she'd printed HURRY AND GET WELL.

This was the longest since the attack I'd been awake,

and it tired me out. Although I struggled to keep my eyes open, they kept drifting shut. "I think I need to sleep a bit."

"You do that."

"I don't want to." If I fell asleep I'd be wasting the precious minutes Drew was with me, and I most definitely didn't want to do that. "I'll miss seeing you."

"I'll be here when you wake."

"Promise?"

"Promise." He leaned forward and kissed my cheek.

It felt wonderful to have him close. The battle was already lost, though, and I could feel the pull of sleep and was unable to resist.

Time was of little consequence, and I woke to the sound of whispered voices. Drew's I recognized right away. The second voice was vaguely familiar. I tugged at my memory for a name.

"How is she?"

Drew answered. "Better. She was awake earlier, and we spoke. She seems to stay awake longer each time. That's a good sign."

"I'm glad to hear it."

It took a moment, but I recognized the woman's voice as belonging to Linda Kincaid.

"Everything ready at the apartment?" Drew asked.

"Yes, we have all of her belongings moved in. Lilly is there now unpacking. Everything should be shipshape for Shay once she's released from the hospital."

I should let them know I was awake, but it was easier to soak in the warmth and the soft voices and relax.

"I'm grateful," Drew said.

I was, too. With no idea how long it would take me to

recover from this surgery and my other injuries, it would be weeks before I could have found the energy to pack up and move. Having everything prearranged and managed for me was a totally unexpected gift.

"Are you sure you're doing the right thing, Drew?"

I heard the hesitation in Linda's voice.

"What makes you ask?"

An edge of defensiveness etched his words, I noticed, as if he resented Linda's question.

"I know you're fond of Shay."

"It's beyond being fond. I deeply care about her."

He does? A warm sensation fanned out from my heart. More than anything I wanted Drew to know I felt the same way about him.

"What's the problem?" Drew asked.

Linda paused as though considering her words carefully. "Don't misunderstand me, Drew. I think Shay is great, it's just that word has spread that she's been in prison."

Drew was silent, but even with my eyes closed I could feel the frustration radiating off him.

"And?" he pressed.

"And, well . . . there's talk."

"What kind of talk?" His voice was tight.

"Some of the church members have wondered how trustworthy she is. Having her live in that basement apartment has raised several eyebrows."

"Are you one of the people who has questions?" Drew asked.

When Linda didn't respond right away, I knew her answer, and my heart sank.

"My concern is not about Shay," Linda continued. "I

wonder how appropriate it is for you to associate with her when there are other women—"

"More appropriate choices, you mean?" Drew finished for her. "I appreciate you mentioning this. I suppose I shouldn't be surprised. At the same time, I know that once my church family has a chance to know Shay, they'll have a change of heart. She's an amazing woman, and with time, the congregation will recognize that as well."

"You're sure of that, Drew? I'd hate to have the issue of Shay in your life raise questions with the congregation about your role as our pastor."

This time Drew seemed to be the one searching for the right words. "That surprises me, Linda. I tend to think better of my church family, but if what you say happens, then so be it."

Linda seemed to be speechless. "Drew," she said, shock vibrating in her voice. "Are you seriously saying you'd leave the church for this woman? A felon, a woman with a tainted past, an ex-con?"

"Yes." Drew didn't waver in his decision.

A stunned silence followed before Drew spoke again.

"This shocks me, Linda, because I've always seen you as someone with generosity of spirit. In your defense, you don't know Shay as well as I do. For as long as I've known her, she's never once taken advantage of others. I've never heard her speak a negative word against anyone. She's caring, considerate, genuine, and a hard worker."

Linda's response came quickly. "Drew, please, don't misunderstand me. The only reason I mention this is because I felt you needed to know."

"And I appreciate it."

"One of the elders might approach you about having Shay move into the church. You squelched the idea when it was first presented and then went ahead and rented the space to her with no further discussion."

"I sent the elders an email. It had previously been discussed and I couldn't see that there would be a problem. If the subject comes up at the next meeting, I'll deal with it then."

The talk of Drew resigning as pastor because of me had my mind screaming. I refused to even let him consider such a thing.

"Lloyd and I will do everything within our power to make sure nothing gets in the way of Shay moving into the apartment," Linda assured Drew. "I just felt you should know that there's been talk."

I continued to pretend to be asleep until I heard both Drew and Linda leave. My heart sank with what I'd overheard. While I loved the idea of living close to Drew, I didn't want to hurt him or his career. I was falling in love with him, and the one thing I couldn't, wouldn't, do was put him in a position where he had to choose between me and the church he served.

CHAPTER 22

Drew

I'd spent an uncomfortable afternoon dealing with questions from Alex Turnbull, one of the elders, regarding Shay living in the basement apartment. Linda had been right about the elders having questions and concerns about renting the apartment to her. I spent over an hour talking to Alex—an hour I didn't have to spare.

At the end of our discussion, Alex remained skeptical. Thankfully, he was agreeable to giving Shay a chance, and not to bring my decision up before the board as a matter of concern. For that I was grateful.

When I returned to the house, Mark sat in front of the television, deeply involved in a videogame. My son seemed to spend more and more of his time involved in these games. I'd tried to get him interested in other activities, but he showed no inclination for anything else. I had few complaints when it came to my son. He got good grades and seemed to get along well with others. He did have that one incident where he'd gotten the black eye. He'd never told me the full story of what had happened. It seemed he preferred to put the entire episode behind him. I understood and respected his decision. I had to accept that he was simply an indoors kind of kid. I loved my son for who he was, and while I would have liked to see him more physically active, I wasn't going to push him into something he didn't enjoy.

Sarah was nowhere in sight and I suspected she was at Shay's, who had been home from the hospital a week now. My daughter spent as much time as she could with Shay. It was good for them both. Shay was bored and restless and Sarah helped keep her occupied. And Sarah thrived on Shay's attention. My daughter was hungry for a mother and had taken to Shay from the first moment they'd met.

"Where's Sarah?" I asked my son as I walked into the house. I expected company any minute and put on coffee.

Mark ignored me. "Son. Sarah?" I repeated my question, louder this time.

Without looking away from the television screen, Mark answered, "She went over to see Shay."

As I'd suspected. Shay wasn't up for lengthy visits just yet. She remained weak, but was determined to return to her classes and work as soon as she could manage it.

I appreciated all the help given to Shay. Several of her friends had stepped up to lend a hand. Lilly Palmer, Sadie and Alice, and a few others I wasn't as familiar with made frequent visits to check up on her. There wasn't much for them to do other than offer support, love, and encouragement.

I'd made more than a few visits myself, needing the reassurance that she was doing well. I knew Mark had been over to visit her, too, which surprised and pleased me. They apparently worked on questions of logic and played games involving math puzzles. Not my thing, but the two of them seemed to enjoy that intellectual stimulation.

I would've liked to spend more time with Shay myself, but that was impossible. My responsibilities at the church kept me away. I'd been at the hospital nearly 24/7 and was well behind with counseling appointments and other pastoral duties.

At last report Shooter remained on the loose, evading police detection. I'd been in contact with the authorities regarding his whereabouts. Sightings had been reported in the Seattle area, but no arrest had been made. He was a slippery devil, but he wouldn't be able to avoid capture forever.

Because they were worried about Shooter finding Shay again, Richard and Chuck had made a point of standing guard over the church area with the promise to report any suspicious activity. Thus far, thankfully, they'd seen nothing.

"You going to visit Shay?" Mark asked.

The idea of seeing Shay strongly appealed to me. "I will later. I have a couple friends stopping by in a few minutes."

"Who?"

"You don't know them. Their names are Richard and Chuck."

"They new at church?"

"No . . . I met them through Shay. They live on the streets."

If that information fazed my son, he didn't show it. To this point, he had yet to look up from the video screen, intent on slaying dragons or some creatures from outer space, I couldn't tell which.

A couple minutes later, just as I'd said, the doorbell rang. I opened the door to Richard and Chuck. Richard came into the house, but Chuck stayed on the other side of the threshold.

"I'll keep watch," Chuck announced.

Richard looked hard at his friend. "You said—"

"I'll stay out here," Chuck insisted. He peered inside the house, and that seemed to be enough to dissuade him from coming inside. The more I'd come to know Chuck, the more I realized that he was uncomfortable in enclosed spaces. He preferred sleeping outdoors even on the coldest of nights rather than going into a shelter. Both Richard and I had tried to reason with him, to no avail. I didn't know what had caused this with Chuck and he wasn't talking.

Even when it came to visiting Shay at the hospital, Chuck hadn't been by once. Richard had mentioned it all had to do with the elevator and that his friend preferred to wait outside.

"I won't be long," Richard said as he came into the house. He removed his knit cap, which had several holes.

He looked a bit uncomfortable himself, I noticed. Without asking, I poured him a cup of coffee, added cream and sugar, and set it on the kitchen table.

Richard's gaze scanned the room.

"That's my son, Mark," I said.

Mark sat with his back to us but raised his arm in greeting.

"Hi," Richard said shyly, as if he didn't want to disrupt Mark's game. Pulling out a chair, Richard took a seat and cupped the mug with both hands while staring down at the brew.

I took the seat across from him and had my own cup. "I understand you're the one who's been keeping an eye out for Shay's brother?"

Richard nodded. "Didn't know it would lead to this."

"Of course not. None of us would have guessed something like that would happen. Don't blame yourself. Hurting Shay is on Shooter, no one else."

Richard cocked his head to the side. I knew he wanted to believe me but felt terrible that Shay had been hurt.

"What made you want to find Caden?" I asked.

Rotating the knit cap in his hand and keeping his gaze focused down, Richard mumbled, "Shay brought me coffee. She didn't need to do that. That guy, Frankie, who owns the café, he didn't want me around. I wasn't hurting nobody. There's this grate there, see. It has warm air coming out of it, and nights when I can't get in the shelter it's the warmest place to be."

"I understand."

"Didn't think there was anything I could do for Shay, to thank her, you know. I don't have much and what I got I need."

"Of course," I agreed.

"One time she mentioned her brother. Told me she hadn't heard from him the whole time she was in prison and I thought, you know, that maybe if I found him that I could help him, steer him toward folks who could get him help. I mentioned it to Shay once and she thanked me real nice, but then she said it would be best if Caden sought the help on his own."

"Caden needs to want to get well himself," I told him.

"I know," Richard was quick to tell me. "But I've lived on these streets. I know how down a man can get when you start to believe there's no way out, no one who cares. I've been there. If anyone can reach Shay's brother it would be me. I wanted to do that for her to thank her."

"It was a thoughtful thing to do."

"Never knew it would lead to her getting hurt."

"How'd Shooter ever find her?" That question had played heavily on my mind.

"Think it was an accident that he did," Richard said. "Like I explained, I put the word out, but I promise you I never gave anyone information about Shay. The only thing I can figure is that Shooter had come looking for me and got lucky when he happened upon Shay that morning. No siree, I had all contact come to me. Not Shay."

Richard had worried some might place the blame on him for what had happened to Shay. I didn't, and I doubted anyone else had, either. Especially Shay.

"What did Shay tell you about Caden?"

Richard shrugged as if unwilling to share confidences.

"I know he's the one she stole the money for." Although she'd never justified her actions, Shay had to have known at the time that she'd be prosecuted. She'd sacrificed herself for the sake of her brother.

"And I know, Richard, that Shay has decided it would be best to keep her distance from her brother as part of her recovery, and frankly, I agree. Have you had any success in finding him?"

"Nope, sorry. I found out what I could, which wasn't much. Last I heard he might be living in San Francisco, and that's a big *might*. The guy who told me was high at the time so I wouldn't count him as a reliable source."

"Keep your ears open if you would. Caden is a threat to Shay. My top priority is to keep her safe."

"I agree. If I hear anything you'll know about it."

"I appreciate that."

Richard drank down the rest of his coffee and stood. "Got a cup of that I can take to Chuck? Not a fancy mug like this, a throwaway one?"

"Sure thing." I prepared a cup for Chuck the same way that Richard liked his coffee, thinking his friend would as well. All I could find was a disposable cup meant for cold beverages. Richard didn't seem to mind, though.

Seeing that Richard had already been on the search for Shay's brother and found nothing but dead ends, it left me wondering who else I might be able to ask about Caden's whereabouts, not only to be assured of Shay's safety but also to help her brother if he was willing.

The following Wednesday before basketball with my guy friends, I asked to speak with Kevin Forester at Hope Center.

"What's up?" Kevin asked when I entered his office. He appeared surprised to see me, knowing we were only minutes away from meeting on the court.

Scooting out the chair across from his desk, I took a seat, indicating that this might take a few minutes.

"Everything going okay with Shay since she's out of the hospital?" Kevin asked.

"She's doing great. Eager to get back to work and her classes."

Kevin leaned back in his chair. "I told her she's got a job here as soon as she finishes her schooling."

"She told me." The faith and trust Kevin and the others had placed in her and her ability had gone a long way toward the emotional healing that had taken place in Shay.

As was his habit after small talk, Kevin patiently waited for me to get to the crux of my visit.

"I need you to do something for me."

My friend didn't hesitate. "Sure. Anything."

Kevin didn't even know what I was about to ask and had already agreed. That said a lot about him as my friend and about the strong bond we shared. I didn't have a lot of close friends. I worked with the elders at the church and was friendly with others, but there remained a separation, a distance, between us. Not so with Kevin. We were on an even playing field, comfortable enough with each other to share confidences, our fears and concerns. Had the situation been reversed, I would do whatever I could to help Kevin, should he ask.

"What do you need?"

"Shay has a brother. He was the reason she was attacked. I want to find him. Get him off the street if possible."

Kevin folded his hands across his stomach. "I know about Caden."

"You do?" Encouraged, I sat up straighter.

"Richard thought he might be living in the San Francisco area."

"That I wouldn't know," I said, grateful I didn't need to fill in the details to Kevin. "What I do know is what Shay told me. She's got a new life now and is looking to avoid contact with him, which in my opinion is a good idea. I want to make sure he doesn't have any access to her. If he does happen to be in the area, I was hoping you could get him into some kind of program."

"Drew, of course, but Caden has to want help. Forcing it upon him won't do any good. He has to be ready."

I knew that but was hoping to keep Shay safe, and that meant keeping her brother away from her as best I could.

"If the opportunity arises, and frankly I hope Caden is in the Bay Area and as far away from Shay as possible, but anything you could do would be appreciated."

Kevin sighed and I could sense his concern. Dealing with drug addicts wasn't my area of expertise. I took eighty- and ninety-year-old widows to lunch. It was only since I'd met Shay and reconnected with Kevin that I'd had anything to do with street ministry, other than my time in the seminary.

"Richard has feelers out and is as concerned as I am. If Caden is in the area, then I believe Richard will do everything within his power to find him and steer him to you."

"He's definitely our best resource, but it's a big if, seeing that all Richard has is a name. It isn't uncommon for men like Caden to change their names, especially if someone like Shooter or law enforcement is looking."

I agreed. "I have something that will help." I reached for the photo I had of Caden and handed it to my friend. "Lilly found this when moving Shay into the church apartment. I had a copy made. Richard has one, too."

Kevin stared at the photo for several moments. "I'll pass this around the shelters and do what I can."

"I appreciate it."

Kevin straightened slowly. I assumed he was getting

ready to head for the basketball court. We'd be a few minutes early, but that would give me a chance to warm up.

Instead, Kevin had a question of his own. "So how are you?"

I gauged how close to the truth I should be. The fact was, I was better than I had been but still had a ways to go. Katie's death had nearly killed my faith in a loving God. For four long years I'd continued to struggle with that question.

Everything had changed for me after I'd met Shay. We'd found each other at exactly the right moment. I believed there were no accidents in life.

"How am I?" I repeated Kevin's question. "Better, Kevin. Much better, and a lot of that has to do with Shay."

My closest friend grinned. "I see the changes."

"The thing is, I'm at a loss as to what to do with my feelings for Shay. She makes me happy. The children love her. But when it comes to romance, I'm all thumbs. You got anything to help me?"

This time Kevin laughed. "Sorry, you're on your own, but I'm confident you'll find your way. You did with Katie."

CHAPTER 23

Shay

Being back at work and school made me feel almost human again. My hair was growing back and I could look at myself in the mirror and not cringe. I was beginning to look like myself.

My appearance had changed since I'd been released from prison. It wasn't the way I wore my hair or that I used a different brand of makeup. No, the changes were internal rather than external. I was happy, happier than I could ever remember being since I'd lost my mother. On top of that, I was falling in love with Drew and his children. Living close to them was wonderful. I saw Sarah nearly every day; I'd been motherless, too, and could identify with her, young as she was. Mark wasn't as easy to get to know, but we'd bonded over videogames and enjoyed putting together jigsaw puzzles. He wasn't as keen to share his feelings, but I was fine with that. He was a teenager and still finding his way. I didn't know if he was so quiet and withdrawn due to the loss of his mother or for some other reason. So although I was tempted, I never plied him with questions, determined to accept him as he was.

True to his word, Drew insisted on driving me to work in the mornings and then Frankie personally escorted me to the bus stop when I'd finished my shift and waited until I was safely on board. For my night classes I was able to catch a ride with one of my fellow students, which worked beautifully.

When I first returned to my regular routine, I lived in constant fear of running into Shooter a second time. If that happened, I didn't expect to come out of the encounter alive. After the first few days I had an epiphany of sorts. I decided I could either live my life in fear or I could—simply put—live my life. I refused to look over my shoulder or stop before turning every corner to make sure I was safe. I chose instead to breathe easy, and to put my trust in God. It was either that or I would soon be afraid of my own shadow.

That decision made a world of difference in my attitude. Living in the church apartment had been life-changing, too. Drew claimed it was small. Apparently, he'd never seen the inside of my tiny house. The apartment had to be four times the size of my previous living space. At first I didn't know what I would do with all this room. Gradually I started filling it up with stuff. I'd lived without things for so long that this was sheer joy. When I'd first moved in, I'd wander from room to room amazed and thrilled that this apartment was really mine.

Because I loved my new home and enjoyed living close to Drew and the children, I wanted to prove to his church family that they had made a good investment in me. Getting involved was the one way I could think to reassure the elders and any others who had concerns about me that I was trustworthy. I would never do anything to hurt Drew. I owed him so much. To show my appreciation I volunteered in the nursery once a month, taught a Sunday School class, and signed up to be the coordinator of Vacation Bible School, which was scheduled for late in June. I wanted to join the choir but practice was on Wednesday, a school night.

Saturday morning, I walked down to Pike Place Market, which was one of my favorite places in all of Seattle. The market carried fresh vegetables and fruit. Shopping there was an experience all on its own and I loved it. The walk would do me good.

As I trudged uphill after my shopping excursion, my heart warmed with thoughts of Drew. He'd been wonderful in every way. I was falling for him and I was fairly certain he held strong feelings for me, too. Neither of us had spoken of it, but I knew. How could I not, after all the time he'd spent at the hospital with me?

The frustrating part was that neither of us acted on those feelings. And this lack of physical contact was driving me nuts. We'd only kissed a few times.

Kissed!

We'd come close several times lately but had always been interrupted, either by Mark and Sarah or by someone from the church. It'd happened a dozen times or more since I'd moved into the church apartment. Although he never spoke of it, I knew Drew felt as frustrated as I did. In some unexplainable way, I think we were both a little afraid of what would happen once we spoke openly about what we felt for each other.

I knew it would happen soon, though.

Loaded down with shopping bags, I plodded toward

the church. As I started down the walkway to my apartment, I saw Drew walking between the church and the parsonage. Just from the way his shoulders were hunched forward, I knew something had happened. Quickening my pace, I hurried to meet up with him.

"Drew." I called out his name, but he either didn't hear me or had chosen to ignore my call.

Undeterred, I half trotted, the bags of groceries bouncing in my arms as I rushed to meet him.

"Drew," I shouted, louder this time.

He looked up and seemed startled to see me. Right away he stopped and waited for me to join him. Pain was etched across his face.

"Shay." My name was a tortured whisper.

I hoped he would share whatever had happened that had so clearly upset him. "I tried to catch you, but you didn't hear me."

He wiped a hand over his eyes. "Sorry . . . I'm a bit preoccupied."

I hesitated, not wanting to pry but at the same time wondering if there was any way I could help. "Anything I can do?" I asked.

He looked as if the weight of the Great Wall of China was balancing on his shoulders. In all the time I'd known Drew, I'd never witnessed a look of devastation in his eyes, not the way I did now.

"I need to leave town for a few days."

"Okay." My biggest fear was that whatever this was, it had to do with what had happened to me. I shifted the groceries, their weight cutting into my forearms.

Automatically, Drew took the bags from me. I started walking toward my apartment. It was easier to ask when

I didn't need to look into his eyes. "This doesn't have anything to do with Shooter, does it?" He placed his hand on my shoulder, stopping me.

"No. I just heard the news that a dear friend, a man I consider my mentor, has died."

"Oh Drew, I am so sorry. Is this the man who you drove to Spokane to visit a few weeks back?"

He nodded and whispered, "Yes. Joe's death was expected, but that doesn't take away the shock of it."

I unlocked the outside door and held it open for Drew. He set the bags down on the kitchen countertop. When he turned away, I saw tears glistening in his eyes. He pinched the bridge of his nose. "I'm grateful I had the chance to see Joe when I did."

Clearly Joe was someone close and dear to Drew. It hurt me to see him in such deep emotional pain.

"Would you be willing to stay with Mark and Sarah for a few days?" he asked, making an effort to control his emotions.

"Of course."

"Linda Kincaid would do it, but she's done so much already for the children and me. I hate to rely solely on her."

"Drew, I love Mark and Sarah. I'd be happy to stay with them."

"Thank you." The words sounded as if they were choked out.

It about killed me to see him grieving like this. Because I knew he was hurting, I didn't question my actions and reached for him. I slipped my arms around his middle and held him against me, wanting to absorb his loss, take it away as best I could.

It took a couple seconds for him to respond. When he did, his arms circled me, crushing me against him, holding me so tightly that I found it hard to breathe. My ribs had healed, but his fierce embrace nearly caused me to gasp.

I felt the moisture from his tears against my neck and knew this show of emotion embarrassed him. That I could offer him comfort was enough. I gently rubbed his back, silently letting him know that I understood.

How long we stood with our arms around each other I couldn't even guess. It might have been only a few moments or it could have been much longer. When he did release me, I noticed that his eyes remained red, but they were dry now.

"Thank you," he whispered.

"When do you plan to leave?" I asked, brushing imaginary lint off his shoulders just for an excuse to touch him.

"As soon as possible."

"This afternoon?"

He nodded. "I need to make a few calls and get someone to preach for me in the morning."

"I'll do it," I joked.

That produced a smile, which was what I intended.

"Thanks for the offer, but I have a few contacts I'll ask first. If all else fails, then you're on."

I knew he was teasing, looking for a way to lighten the mood. "Do the kids know?"

He shook his head. "Not yet. I got the word less than ten minutes before I saw you."

"Go make your phone calls and I'll pack up a few things to take over to the house with me."

"Okay." He started for the door, paused, and then turned back. His eyes were filled with purpose and intent. When he reached me, he gently took me into his arms and lowered his mouth to mine.

All these weeks I'd been waiting for this moment. Drew's lips were on mine, warm, tender, demanding. I opened to him and wound my arms around his neck, standing on the tips of my toes, needing to be as close to him as possible. This was good. So very good. I twined my fingers in the short hairs at the base of his neck, loving the feel of him, the taste of this man who had my heart in the palm of his hand. I'd loved before, unwisely, and for all the wrong reasons. I'd never experienced love like this, a love that touched my heart but made its way into my soul. When he broke off the kiss, he braced his forehead against mine and looked deep into my eyes.

"I've wanted to do that for weeks."

I smiled, letting him know that I'd been waiting all this time. I kept my hands at the base of his neck, treasuring these moments.

"I might serve God and the church, Shay, but I'm still a man and I want you so desperately it's eating me alive."

I grinned and leaned my forehead back against his. "I want you, too."

He closed his eyes as though relieved. "I've hoped you did."

He kissed me again and again, as if he couldn't get enough of the taste of me. I didn't know how anything could ever be this good. Closing my eyes, I drank in the scent of him, the unique blend of citrus and wool and something else I couldn't identify.

"I'll let the kids know you'll be staying with them," he

said, as he reluctantly released me from his embrace and stepped back.

I nodded. "It won't take more than a few minutes to put together a few things to take to the house."

"Sleep in my bed," he whispered. "I want to think of you being there while I'm in Spokane."

"Okay."

He maintained eye contact and sighed. "I need to go."

"I know."

His eyes drifted shut. "You have no idea how hard it is to leave you right now."

He was wrong. I had a very good idea of how difficult it was, seeing as I was experiencing the same reluctance.

Thirty minutes later I was at Drew's. Sarah raced to my side as soon as I entered the house. "Dad said you're going to live with us."

"Just while your dad is away."

Sarah's face fell as she gripped hold of my hand. "Did you know my uncle Joe died? He was old, more like a grandpa than an uncle. But he loved us and we loved him."

I wrapped my arm around Sarah, gave her a gentle squeeze, and told her I was sorry.

"Hey, Mark," I said, addressing the teenager who was on the floor in the living room in front of the television. The TV was on, but he was involved with his iPad.

"Hey," he returned, without looking at me.

"Anything special you'd like for lunch?" I asked them both.

He shrugged and continued with his game.

"Spaghetti," Sarah suggested.

"I hate spaghetti," Mark muttered.

Rather than get involved in a sibling squabble, I suggested, "Why don't I cook a dish everyone will enjoy? What do you think of tacos?"

"I like tacos," Sarah said eagerly. She was already in the kitchen and took out a large frying pan from the drawer next to the stove.

Mark remained silent.

"Mark," I said, attracting his attention. I walked over to where he lay and saw that he was playing Candy Crush. "Tacos okay with you?"

He shrugged. "I guess."

"Do you have a better idea?" I asked, hoping to draw him into a conversation.

"Not really."

"Then tacos it is."

Drew came out of the bedroom with an overnight bag. He hugged Sarah and patted Mark on the shoulder. "You two be good for Shay."

"I'm always good," Sarah insisted righteously. "Mark is the troublemaker."

Mark tore his gaze away from his game long enough to glare at his sister. "Am not."

"Kids," Drew said stiffly. "Do as I say. Shay doesn't need to put up with your fighting, understand?"

Sarah nodded and Mark did, too, but with some hesitation.

"I'll call once I reach Spokane," he promised as I walked him to the door.

It was hard for me to let him go. I delayed him with a

question. "You found someone to preach for you Sunday morning?"

He nodded. "Kevin Forester agreed to step in."

Knowing Kevin as I did, I suspected it would be a wonderful sermon. "Drive carefully," I urged.

Drew stood by the door, suitcase in hand. He lowered it to the ground and hugged me. "Thank you," he whispered softly. As he drew back, his look was tender and warm.

"It's all right if you want to kiss Shay," Sarah announced, coming over to stand next to us.

We broke into smiles. It was nice to know we had Sarah's permission.

Drew took full advantage of it, lowering his lips to mine and leaving me with a kiss that would stay with me long after he was out the door.

CHAPTER 24

Drew

Joe's funeral took place on Wednesday and I was back in the church office Friday morning. It'd been an emotional time. I'd connected with Shay and the kids every day while I was gone. Our conversations were short, but exactly what I needed to see me through the loss of my mentor and friend. Joe left a legacy through me and the other pastors he'd mentored through the years. He would not be soon forgotten.

I'd been in the office less than an hour when Linda Kincaid paid me a visit. One look at her and I knew something was on her mind.

"Good morning, Linda," I greeted. Mary Lou had alerted me to the fact that Linda had asked to be notified once I was back.

"Morning," she said, crossing her arms and getting straight to the point. "I understand you had Shay stay with the children."

"Yes. Is there a problem?" Not that it was any of her business if she thought so. I wasn't looking to be confrontational, so I kept my opinions to myself.

"It probably wouldn't have been a problem if Sarah hadn't told half the church that Shay had moved in and was now living with you."

"She said what?" I hadn't heard about this.

"You heard me right. And let me tell you that news spread faster through the church than spilled milk on a marble floor."

Although this wasn't funny, I had the almost irrepressible urge to laugh. I could just imagine what people were thinking and, knowing human nature, how eager they were to think it.

Linda shook her head and sank into the chair across from my desk. "I did my best to quell the rumors."

"I appreciate that," I assured her, and I did, while at the same time finding it amusing. Leave it to my innocent nine-year-old daughter to misconstrue the facts and lead others down the path of speculation and gossip.

"This is nothing to laugh about, Drew."

"Oh come now, Linda, you mean to say you don't find this a little bit funny?" She was taking this far too seriously. I'd always known her to have a good sense of humor, if not a bit dry. She could take a joke as well as the next person, or so I thought.

"The thing is, Drew, you need to be more careful."

"Careful?" We'd already had this conversation once. As far as I was concerned, Shay had more than proved herself. "What do you mean?"

Linda exhaled a deep breath. "Don't you see? By asking Shay to stay with the children, you put yourself in a vulnerable position. I like Shay well enough, and you know I love Sarah and Mark like my own grandchildren and love you like a son. That said, I'm going to speak frankly."

"I wouldn't expect anything less," I said and gestured for her to continue. "I respect your opinion."

"Everyone knows how you feel about Shay. You haven't made any effort to hide your feelings. I'm happy for you, Drew. There's been a real change in you since you've met Shay. You're happier than you have been since we lost Katie."

"Thank you. You're right, I am happier and so are the children. Have you noticed the way Sarah clings to Shay? She's made a world of difference in my daughter and in Mark, too."

"I have seen the changes, and that's why it pains me to say this."

I gestured for her to continue. If there were issues I needed to resolve, I would face them head-on. I trusted Linda to be honest and direct with me.

I read the regret in her eyes and the serious look about her. Whatever had happened had my friend worried. I couldn't believe Sarah's innocent ramblings could have stirred up a hornet's nest.

"You're the spiritual leader of this church and the congregation looks to you to be their guide, both spiritually and morally."

"Are you seriously asking about my physical relationship with Shay?" I asked, finding it almost humorous. I didn't see how anyone could fault a few stolen kisses and misconstrue those kisses as falling down the slippery slope of sexual indiscretion.

"Heavens, no," she returned, aghast. "It's the impression, the implication that your involvement with Shay is improper for a man of your standing. She presents the near occasion of sin."

"What?" I couldn't help it, I laughed out loud. *Near occasion of sin?*

Linda's cheeks burned a bright shade of red. "Drew, please, this is no laughing matter. The bottom line is that Shay isn't the kind of woman any of us expected you to show an interest in, especially after Katie . . ."

The humor in me vanished. I took in a deep, calming breath, doing my best to remain composed. "That was below the belt."

"Was it?" Linda asked.

"What do you expect from me?" I demanded, losing my cool.

"Not her."

"Why?" I asked, genuinely surprised that we were even having this conversation. "Isn't Shay Christian enough for you? If Christ was standing here this moment, do you have any idea what He would say, because I do. He'd look you straight in the eye and ask whomever among you was free from fault to throw the first stone."

"I know what you're saying, Drew—"

"I don't think you do," I said, cutting her off.

"I do, but there are others and they are disappointed in you. When Katie was alive—"

"Katie would have loved Shay. She would have thrown out the welcome mat and taken Shay under her wing." To remain seated was impossible, and I rose to my feet and walked around to the front of my desk so that we could face each other eye to eye.

"Do you seriously believe Katie would want her children associating with Shay? Seriously, Drew."

I did my best to put my personal feelings for Shay aside and look at this from Linda's viewpoint. From what she was saying, she wasn't the only concerned voice, either. When I first met Shay, well over a year ago now, I wouldn't have introduced her to my children. At Shay's graduation ceremony, I'd hesitated to include Mark and Sarah. The reason I'd brought them was because I'd made the mistake of mentioning it to Sarah and she'd been eager to go.

Searching for a response, I thought about Katie and how she would feel having Shay associate with our children, and in that moment, I had my answer. I knew my wife. I deeply admired the way Shay cared about others, her willingness to volunteer wherever needed. A sense of peace came over me and I relaxed.

"I believe Katie would be the first person to love Shay because she had the ability to look for the good in others. That's something she taught me and, Linda, there's so much good in Shay. It hurts me that you and others in the church don't see it the same way I do." And Sarah. My nine-year-old daughter had recognized it in Shay from the beginning. How like her mother my daughter was. Until that moment I hadn't realized it.

"I do see the good in Shay," Linda countered. "But I'm only one person. There are others who are blinded by the fact that she has a felony record and spent time in prison."

"I feel sorry for them," I whispered.

"Drew, do you think I wanted to have this conversation with you? I felt it was necessary because I'm afraid what will happen in the church if you continue your relationship with her."

That gave me pause. I took in a deep breath and realized that if it came to choosing between my role as pastor at Seattle Calvary and having Shay as part of my life, then as painful as it would be, I'd choose Shay.

"I appreciate everything you've told me. I know it hasn't been easy. But I'll take my chances." I trusted that in time my church family would come to love Shay the same way they had Katie.

Linda took a moment to absorb my words. "I know Shay is working hard to prove herself."

"Perhaps too hard. In time the church will notice how much of herself she's given to this congregation, all the volunteer hours she's put in despite her work and school schedule."

"I . . ."

"This latest sermon series has brought more people into the Sunday service, and do you remember who gave me the idea? It was Shay, in case you've forgotten."

"I know . . ."

"As long as I am pastor of this church, we will welcome one and all. I refuse to focus on our past mistakes; God takes each one of us exactly where we are and so do I. Instead of focusing on the past, I prefer to look at the potential God has given each of us. As far as I can see, He's doing fine work in Shay."

"Will you give me a chance to speak now?" Linda asked pointedly.

I gestured for her to have her say. "Go ahead."

"I'm making no judgments," Linda insisted. "If you're in love with Shay, then so be it, but I feel you need to consider the consequences."

"I am in love with her." I realized that was the first time I'd said the words aloud. I did love her. If I was willing to put my future on the line for her, then that told me everything I needed to know.

Linda paled slightly. "Are you going to ask her to marry you?"

That was a loaded question. "I don't know yet. It's early in the relationship, but at some point I probably will."

"That might cost you," she said. "I'm afraid the elders will call for a vote of confidence if matters go that far. It isn't what I want, but I feel you should have fair warning."

"Then so be it." I refused to back down to threats, veiled or otherwise, although I believed Linda's intentions were good. If I was asked to stand before the elders, then I'd cross that bridge when necessary. My hope, naturally, was that it wouldn't come to that. I trusted Shay and knew that if given the chance, Shay would win them over.

"Drew, do you understand what I'm saying?"

"I do," I returned confidently.

Linda seemed more concerned than I was, and I wanted to reassure her.

Before I could say anything, she said, "If it comes to that, I want you to know Lloyd and I will do everything within our power to make sure that doesn't happen."

"I appreciate your support."

Linda shook her head slowly, as if she had yet to fully grasp what had transpired between us. "You genuinely love her, don't you?"

"I didn't realize how much until just now."

Linda had never been the kind of woman who wore

her heart on her sleeve, so it surprised me when she reached out and gave me a big hug. Taken aback as I was, it took me a couple moments to respond.

"I hope Shay realizes how fortunate she is."

Linda had it all wrong. I was the fortunate one. I didn't expect her to understand, at least not yet, but she would in time.

If my morning meeting with Linda wasn't enough to complicate my day, a phone call from Kevin later that same afternoon did.

"Glad to hear you're back," Kevin said after I picked up the call.

"It's good to be back." That was a slight exaggeration. My mind had been caught up on the conversation with Linda that morning. I'd tried not to let it get me down. Although she hadn't mentioned names, she didn't need to say who the rabble-rouser was. Alex Turnbull served as the head of the church council and he'd questioned Shay's "acceptability" from the start. He'd been the one to put up the biggest fuss about renting her the apartment. The most annoying part of his censure was that he'd been the elder who'd proposed that the church rent the space in the first place.

I was tempted to tell Kevin about my morning confrontation but decided against it. Later, if I needed a sounding board I'd go to him as a friend. I didn't need his advice; I'd made my decision when it came to having Shay in my life and that wasn't going to change.

"I have news for you," Kevin said enthusiastically. "Good news."

"I could use some," I admitted. Kevin would think I was emotionally down because of Joe's death. I didn't enlighten him otherwise.

"Thought that might be the case." He paused for dramatic effect. "I believe I've found Shay's brother."

"You know where Caden is?" I could hardly believe it'd happened so quickly.

"As I suspected, he changed his name. He goes by Shane now. As soon as I had my contacts pass his photo around I got hit after hit."

"He's in Seattle?"

"Right here."

This was a good news/bad news scenario. My hope was if we reached out to Caden he would recognize the help Kevin offered and accept the opportunity presented to him. I would avoid any mention of Shay. All I wanted was the assurance that she would be safe.

"As Richard suspected, he's in one of the homeless camps," Kevin said, cutting into my thoughts. "In fact, it was one that we visited last month."

This was almost more than I could assimilate. Caden had been living in Seattle in a homeless camp—the very one Shay and I had visited while out with the Search & Rescue team. I had to wonder if he'd seen his sister the night we were there and if he'd hidden when he caught sight of her. I hated the thought that he might already know she was in the area.

"I want to be there when you talk to him," I said, determined to see Caden for myself. I hoped to learn what I could about the man and where he was mentally. Keeping him away from Shay was my first priority, but now that I'd learned that he might possibly know she was living in the area, I was concerned. For all I knew, Caden could be looking to find her, looking to play on her sympathies again, and that was something I wanted to avoid. I'd let Kevin do the talking but I wanted to be there when he spoke to him.

"Working on it, brother. I reached out to Richard and Chuck and asked if they could arrange a meeting."

"When?" My eagerness made me edgy and anxious.

"No time like the present. If we wait and he gets word it might be enough to spook him."

"I'll clear the rest of the day."

"Good. Meet me at Hope Center."

I was already on my feet. "I'm on my way." Grabbing my coat, I called out instructions to Mary Lou and headed for the door.

My heart pounded hard with anticipation when I met up with Kevin, who drove to the homeless camp. Right away I saw Richard sitting in an open area where a couple of card tables had been arranged close to an open fire pit along with a few chairs. Richard sat with Caden by the fire.

As Kevin and I approached Caden, he turned questioning eyes to Richard. "Hey, man, what's this?" he asked.

"Friends, man. These are friends."

Caden was dressed in a thick sweater with a long-sleeved shirt underneath. The sweater elbows had big holes. He had to be chilled to the bone in the winter cold. He apparently didn't own a coat.

"Hi," I said, smiling at Caden.

He didn't respond. If I was looking for any family resemblance, none was visible. He'd changed from the fresh young man in the photograph Lilly had found. Staring at him now, with his yellowed teeth, straggly hair, and baggy eyes, he looked several years older than Shay instead of being her younger brother.

"I'm here to help you," Kevin told him.

Caden snickered. "Sure you are."

Kevin continued talking, but I noticed that Caden focused his gaze on me. His eyes narrowed and he frowned as if he was trying to place me. It was then that I knew he recognized me from the night I'd been on the rescue mission. If that was the case, then he must have seen Shay that night as well. My heart sank.

Recently, Caden had been talking to Richard and Chuck. A chill came over me at the implication. Both men had been with Shay that night, leading her through the camp. I had to believe Caden had seen her with them as well as with me, which might explain his willingness to agree to this meeting. It could mean that Caden was looking for a way to connect with Shay, use her.

"Who are you?" Caden demanded, focusing his attention on me.

I was about to tell him I was no one when Richard spoke up. "That's Pastor Douglas. Show him some respect, man."

"Pastor Douglas," Caden repeated slowly.

Kevin continued. "We're here to let you know that there are programs available to help . . ."

Caden held up his hand, stopping him. "Not interested."

"These are good people," Richard insisted. "Least you can do is listen."

"Already told you I'm not interested." With that he stormed away with a cynical smile twisting his mouth.

My heart was in my stomach. I had a terrible feeling that in looking to protect Shay, I might have done the exact opposite and put her at risk.

CHAPTER 25

Shay

A loud knocking sound startled me and woke me in the middle of the night. Rolling over, I glanced at the bedside clock and saw that it was barely three. A shot of adrenaline had me bolt upright in bed. My immediate thought was that Shooter had found me. Then reason took over. If it was Shooter, then it was highly unlikely he'd knock. His style was to ambush and attack. Whoever it was, it sounded urgent. Maybe something was wrong with Drew or the children.

Hurrying now, I turned on the lights and headed into the living room. Thankfully, the door had a peephole and a porch light that illuminated the area. Drew had added a bright one as a safety measure that shone across half the yard. If it was Drew at the door, I wanted proof, although I couldn't imagine why he wouldn't phone first instead.

A man stood on the other side, wobbling back and forth on his feet as if struggling to find his balance. At first I didn't recognize him and assumed he was one of Richard or Chuck's friends.

Then I did.

It was Caden.

My brother.

My heart nearly burst inside my chest. I had wondered how I'd feel if I ever saw him again. Early on in my recovery I'd made the decision to avoid anything to do with my brother. As painful as it was to cut him free, I had to do what was best for my own emotional well-being.

I didn't know how he'd managed to find me. My heart clenched at the sight of him and I struggled with what to do. As much as I wanted to turn my back and ignore him, I found I couldn't. I didn't know what he wanted, but I was stronger now and unwilling to be drawn into his drama. Then, I reasoned, if he had come to me, he must be desperate.

I undid the lock and opened the door. Caden pointed at me, then staggered a few steps. "Aren't you going invite your baby brother inside?" he demanded.

"No. Go away, Caden, you're drunk." I took an involuntary step back. Even in the cold of the night, he reeked of alcohol. It'd been over four years since I'd last seen him and I almost hadn't recognized my own brother. The years hadn't been good to him, which led me to believe he was still hooked on drugs. "Caden, oh Caden, what's happened to you?" I whispered, my heart breaking at the sight of him.

"I need my big sister. Won't you help me, Shay? All I need is a few dollars to see me through."

"Caden, I can't . . ."

"Look at you in this fancy apartment, living the good life while your baby brother is sleeping on the street."

He staggered forward and tried to grab hold of my

shoulders. I managed to catch him by the shoulders so he didn't stumble.

"I've been looking for you," he said, slurring the words. "Needed your help but you didn't want to see me, did you?"

"Caden, please, you have to understand, I'm not the same person I was four years ago. I've changed. I—"

"Bet you didn't think I'd find you, did you?" he said, cutting me off. "Thought you could hide from me. Well, I'm smarter than you think. Smarter than you realize."

I blinked, not knowing what to say or even if I should comment.

"I saw you, you know, that night you were out with that rescue team. Saw you with him."

"Him?"

"That pastor friend of yours. He came . . . him and that other do-gooder, thinking they could help me. I recognized him and then followed him. I saw the two of you." His laugh was maniacal. "You got something going with that preacher, don't you? Imagine what Shooter would think if he knew. He'd laugh his fool head off. I did."

I bristled, disliking his tone. I wondered if Caden knew what Shooter had done to me in an effort to find him. Probably not. "It's time for you to leave," I said as forcefully as I could and attempted once more to close the door.

"I ain't leaving until you give me some money. Don't tell me you don't have it, living in this fancy place."

I could see it wasn't going to be easy to persuade him to walk away. I toyed with the idea of giving him a twenty and just as quickly changed my mind. If I started giving him money now it would be only the beginning. Soon he'd be coming to me for funds for his drinking and drugs and his needs would be endless. I couldn't give in, no matter what.

"I can't, Caden. I'm sorry, but I can't give you any money."

He blinked and scowled as if he didn't believe me. His arms flung out as if he had trouble maintaining his balance.

Taking advantage of the opportunity, I started to close the door. Caden was too quick for me and put his foot in the way, stopping me. "Didn't I tell you I wasn't going to leave until you gave me what I came for? I can stand here all night if need be, but I'm not leaving until you do what's right for your family."

I shook my head, using every bit of determination I possessed to turn my back on my brother.

"Please. You're my sister," he pleaded, changing tactics. "You need to help me; it's your duty. It's what Mom would have wanted you to do."

As hard as it was not to give in, no way would I let my brother manipulate me. "No, Caden, what Mom would want is for you to be clean and sober, and the last thing she'd want is for me to enable you to continue on this path of self-destruction."

"Okay, fine," he said, cursing at me, calling me terrible names. I regretted opening the door now and tried again to close it. Despite being drunk, Caden was surprisingly strong. As hard as I pushed, I was unable to get the door to budge.

I wasn't going to allow him to verbally abuse me. "It's

time for you to go, Caden. Leave me alone and don't come here again."

He growled at me like a rabid beast.

I saw a police cruiser stop on the side of the street. The light Drew had installed must have illuminated the area, which was easily viewed from the street. "The police are here—"

"Cops. You bitch . . ." Again with the foul language, all directed at me. My brother used every foul word I had ever heard.

"Leave." I shoved with all my might, hoping to close the front door. Caden yanked me forward and then, gasping with surprise and shock, I stumbled out into the cold. That was when my brother took a wild swing at me. Thankfully, I was able to step back in time to avoid getting hit. The action caused my brother to lose his balance and stagger sideways. It was a major accomplishment that he managed to remain upright, although he stumbled several feet before he could stop himself.

I groaned inwardly when I noticed two police officers getting out of their cruiser and running across the lawn.

As soon as Caden saw the police, he cursed me again and took off in a desperate run. One of the officers raced in pursuit while the second approached me.

"Are you okay?" the female officer asked.

"I . . . think so," I said.

"We saw what happened. Do you want to press assault charges?"

"No. He's drunk or worse." I wanted to explain that I hadn't seen him in years but I didn't get a chance. When Caden realized he wasn't going to be able to outrun the officer, he turned to face the man and reached for a knife.

As soon as the female officer saw the weapon, she left me to assist her partner.

I couldn't see what happened next, but I heard the officer call into her mike, "Officer down, officer down."

The policeman who had gone after Caden was on the ground, grabbing hold of his side, and the female officer had her gun drawn on Caden. I realized then that my brother had stabbed the first officer.

My first thought was to try to help, to do what I could to talk to my brother, calm him down. Instinctively I realized any effort I made would simply add to the chaos. The only thing I could do was stay out of the way.

Sirens blared in the distance. Caden was restrained and arrested and the injured officer was taken by an aid car to a local hospital. I was in the middle of being interviewed when Drew came out. I'd never been so grateful to see anyone.

He ran across the yard and grabbed hold of me in a fierce hug. "What happened? Dear God, are you all right?"

"I'm fine. It was Caden."

"Sir," the female officer intervened, "if you could wait a few minutes, we need to finish our interview?"

Drew didn't release me but held me close to his side. I noticed he was trembling. I knew that seeing the police and the aid car had given him a fright. He must have assumed the worst.

To the best of my ability, I answered the officer's questions. Before they finished, I had a few questions of my own. "What will the charges be?"

"He's under arrest."

That much I knew, seeing that he'd been hauled away in handcuffs.

"He'll be charged with assaulting an officer, public drunkenness, and resisting arrest."

This wasn't sounding good.

"He's looking at some serious jail time," she told me.

I closed my eyes, wishing things had turned out differently. Reading between the lines of what Caden had said, Drew and Kevin had found him and offered him help. It was clear Caden wasn't interested. That being the case, there wasn't anything I could do for him. I certainly wasn't giving him money. He assumed I was an easy touch. I had been at one time, but no more.

After the police left and the medical people had driven away, my pulse gradually returned to normal. Drew's arms were around me as he whispered, "Let me make you a cup of coffee so we can talk this out."

Sleeping now would be impossible, and it wasn't that long before I was due at the café. "Okay."

Drew waited while I changed into my work uniform, and then, taking me by the hand, he walked me back to his house. The children had managed to sleep through the commotion, which was a blessing. Drew pulled out a stool at the kitchen counter, then drew me into his arms, sighed, and kissed the top of my head.

"You can't imagine what went through my head when I heard those sirens and saw that police car pull up. I think I died a thousand deaths until I realized that it wasn't there for you."

My arms circled his middle and I hugged him close. "My brother was half out of his mind."

"He was drunk, Shay, and probably high, too."

After what had transpired in the last hour, there could be no doubt Drew was right. "He said something about you and a man I can only assume was Kevin coming to talk to him. That wasn't you, was it?"

Drew went still and a look of regret came over him.

"It was you?"

He nodded.

"And Kevin?"

Again he nodded.

"When did this happen?"

"I'm sorry, Shay. I would have mentioned it, but—"

"When?" I asked again, needing answers. I'd already guessed his reasons, but I wished he'd discussed his plans with me first and given me a warning. I knew Richard had made it his mission to find and help Caden. My homeless friend seemed to think he was doing me a favor. I'd tried to explain that it was best if Caden stayed out of my life. Richard accepted that but still thought he might be able to help my brother. I'd reluctantly agreed, with the promise that Richard not tell Caden where I lived.

"Kevin spoke with him this afternoon, but your brother remembered me from before and knew we were connected."

"Richard found him and told you?" I asked, wondering why my friend would mention it to Drew.

Drew looked uneasy. "I helped Richard. After what happened with Shooter, I wanted to do everything I could to protect you. I thought if Richard found Caden that Kevin could talk him into getting into a rehab program."

Drew's intentions were good, I realized. He'd never meant to lead Caden to my doorstep. The entire situation had blown up in his face and, unfortunately, mine.

"Lilly found a photo of you and Caden when she moved you to the apartment," Drew confessed. "She showed it to me and I made a copy and took it to Kevin. Once we had the photograph, it didn't take long for one of his contacts to locate him. Caden is going by the name Shane now."

"I wish you'd discussed all of this with me first." I gestured with my hands, letting him know this all might have been avoided if I'd known what Drew had done. His intentions were well-meaning, but it would have helped had I been aware that Caden was living in the Seattle area. The last I'd heard he was in California. From the first I'd hoped to avoid a confrontation with Caden, although one was probably inevitable at some point.

Drew held my eyes, his own wide and pleading for understanding. "I wanted to tell you about Caden before Kevin and I went to see him, but there wasn't time; this could well have been our only opportunity."

"I wish I'd known . . . I would have been better prepared."

"I know . . . the situation got out of hand. I don't know how he found you."

"He followed you and he saw the two of us together."

Drew paled and he briefly closed his eyes. "In looking to protect you I led him to your front door. Shay, I am so sorry." He wrapped me in his arms and held me tight against his torso. "I feel dreadful that this happened to you. It's all my fault."

"Stop," I whispered, unwilling to let Drew shoulder the blame. Knowing my brother, eventually he would have found me. He wouldn't have easily given up. I noticed that Caden hadn't asked about me or what had happened after he disappeared when he got the five thousand dollars. All Caden was concerned with was his next high, whether from drugs or alcohol.

"Kevin offered to help him, get him into rehab, but Caden didn't want anything to do with that."

That came as no surprise. It would take more than a few words to reach my brother. He was lost, trapped in a web that held him in a tight grip. He was at a point where he couldn't see a way out of the black hole into which he'd fallen. He was lost and hopeless, angry and defiant. I couldn't take on his problems, but at the same time I couldn't stop caring what happened to him.

"I know you don't want to hear this, but I believe jail might be the best thing for him now. It will sober him up. Once his head is clear he might be willing to listen to reason."

I lowered my head to our folded hands. "I hope you're right."

Leaning forward, Drew kissed my cheek. "I would never intentionally do anything to hurt you, Shay. I love you."

My head came up. I knew how I felt about Drew but had never told him. I held his look, uncertain I'd heard him correctly. His smile was gentle, and he seemed to be awaiting a reaction. "Did you just say you love me?"

"So much it frightens me."

A smile broke out across my face and I leaned forward and pressed my lips to his, savoring the sweetness of the moment. "I love you, too, Drew Douglas, so much. Let's be frightened together."

CHAPTER 26

Drew

Following the events of the early-morning hours, I wasn't prepared for the media ruckus they caused. By morning all the local television news channels and a couple of the national news networks had picked up the story of the police stabbing. I switched channels several times and each station used the incident to headline the newscast. Like a deer trapped in headlights, I stood in front of the television, riveted to the scene. The church and yard played prominently in the telecast and I groaned inwardly as one report followed another.

When I looked out the window, I saw two news trucks parked outside the church with reporters standing in front of cameramen as they gave their live report.

By the time I got to the office, the phone was ringing off the hook. Mary Lou had been so busy answering calls that she hadn't had time to remove her coat. Feeling bad for her, I brewed her coffee and took a cup to set on her desk. She sighed and thanked me with a small smile.

Before she could ask, I told her, "I won't be accepting any interviews."

"Got it," she said and sounded relieved.

As soon as there was a lull, she approached me. "For the love of heaven, what happened?"

I responded in the simplest of terms. "Shay's brother found her and attacked a police officer when they came to break up the disturbance."

"The latest report from the news media is that the police officer required surgery and is reportedly in critical condition."

This was even worse than I had imagined. Shay and I had been unable to get any updates on the extent of the officer's injuries this morning, which was understandable. What little information I'd discovered, I'd learned on the morning newscast, and that had been sketchy.

Kevin stopped by the church and we sat in my office with the door closed. I appreciated his support. He talked for several minutes and then we prayed together.

"Nothing happens without a reason," my friend assured me. "I know it's hard to look at this mess and believe that God is in control, but He is."

It wasn't as though I doubted him, seeing as I'd uttered those same words myself, countless times.

"How's Shay handling this?"

"She was upset, and rightly so," I told him. "I should never have contacted Caden without letting her know what we were doing."

Kevin stroked the side of his cheek and nodded, silently agreeing with me.

"I wanted to protect Shay. I never considered that Caden would seek her out . . . I should have realized . . ."

"Realized what?"

"Caden recognized that I was with Shay the night we were on the rescue mission. He followed me and I led him right to her."

"You couldn't have known."

"That doesn't lessen my guilt. I don't know what would have happened if that police cruiser hadn't gone by when it did."

Kevin sighed, slowly releasing his breath. "I'll stop by the jail and find out what I can from Caden and what I can do to help with his defense. If he isn't willing to talk, which I suspect he won't be, then I'll see what his defense attorney has to say."

"I'll go with you, but I want to make sure Shay knows what we're doing." I'd already mishandled the situation and I hoped to learn from my mistake.

Kevin nodded. "Good idea."

He stood to leave and I walked him to the door. When I opened it, I saw Linda Kincaid standing by Mary Lou's desk, chatting with her. She looked up when the door opened and Kevin came out of my office. Her eyes were dark and serious, and I sensed trouble brewing.

Not that it was unexpected. I realized the minute I saw the news broadcasts that morning that there would be plenty of blowback from this.

For Shay. And for me.

"Come in," I greeted Linda. "Would you like some coffee?"

She shook her head. "This isn't exactly a social visit, Drew."

"I figured." Stepping around to my side of the desk, I took my seat. I had the distinct feeling I was going to need to sit down for this. "I take it you heard about the incident with Caden Benson."

"Heard about it?" she repeated with her arms crossed. She stood on the other side of my desk like a marble statue, an unmovable force. "It was all over the news this morning, as you're no doubt aware."

"Is there still a camera crew outside the church?" I asked. I hadn't looked since I'd come into the office.

"No, thank God."

I felt the same, although I didn't say it. I expected the television reporters would return for the noontime broadcast, and probably again this evening. Lead stories for the top of the hour were dissected and repeated. Every tidbit of any update was announced as a major revelation. These reporters were not about to be denied.

Linda started pacing in front of my desk. "Did I not warn you about moving Shay into that apartment?" she demanded, her voice raised and irritated.

"As I recall, you did mention your opinion."

"Which you ignored."

I met her look and didn't flinch. "It was for Shay's safety."

"That doesn't seem to be working well, does it?" She marched back and forth and then stopped and shook her head as if she wasn't sure what to say next. "You aren't thinking with your head, Drew."

"I love Shay." I was tired of defending my decisions to Linda. I'd tried to look at it from her perspective, but it didn't change the way I felt about Shay or the need to keep her safe.

"I'm afraid loving Shay is going to cost you your ministry," Linda snapped.

The words hung in the air like launched hand grenades.

I had a good idea of what was about to happen and why. I straightened my shoulders, determined to meet this news head-on.

"I tried to explain it before," she reminded me, gesturing helplessly with her hands. "I did my best to make you understand the risk you were taking by moving Shay into that apartment."

"I never knew you to be one to say 'I told you so,'" I said, without emotion. Nothing anyone could have said would have changed my mind. Even knowing what I did, I didn't have a single regret. It certainly didn't help that the church grounds and the church were all over the news this morning, and not exactly in the best light.

I'd watched the news reports and cringed. The first reporter had talked about the homeless problem in Seattle while standing directly in front of the church steps, as if to say the church had basically ignored the needs of the people on the street.

"So tell me. What am I looking at?" I asked, bracing myself for the worst, already knowing it was coming.

Linda sank into the chair with a defeated look. "I'm sorry, Drew."

"Tell me."

Linda sighed. "Alex is calling for a vote of confidence with the church council."

My shoulders sank. A vote of confidence was basically the elders telling the congregation they had serious doubts about the leadership abilities of the pastor. If the vote went against me, it would mean changes in leadership. A pastor needed the support of the church council. If I did manage to survive, then there would be bridges to build and relationships to repair. Even a call for a vote was devastating. For the unity of the church, no matter which way the vote went, it would be best for me to resign.

"I see," I said, my heart aching. It hurt that the men and women I trusted and had served with through the years were basically telling me that they no longer believed I was qualified to lead our church.

"He's asking for a vote with the elders," Linda continued. "That doesn't mean it will come to pass."

Words escaped me. I knew what was to follow. I would be asked to meet with the elders. Alex would state his case and the eleven others would vote. If the vote went against me, it would go to the congregation.

"Lloyd is doing his best to make sure this doesn't happen."

"I appreciate it," I whispered, but as far as I could see the die was cast.

"I'm sorry, Drew. You don't deserve this. Neither does Shay."

Her irritation was replaced by sympathy and understanding. Linda had always had my back, even now, when it looked like everything was against me.

"I'm grateful you let me know," I said, accepting that I would need to prepare myself for the upcoming storm of controversy and speculation.

We talked for several minutes more and Linda did her best to reassure me. After she left I sat and stared into space, letting the worry and the doubt build up in my mind.

Sometime after one, Mary Lou knocked on my door. "Would you like lunch?" she asked, looking concerned.

I didn't realize the time. Shaking my head, I declined. "I'm not hungry."

By now I was sure Mary Lou knew what was brewing within the church. She wore a worried frown. "Anything I can do, Pastor?" she asked.

I shook my head. My two-o'clock counseling appointment canceled. I suspected that Mary Lou might have had something to do with that. Either way, I was grateful.

As soon as my head was clear, I went into the church sanctuary and sat in the front pew. I'd been here many times, especially in the months following Katie's death. It was the place I came when my heart was heaviest. It seemed loving Shay would come at a high price, but if my role as pastor was what it cost me, then it would be worth it.

Shay had brought light back into my life, she'd revived my faith and loved my children, and they loved her back. Every minute I spent with her brought me happiness. Seeing the strides she'd made in her life made me proud of her. Deep down I knew that Katie would have loved her, treasured her as a friend. I sat for so long that I lost track of the time.

I heard the door open but didn't look up, hoping whoever had come inside would get the message and leave me alone. I wasn't in the mood to talk.

After a few minutes, I felt someone sit down close to me. Even with my eyes closed I knew it was Shay. She reached for my hand and laid her head against my shoulder. Not a word passed between us and yet I felt the heaviness lift from my heart simply having her close to my side.

I heaved a sigh as the ache of uncertainty returned. I would do my best to move on and follow wherever the road took me next. It was all I could do. The decision wasn't in my hands.

When I finished my prayers, I raised my head, and Shay's was lowered in prayer, too. She seemed to sense that I'd finished.

We left the church together. In the hallway between the sanctuary and the office, she paused and gripped hold of my arm, looking up at me, her face bright with unshed tears.

"I'm so sorry, Drew."

Brushing the hair away from her face, I stared down at her, unable to disguise the love I felt for her. "Who told you?" I asked, surprised she knew the details of what was happening.

"Linda stopped at the café."

I could only imagine what she'd said, and that irritated me to no end. I wanted to make sure Shay was protected from all this. Her faith was new, fragile yet, and this could destroy her. "You are not to blame, understand? I don't know what Linda told you—"

Shay stopped me. "Linda said you would probably appreciate a visit from me this afternoon. She didn't tell me anything until I asked her."

"She did?" I had misjudged my friend. I'd assumed she'd gone to Shay and laid the blame at her feet, which would have been grossly unfair.

"Linda loves you like a son, Drew. You and the children mean everything to her. I realize I'm not the woman she wanted for you, but she respects you enough to do her best to accept me."

I brought Shay into my arms, content to simply hold her, soaking in her comfort and her love.

"I talked to the prosecuting attorney about my brother this afternoon before I saw Linda. He'd just been assigned the case. Caden's been given a court-appointed attorney. That's all he could tell me at this point. I don't want any contact with Caden, but I do want to know what will happen to him."

The fact that she continued to care about her brother after what he'd done spoke volumes. I hoped that once Caden was sober and in his right mind he'd appreciate Shay and not see her as a means to getting him his next fix.

Depending on the degree of the charges against him and the jail time he faced, I would do what I could to get him into a drug rehab program. Caden was going to need all the help he could get.

When I returned to the office, Mary Lou gave me a sympathetic look. "An emergency elder meeting has been called for tonight."

So soon; it was what I should have expected. Mary Lou told me the time. "Thank you," I said.

I noticed Shay biting into her lower lip. Actually having Linda tell her what was happening was a blessing. It saved me from having to explain, knowing she would blame herself.

"I'll stay with the children," she assured me. "Do you want me to say anything to them about this?"

I shook my head. "Not yet. This meeting involves the elders who will vote first. It could all end tonight if the vote goes my way. No need to upset the children or give them reasons for concern." I wasn't sure Shay understood the inner workings of the church. It wasn't necessary for her to know all the details. Having her support and love was all I needed to see me through this.

That evening, as I stepped into the meeting room, twelve elders awaited my arrival. Alex Turnbull sat at the head of the table. He greeted me stiffly and asked me to take a seat. He waited a moment and had his say first, outlining what he considered my shortcomings and how my behavior had an adverse influence in the community. He went on to claim that my relationship with Shay had brought undesirable attention to the church. The incident this morning had been a prime example. In closing, he stated that he had seen homeless men sitting within our midst during the Sunday service.

He was referring to Richard, whom I'd seen slip into the eleven-o'clock service and take a seat in the back pew. I'd been amused and pleased to see him singing the closing hymn at the top of his lungs. Although he was in the far back of the sanctuary, I could hear him from the pulpit. I loved having him in church and knew in my heart that God did, too. He'd brought a couple other men in the last week and I had welcomed them one and all.

"Do you have anything you'd like to say in your defense?" Alex asked, after I'd answered several questions.

Every eye in the room was on me as though they expected a heated rebuttal. I had none to give. "No, everything you said is true, Alex. The only thing I would like to add is that as long as I am pastor of this church, these doors will be open to all who enter. Other than that, I have nothing to say."

Alex Turnbull looked surprised. "Fine, then, let's take a vote."

CHAPTER 27

Shay

From the smile on Drew's face when he walked in the door, I knew the vote had gone his way. The relief I felt nearly overwhelmed me and I felt tears burn the back of my eyes. Until that very moment I didn't realize how tense I was about the elders' decision. Pressing my hand over my heart, it was all I could do to keep the emotions at bay.

Drew came to me and wrapped me in his arms, holding me close. "It's good. Everything is good."

My heart was too full to speak. I buried my face in his neck and took in several calming breaths, needing that time to compose myself. It went without saying that Drew was relieved, too.

Although they didn't know what was happening that evening or why their father had an unexpected meeting, both children seemed to sense the tension. Sarah had been demanding and needy all evening and Mark had been withdrawn, which had become the norm with him. I worried about Drew's son. He seemed to keep more and more to himself these days. I'd mentioned it to Drew once and he'd talked to Mark, but it didn't seem to have done much good.

Sarah peeked out from the hallway, dressed in her night-gown. She'd gone to bed earlier, but she'd made one excuse after another to get up. "Are you going to kiss Shay, Dad?"

"Probably," Drew told his daughter.

"Can I watch?"

"Absolutely not. You're supposed to be asleep by now. You have school tomorrow," he reminded her and tried to look stern. He failed and I could see that he was struggling to hold back his amusement.

"I'm not tired. Besides, I want to see you kiss Shay."

While Drew put Sarah back to bed, I poured us each a glass of iced tea and set out a plate of oatmeal-raisin cookies that Sarah and I had baked that evening. Needing a distraction, I'd suggested baking, and Sarah had been more than eager to help. I'd asked Mark to join us, but he claimed he wasn't interested.

Drew devoured the cookies. I knew he hadn't eaten dinner and I strongly suspected with the vote hanging over his head that he'd gone without lunch, too. As we sipped our tea, Drew told me the gist of how the elder meeting had gone.

It seemed Alex Turnbull was the only one who had any overwhelming concerns regarding Drew's competency to continue as pastor. The remaining elders had listened carefully to Alex, asked questions of Drew, and then voted. From what he said, Drew didn't put up a lengthy rebuttal; he didn't feel it was necessary. My name was mentioned but only briefly.

"I can't tell you how sorry I am that this has hap-

pened," I told him. I'd never meant for any of this to fall
on his shoulders. He should never have become involved
with Caden. From the first, I'd made it perfectly plain
that Caden was bad news. I couldn't imagine what had
led him to seek out my brother.

"All is well that ends well," Drew assured me, gently
brushing the hair from my face and looping it behind my
ear. His touch was gentle, loving. "Everything happens
for a purpose."

"True, but you should never have involved yourself in
this, especially without me knowing."

Drew agreed and apologized again. I accepted, determined to put this in the past. He'd paid the price and so
had I.

As a result of all this hullabaloo, I felt I needed to make
friends with the very people who had doubts about me
and my relationship with Drew. The first person I wanted
to start with was Linda Kincaid. This was an important
relationship. Linda didn't openly dislike me, although I
wasn't sure she trusted me.

Thursday evening of that week, I joined Linda Kincaid
and a couple other volunteers at the Bring-a-Meal night
at Hope Center. It was while I was a resident there that
I'd met Linda the first time. That seemed like a lifetime
ago now. Since I'd started attending Drew's church, I'd
volunteered to work on the kitchen crew twice and both
times Linda told me that she had all the volunteers she
needed. I tried not to take her rejection personally. She'd
never been openly unkind, but I had the feeling that she
would rather not have me.

When I phoned to tell her I was available for that Thursday night, I recognized her hesitation. Knowing how important Linda was to Drew and how much she loved the children, I wasn't going to be easily turned away this time. In the end she agreed to let me help, although she'd made it sound as if she was doing me the favor.

After I finished my shift at the café, I headed to the church. Linda and the two other volunteers were busy making dinner for the women at Hope Center. Stephanie and Kelly were good friends and the two of them chatted away and basically ignored me. It wasn't intentional, I knew. It had been awhile since they'd last talked and they were catching up. As soon as they realized they'd excluded me from the conversation, they did their best to include me. I appreciated their effort.

The menu for the evening was roast beef, mashed potatoes, green beans, salad, and red velvet cake.

"Where would you like me to start?" I asked Linda once all the ingredients for the meal had been set out. I'd washed my hands and rolled up my sleeves, ready to dig in.

"How are you at peeling potatoes?" Linda asked, giving me the least welcome task.

"An expert," I assured her with a smile, eager to prove myself.

"Then have at it." Her smile was strained. I knew I wasn't her favorite person and appreciated that she was trying. But then so was I.

Stephanie put on the playlist from her phone and soon the three of us were dancing around the kitchen, laughing and having a good time. The only one who showed any restraint was Linda, who didn't even tap her toes.

Once the meal was ready, we loaded the food into the

church van and drove over to Hope Center. Lilly Palmer met us at the door and led us to the cafeteria. Her eyes met mine and I saw the worry there.

We'd talked several times in the last week, mostly about my brother and what had happened at the church with Drew. Lilly had helped me talk through my emotions with both incidents.

"Everything coming up roses?" Lilly asked, helping me cart in the large containers of food. The residents had started to line up with their trays. Stephanie and Kelly helped serve while I filled the drink glasses. Linda supervised.

"Everything's great," I responded, laughing softly. Lilly was a dear friend and I was grateful every day for her support and encouragement.

"Have you been able to find out anything about your brother?" she asked as she helped cart out the carafes of coffee.

I shook my head, thoroughly depressed when it came to Caden and his troubles. I'd talked to both the prosecutor and his court-appointed defense attorney and learned what I could. It didn't look good for Caden. Thankfully, the police officer would make a full recovery from his injuries in time.

No way was my brother going to avoid prison. I knew jail time might be the only way he would get sober.

The dinner went well with all of us working together. It was hard to believe that I had once been one of these women, struggling to find my place in society, weighed down by rejection from the very ones who were supposed to love and care for me. Like many of them, I had made poor choices and had low to no self-esteem. I wasn't that person any longer, and seeing these women showed me just how far I'd come.

As we finished loading up the van, I saw Linda on her phone, deep in conversation. She frowned and closed her eyes before righting herself. While Stephanie and Kelly dealt with cleaning up the kitchen and clearly didn't need me, I went out to talk with the residents.

Stepping up to a table full of women, I told them my own story and saw their eyes widen with what I could only describe as hope.

"You were part of Hope Center?" one of the women asked me.

"Sure was. Arrived with a lot of attitude, too."

"That she did," Lilly verified, coming to stand beside me.

I smiled at my friend. "I remember the first day I was here, when Lilly told me she was going to be the best friend I ever had. At the time I wanted to laugh in her face, but you know what, she is."

"Hate to tell you this, but I say that to all the women."

I smiled because I knew that was probably true.

Lilly placed her arm on my shoulder. "Shay didn't have an easy time of it at Hope Center, but she stuck with it. She's proven that taking a negative and making it a positive is possible."

The women gathered around the table nodded.

"You'll be seeing more of Shay," Lilly continued. "Starting in June, she'll be working as a bookkeeper at Hope Center."

"As soon as I finish my accounting classes, which Lilly suggested I take. When I first came to Hope Center, I was afraid to dream of anything good happening in my life. Lilly asked me to come up with a dream and I told her I'd only be setting myself up for failure. Do you remember what you told me?" I asked her.

"Sure do. The same thing I've told these women. Any dream will do. Allow yourself to dream."

I felt someone come up behind me and discovered it was Linda. "The van is loaded. It's time for us to leave."

After hugging Lilly goodbye, I headed out with Linda and the other two.

I sat in the front seat with Linda. Stephanie and Kelly were in the back, chatting away.

"I didn't mean to rush you," Linda murmured.

"You didn't." I noticed that her hands were holding on to the steering wheel in a death grip. She'd seemed to be in a rush ever since she'd taken that phone call. I'd noticed that she'd grown quiet and intense afterward.

Not sure if I should say anything about the call or not, I watched her out of the corner of my eye and then decided I had to say something to break the tension. "Linda, I don't mean to pry, but did something happen earlier?"

"What do you mean?" she asked defensively.

"I saw you on the phone," I said. "I noticed since then that you've become quiet and tense."

"Sorry, it's just that . . ."

"Just that?" I prompted when she didn't finish.

"Lloyd called. I put a load of wash in before I left this afternoon. Our washer is in the basement, and it seems that a pipe burst. The basement is flooded."

"Oh no. How bad is it?"

"I don't know. Lloyd is trying to deal with it, but it's too much for him to handle alone."

We arrived at the church and I realized that after working all afternoon getting the meal ready to deliver to

Hope Center, Linda was headed home to clean up a huge mess in her basement.

"Let me help," I said.

"Help?" she asked, as if she didn't know what I was talking about.

"With your flooded basement."

She paused, as if she didn't hear me correctly. "It's late. You were up early this morning and—"

"You have given yourself to the church, to others, to Drew and to his children. I think it's time someone stepped in and gave you a hand."

Linda continued to stare at me as if she didn't know what to say. "I can't let you do that."

"You can and you will. Now let's head to your house and tackle this mess. I'm young and I don't need a lot of sleep. If I were you I wouldn't hesitate to take advantage of my generous offer."

She cracked a smile. "I probably should take you up on it."

"Yes, you should. As for me being up early, I think you were probably up at around the same time. Let me do this for you to show my appreciation for all you've done for everyone else."

To my utter surprise, Linda tossed her arms around me and hugged me. "Thank you," she whispered.

"Let's get to it," I said.

The van had been unloaded and I followed Linda to where she'd parked her car and we drove to the house. Going down to the basement, we found Linda's husband wading around in water, looking exhausted and unsure what more he could do on his own. He had a push broom in his hand and was sweeping the water toward a drain.

"The cavalry has arrived, and looks like we got here in the nick of time," I told him.

Lloyd blinked. "I hardly know where to start."

Stacks of magazines were soaked through, as well as boxes that had been on the floor. To put it mildly, the basement was a mess.

We worked together for an hour until it was clear that Lloyd was too tired to continue. Linda sent her husband upstairs to brew coffee. Fifteen minutes later he carried down a cup for each of us, apologized, and then left.

Linda and I worked companionably, sorting through the boxes, taking out what could be salvaged.

"I heard Lilly mention that you're going to be working as the bookkeeper for the center."

"Yes, I'm excited to get back into the kind of work I enjoy. This is an opportunity I never expected to have."

She didn't say anything for several minutes. "Lloyd counts the money from the collection every Sunday after church, which is one of the reasons we're often the last people to leave."

I knew the Kincaids donated a great deal of their time to the smooth operation of the church.

"He's going in for surgery next Wednesday and will be out of commission for a couple weeks. He asked me if I'd take over the task for him. I was wondering if you'd be willing to step in for me."

The suggestion was much more than counting out the offering. Linda was saying I had her trust, that she believed I was capable and honest. "I'd be honored."

"Good. That's one less thing on my plate," she said a bit gruffly.

Not letting her see my smile, I continued working. I'd

met women like Linda before. They liked to be in control, and giving up even one small piece of their control was difficult.

"I'll let Drew know that you'll be putting together the church deposit," she said.

I realized this was her way of letting Drew know that she accepted me as worthy of his love.

And to think, all it took was three hours spent in a flooded basement.

CHAPTER 28

Drew

My sermon series inspired by popular movies had gained a lot of local attention. The religion editor for *The Seattle Times* had heard about it, and unbeknownst to me visited the church one Sunday. The next week he wrote his column about the topic of my message. Since then, every pew in the church had been filled for the last two weeks.

Again, I had Shay to thank for the idea, which had inspired other similar ideas. I'd decided my next sermon series would be on ten of the most popular downloaded songs from iTunes. I'd been listening carefully to the lyrics. I believed songwriters were the sages of their generation and said a lot about the society in which we live. I'd done a bit of research on the artists' backgrounds along with their lyrics. My goal was how best to relate the words of the music to Scripture and then apply it to life.

I stood in the lobby as the choir sang the final hymn, preparing to greet my church family as they exited the building. My heart was full. For the first time in a long while I felt effective as a pastor. My sermons were being well received and I seemed like I was reaping the rewards of the years I had invested in the ministry.

As I was getting ready to head over to the house for dinner, Alex Turnbull sought me out. His look was dark and serious. For just a few minutes I was tempted to turn away. Alex had been a thorn in my side even before the incident involving Shay and her brother. He'd made his opinion of Shay clear. He wanted her gone, and if not her, then me.

To be fair, I had to admit that he'd accepted the defeat of his vote of confidence with good grace. I appreciated that he didn't hold any resentment. He'd accepted the support of the other elders and had gone out of his way to show his support since that time.

"Do you have a few minutes, Pastor?" he asked.

Making a show of checking my watch, I let him know my family was waiting for me to join them for our noonday meal. I'd already left them waiting longer than I planned.

"It won't take more than a couple minutes," he insisted.

"Sure." It was probably best to discuss this now rather than later, I reasoned.

He hesitated, which was odd, seeing that he seemed eager to chat. "This is a delicate matter. Perhaps it would be best if we talked about this in your office."

Apparently this was more serious than I realized. "Sure."

Alex followed me to my office and entered after me, closing the door. I leaned against the edge of my desk.

"I realize, Pastor, that you and I have had our differences over the last few weeks. I hope you understand this has nothing to do with any of that."

While it was true we tended not to agree, especially when it came to Shay, I didn't hold any resentments. I let Alex know that. "True enough, but I also accept that you have always had the church's best interests at heart, as do I."

"I appreciate you saying that."

"The church is doing well," I commented. "Better than it has in a long while."

No denying that attendance was up substantially. "But you're here because you believe there's a problem," I said, urging him toward the reason for this meeting.

Alex stiffened and stared down at the carpet for several seconds as if gathering his resolve. "It gives me no pleasure to tell you this."

"What is it, Alex?" He was beginning to worry me.

"It's about Shay."

My relaxed pose instantly dissolved and I straightened and crossed my arms. It bothered me that he'd targeted Shay almost from the first moment she'd come into my life. I couldn't imagine what she had ever done to deserve this man's dislike. "What now?" I demanded.

Alex met my eyes and I read a mixture of emotions, the most prominent one was regret. "I know you think I carry hard feelings about what happened with her a few weeks ago. That incident with her brother."

"She had no control over that situation, as you well know." I refused to let Alex blame Shay for her brother's behavior, especially when I was the one who had led him to her.

"I was never keen for the church to rent her the apartment. In the last few weeks, though, I've had a change of heart."

I relaxed somewhat, encouraged by the news.

"Shay has been great," Alex said. "I've kept a close eye on her and there's nothing she isn't willing to tackle. She volunteered to work in the nursery this morning, rocking the babies when the woman who was scheduled had to stay home with a sick child.

"Last week, Shay filled in for one of the Sunday school teachers at the last minute."

I knew about both incidents. The children in the Sunday school class had loved Shay. She'd been creative and fun. She'd told the story of the Good Samaritan and asked the children what they would do if they saw someone in need. Then she had them write letters she planned to give to Richard and Chuck to let the men know they were loved.

This morning I noticed the bin for the collection for the food bank was full and I was convinced it was because Shay had opened the children's eyes to the needs of those less fortunate.

"When I saw that Lloyd Kincaid wasn't able to fulfill his duty because of his recent surgery, I was mildly surprised that Linda asked Shay, on Lloyd's behalf, to fill in for him."

Lloyd counted the money from the collection basket and readied the bank deposit for Monday morning.

Uncrossing my arms, I grew still and struggled to hide my defensive posture. "Why are you surprised, Alex?"

The head elder clenched his hands into tight fists, clearly uncomfortable and irritated. "It isn't a secret that Shay went to prison for embezzlement."

"She's never tried to hide it," I reminded him.

Alex gestured with his hands. "Most churches wouldn't ask someone with that kind of history to count and deposit donations."

"Were you aware that Hope Center plans to hire Shay as their bookkeeper?" I asked him. This was my way of letting him know that Hope Center trusted Shay and I didn't feel we could do any less.

Alex nodded. "I heard. But bookkeeping is a bit less tempting than dealing with cash on hand, don't you think?"

"What are you saying, Alex?" I asked, growing tired of this discussion.

He exhaled and pinched his lips together before he spoke. "Pastor, I am concerned for Shay, fearing she is being put in a position of temptation."

"Shay would never steal from the church." I would stake my retirement fund on it. "The only reason she stole the money was to save her brother."

Alex nodded. "Her brother is in trouble again, isn't he?"

It was hard for me to control my patience. "Yes, but Shay has no contact with him. Alex, please, what's your point? My family is waiting."

With a look of deep concern, he edged toward me. "Last week before the collection was given to Shay to count out for the bank deposit, I added up the cash donation myself."

Cash wasn't uncommon, but most parishioners contributed to the church either online or by writing a check. The cash donations generally came in small bills.

"And?" I asked, seeing that there was obviously more Alex had to tell me.

"It came to three hundred and twenty-five dollars in cash."

"And?"

"The deposit slip showed only three hundred dollars. Twenty-five dollars was missing."

"You could have easily added the amount incorrectly," I insisted.

"I thought the same thing," Alex agreed. "I wrote it off as a problem with my addition. Twenty-five dollars isn't a large amount. However, to err on the side of caution, I decided that I would do the same thing this week."

"Without Shay knowing what you were doing?"

"Correct."

"And?" From the flow of this conversation, it didn't take a genius to figure out what he was about to tell me.

"There was a hundred-dollar discrepancy."

My heart fell and I closed my eyes while I struggled to find a plausible explanation. "The elders gather the collection plates," I offered, although there wasn't one I wouldn't trust with my life. I'd known these men and women for the entire time I'd been at Seattle Calvary and found them completely trustworthy.

"Unfortunately—or fortunately, as the case may be—I was extra-careful to keep tabs on the money collected today. The only person who had access to the cash is Shay."

"You're sure?" I had a hard time believing it.

"Positive."

With nothing more to say, I nodded. "I'll take care of it."

Alex reached out and touched my sleeve. "Drew, I really didn't want to be the one to tell you this. It hurts me, knowing how much faith you've put in her. I know you have strong feelings for Shay."

"I do."

To his credit, Alex looked utterly miserable. "I'm sorry."

As best I could, I accepted his apology. I'd take a day to mull this over before I confronted Shay. While everything within me screamed she would never steal from the church, I also knew Alex wouldn't stoop to lying about something this serious.

To complicate matters, Shay was at the house with the children. It had become part of our routine for her to join Mark, Sarah, and me for Sunday dinner.

My thoughts were heavy as I walked toward the house, my steps slowing with regret and worry as I approached.

Sarah had the door open even before I got to the porch. "We've been waiting and waiting."

"Sorry, sweetheart, I had a quick business meeting." I kissed the top of her head as I entered the house.

"I'm hungry and so is Shay."

"Where's Mark?" I asked. Generally he was one of the first to the table. He'd been going through a growing spurt and seemed to be hungry all the time.

"In his room. I don't think he's feeling well," Shay told me.

Welcoming the excuse to escape for a few minutes, I sought out my son. Sure enough, he was lying on top of his bed, looking miserable. I sat on the edge of his mattress and pressed my hand over his forehead. "You feeling sick, buddy?"

"Yeah." If he wasn't playing his videogame or had his face stuck in his iPad, I knew something was wrong.

He didn't feel feverish. "Upset stomach?"

Mark nodded. "Yeah. It's cramping. You aren't going to force me to eat chicken noodle soup, are you?"

"Not unless that's what you want."

"I'd rather stay here and sleep, if that's all right."

"Sure. Call me if you need anything."

"Thanks, Dad."

Although Mark was at the age where he didn't appreciate displays of affection from his father, I leaned down and kissed his forehead.

"Dad," Mark groaned. "I'm not a kid."

"You'll always be a kid to me," I said, struggling not to smile. His grandmother had knit him an afghan that was neatly folded at the foot of his bed. I reached for it and pulled it up over Mark's shoulders. As soon as the knitted piece settled over him, Mark's eyes drifted shut.

I closed the door as I left his room.

"Is Mark okay?" Shay asked as she finished dishing up the pot roast and potatoes with carrots.

"He might be coming down with something. He wants to sleep, and I think that's probably a good idea."

Shay carried the platter over to the table and sat down with Sarah on one side and me on the other. She automatically stretched out her arms for the three of us to link hands while I said the blessing.

For a moment, my words faltered before I could continue. When I finished, I opened my eyes and looked at Shay.

She must have noticed my scrutiny because she caught my eye and smiled softly. Looking at her now, so breathtakingly lovely, I found it hard to look away. It seemed impossible to believe she would steal from the church. Steal from me. Surely she understood what that would do to our relationship.

Although dinner was cooked to perfection, I had little to no appetite. Sarah insisted she play a game of Yahtzee with Shay after we finished with the meal. I was grateful, unsure if I would be able to keep up the pretense that nothing was wrong much longer.

"I'll do the dishes," I volunteered.

"We should all help," Shay suggested.

"Dishes?" Sarah moaned as if I'd asked her to clear the church parking lot of snow with a single shovel. "Daddy, please. I've been wanting to play Yahtzee forever, but Shay said we had to wait until after dinner."

"It's fine," I insisted. "I'll do the dishes."

Shay and Sarah played the dice game and I used the time stacking dishes in the dishwasher as an excuse to avoid talking to Shay.

She noticed, though. I knew she would. I'd never been good at hiding my feelings.

After I finished the dishes, I checked on Mark and wasn't surprised to find him asleep. If he wasn't feeling better in the morning, I'd keep him home from school. I left my son's bedroom and carefully closed the door so I wouldn't wake him. I found Shay standing behind me in the long hallway.

"Mark's sleeping," I whispered.

Shay's gaze held mine. "Any problems over at the church?" she asked.

Her question left me wondering if she knew about the

missing money. Made me wonder why she hadn't mentioned it.

Stop.

I would ask her. That was the fair thing to do. But first I needed to consider how best to pose the question. For me to ask was major. I wanted her to know I trusted her and believed in her. At the same time, if something had happened that I didn't know about, some reason she would need that money, then I had to give her the space to explain. How I approached her would take consideration and I needed to mull it over.

"Drew? Church? Problems?"

"Nothing I can't handle," I answered, hoping that would be the end of her questions.

Her eyes bored into mine.

She knew.

I could tell simply by the way she looked at me. Right away I detected a subtle change in her. For the first time since I could remember, she couldn't look me in the eye. My stomach muscles tightened and it felt as if a three-hundred-pound man had climbed onto my back and was pressing me down. I struggled not to slouch forward.

Soon after our brief exchange, she left. For the first time in a very long while, I was grateful to see her go.

What Alex hadn't said, but seemed to imply, was that each week the amount would rise. The first couple weeks were probably a test to see how much the thief could get away with before anyone noticed.

My heart was sick. It was almost as if I had a case of the flu.

"Daddy?" Sarah said, coming to sit next to me. "Are you sick, too? Like Mark?"

I offered my daughter a soft smile and placed my hand on the top of her head. "I'm not feeling good, either, I'm afraid."

"Do you have the flu?"

"I don't know." How could one explain to a child that what I suffered from was a troubled heart?

CHAPTER 29

Shay

I received word via Caden's attorney that my brother wanted to see me. It took me a long time to make the decision. I knew that after several days in jail, he would be sober. I was stronger now, more sure of myself, and unwilling to risk my future to enable my brother to continue in his destructive lifestyle. This wasn't the first time he'd asked to see me. Following his arrest, he'd made several attempts to reach me. For my own emotional well-being, I'd refused. I felt ready now.

Monday afternoon, as soon as I'd finished my shift at the café, I headed over to the county jail and put in my request to see Caden. It took fifteen minutes before I was approved. When the clerk returned, she apologized for the delay. I suspected the waiting time was because of my own felony conviction. I was smart enough not to ask.

After another wait of ten minutes or longer, Caden was led out in an orange jumpsuit, wearing slip-on shoes with white socks. He didn't look at me but kept his eyes lowered. Seeing that he'd been the one who asked to see me, I remained silent, patiently waiting. The last time I'd talked to my brother had been the night he'd shown up at the church apartment. He'd been high on drugs and/or alcohol and abusive, wielding a knife, which he might easily have used on me. With that in mind, I was content to wait him out.

An uncomfortable amount of time went by before Caden looked up. He offered me a sad, broken smile. "Guess you're mad," he said.

I shrugged in reply. I certainly had every right to be angry. If not for the counseling I'd received at Hope Center, I would be ranting at him now, filled with righteous indignation, spewing my anger at him. Over the last sixteen months I'd learned how to accept my own responsibility in what had happened, when I'd stolen money from the bank. And with help I'd found a way to forgive him, not because he'd asked or because he deserved my forgiveness. I'd done it for my own peace of mind, to unburden the heavy load of resentment, refusing to cart it around any longer. That didn't mean I was willing to be drawn back into his craziness, however.

"Why'd you come?" he asked next.

"You asked and you're my brother."

"Not much of one, though."

I didn't disagree. "I've been praying for you, Caden."

"Praying?" he repeated. "You pray now?" He made it sound like I'd taken up sword-swallowing.

"I do."

His eyes widened, as if he found this hard to believe. "Next thing I know you'll become one of those women preachers you see on TV, carting around a Bible."

"I have a Bible," I admitted freely, "and, even better, I read it."

Caden's mouth sagged open. "What happened?" he

cried, as if I'd announced I'd been captured by aliens and been zoomed up to their spaceship.

"I have a new life now."

"What happened . . . I mean after you got out of prison? You said you're a different person, and I can see that you are."

Condensing the story as much as possible, I relayed how I'd been released from prison with only a few hundred dollars to my name and had walked into the church, where Drew had found me. I went on to explain how Drew had helped me to get into the program at Hope Center. Caden listened intently as I explained what had happened in the time since I'd graduated out of the program.

My brother held my look for several awkward moments while I told him about my current job at The Corner Café, my bookkeeping classes, and my hope of being hired to work at Hope Center in a few months. He didn't ask questions or speak until I was finished.

"Sounds like you have a great new life now."

"I have a promising future that's filled with opportunities I never had before."

A look of sadness settled over him. "I'm a big loser, Shay . . . I'm—"

"You're not a loser," I said, cutting him off. "You can have a decent future, too."

"A future in prison, you mean. I stabbed a cop, Shay. They don't write that off with a slap on the wrist. It doesn't matter that I was high. I'm looking at some serious time."

I couldn't deny his reality. "You're probably right." I didn't want to raise his hopes, but I knew both Kevin and Drew were working behind the scenes, talking to the prosecutor and Caden's court-appointed attorney, offering alternative solutions to a lengthy prison sentence. No matter what connections my friends had, the bottom line was that my brother was looking at time in prison.

"It's what I deserve," Caden whispered, his head lowered. "Especially after what I did to you."

I wasn't about to excuse his behavior or write it off either. "I agree it was low. You threw me under the bus, little brother."

He chanced a look at me. "Would it help if I told you I regret it? But Shay, I didn't have any choice. If you didn't give me the money, they were going to kill me."

I didn't want to talk about the past. He wasn't ready to accept responsibility for his actions and I wasn't going to rub his face in his mistakes. I'd paid the price for being stupid and allowed him to sabotage my future. But one thing I'd learned through all this was that even the most negative events in my life—prison, nearly landing on the streets of Seattle, homeless and lost—I had turned them all into something good.

If none of that had taken place, I might never have met Drew, might never have received the counseling and emotional healing I needed to become the person I am now.

"I don't hold any resentment toward you, Caden. I have a new life now. I've met a good man. I'm happier than I can ever remember being since Mom died."

"You in love with one of those preacher guys?"

"I am. How did you know?"

For the first time since we'd started talking, my brother smiled. "Don't think he could hide it. Protects you like a wolverine. The other guy had to hold him back when I

mentioned you were lucky I didn't take the knife to you."
He glanced up, guilt written on his face. "I . . . I do crazy
stuff when I'm high. I don't mean for it to happen, but it
does."

He didn't need to explain, I'd seen the evidence.

He snickered softly and shook his head. "You and a
preacher? Really? I find that hard to believe."

"Believe it, Caden."

"You going to marry him?"

"It's too soon to say." I hoped that was where the future would lead, but I feared we were about to enter a
rocky road in our relationship. Time would tell.

My brother released a long, slow sigh. "I'm happy for
you, Shay."

I smiled, warmed by his words. "Thank you."

For the first time since he'd walked into the room,
Caden showed evidence of a grin. "You look good."

"Thanks." I felt good, too, better than I had in years. I
was in control of my own life and when I looked at the
future, I could do it with a smile and not cringe with pes-
simism at what I feared awaited me.

"I mean you look really good."

My brother wasn't one to freely hand out compli-
ments. "If that's the case, then you should know this is
the way someone looks when they don't shoot drugs or
drown their sorrows in the bottom of a bottle."

"Is that a dig?" he asked.

"Not intentionally. It's a statement of fact."

My brother let those words soak in for several minutes. "I'm clean now."

"Stay that way," I advised. "No high is as high as being
clean and sober, brother."

He nodded. "It isn't easy."

I knew that, too. "Nothing of value ever is, but I'm here to tell you that you can break completely free with help from your Higher Power."

Caden's forehead folded into a thick frown. "Are you attending one of those twelve-step groups now, too?"

"No." Drugs had never taken control of my life, and for that I was eternally grateful. Shooter had been disappointed when I wouldn't use with him. It'd been a constant source of conflict between us. Occasionally, I'd give in to his demands, but drugs had never given me the same high they did others. In retrospect, I believed this had been God's protection in my life.

"Guess three years in prison did that for you."

It would be too hard to explain and so I didn't try. "I got word about Shooter," I said.

Caden's head shot up. "The police found him?"

I nodded. "They caught him in Oregon. He's being transported back to Washington state."

My brother paled. "He's the reason I needed to see you. Shooter will kill me if he gets a chance."

"Which is why you decided to change your name to Shane?"

Caden nodded. "Always liked that name better anyway. Don't know what Mom and Dad were thinking naming me Caden."

"It's a good name."

"So is Shane."

I wasn't going to argue with him. Caden, Shane, or whatever else he chose to call himself was fine by me.

"I don't feel I have the right to ask you for anything," Caden said.

He didn't, but I would do what I could to help him. "I'm listening."

My brother exhaled, as though he found it difficult to speak. "It's not asking you for money, if that's what you're worried about."

"Good, because I'm not giving you any."

"Would you talk to my attorney for me?" he asked.

It seemed my brother thought I had some influence with the prosecutor. I didn't. "About . . . ?"

"All I want is to be sent to a different prison than where Shooter is. If they can't do that, then it will be a death sentence for me."

Seeing that I'd already had one nearly disastrous run-in with the drug dealer, I could understand Caden's fears.

"I'll ask," I assured him, "but don't expect miracles."

"I'd appreciate whatever you can do."

"No promises."

"I understand."

I nodded. Now that we'd arrived at the reason he'd asked to see me, I was ready to go. It surprised me when Caden continued the conversation. It was almost as if he was looking for an excuse to keep me close.

"What's the name of that preacher . . . the one you like."

"Drew."

"He's the taller one, right?"

Both men hovered around six feet, but Drew was definitely taller. "Yeah, what about it?"

"He's been to see me a few times."

Drew hadn't mentioned it, but it sounded like something he would do. That Caden would be willing to talk to Drew surprised me. Knowing that, Drew probably thought it was best that I not know.

"You been listening to what he has to say?"

"Not really," Caden said with a shrug. "I like the other guy better. He knows street life. Your Drew, he just wants to be sure I understand that I'm to leave you alone. If you tell him I asked to see you, then you'd better explain why, otherwise he might make things bad for me. Worse than they are already."

"Drew wouldn't do that."

Caden snickered. "He's real protective of you. I'm glad of that."

Nothing could have hidden my smile. When push came to shove, I knew that Drew wouldn't doubt me about that missing money. We hadn't spoken of it, but the conversation needed to happen and we both knew it. It felt like a dark cloud hung over my head while I decided what I was going to say and do.

"You've got a couple white knights in your corner."

"I know, Drew and—"

"Not them," Caden said with a snort. "Those homeless guys. Dumb and Dumber."

"Hey, those two are my friends."

"You're telling me? They look at themselves as some kind of guardians, watching out for you."

Keeping a smile off my face would have been impossible. These people were my family now and I loved them. "You should be so lucky to have friends like those two, Caden. Perhaps one day you will."

He gave me a funny look and then shrugged. "Maybe you're right."

I already knew that I was, at least in this instance.

CHAPTER 30

Drew

"Shay, can we talk?" I asked her Monday afternoon. I'd waited until she was back from an errand she'd run.

"Of course." I suspected that we both knew where this conversation was headed. I saw her tense up. That did little to settle my own nervousness. I was certain Alex hadn't mentioned the missing funds to anyone other than me. The only way Shay would know about it was if she'd taken the money herself, or if she knew who'd done it. I couldn't make myself believe that she would risk her future for less than two hundred dollars.

She sat at my kitchen counter while I took the time to brew us each a cup of coffee. When I'd finished, I turned to face her and handed her the first cup. I held my mug with both hands, letting the heat warm my palms, deciding how best to start our conversation.

We stared at each other for several moments before I spoke. "Shay, is there something you'd like to tell me?" I asked her.

I could see the hesitation in her eyes. "You're asking me about the missing money, aren't you?"

I nodded. "What do you know about it?"

Shifting uncomfortably on the stool, she avoided eye contact. "Do you think I took it, Drew?"

"No."

Immediately her shoulders relaxed. "Thank you for that."

"But you know who did." It wasn't a question. She had to know.

"I'm not at liberty to say."

Disbelief flooded me. "Excuse me?"

"You have perfect hearing, Drew. You don't need me to repeat that, do you?" she asked.

Dumbfounded, I continued to stare at her. "Do you have any idea of what's at stake here?"

She lowered her eyes and nodded. "Yes," she whispered, "I do."

I ran my hands through my hair. "Help me to understand, then, because the consequences for you could be beyond my control. I'll do what I can to protect you, but, Shay, there's only so much influence that I have."

"I understand."

"I need more. We can't leave it like this. You can tell me."

She closed her eyes as if struggling within herself. "I promised I wouldn't."

Unbelievable.

"We all make mistakes," she told me. "This person is sorry and intends to make it right. I promised I would keep this knowledge to myself until they could do that. It makes me feel good knowing you believe I wouldn't steal from the church. Thank you for your trust."

I set the mug on the counter and tossed my hands in the air. "Shay, you're not listening to me. I believe you, but that doesn't mean the elders will have the same confidence in you. As your pastor and as the man who loves you, tell me who took that money." My patience was reaching its limit and my voice rose as I spoke.

She paled and I noticed how her hands went white holding on to the mug with such force; it was amazing the ceramic didn't crumble, allowing coffee to spill over the kitchen counter. "I gave my word," she whispered. "This isn't easy for me, either. I've talked to Lilly about it—"

"Were you willing to give the name of the offender to her?"

"No. I've kept my word and I fully intend on keeping it. All I have is my word, Drew, and it has to mean something."

The frustration was getting to me and I rammed my fingers through my hair. "What did Lilly tell you?"

"She said the decision was mine, and I've made up my mind. I don't mean to be evasive, but my word is my word."

Holding her look, I tried again. "I'm absolving you from whatever promise you made."

For what seemed like an eternity, she said nothing and then slid off the stool. "I'm sorry, Drew."

She started to leave. I couldn't let her do that, not without giving me the answers I needed.

"Shay, please, don't go."

For a second I thought that would stop her. Her steps slowed and she seemed to hesitate, but then continued to the door without looking back.

I watched her leave, caught between shock and disbelief.

—

Although I didn't have an appointment with Kevin, I showed up at Hope Center on the off chance he would have time to talk me through this situation with Shay. I was stunned that she wouldn't tell me what she knew.

Once at Hope Center I walked, almost in a trance, down the hallway to Kevin's office. The door was closed and I let myself in. His assistant looked up, surprise written on her face.

"Pastor Douglas? Do you have an appointment? Did I miss something?"

"No. Is Kevin available?"

My friend must have seen me through the glass partition because he stood up from his desk and walked around the enclosure. "Drew? What's happened? You look like you've just lost your best friend."

"Seeing that you're my best friend, I'm glad to report you're still alive and kicking," I said in a lame effort to crack a joke. "You got a few minutes?"

"Sure. Come on in." He ushered me inside his office.

Depressed and deeply discouraged, I slumped down in the chair across from his desk.

Kevin didn't waste any time getting to the heart of my visit. "What's the problem?"

I found it difficult to speak. "It's Shay."

"Did something happen?" His eyes revealed his concern.

It looked like he was ready to stand when I motioned for him to remain sitting. "Something happened at the church. Shay was counting out the donations and making the deposit slip. Money has turned up missing for the last two weeks."

Kevin looked as stunned as I was when Alex first told me. "You don't think Shay is responsible."

"No. No way."

His shoulders sagged with relief. I would never come to him if I had even a hint of suspicion that Shay might be responsible for the missing funds.

"Then what's the problem?"

"She knows who's responsible and refuses to tell me."

Mulling this over, Kevin leaned back in his chair. "Who told you about the theft?"

"Do you know Alex Turnbull?" I asked, knowing he probably did.

"I do. He's a good man."

"Alex came to me on Sunday. Lloyd Kincaid had surgery to correct a bunion and will be out of commission for a few weeks. While he's recuperating, Linda asked Shay to count the offering for Lloyd and get it ready for the bank deposit on Monday."

Kevin gestured with his hands, as if that shouldn't be a problem.

"Alex knows Shay was in prison for embezzling and worried that Lloyd had put her in a position of temptation. He decided to count the cash offering before handing it over to her."

Sitting straighter in his chair, Kevin sighed audibly. "And money turned up missing."

I felt the heavy burden of what I was about to tell him. "Twenty-five dollars the first week and a hundred the second."

Making a steeple with his fingers, Kevin rested them

beneath his chin and frowned. "She's willing to keep her silence, even knowing what it might cost her and you?"

I feared Shay didn't fully understand the consequences of what she was doing. If the church believed she was the guilty party, then they would never accept her as my wife. Even if we were to marry sometime in the future, there would always be speculation and doubts about her. About us.

"She refused to tell me. She gave her word and insists the person who took the money wants to make it right. She promised to give them that chance."

"Second chances," Kevin whispered.

"What?" I asked, not quite hearing him.

"Shay was given a second chance and now she feels obligated to offer that same opportunity to someone else. I understand why she's doing it, but I have to believe she has no idea of what she's risking."

"I know she doesn't understand what this misplaced loyalty could cost her, otherwise she'd listen to reason."

Kevin's shoulders sank as the weight of my words settled on him. "This makes me sick at heart."

I couldn't begin to tell Kevin what it did to me. I'd barely slept Sunday night stewing about how best to handle this situation. I'd wanted to talk to her first thing that afternoon, as soon as she was off work, but she hadn't returned to the apartment. I'd kept an eye out for her and was certain she'd purposely stayed away, avoiding me.

"What are you going to do?" Kevin asked me next.

That was the million-dollar question. I had no clue. "Alex hasn't wasted any time. Just before I drove here, I got word that he has called an elder meeting tonight."

"Will the elders want to press charges?"

I hadn't considered that. They were likely to charge Shay, especially if she refused to name the person responsible. Naturally, I'd fight that and hope that I had enough influence to prevent that from happening.

"Seeing as it isn't a major amount of money, I'm hoping I can get the elders to agree not to get the law involved." I'd refund the money myself before I'd let that happen. No way would I let Shay be charged.

"What about allowing her to continue living in the apartment?"

That was another thing I hadn't considered. "It's possible that will be a consequence. Again, I'll do what I can to prevent that, but I don't know if I can." My heart sank. The ramifications of this were hitting me like hail, falling from the sky and crashing against me. Unavoidable, damaging, and painful hits, one right after another.

My fears compounded with every heartbeat. "They won't believe her. What is it people say?" I asked the rhetorical question. "Once a thief, always a thief?"

"I know you'll do everything within your power to protect her."

That went without question. Of course I would. I loved Shay. This misplaced loyalty she had toward the thief was going to hurt us both. I'd already tried once to get her to understand all that she was putting at risk but to no avail. I wasn't certain that I would be successful in a second try, either.

Several moments passed before Kevin spoke. "This has badly shaken you, hasn't it?"

Rather than respond verbally, I nodded. The only thing I could even think to equate it to was when Katie was first diagnosed with cancer. We knew the road we were about to face and that there would be struggles ahead. It hadn't ended well for my wife and my fears were rampant when it came to my future with Shay.

"Who could it be?" I asked, knowing Kevin had no more clue than I did. I rubbed my hands down my face. "I fell in love with her when I thought it was impossible to ever love again."

To complicate the situation, I wasn't the only one who'd come to love and trust her. My children loved her, too.

"Sarah," I whispered, without realizing I'd said her name aloud.

"What about Sarah?"

Caught off guard, I looked up. "Just the other day she asked me if Shay could be her backup mother."

Kevin grinned. "She always did have a wonderful way of expressing her thoughts. Did you come to me looking for advice?" Kevin asked.

"Please." If my friend had a solution, I was more than willing to hear it.

"You've endured worse. You and Shay will get through this, too."

I wanted to believe that was possible, but doubts had started to creep in, strangling my hopes for the future. If the person responsible didn't step forward and make it right, I didn't know what would happen between Shay and me.

Before I left his office, Kevin patted my back. I was grateful for his advice and encouragement.

—

Following my visit to Hope Center, I returned to the office and stayed late. Mary Lou left at five and I made a quick trip to the house to make sure Mark and Sarah had dinner, but I had nothing to eat myself. My stomach had been in knots ever since my talk with Alex, my appetite nonexistent. I hadn't eaten more than a sandwich all day.

The elder meeting was scheduled for seven o'clock, which gave the church council enough time to get home from their day jobs and grab a quick bite of dinner. Once everyone was assembled, I explained the situation.

There were plenty of shocked faces. I explained that I'd talked to Shay and she'd told me she hadn't taken the money. I believed her. As I spoke I saw the look of the men and women around the table. They had doubts. To be fair, I didn't blame them. I went on to explain that she knew who was responsible but had promised that she wouldn't tell. In return, the thief would make restitution.

The room erupted in discussion, and from the tidbits I heard, a few were willing to accept Shay's word. Right away a proposition was brought before the council. It didn't take long for a decision to be made. It was unanimous that Shay would no longer be allowed to rent the apartment.

The elders left and I remained in the small conference room, my head in my hands. Hearing a noise, I glanced up and saw that it was Alex Turnbull.

"I want you to know how sorry I am, Pastor," Alex said.

"I know. I appreciate how hard this has been on you as well."

Alex drew closer to the table. "I hope you know that I

have no hard feelings toward Shay. I realize you care for her."

I couldn't deny it. Not only was I devastated, my heart was broken. The full impact had yet to hit me. I didn't know how I was going to break the news to Mark and Sarah. The more I thought about it, the more depressed I became. I toyed with the idea of simply letting them think Shay was moving away and avoid telling them why. I guess I'd figure out what to say when the time came.

"Pastor, would you like me to be the one to tell Shay?" Alex asked, breaking into my thoughts.

It would be easier on me for sure, but as uncomfortable as it would be, I felt I needed to be the one to do it.

A part of me was curious to find out why someone as intelligent as Shay would risk so much because of a promise. Second chances. She would always be willing to give someone else another chance. Admirable and devastating, both at once.

"Pastor?" Alex asked, once more interrupting my thoughts.

"I appreciate the offer," I told him, "but I need to be the one."

Alex nodded as if he understood. "Would you like me to come with you?"

I considered it but only briefly. "No. I was the one who offered to let Shay move into the apartment; I'll be the one to explain that she needs to leave before the end of the month."

We talked for a couple minutes longer. I knew I should get back to Mark and Sarah, but I didn't want this task hanging over my head a minute longer than necessary.

My steps were filled with dread as I walked around to

the front of the apartment. The porch light was turned on, which generally meant Shay was home. I knew she often stayed up late studying on nights she wasn't attending classes.

I don't know how long I stood outside her front door before I found the courage to knock.

It took only a minute or two for Shay to answer. Her eyes widened when she saw it was me.

"Drew?"

"Shay," I said, my heart pounding with a heaviness I had only rarely experienced. "We need to talk."

CHAPTER 31

Shay

"Come in," I said, ushering Drew inside my apartment. He looked pale and drawn. Earlier I'd seen several cars pull into the parking area. I didn't know of any scheduled meeting, but I wasn't privy to all the inner workings of the church.

Drew stood with his hands tucked in his back pockets as if he wasn't sure what to do with them.

My stomach tightened with anticipation. I had a feeling I knew what was coming.

We stood staring at each other for several minutes before Drew got to the reason for his visit. I didn't invite him to sit; I preferred to face whatever he had to say while standing.

"Shay," he said, softly, tentatively. I detected a pleading quality to his voice. "I'm going to ask you again . . . no, not ask, I'm pleading with you. Will you tell me what I need to know? Who took that money? This isn't the first time, is it? This has been ongoing for a while, hasn't it?"

He didn't give me a chance to answer.

Plowing his fingers through his hair, he paced the compact living space as if the thought had only recently occurred to him. "This is slowly starting to make sense. Lloyd, bless his heart, is good. But it would be easy for someone to take funds without him knowing. Someone. Anyone could steal before Lloyd made the deposit." He paused and looked up, his eyes rounding with the thought. "You're protecting whoever this is, Shay. I can't allow you to do that. You need to tell me who's responsible."

I carefully considered my response, weighing my options. "I already told you, I can't."

"Shay, please."

I wavered, and I saw that it gave Drew hope. "Please don't ask me again."

"Did you speak to this person?"

"You know I did."

"Recently?"

"Yes." I was afraid of saying too much for fear he would guess. It would devastate him and I refused to do that.

"Today?" he pressed.

Rather than answer verbally, I nodded.

His shoulders sank. "It's Linda, isn't it?"

My eyes slammed shut. "Don't do this, Drew. Don't play this guessing game with me. I can't and I won't tell you, so don't ask me again."

Disappointment flashed in his eyes as if he'd hoped for more. More was something I couldn't give him. I looked away, refusing to meet his gaze.

"Do you have anything else you can tell me?" he asked, his words weighed down with what sounded like disappointment and frustration.

"No. Nothing," I whispered past the lump in my throat. He didn't understand how unbelievably hard it was for me to maintain my silence.

"I had hoped that out of respect for me, you would trust me enough with the truth."

I exhaled and briefly looked up. "You can't guilt me into breaking my word, Drew. Eventually you'll learn the truth."

"What if I don't? What if this person refuses to come forward? Then what?"

I had no answer. There was no guarantee I would be exonerated. I hoped, I trusted, but at this point that was all I could do.

Drew walked to the other side of the living area and rammed his hands through his hair.

"You claim you love me."

"I do." With everything in me, I longed to shout from the rooftops how much I loved him.

"Then please tell me the truth. Once I know, then I can make everything right again."

"Now you're trying to bribe me. Drew, don't you see what you're doing?"

"I'm desperate, Shay. Desperate," he repeated.

I had to bite down on my tongue to keep from speaking.

"Why won't you look at me?" he demanded.

"I can't," I whispered as tears clouded my eyes. If I looked at him, he might be able to persuade me to give up the name, and I couldn't do that. The risk was too high.

"Was it for Richard or Chuck?"

I nearly laughed out loud. He was drawing names out of a hat. "No. You know better than to suggest either of them."

"Your brother?"

"That's equally ludicrous. Caden is in jail. It's highly unlikely he could be responsible."

He threw his hands in the air. "Then who?" Drew walked to the other side of the room, his back to me. We stood on opposite sides of the apartment. After what seemed like an eternity, he said, "The elders met tonight."

That explained the cars in the parking lot.

"It was decided that the church would cancel their month-to-month lease with you effective at the end of this month."

"You're asking me to move?" I was stunned. Perhaps I shouldn't have been, as I realized there would be some form of consequence.

"You'll have to make other living arrangements. The apartment needs to be vacated by the first of the month."

"That's only ten days."

"I know."

"I don't have anyplace else to go."

He closed his eyes and then started toward the door. "I'm sorry, Shay."

My heart was beating with the speed of a horse in the Kentucky Derby. I stopped him. "Drew, please," I said, struggling to hide my panic. "I have one question."

His hand was on the door, but he paused and didn't open it as he waited.

"How did you vote?" I asked.

He didn't answer right away. Nor did he turn around to face me. "I abstained."

Deep down I'd known.

—

The next day, I started my early-morning shift at The Corner Café, amazed that I could handle the counter, take orders, and deliver meals without any incident. My mind and my heart were at odds with each other.

I'd taken a gamble, and it seemed I'd lost and I'd lost big.

Now I had two unpleasant tasks facing me. First and foremost, I needed to find other living accommodations, and the sooner the better. The Seattle housing crisis was well known. Finding an apartment, especially a low-rent one, would be next to impossible. The waiting lists for apartments were said to be months, if not years. The best I could hope for was to find a room to rent.

Next on my list and equally important had to do with Hope Center. I needed to talk to Lilly Palmer, and I hoped she would be able to convince Kevin Forester to not take the bookkeeping position away. With everything that had happened, it wouldn't surprise me if I learned I was no longer being considered for the job. If I lost that opportunity, I didn't know what I'd do.

I'd made arrangements for Sadie to cover the second half of my shift, so I could stop at the Center, as well as search for housing. As I was getting ready to leave, she sought me out. "You okay, girl? You don't seem yourself."

"I'm fine," I said, stretching the truth. "Got stuff on my mind."

She didn't look convinced. "What's this I hear about you needing to move before the end of the month? What's up with that? I thought you had an apartment at the church."

"I don't any longer."

"What did you do, throw a drunken party on church property?"

Despite the concerns I'd been carrying with me since Drew's visit, I couldn't hold back a smile. "Not exactly."

"Well, you must have done something to raise a few eyebrows, seeing how you need to be out that soon."

"You know anyone looking for a lodger or a room-mate?" I asked, rather than address her comment.

Sadie shook her head. "Sorry, I don't."

My shoulders sank. I had only nine days, and time was ticking away at an alarming rate.

"Don't you fret, though," Sadie interjected. "You can room with me and the cats until you find a place."

While I appreciated the offer, I'd heard more than one comment about Sadie and her felines. Alice teased that Sadie had her own cat house. "Thank you," I said, and impulsively hugged her. "But I'm allergic to cats."

"Not good, and with four of them you'd likely need an oxygen mask before the end of the first night."

"Probably," I agreed.

"You could sleep on my couch if you have to," Alice chimed in. "I'd offer you a bed, but with three kids there isn't a spare mattress in sight."

I couldn't stop myself from tossing my arms around these two wonderful women in a group hug. They'd had my back from the very first day I'd started working at the café, and I loved and appreciated them.

"Hey, hey," Frankie called out from the kitchen. He waved a spatula at the three of us. "What's going on out there? This isn't a love-in, you know. I'm running a café here, so if you three are into something kinky, I'd prefer you didn't do it in front of the customers."

No one bothered to mention that the café was nearly empty in that lull between breakfast and lunch. Those sitting in the booths were dialed into Wi-Fi on their laptops or glued to their phones.

I thanked Frank for letting me take a half day, clocked out, and reached for my coat and backpack, ready to walk over to Hope Center, which was less than a mile away. I could have taken a bus, but I wanted the exercise to clear my head.

This conversation wasn't one I looked forward to having, especially if it was going to be bad news. All I could do was pray that Lilly and Kevin would have more faith in me than Drew and the church elders.

Then again, perhaps I was asking too much.

As I left the café, I noticed a small figure huddled against the side of the building. I looked again and realized it was Sarah.

"Sarah?"

As soon as she heard her name, the nine-year-old raced toward me, her arms opened wide.

Squatting down to catch her, I reached for her as she threw herself into my embrace, her thin arms locking around my neck.

"Sweetheart, what are you doing here?" I asked gently, cupping the back of her head as I held on to her.

Instead of answering, she buried her face in my neck, sobbing her little heart out.

"Tell me what's wrong," I pleaded.

"Don't you love us anymore?" Sarah asked, crying so hard it was almost impossible to make out the words.

"Of course I love you. I'll always, always love you."

"But Daddy said . . ."

"What did he say?" I asked gently when she didn't finish her thought.

"He said you were moving and that we might not be able to see you anymore."

My hold around her tightened and I felt my own throat clog with tears. "That doesn't mean I will stop loving you, though. That would never, ever happen, no matter where I live."

"I don't want you to leave us," she cried, her arms tightening around my neck as if snuggling against me would prevent me from going away.

I didn't want to go, either, but I couldn't tell Sarah.

"Can I go with you?" she asked, raising her head enough to look at me, her beautiful face full of hope.

I couldn't speak, and answered her with a shake of my head.

Sarah brushed the tears that leaked from my eyes. Her fingers rubbed at my cheek. "Why would you move?" she asked.

"Sometimes that's what adults need to do," I said in a way I hoped sounded normal and reassuring.

"Don't go, Shay. Please don't go."

Overwhelmed with sadness, I pressed the side of my face against hers.

"Please, Shay. Don't you know how much we love you?"

"I know, sweetheart. Sometimes things happen that make it necessary for people to leave."

"Don't, please don't leave me."

Sarah was breaking my heart. I straightened. "Wait a minute. Aren't you supposed to be in school, Sarah?" I asked.

Sarah looked down at the sidewalk. "I ran away," she admitted.

"Oh Sarah."

"I decided I want to live with you."

"Sweetheart, as much as I love you, as much as I would like that, I can't take you with me."

"Please, Shay. Please. No one else can fix my hair right and Mark is stupid and Daddy is sad. Don't make me go back, Shay. Please let me come with you."

CHAPTER 32

Drew

My mind wasn't on sermon preparation the morning after I'd confronted Shay. I'd hoped that once we'd talked, she'd be willing to give up the name, which would vindicate her. The fact that she'd refused had torn me up inside.

That didn't compare to what happened when I told Mark and Sarah that Shay would be moving. Right away Sarah had burst into tears, which had quickly escalated to near hysterics. I'd spent most of the night calming her down.

Mark hadn't taken the news any better. He'd plied me with questions. Because he was older I'd told him the truth, that Shay refused to give up the name of the thief. My son had gone quiet and sad, which was almost exactly the way I'd reacted since my confrontation with Shay. It was hard to believe she would be this stubborn, and even harder to accept.

My Bible was propped open in front of me as I tackled writing Sunday's sermon. But my heart wasn't in it. I felt devoid of spiritual insight.

Empty.

I didn't feel like I had anything left to offer others. I knew myself well enough to know I'd muddle through. I had years of preaching experience. But I'd simply be going through the motions.

As I stared down at the Bible opened on my desk, my mind refused to let go of what had happened the night before. My children loved Shay. I loved Shay. It made no sense to me that she would stay silent when her entire future was at stake. I'd wanted to take her by the shoulders and shake her and demand that she give me a name.

The phone rang in the distance and I waited for my assistant to pick up the call. Mary Lou buzzed me on the intercom.

"It's the school calling," she said.

Oh great. Sarah had been emotional that morning and refused to eat breakfast. My guess was that she had a stomachache now and wanted to come home. That meant I was going to have to give up the rest of my day, not that it would be any great loss, seeing that I hadn't written more than a few lines of my sermon anyway.

I picked up the receiver. "This is Drew Douglas," I said.

"Yes, Mr. Douglas, I'm calling to confirm that Sarah is home sick today."

A chill went down my spine. "No. Are you telling me she isn't at school?"

The line went silent. "Mr. Douglas? Sarah didn't show up for class this morning."

My heart rate accelerated, but I was convinced it was an error. "I'm sure there's a mistake. Please recheck."

"I have the report right here in front of me. Sarah's teacher, Mrs. Janachek, shows Sarah as absent."

"That can't be right. I walked her to the bus myself." None of this was making sense.

"Did you see her get on the bus?"

"No," I admitted reluctantly. I'd waited only until one of the other children and another parent showed. I pressed my hand to my forehead to think this through. I stood up from behind my desk. Something was very wrong and I needed to find out what it was pronto. "I'm coming to the school. I'll be there within the next ten minutes."

Sarah was missing.

My daughter had been distraught this morning, and because I was upset, I hadn't paid enough attention. Because she was hurting, Sarah could easily have been lured away by a predator.

By the time I reached the school, the scenarios going off in my head were enough to cause a panic attack. The principal at the elementary school was quizzing one of Sarah's friends when I arrived. Heather rode the bus with my daughter. She'd been at the bus stop that morning when I left Sarah.

"Hi, Heather," I said, noting how frightened the other child seemed to be.

"Hi, Pastor Douglas."

Mrs. Thalheimer, the principal, spoke. "According to Heather, Sarah said she'd forgotten something at home and needed to go back. This happened just before the school bus arrived."

I slammed my eyes closed. Not once had I thought to check the house. I should have guessed that was what had happened. My daughter had been upset that morning; we all were. It was only natural that she'd want to skip school. My relief was instantaneous.

"She must be at the house," I said.

"Please call and let us know that Sarah is safe," Mrs. Thalheimer said, and walked me to the door. "If not, I believe we should notify the police."

"Yes, of course." The panic hadn't left me as I rushed to the house. Nothing would take away the sick feeling in the pit of my stomach until I found my daughter.

Only the house was empty. I checked every room twice, racing around, calling her name, growing more desperate by the minute.

I reached for my phone to notify the police of a missing child. My second call would be to the school to let them know I hadn't found Sarah.

Holding the phone in my hand, it rang unexpectedly, startling me. When caller ID told me it was Shay, I experienced a mixture of emotions. Some relief, some irritation. With a missing nine-year-old, I didn't have time to deal with Shay. I almost let the call go to voicemail.

"Yes," I said impatiently.

"Sarah's with me," she said, without any exchange of pleasantries.

"Sarah's with you?" I repeated, overwhelmed with gratitude and relief. "Where are you?"

"The café. We're having a bite to eat."

"What?" I nearly exploded. Shay made it sound like the two of them were on a field trip, while I was a hairsbreadth from losing my mind and calling the police.

"She was waiting for me outside the café at the time I normally take my break," Shay explained, remaining calm and coolheaded.

I, on the other hand, was about to gnaw off my fingers. "Stay there," I said, doing my best to settle my rampaging emotions.

"Okay. We'll stay put."

I could hear Sarah protesting in the background that she wanted to be with Shay.

"I'll meet you at the café," I told her, and was already on my way out the door.

"Will you be long?" she asked.

"Give me ten minutes."

I hung up and immediately contacted Mrs. Thalheimer at the school. "I found Sarah," I told her, breathless, as I raced toward my vehicle. "She's with a family friend."

"Is everything all right?" the school principal wanted to know.

"It's fine," I told her, although it wasn't. As best I could figure, Sarah had decided to run away.

Nothing felt right and I knew what I had to do.

I found Sarah and Shay sitting in a corner booth when I entered The Corner Café. Sarah was eating French fries. I noticed Shay hadn't ordered anything for herself.

Shay's eyes locked with mine and she offered me a sad smile. Her look went through me like a laser beam. I felt it all the way through my body. A part of me wanted to talk to her then and there, plead with her one more time, but I needed to deal with my daughter first.

Sarah glanced at me as I approached and her eyes were rimmed with tears. Right away she turned toward Shay, as if seeking her help.

Sliding into the booth next to my daughter, I placed my arm around her shoulders and hugged her.

"Shay told me I had to tell you I'm sorry."

"Are you sorry?" I asked.

She answered with a stubborn tilt of her chin. "No, and you can ground me if you want, but I wanted to be with Shay."

"There are consequences, Sarah, when we do what we know is wrong," I said.

Sarah hung her head. "I know you're mad." As though to comfort Shay, Sarah stretched her arm across the table and patted Shay's hand. "I had to talk to Shay before she moved. If she was going to leave us, then I wanted to tell her that I'd go with her."

My gaze met Shay's. All I could read in her eyes was pain and sadness. "And what did Shay tell you?" I asked my nine-year-old.

Sarah's shoulders slumped forward. "She told me I couldn't."

"I see."

"I don't want her to leave us, Daddy."

"I don't want her to leave us, either."

Shay's eyes shot to mine, filled with questions. Mine were filled with love. "I thought it would be all right if she went away," I said, addressing my daughter, "but I realize now that it would never be the same for any of us without Shay." I didn't know what that would mean for any of us, how my church family would react to having her as part of my life, but at this point I was past caring.

Grabbing a napkin from the dispenser, Shay dabbed at her eyes.

"Do you know why it would be hard to let her move away?" I asked my daughter.

"Because we'd miss her?" she guessed.

"For sure, but there's an even stronger reason."

"Because we love her?"

"Yes, we love her and she's important to us."

Sarah's face lit up with a huge smile. "Will you stay with us?" she asked Shay. "Please say you will."

"I'll see what I can do," Shay whispered, as if she was having a difficult time finding her voice.

"Finish your fries, Sarah, so I can drop you off at school. Don't you have a spelling test this afternoon?" I knew that because I'd gone over her spelling words with her the night before.

I stole a couple fries when Sarah wasn't looking, but she caught me and teasingly slapped my hand. "You can have one if you ask nicely, and say 'pretty please.'"

"Pretty please," I said and reached for two, giving one to Shay.

Shay grinned and accepted the fry from my fingers. As soon as her hand was close, I curled my fingers around hers and squeezed gently.

I asked Shay to accompany me to Sarah's school, and she did. She waited in the car as I escorted Sarah into the building. Afterward I drove to the house, preferring that we talk privately there instead of at the church office.

We both had little to say while in the car. As soon as we were inside the house and the door was closed, I pulled Shay into my arms and simply held her. God help me, I couldn't let her go. For the life of me, I didn't know what was going on with her and the missing money. We'd deal with that later, if at all.

I kissed her, tasting the salt of her tears on my lips. She felt so good in my arms and I knew this was where she was meant to be. Running my fingers through her hair, I angled my mouth over hers, kissing her again and again, unable to get enough of her, needing more, wanting more. I don't know what I was thinking to send her out of my life. I needed her. My children needed her. Yes, there'd be consequences, but I'd face those, we'd face them together.

Her arms were around me, holding on as if we were locked together in the middle of a stormy sea, rocking in a small life raft. I leaned my forehead against hers, breathing in the scent that was uniquely hers.

"I don't know why you won't answer my questions. Nor do I know why you think you can't tell me what you know about that missing money. For whatever reason, that's important enough to keep your promise. I'll honor that with you."

Tears filled her eyes and spilled down her face. "I trust this person. I know in the end it will be made right."

I hoped she was right, because she was taking a tremendous risk.

Her hands cupped my jaw and she kissed me again hard and long, twisting her mouth against mine. "Thank you," she whispered.

"I'll help you find someplace else to live," I offered.

"I can't stay in the apartment?"

"I'm sorry, Shay, so sorry. That decision isn't mine."

I felt her disappointment and it hurt me to have to tell her that there was nothing more I could do about the board's decision.

"I understand."

"I'll help you as best I can."

"Both Sadie and Alice offered to let me stay with them until I could find a new place."

Inspiration struck. "I'll talk to Linda Kincaid. She

seems to have connections everywhere. What's most important to me is that you know that I trust you and I love you."

"I love you, too."

"I'm sorry I pressured you."

She planted her forehead against my chest. "Thank you," she whispered, her voice cracking with emotion. "It means everything to me."

We talked for an hour or longer. I made a few phone calls and then brewed us each a cup of coffee.

As we spoke I realized how close I'd come to losing her. Sarah and Mark had been the ones to give me a wake-up call. Their love for Shay was as strong as my own.

"Sarah and Mark need you as much as I do."

The back door opened. Mark was home from school. The afternoon had flown by; I hadn't realized how late it was.

For a moment my son looked shocked when he saw Shay.

"Shay," he whispered, his eyes brightening with surprised joy. "You didn't move."

"Not yet," she told him, "but I'll need to find somewhere else soon."

Mark nodded and headed straight to his room.

Never one to verbalize his thoughts, Mark wouldn't say much one way or the other. He didn't need to. I could tell how pleased he was to see Shay. I'd explain later that despite the move, Shay would remain a part of our lives.

CHAPTER 33

Shay

With only a few days to pack up my clothes and the other belongings that I'd managed to acquire, I collected boxes from the café. Frankie saved the best of the produce boxes for me and I was grateful. Seeing that I couldn't exactly cart them home on the bus, I chose to walk. It was only a matter of six or so blocks, although it made for an awkward trip.

Saturday morning, following my shift, I had two more of the boxes with me as I approached the church. Mark was outside with his dad working in the yard when he noticed me, and he stopped what he was doing and stared as I headed toward the apartment.

I smiled at Mark encouragingly.

He said something to his father and then approached me. "Do you want some help carrying those?" he asked.

"Sure." I handed him the smaller one.

"I hate that you're moving," Mark said, setting the box on his shoulder.

"Yeah, me, too."

"Do you have another place yet?" he asked.

"No, but I'm working on it." I set the box down and reached for the apartment key to open the door.

"Where will you go?" he asked, sounding worried.

I was surprised his father hadn't told him. "I'm moving in with the Kincaids until I can find a place of my own."

"Oh."

Sarah saw the two of us and raced across the yard. "Can I help, too?" she asked, her face bright and eager.

"We got this," Mark told his sister.

"I didn't ask you," she grumbled at her brother. Turning to me, she asked, "Can we bake cookies later?"

While I should take the time to pack, I wasn't about to waste the opportunity to spend time with Sarah. The Kincaids were kind enough to allow me to move in with them and I was more than grateful. The one negative was that they lived several miles from Drew and the church. Getting to and from my classes was going to be a hassle. I would no longer have my ride and bus service to their neighborhood, especially that late at night, wasn't the best. It would add an extra hour or longer to my day.

"What kind of cookies do you want to bake?" I asked.

"Can we do sugar cookies this time?"

"You got it."

Drew called his daughter and she raced back to her father while Mark continued with the box into the apartment.

"Thanks, Mark."

He hesitated after setting down the box. Glancing around the apartment, he saw that I'd packed and stacked the others, preparing for the move. I saw him swallow hard, as if struggling to hold back tears.

I wasn't sure how he'd feel about me hugging him, but I refused to hold back any longer. My arms went around him and I brought him close to me and kissed the top of his head. "It's going to be fine," I whispered.

"You . . . you love us."

"I do. More than anything, more than I've ever loved anyone . . . even more than I love my brother."

"Sometimes I think my mom sent you to us."

Tears sprang to my eyes and I fought to hold them back. "I don't think anyone has ever said anything that means more to me. Thank you, Mark."

His young arms came around my waist and he hugged me and started to sob. "You didn't tell. Even when it meant the elders would make you move."

My own grip around him tightened. "I promised I wouldn't. I keep my promises."

"You . . . you should have told on me," he managed between sobs.

It was easy to see that the last week had been torturous for him. "You made me a promise, too, remember. You assured me you'd do the right thing."

"But I didn't," he sobbed, his thin shoulders shaking. "I let you take the blame. I . . . was afraid."

"I know you were," I whispered, trying hard to keep the tears out of my voice. "I hoped you'd tell your father the truth and why you took that money." He hadn't shared his reasons with me and I hadn't pressured him. I knew it had to be a heavy weight on his thin shoulders to carry this burden.

He pulled away and wiped the tears from his face,

smearing them down his cheeks. "They were going to beat me up again," he said, sniffling now.

"Who are they?" I asked.

"Those boys you saw, remember?"

I'd been right. The afternoon Mark had come into the café, I'd seen those other kids and wondered. Mark had come not out of any interest in seeing me. It'd been an effort to escape those bullies.

"At first all they wanted was for me to do their homework. I did, but it wasn't enough. Then they took my lunch money away from me."

That helped to explain why Mark was always so hungry when he came home from school.

"Your dad put you in karate classes. Why did you drop out?"

Mark ran the back of his hand below his nose. "One of the boys was in the same class and he made fun of me. I'm not very athletic and there was a girl in that class and—"

"You don't need to say anything more, I understand." Poor Mark was caught between a rock and a hard place.

My door opened and Drew came into the apartment. He paused when he saw his son openly weeping.

"Hey, you two, what's . . ." He stopped mid-question.

Mark straightened, looked at his father, and burst into tears again. Immediately I brought him back into my arms.

"Mark?" Drew asked, frowning. When his son didn't answer, he looked to me. "Shay?"

This wasn't for me to tell, and so I remained silent.

Gradually Mark pulled away from me, squared his shoulders, and faced his father. "Dad," he said, struggling to speak as if the words were stuck in his throat. "I took the money, not Shay. She knew and she confronted me and we talked. I knew it was wrong, but I didn't want her to tell you and so I said I would. I made her promise not to tell anyone." He swallowed hard and continued. "I promised her that I would tell you and . . . and then I didn't and then I learned Shay was going to have to move and I got scared and I didn't know what to do."

Drew's eyes widened in shock. He froze as if he didn't know what to say. "Why, son? Why would you steal?"

Mark went to his father and Drew immediately wrapped his arms around his son, comforting and hugging him, holding him tightly in his embrace.

It was evident that the guilt and anguish of the last week had broken the young teen. His sobs echoed in the room. After a few moments, Drew looked up and his eyes captured mine.

"And you refused to break your promise to my son," he said, as though it was more than he could comprehend.

Again, I nodded. "I told you I trusted the person responsible. Mark had made a promise to me, too, and I knew he would eventually own up to it. More important, I wanted him to tell us why he was desperate enough to steal. You and I both know Mark isn't a thief. There had to be a solid reason for what he did." I reached out and patted Mark's back. "It's time to tell your dad."

"Can you explain it to me, son?" Drew asked.

I was about to suggest that we all sit down and I'd make us tea, but unfortunately my cups were packed away and for that matter, so was the tea.

"I . . . I told Shay a lot of what's been happening, but I'll tell you, too."

The two headed toward the door so they could speak privately.

"Send Sarah over," I called after him, knowing Mark wouldn't want his sister listening in on the conversation. Being bullied was embarrassing enough without his sister knowing. "Tell her I need help packing."

Drew's eyes held mine for an intense moment. "You mean unpacking. No way are you moving now. I'll see to that personally."

"Send me Sarah," I said, unwilling to press the point. The last thing I wanted was to put Drew in an awkward position, going up against the elders and their decision. If I needed to vacate the apartment, then I would.

Drew had his arm around his son and, looking over his shoulder, he mouthed, "Thank you."

Within a few minutes Sarah came racing over to the apartment. "Dad sent me over," she announced breathlessly. "What's going on with him and Mark?"

The kid was no dummy. Right away she'd sensed something wasn't right. "Did Mark do something bad?"

"What makes you ask that?" I asked, hedging the question.

"Because," she said, as if I should already know, "Dad took Mark into his bedroom. He only does that when we've done wrong and for serious talks. It usually means we're going to be grounded. When Dad takes us into the bedroom, it's important."

"If you must know . . ."

"I do," she said eagerly.

"Then I can tell you that your brother did the right thing."

"He did?" Her eyes went wide as if that was hard to believe.

I hid a smile. "Mark has been going through a lot at school lately."

Sarah frowned as if reviewing the last several weeks. "He's been a jerk for a long time."

"Mark's going to be better now." I wasn't sure how Drew would handle the bullying situation, but I had complete trust that he would take care of it.

Sarah sighed as though gifted with great wisdom. "I kind of figured something was up with him. Mark's been too quiet. You know what they say about kids who are too quiet, don't you?" She didn't wait for me to answer. "They're up to no good." She narrowed her eyes as if to gauge how much information she could get out of me. "Are you going to tell me what's up?"

"Nope."

She grumbled under her breath. "That's what I thought you'd say."

Sunday morning, Drew met with the elders before the church service. Mark went into the meeting with him. I can only imagine how difficult it was for the young teenager to stand before the church elders and confess what he'd done.

Although I wasn't privy to what was said, Drew came out of the meeting smiling. From the way his gaze flew to mine, I knew that all was well. As the organ music started to play, Mark slid into the church pew and sat next to me. Sarah was on one side and Mark on the other.

My heart was bursting. As Drew stepped up to the pulpit, his eyes zeroed in on the three of us, his gaze warm and full of love. I'd never known love like this. I resisted the urge to plant my hand over my heart so I could hold on to this indescribable feeling.

The sermon was one of Drew's best. He spoke on redemption and what it meant. I felt as though I'd been redeemed. The woman who'd stepped out from behind those prison walls and the one I was now were two completely different people. And to think it had all started right here in this church a little over a year ago now.

When the final hymn was sung and the congregation emptied the pews, Alex Turnbull, the head elder, wove his way in my direction. I remained in my seat and waited for him.

"If you have a few minutes I'd like to talk to you."

"Of course," I said.

I sent Sarah and Mark to the house with instructions to get the table set and ready for the afternoon meal.

Alex waited until the children had left. He sat next to me, looking down at his hands as if going over in his mind what he wanted to say. "Shay, I owe you an apology. I misjudged you from the beginning."

This was a surprise, and I wasn't sure how to respond.

"I have no excuses or justifications I can offer. I was wrong. That said, I hope you can find it in your heart to forgive me."

"Alex, of course. I understand. We have all fallen short. Isn't that what Scripture says?"

Alex grinned. "That being the case, there are a lot of

short people in this world and right now I feel like a very small person."

I smiled back. "I think you're being much too hard on yourself."

"I am undeserving of your generosity of spirit, Shay," Alex continued.

I patted his hand. "We're square, Alex."

Another one of the elders approached us and I knew Alex had further obligations. We hugged before he left.

As I started to exit the pew, I saw that Linda Kincaid stood off to one side, waiting for me.

"How's Lloyd recuperating?" I asked, happy to see her. Her willingness to put me up until I found an apartment spoke volumes. Her faith and trust in me would not easily be forgotten.

"He's taking advantage of me, but it's okay because I don't mind spoiling him." The smile drained from her face as she grew serious. "I heard," she continued, lowering her voice to a near whisper, "that you won't be moving after all. I have to say, I'm a little disappointed. I was looking forward to having you as a houseguest."

It probably wasn't proper to burst out laughing inside church, but I couldn't help myself. "If I were you, I'd call it a lucky escape."

Linda laughed, too, but once again the humor left her and she grew serious. "After Katie died, I worried about Drew and what would become of him and the children. I prayed God would send him a special woman, one who would bring joy back into his life and who would love his and Katie's children. I'll admit, you weren't exactly what I had in mind."

I laughed again. "I don't think I was who Drew was expecting, either."

"I don't think I agree with that. You were just the right woman for him and for those children. You've opened my eyes and many others', too. Drew is a smart man. He loves you, and for what it's worth, so do I."

To me that was solid gold. I impulsively hugged Linda and thanked her. "You're going to make me cry," I whispered.

"Hey, hey, what's going on here?" Drew asked, joining us.

"It's a lovefest," Linda answered, sharing a smile with me.

Drew put his arm around my shoulders and brought me close to his side. "You ready to head over to the house?" he asked.

"You're finished?"

"I am. Seems you're going to need someone to help you unpack and get situated again."

From the happy look he'd sent me after the meeting with the elders, I hoped that was the case. Linda confirmed it.

As we walked toward the house, I questioned Drew. "Is Mark okay?" It couldn't have been easy for him to stand before the church council and confess what he'd done.

"He did great. I'm proud of him. He told them what you'd done and how awful he felt about letting you take the blame. I haven't quite figured out what to do about the bullying. I'm going to make an appointment with the school counselor as soon as it can be arranged."

"That's a start."

"This harassment of my son is going to stop and it's going to stop now."

Drew's arm was around me as we walked toward the house where the children waited. "Thank you for what you did for Mark," he whispered.

I pressed my head against his shoulder, savoring his appreciation, loving him.

"Thank you for loving me and my children," he whispered, and kissed the top of my head. "This is only the beginning of our journey together, Shay. I can't wait to see where God will lead us next."

I mulled over his words as a sense of deep joy filled me. I reflected back on my time at Hope Center when Lilly had asked me what my dreams were and, at that point, I couldn't think of a single one. Little did I understand at the time what was in store for me. While participating in the program at Hope Center I'd learned to dream again. Now, I realized, my reality had far and away exceeded my expectations. Lilly once told me that any dream would do. As I looked around me, I had more than a handful of dreams, and every one of them seemed to be coming true.

#1 *New York Times* bestselling author
Debbie Macomber delivers an inspiring novel
of friendship, reinvention, and hope in

A Girl's Guide to Moving On

An affirmation of the ability of
every woman to forge a new path, believe in love,
and fearlessly find happiness.
Continue reading for a special sneak peek.

Available now from Ballantine Books

CHAPTER 1

Nichole

The first step in our *Guide to Moving On* was also the most enjoyable. Every other Saturday I spent the entire day at Dress for Success, a gently-used-clothing boutique. I loved dressing these ladies, whose courage inspired and stirred me. Many had come out of abusive relationships or were looking to get off welfare and find their place in the workforce. It was a joy to fit them with a wardrobe that gave them confidence and the hope that they could succeed.

"Would you look at me?" Shawntelle Maynor said, as she studied her reflection in the mirror. She turned around and glanced over her shoulder, nodding, apparently liking what she saw. "This hides my butt good."

Shawntelle was a good five inches taller than my own five-foot-three frame. Her hair was an untamed mass of tight black curls raining down upon her shoulders. She critically studied herself in the outfit I'd put together for her first job interview.

I found it hard to believe the difference clothes made. Shawntelle had arrived in baggy sweatpants and an oversized T-shirt. Now, dressed in black slacks and a pink Misook jacket, she looked like a million bucks.

"Wowza." I stepped back and reviewed my handiwork. The transformation was stunning.

"I need help with this hair," she said, frowning as she shoved it away from her face. "I should have known better than to let Charise cut it. She was all confident she could do it after watching a YouTube video. I was crazy to let her anywhere close to my hair with a pair of scissors." Her fingers reached up and touched the uneven ends of her bangs, or what I assumed must be her bangs. "I thought it'd grow out, and it did, but now it looks even worse."

"I've already made you an appointment next door." The hairstylist in the shop next to Dress for Success volunteered to give each woman at the boutique a wash and cut before her job interview.

Shawntelle's eyes nearly popped out of her head. "Get out of here. Really?"

"Really. When's your interview?"

"Monday afternoon."

"Your hair appointment is set for ten. Does that time work for you?"

Her smile was answer enough. Shawntelle had recently graduated from an accounting class and was looking for her first job. She had five children and her husband had deserted the family. The agency had gotten her an interview with a local car dealership. She'd gone through several practice interviews, which had given her a boost of confidence. Now, with the proper outfit, she beamed with self-assurance.

"I never thought I'd make it without LeRoy," she whispered. "But I am and I refuse to let that cheatin' scumbag back. He's screwed me over for the last time."

I smiled at the vehemence in her voice. I was walking this same rock-strewn path. In addition to my volunteer work, I was a substitute teacher for the Portland School District. My degree was in French literature with a minor in education, which qualified me for a teaching position. Unfortunately, no full-time positions were available, so I filled in as needed.

Thankfully, Leanne was available to watch Owen for me and as a backup there was a drop-in daycare center down the street from our apartment building. I eked by financially, in stark contrast to the lavish lifestyle I'd become accustomed to while married.

I had to remind myself I was still technically married. The final papers had yet to be drawn up to Jake's satisfaction. My husband had made this divorce as difficult as possible, thinking he could change my mind. He'd been persistently begging me to reconsider. When he finally realized my determination to see this through, he'd set up every roadblock he could, dragging out the settlement hearings, arguing each point. Our attorney fees had skyrocketed.

Divorce is hard—so much harder than I'd ever imagined it would be.

"You'll call after the interview?" I asked Shawntelle, determinedly pushing thoughts of Jake out of my mind.

"You got it."

"You're going to do so well." I gave her arm a gentle squeeze.

Shawntelle turned and wrapped me in a hug. "Them Kardashian chicks ain't got nothin' on me."

"You're beautiful." And I meant it.

By five I'd finished for the day and I was eager to get back to my son. Leanne had taken Owen to the park. At nearly four my little man was a ball of explosive energy. I imagined my mother-in-law was more than ready for a break.

I got in my car and started the engine when my phone rang. I drove a ten-year-old Toyota while my soon-to-be ex-husband was in a nearly new BMW, a car I'd bought him with the inheritance I'd gotten after my parents died. That was another story entirely, and one I had to repeatedly push out of my mind. Rule number three: **Let go in order to receive.**

I frantically searched through my purse until I located my phone. Checking caller ID, I saw that it was Jake. No surprise. It seemed he found an excuse to call me just about every day. I was able to remain civil, but I resented his efforts to keep me tied to him. Friends had been all too eager to tell me he hadn't changed his womanizing ways. Now that I was out of the house my husband didn't bother to hide the fact he was a player.

This was supposed to have been his weekend with Owen, but he had a business trip. Or so he claimed. Because of what I knew, I'd become suspicious of everything he said.

"Yes," I said, making sure I didn't sound overly friendly. It was difficult to maintain an emotional distance from him, especially when he worked overtime to make it hard. Jake knew all the right buttons to push with me. Through the negotiations for the divorce he'd played me like a grand piano.

"Hi, sweetheart."

"You have the wrong number," I said forcefully. Every time he used an endearment I wondered how many other women he called "sweetheart."

"Come on, honey, there's no need to be bitter. I'm calling with good news."

Sure he was. "Which is?"

He hesitated and his voice sank lower, laced with regret. "I've signed off on the final negotiations. You want a share in the house, then fine, it's yours, but only when I choose to sell it. That's what you asked for, right?"

"Right." Which meant this bitter struggle was over and the divorce could go through. Twenty-five months after I'd filed we could sign the final papers.

"You signed off?" If that was the case I'd be hearing from my attorney shortly, probably Monday morning.

"It's killing us both to drag this out any longer than it already has."

From the minute I'd moved out of the house Jake had believed he could change my mind. I'd gladly given up living in the house despite the fact that my attorney had advised me to stay put. All I asked for was my fair share of the proceeds when he chose to sell it.

I wasn't interested in living in that plush home any longer. My life there with all the expensive furnishings and designer details had been a sham. The memories were too much for me. Sleeping in our bed was torture, knowing Jake had defiled it. For all I knew he may even have made love to another woman in that very bed. Besides, holding on to the house would be a financial struggle. I needed to break away completely and start over. Jake had been surprised when I agreed to move out. I'd used the house along with the country-club membership as bargaining chips in the settlement agreement.

"Aren't you going to say anything?" Jake asked.

I wasn't sure what to say. "I guess this is it, then," I whispered, staggering against a wall of emotion. My attorney assured me that eventually Jake would cave. It was either that or we would be headed to a meeting with a court-appointed negotiator. I was willing, but Jake had balked. Neither one of us wanted this to go to trial. The attorneys and the divorce proceedings were expensive enough.

"Yeah. It'll be final soon," Jake said, his voice so low it was almost a whisper. His words were filled with regret.

"Final," I repeated, and bit into my lower lip.

"You okay?" Jake asked.

"Yeah, of course." But I wasn't. After all this time one would think I'd be glad this bickering and madness were about to end. I should be over the moon, eager to put my marriage behind me. I was more than ready to move on. Instead my heart felt like it was going to melt and a huge knot blocked my throat.

"I thought you'd want to know," Jake said, sounding as sad and miserable as I was.

"Thanks. I've got to go."

"Nichole . . . Nichole . . ."

I didn't want to hear anything more that he had to say, so I ended the call. With tears blurring my eyes, I tossed my phone back inside my expensive Michael Kors purse. A purse I'd purchased because Jake insisted I deserved beautiful things. Now I understood he'd wanted me to have it because he'd felt guilty. As best I could figure, I'd bought the purse shortly after he learned Chrissy was pregnant with his child.

Wiping the moisture from my cheek, I put the car in reverse, stepped on the accelerator, and immediately backed into a ditch.

CHAPTER 2

Nichole

I don't know how long I sat in my car with my forehead resting against the steering wheel. I was embarrassed and shaken, and it wasn't only from the accident. My marriage was over. I thought I was ready, more than ready. The reality of it hit me full force; a deep sense of loss and unreality swamped my senses.

"Nichole, are you all right?"

A disembodied voice came at me. When I lifted my head I found Alicia, the hairstylist standing alongside my upended car. When I didn't answer right away she knocked against the driver's-side window.

"Nichole. Nichole."

I lifted my head and nodded. "I am such an idiot."

"Are you hurt?"

I assured her I wasn't.

"You're going to need a tow truck to pull you out of here."

I figured as much.

"Do you have Triple A?"

I shook my head. It was an added expense I couldn't afford.

"Do you want me to call someone for you?"

"Please." Still I remained in the car, praying I hadn't done any further damage to my vehicle.

Alicia hesitated. "Are you sure you're all right? You didn't hit your head or anything, did you?"

"No, no, I'm fine." I wasn't. I wasn't anywhere close to okay, but that wasn't due to the fact my car was head up in a ditch.

Alicia hesitated and then left me. Breathless, she returned a few minutes later. I remained seated in the car, clenching the steering wheel. She opened the driver's-side door. "Potter Towing will be here within thirty minutes."

I nodded. "Thanks."

"You need help getting out?" She studied me as if unconvinced I hadn't suffered a head injury.

I sniffled, ran my hand beneath my nose, and shook my head. "I'm not hurt, just a little shook up."

"Listen, I'd wait with you, but I'm giving Mrs. Fountaine a perm and I don't want to leave the solution on too long. Denise has gone for the day, so I'm all alone."

"Don't worry; go take care of Mrs. Fountaine. I'll be okay." I wanted to blame Jake for this but I was the one who hadn't looked where I was going.

Just as Alicia promised, a tow truck pulled into the parking lot about twenty-five minutes later. By then I had climbed out, had collected my purse, and was pacing anxiously, waiting. I'd called Leanne and told her what happened.

"You're sure you're okay?" Leanne asked, and I could hear the concern in her voice.

"No, no, I'm perfectly all right. I just wanted you to

know I'll be later than usual. Look, I need to go, the tow truck just pulled up."

"Don't worry about Owen. He's doing great. Take your time."

I disconnected just as a hulk of a man jumped out of the tow truck. He had on greasy overalls and a sleeveless shirt. Both arms revealed bulging muscles and full-sleeve tattoos. His eyes were a piercing shade of blue as his gaze skidded past me to my car.

"How'd that happen?" he asked, studying the position of the car.

"I wasn't drinking, if that is what you think."

He shook his head and grinned. "You mean to say you did that sober?"

For the first time since I'd ended the conversation with Jake, I smiled. "I guess it does look like I was on something."

His smile was friendly, lighting up his eyes.

I wrapped my arms around my waist. "How much is this going to set me back?" I asked.

He named a figure that caused me to swallow a gasp. "I'll need to put it on my credit card." I had one I used only for emergencies. I'd once been free and easy with money. I could afford to be then, but no longer.

"I can give you a discount for cash," he told me as he pulled out a thick wire cord and hooked it onto the car's bumper.

"How much of a discount?"

"Ten percent."

I did a quick calculation in my head. "What about my debit card?"

"Still got to pay the bank fees with that. Cash only."

"Will you take a check?" I had a checkbook in my purse.

He paused and glanced over his shoulder. "Is it good?"

I was pissed that he'd ask. "Yes, it's good."

"Then I'll take your check."

Big of him.

"I know Alicia," he said as he walked back to his truck. "She said you work at that used-clothing place." He motioned with his head toward the shop.

"It's a volunteer position, so it isn't like a job."

"Yeah, that's what she said. She said it's a shop that dresses women looking for work. Guess you must have a good eye for that sort of thing."

He didn't expect an answer and I didn't give him one.

Once the car was connected to the tow truck, it took only a few minutes to bring it out of the ditch. He waited to make sure the engine started and I hadn't done any further damage.

I set my purse on the hood of the car and pulled out my checkbook. He took the check, folded it in half. He looked at me and then paused before slipping it into his pocket. It seemed like he had something he wanted to say. I waited and then realized he was probably worried about the check.

"It's good," I assured him again, annoyed that he seemed to think I'd stiff him. Maybe he'd gotten stiffed before.

"Anything more I can do for you?" he asked.

"Nothing. Thanks. I need to get home."

He gave me a salute and said, "It was nice doing business with you, Ms. Patterson."

"You, too, Mr. . . . ?"

"Nyquist. Call me Rocco."

"Rocco," I repeated with a smile. "Thank you for your help, Rocco," I said, eager now to be on my way.

As soon as Leanne answered the door, Owen dropped his toy and raced into my waiting arms. I got down on one knee and my son hugged my neck, squeezing tightly.

"Did you have fun at the park?" I asked.

"Grandma took me on the slide."

"Was it scary?"

He nodded and then, typically, the first question he wanted to ask was about dinner. "Can we have hot dogs for dinner?"

"Sure." Wieners were his all-time favorite meal, along with macaroni and cheese. Good thing, because with what I'd been forced to pay for the tow, we were going to need to cut back on groceries.

"Did you have a good day?" Leanne asked.

I nodded. "It was great." And it had been until the call from Jake.

I didn't tell her about our discussion. I would later. Her divorce had been finalized eighteen months ago. Sean had made it as easy as possible, giving her whatever she wanted. He seemed almost glad to be out of the marriage. I was envious Leanne hadn't been dragged into this emotional minefield Jake seemed intent on putting me through.

That was until I found Leanne crying nearly hysterically one afternoon, shortly after she'd signed the papers. It hadn't been kindness or guilt that had prompted Sean's actions, she'd told me. Sean said he was simply glad to have her out of his life. According to him, she'd gone to seed and he'd lost all desire for her years ago.

If I hadn't disliked my father-in-law before, then I detested him now. How a man could be so thoughtless and cruel to a woman who had shared his life all those years was beyond me. Leanne was a beautiful woman. Yes, she was a few pounds overweight, but it didn't distract from her overall appearance or beauty. She was kind and thoughtful, loving and generous. I admired her more than any other woman I'd ever known.

Owen collected his things and we walked across the hall to our two-bedroom apartment. It was about a third of the size of our home near Lake Oswego. I missed my garden and the flower beds. Gardening had become a passion of mine. When Owen and I could manage it, I'd buy a house and plant another garden.

Happy to be in his own home, Owen raced around the living room, his chubby legs pumping as he ran circles around me. I hoped it would tire him out enough that he'd go down for the night without a problem. I read to him each night, and the stack of books grew as he wanted to listen to all his favorite stories. I knew Jake didn't read to him, because Owen complained that he didn't.

We ate wieners for dinner along with green beans that Owen lined up on the tabletop in an arch above his plate. I managed to bribe him to eat two of the green beans. Getting him to eat his vegetables was an ongoing battle.

After reading him his ten favorite books, he settled down for the night. It'd been quiet all evening, which was unusual. I hadn't gotten a single call, which made me wonder if I'd let my battery run down. I probably needed to charge my phone. But when I dug through my purse I couldn't find it.

Immediately a sense of panic filled me. I needed my phone. Thinking I must have somehow missed it, I emptied the entire contents of my large purse and sorted through each and every item.

No phone.

I stood with my hand over my heart when the doorbell chimed. From the peephole I saw it was Rocco, the tow truck driver, standing on the other side. He must have known I was checking because he held up my phone as if to explain the reason for his visit.

Unlatching the door, I heaved a sigh. "Where did you find it?" I asked, with a deep sense of relief.

"After you drove off I saw it lying there on the blacktop and realized it must be yours. I got your address off the check you wrote."

"Of course. Come in."

He stepped into the apartment and his bulk seemed to fill the entire room. His size was intimidating. I figured he had to be at least six-four. He'd cleaned up and changed out of his coveralls. Now he wore a T-shirt and faded blue jeans that emphasized his long legs.

"I just realized I didn't have my phone and was going into panic mode. Thank you." I clenched the cell to my chest.

"No problem." He stuffed his hands into his pockets. His sleeves bulged with his muscles. I wanted to examine his tattoos but didn't want to be obvious about it. It made me curious if he had more tattoos elsewhere on his body.

"Daddy?" Owen said, racing out of his bedroom. The

doorbell must have woken him. Either that or he hadn't been entirely asleep. He came to a screeching stop when he realized the large man standing just inside the apartment wasn't Jake.

Owen's eyes grew huge as he tilted his head back and gazed up with wide-eyed wonder at Rocco.

Rocco squatted down and held out his hand. "How about giving me a high five, little man?"

Owen hesitated for only a moment before swinging his arm into a big circle, slamming it down on Rocco's open palm.

"That's quite a hit for such a little guy."

Owen smiled proudly.

I placed my hands on Owen's shoulders, steering him back toward his bedroom. "Okay, young man, back to bed."

"When will I see Daddy?" he asked, his big brown eyes pleading with me.

"He'll come for you next weekend, buddy," I assured my son. I glanced toward Rocco. "I need to put him back to bed."

He surprised me by asking, "Do you mind if I wait?"

Although I was taken aback, I gestured to the sofa. "Make yourself at home. This shouldn't take more than a few minutes."

Maybe Rocco was looking for a reward for returning my phone. My mind raced with what I could possibly give him. Maybe I didn't want to know.

It probably hadn't been the smartest idea inviting him into the apartment. I was a woman alone, and I needed to be more aware of dangers. Funny, really. As big as he was, I didn't feel the least bit threatened. I'd learned to listen to my instincts and they said I was safe.

Getting Owen down a second time wasn't as easy as I would have liked. A good ten minutes passed.

When I returned, Rocco had turned on the television and had made himself comfortable. He sat with his ankle balanced on his knee and his arm stretched out across the sofa, looking completely relaxed.

"You have coffee?" he asked.

I blinked before I found the ability to answer. "I do." I hesitated.

"Make yourself one while you're at it," he suggested.

This man had nerve. Nevertheless, I brewed us each a cup. He helped himself to milk, digging the carton out of the refrigerator and then putting it back.

Apparently he had an agenda other than delivering my phone. We stood in the middle of my small kitchen, facing each other, each holding a mug of coffee. If he could be direct, then so could I.

"What can I do for you, Rocco?"

He reached inside his pocket and removed the check I had written him earlier. "I have a proposition for you."

Seeing the check sitting on the kitchen counter, I wasn't sure I was going to like what he was about to suggest. "What kind of proposition?" I asked, frowning up at him.

The edges of his mouth curved upward as if he'd read my mind. "Whatever you're thinking isn't it. I have a fifteen-year-old daughter. Her name is Kaylene and, well, she's a typical teenager. That girl has a mouth on her . . ."

"Most teenagers do."

He didn't agree or disagree.

"I substitute teach at the high school. I hear the way they talk."

He arched his thick brows. "Must be hard to tell the difference between you and the students."

I wasn't sure that was a compliment, so I let it go. "What about your daughter?"

Rocco sipped his coffee. "She wants to attend this dance, which, according to her, is a big deal."

"And . . ."

"And I am not letting her out of the house with the dress she bought with her friends."

"And . . ."

"And so I thought we might strike a deal. If you help Kaylene dress for this dance in something I can approve of, then I'd be willing to tear up this check and call us even."

That sounded almost too good to be true. "What will your boss have to say about that?" I asked.

"I am the boss. I own Potter Towing."

"Oh." Then I paused. "I thought you said your name was Nyquist."

"Good memory. I got the business from a man named Potter. Do we have a deal?"

I didn't need to think twice. "Sure." So that was why he'd been so curious about my work with Dress for Success.

Rocco thrust out his hand and I did, too. His huge hand swallowed my much smaller one. As far as I was concerned, I was getting the much better end of this transaction.

Join
DEBBIE MACOMBER
on social media!

Facebook.com/debbiemacomberworld

Twitter: @debbiemacomber

Instagram: @debbiemacomber

Pinterest.com/macomberbooks

Visit DebbieMacomber.com
and sign up for Debbie's e-newsletter!